CONF~~RONTING~~
THE

Suddenly an explos~~ion~~
erupted behind the ~~...~~
howls cut through the night.

Turn and face us, a voice urged through
Trevelyan's mind. The howling stopped and the
wind faded as Trevelyan looked in the direction
of the light.

Welcome, young lord. Trevelyan reeled at the
perfect beauty of the wolf's voice.

"You are the first wolves." The enormity of
what was before him filled the young prince with
giddiness. "You betrayed the gods, dragged them
into the crypts where they lie to this day, tricked
them into inhaling the scent of the black lotus so
they would sleep for an eternity. You were there
when mankind leapt from the dreams of the
sleeping gods and you threatened to destroy us
when we became too much like them."

Warriors of the Unseen, Hand of justice.

"Bloody *paws* of justice! *Fangs* of truth! By
the Unseen, get to it!" Trevelyan shouted. "Why
did you summon me?"

Autumn is dying, the wolf said without
emotion.

The Wolves of Autumn

SCOTT CIENSIN

WARNER BOOKS

A Time Warner Company

WARNER BOOKS EDITION

Questar® is a registered trademark of Warner Books, Inc.

Cover design by Don Puckey
Cover illustration by Daniel Horne

Warner Books, Inc.
1271 Avenue of the Americas
New York, NY 10020

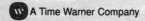 A Time Warner Company

Printed in the United States of America

First Printing: April, 1992

10 9 8 7 6 5 4 3 2 1

PART ONE

Guardian of the Soul

CHAPTER ONE

Blocking out the distant sounds of the battle, Trevelyan Arayncourt stood at the head of the path overlooking the valley of Castle Ranseur. The young merchant prince was two joints of a finger short of two meters, with sharp grey-blue eyes, chiseled features, and silky black hair worn in a tail. His lips were pale, as if the life had drained from them.

A tight-fitting red mesh tunic of his own design was worn over his lean runner's body. Silver armor plating further protected his tight, muscular form. The scabbard hanging at his side was empty. He clutched a black steel *kris,* a combination dagger and swordbreaker with a thick blade notched at regular intervals to snag an enemy's sword and snap it. A black longbow with several dozen arrows was strapped to the young man's back.

The cool Arjunian winds licked the exposed flesh at the back of his neck. It was morning and dozens of his fellow warriors from the city-state of Cynara lay scattered upon the soft moist earth of the castle walk. Some of the soldiers were strewn on the flat stretch of land behind him, others littered the downward slide toward the series of grey and burgundy homes and businesses below the ivy-covered walls and towers of the castle. Men fought on the ramparts, in the courtyard, inside the towers. Warriors swarmed up the ivy. Small fires burned in the village.

A blue-grey mist had settled on the lake beyond the township, nuzzling the underside of the bridge that crossed the waters and led to the mossy high hills. Beyond the distant hills,

3

which stretched as far as the young merchant prince could see in either direction, lay Cynara, his homeland, the capital city of northern Aranhod.

As he gazed into the soft, filtered light reflecting off the rooftops and the waters beyond, looking for a sign of Shantow, the leader of the force from Kintaro that had joined his enemies, Trevelyan wondered if he had made a mistake. The carnage surrounding him was certainly of Shantow's design; the triple-bladed *menuki* crossbow shafts jutting from the bodies boldly proclaimed their Kintaran origins. Yet there was no evidence that Shantow remained behind after dispatching Trevelyan's neighbors and friends.

The prince looked down at his weapon. As a dagger, the *kris* was designed to go in easily and disembowel the enemy when withdrawn. It seemed he would have no use for it at the moment, and so he placed the swordbreaker in its scabbard.

Resting against the smooth trunk of a warped birch tree, the prince looked into the face of one of the fallen men. Only the right side of the man's face was visible, the left ground into the dirt by the impact of his fall. Trevelyan judged the soldier to be three decades older than himself. The old man's clothing was bedraggled. The emblem of Cynara, a lone wolf upon a summit, baying in silhouette against a bloated moon, had been torn to shreds by the blades embedded in the old man's chest.

Despite his age, the fallen warrior had a thick head of soft white, lamb's fleece hair, curled and glowing as it soaked up the bright morning sunlight. A scrappy grey-white beard complemented the heavy arched eyebrow that seemed to continue straight across his heavily lined forehead. There was a sly expression on the man's face despite his current circumstances. His features marked him as handsome and strong, with a flat jaw, broad cheekbones, perfectly straight nose, and sensuous lips that were now dry and cracked.

The old soldier clutched his skrymir, holding the black shaft across his powerful body as if to warn vultures and thieves to beware; he seemed fearless, as if even death in all its horror could not trouble his good spirits. A horseman's hammer and a broadsword lay flat beneath his silver and red uniform. His single, exposed eye was open and he appeared to be staring at Trevelyan. Crimson flecks floated lazily within the dark field of the iris.

Trevelyan did not recognize him. "If only I'd caught up with that flat-nosed devil earlier, I might have saved the lot of you,'' Trevelyan snarled.

The prince closed his red-rimmed eyes as he tried without success to stifle a yawn. He had not slept in two days. When he looked to the old soldier again, the man's expression seemed to have changed to a slight frown.

Trevelyan pushed away from the tree before he became too tired to move. The prince walked past the old man and took a final look at the open plain behind him, then turned as he heard a soft whisper of air and felt the impact of the cold black arrow that had just entered his chest. Staring at the *menuki* shaft in disbelief, Trevelyan felt a twisted fascination as he watched the two thin blades attached to the main shaft suddenly spread apart, rending his chest plate.

Although he felt faint, there was no pain. Trevelyan judged the angle at which the shaft had entered his body: his attacker was hiding high above, in the branches of the tree beside him. Shaken, he reached out to touch the shaft, as if to yank it out.

"Stay your hand, Trevelyan. There are maybe more where that one came from." The voice had a lilting Kintaran accent. As if guided by an outside force, Trevelyan tore his gaze from the gruesome weapon that jutted from his chest and scanned the high branches of the birch. At first he could not see any trace of his opponent. Then one of the shorter branches moved, bending midway, and sprouted black fingers. A face rose up, no longer hidden by the hair that had been brushed down before it, and Trevelyan saw the wide, foolish smile of Shantow Yakima. The crouching man was dressed completely in black and a new bolt was already loaded into his crossbow, ready to fire.

Trevelyan's legs became weak. From the ground, an older voice, low and guttural, hissed, "Lay down and die, boy!"

The expression that painted itself across the face of the merchant prince revealed more annoyance than surprise. "Keep out of this," he whispered as he risked a glance at the old soldier. Although the grey-bearded man had not moved, he now watched Trevelyan with a wistful smile.

There was a rustle of branches. Trevelyan spun around to face his enemy who was now standing only a meter away. The bolt from the crossbow was aimed at the spot between Trevelyan's eyes. Focusing beyond the shaft, Trevelyan looked into Shantow's oval face. The man was barely a year older than Trevelyan, and his silky black hair fell to his shoulders. Beneath his thick black eyebrows were green, almond-shaped eyes, a short, straight nose that flared out and ended flat, and rich, full lips. There was a gentle, expectant sparkle in the Kintaran's eyes.

On the ground, the old man sounded impatient for company. "Come on now, boy. It's what's expected of you. Lay down and die."

"Listen to your compatriot," Shantow said, laughing. "Dead men shouldn't stand around."

"Nor should they butt into the affairs of their betters," Trevelyan snapped, directing his comment to the warrior at his feet.

Shantow's eyes narrowed. "On my honor, Lord Trevelyan, if you force me to fire at this range, the results will maybe be—" The Kintaran stopped, searching for the right word.

"Unpleasant," the old man added jovially.

"Yes," Shantow said. "Like that."

"I'm the prince," Trevelyan snapped as he fought the weakness spreading through his body. "I will die for no man." The skrymir in the old man's hands, all but forgotten by Trevelyan, suddenly shot forward and swept the legs of the merchant prince out from under him. The young man struck the ground hard, the air knocked from his lungs.

Crouching beside the fallen man, Shantow said, "I expect to find you in this position when I return with the death counters at day's end."

"Don't worry," the old man said, ignoring Trevelyan's gasps, "he will be."

Trevelyan tried to move and the hooked tip of the iron shaft held him in place.

"Now stay there and expire, do you hear me?" the older man hissed. Trevelyan lay back, staring at the blades protruding from his chest with a sullen expression. Pressing his lips together in anger, the prince remained silent.

Shantow was impressed. He looked to the grey-bearded man and said, "Delightful. Should you survive and find yourself seeking new employment—"

"He will be," Trevelyan snarled. "I certainly didn't hire him."

With a shrug Shantow got to his feet and started down the path. "What's your name, old man? I'll maybe put in a good word for you with my people."

"Chatham," the grey-bearded soldier replied.

His back turned, Shantow waved his free hand and disappeared from view along the castle walk.

Folding his arms over his chest, just below the triple-bladed shaft, Trevelyan said, "Dammit. I'll never hear the end of this."

"Oh, I don't know. At least it's a nice day for a hero's death, don't you think?"

Trevelyan grunted.

"Not a cloud in the sky."

A long, tired growl escaped Trevelyan's lips as he flicked his fingers at the flat of the skrymir's blade. "Move your weapon. If I have to die, I might as well do it in comfort."

Chatham eased the skrymir back to its original position. The young prince relaxed. "Now you're being sensible."

Trevelyan spoke very slowly, his every word punctuated with his anger. "Just *don't* talk to me."

"Huh!" Chatham spat in mock disgust. "I'm good enough to try to protect your royal backside, but not worthy of sharing a pleasant conversation with, to make the hours pass more quickly."

"Gods," Trevelyan whispered.

"Boy, *you* were the one that set the stupid rules for this tournament. Live with the consequences in silence for all I care," Chatham said as he turned his gaze away.

Trevelyan lay upon the moist earth. The morning sun, harsh and unyielding, was in his eyes. The old man was right, he knew. The rules of the contest had been carefully negotiated with Caulin Ranseur and it was too late to change them. The re-creation of a century-old battle was merely the finale of the week-long festival Trevelyan had sponsored for the enjoyment of the less fortunate in Cynara and Arjunia.

For the safety of the participants, the weapons involved were created by the power of the Forge. Although the discovery and use of magic on Autumn had been limited to the past forty-two years, Trevelyan was only eighteen, and had never experienced a time when magic did not exist. He could not imagine a world in which men could not tap into the core of their planet to draw out the *glaive*, the material they could mold and shape into any physical form they envisioned.

Naturally, objects created by the magic of the Forge had limitations. They did not last more than a day or two, their rate of dissolution dependent on their size and the strength of the caster. Items willed into existence by magic took on a pure black cast and refused any attempts to color or disguise them.

While the casters could manufacture their own clothing with magic, they could only create black, the color of the poor or working class. Wonderful bright colors and splendid fabrics were only available to the wealthy. Nevertheless, objects meant to resemble wood, stone, steel, or any fabric were as durable as the items they duplicated.

Finally, magical creations could not harm any living thing. Armor or shielding created by the Forge protected the caster, but swords, daggers, even triple-bladed *menuki* crossbow shafts only ravaged armor and clothing, leaving flesh unharmed. Thus, barring the occasional mishap due to carelessness, the games were safe, the people happy.

All but Trevelyan. According to his own rules, those "killed" in battle had to lie in the place where they were struck down until evening when the death counters arrived. Breaking the rules meant forfeiture of the considerable deposits each warrior had to put up to enter the games, the price set in accordance with the individual's total worth. The loss of the funds Trevelyan had put up to guarantee his place would have upset the economic balance of the city.

Still, it was only a game, and the only reward Trevelyan or Ranseur had to look forward to was the satisfaction of victory. The appointed governments of Cynara and Arjunia were tolerant of the festival, but unwilling to participate with matching funds or any other meaningful show of support.

Trevelyan thought once more of the Forge, and of his love, Ariodne. The prince had yet to wield the power, although she was quite skilled with it. Women inherited the magic upon their first cycle. For a man, the power to shape reality only manifested when he experienced a true union of souls with a woman. A man's potential was only released through the act when he was pure of heart and knew true love.

The last time they met, Ariodne had been quite anxious to help Trevelyan along in this matter. The prince wanted to marry her first. Unfortunately, Ariodne was a Maven, and not yet twenty-one winters. Her parents were dead, and without the blessing of her guardians, she could not marry for another seven months and thirteen days. The young woman's unrestrained life-style had made her unpopular among her kind; the

Mavens felt they were shielding Trevelyan from heartache by preventing the wedding. To make matters worse, although Ariodne truly loved him, she did not wish to be married.

Trevelyan turned his thoughts away from Ariodne. The sun was boiling the merchant prince well enough without any help from his own angers and frustrations. He wondered how long he had been lying here. Several hours, certainly.

"It's only been twenty minutes, in case you're curious," Chatham said.

"By the earth mother," Trevelyan said as he wiped away the sweat spilling into his eyes. As he turned his face to get a better view of the fallen old soldier, Trevelyan stared at the man's profile. The left side of the man's face was still hidden. "What's your name again?"

"Chatham."

The prince frowned. "If I'd met anyone with a tongue like yours, I'm sure I'd remember him. Who hired you?"

"No one." Chatham laughed. "I put up my stakes just like everyone else to enter the games."

"But you wear the uniform of my elite."

"Really? This old rag?" Chatham snorted. "I found it whipping about in the breeze, tied to a tree branch on the outskirts of town. The armor and weapons were sitting nearby, propped up beside an old well."

"You stole that uniform!?" Trevelyan shouted, rising up on one elbow.

"Helped myself is more like it." Chatham moved his head slightly and looked at the shredded breastplate. "In any case, I doubt that anyone would want it back now."

The prince shook his head, his eyes growing wide in amazement. "The wolves will come and take your hand for what you've done. You know that, don't you?"

Chatham's expression became cloudy, unreadable. "Listen, boy, don't speak to me about the justice of the damn wolves. These clothes and weapons were lying out in the elements for more than five days before I took them. If one of those smelly creatures wants to come and make an issue out of it with me, let him come!"

Trevelyan was stunned by the outburst. The grey-bearded man settled back, making himself comfortable. "Others have far more to fear from the wolves," Chatham said quietly.

Despite the heat, Trevelyan felt a cold hand probing his

body, wrapping around his heart, squeezing it. "I may be one of them," he whispered, unaware that he had given voice to his thoughts until it was too late.

"What crimes have you committed?" Concern flushed the old man's features.

"None," Trevelyan said, cursing himself for opening his mouth. He couldn't understand why he had chosen to confide in the grey-bearded soldier, of all people. "I told you, I don't want to talk."

"So we won't," Chatham said happily.

After more than an hour in the heat, the moist earth drying out and turning hard beneath their bodies, Trevelyan said, "I've had this dream."

"I've had many," Chatham said, his unflagging spirit in evidence. "Dreams, that is. Most of them died without a whimper. Go on."

Trevelyan coughed. His throat was very dry. "I don't know why I'm telling you this."

The grey-bearded warrior threw his free hand in the air. "I'm a stranger. You'll never see me again. What harm is there in telling me about your dream? You obviously don't feel comfortable confiding in your friends. Come on, tell me. What happens in this dream?"

Trevelyan paused, attempting to gather his thoughts.

"Don't try to make it pretty," Chatham said. "I know you're a poet. Forget all that. Just tell me what happens."

"It's about the wolves," Trevelyan said.

"Good," Chatham cried. "By all the sleeping gods, we certainly can't hear enough about them, now can we?"

Anger coursed through the merchant prince. He froze as one of the other "corpses" got to its feet and hobbled toward the bushes to relieve himself. The men had been so quiet that Trevelyan had forgotten he and Chatham were hardly alone on the castle walk.

"I've changed my mind," Trevelyan announced with a boldness he did not feel. In truth, the desire to burden someone else with the dream had been with him for months. Now that it was possible to do just that, he felt vulnerable.

"Just talk low, they won't hear," Chatham said, his voice charged with confidence. "I want to know."

"All right," Trevelyan said softly. "In the dream, I'm asleep in my rooms at Arayncourt Hall. I wake up suddenly, my skin dripping with sweat, my heart beating wildly out of control like a lover about to—''

"Keep it simple and stay to the *point*," Chatham growled. "You wake up. What then?"

The young prince decided to rise above his pride, which had been aroused at the possible slight to his skills as a storyteller. "My attention is drawn to the courtyard, beyond the single tree where my ancestors first kissed, to the moon, which is seen through the wiry, skeletal branches."

Chatham was silent, waiting. The young prince felt a surge of satisfaction that faded quickly. "Then I become aware of the sound of breathing in my room. Harsh, quick, staccato panting. Smells come to me: wet fur, fetid breath. I look around and see that I'm surrounded by a dozen wolves. They crowd in on every side. Logic tells me that except for the mad wolf, who died long ago, the wolves only attack criminals. In the face of the wolves, logic falls. Despite myself, I am afraid."

"What happens then?" Chatham said.

"A single wolf breaks free from the pack and approaches me. Ragged patterns of steel-grey and bone-white fur ripple in the near darkness. The wolf leaps to the bed. I jump back." The merchant prince faltered in his narrative. "An involuntary response," Trevelyan said in his embarrassment.

"I understand."

"The wolf raises its head and pads closer, climbing up my body until its paws are on my chest, its face close to mine. An unusual black configuration marks the fur of its head, covering its features like a mask. A smile comes to my lips as I wonder if the wolf had been burrowing in the soot of a chimney. The wolf, Black Mask as I now think of him, responds to my smile by pulling back his lips and showing me the brilliant white of his fangs. There is perfect stillness in his turquoise eyes. I will never forget them."

"It was only a *dream*," Chatham rumbled.

"Yes, I suppose. Black Mask opens his jaws and speaks to me. No, he *whispers*."

"What did he say?"

Trevelyan shook his head. "I don't know. I can't remember. All I know is that I felt mortal dread and my fear angered Black Mask. I screamed at him. Pleaded with him. He seemed angry that I wasn't listening to his words. Then he threw back his head and howled. Soon his howl was joined by all of his brethren. The sound was so sharp, so intense, that I was struck deaf within seconds. Then the eyes of all the wolves became cold, merciless, and grew brighter, bright as the sun, until I was blinded. But just before my vision left me, I thought I saw something that could not have been.''

"Just a dream, boy. Anything can happen in a dream,'' Chatham murmured. "Go on.''

Trevelyan's heart was thundering in his chest. "The other wolves leaped at the wolf that sat on top of me, pinning me down. As their bodies met, they seemed to merge into a single creation, as if they were but spirits, wraiths, apparitions, visions, insubstantial—''

"I *understand*,'' Chatham snarled.

"Then together as one they faded into my breast. Now my sight was gone. I could not hear. I could not see. If I spoke, if I screamed, I wasn't aware that I made any noise. When I regained my sight I was alone in the room. Moments later my hearing returned with the sound of water rushing through tunnels, then all was silence but for the sounds of the night.

"I looked out the window and could not see the moon. Something obscured it. Then I understood. Black Mask remained, perched on the open window frame. He spoke again. This time—this time I wasn't sure of what he said, but I had an idea. He said, 'Guard your soul.' Abruptly I woke and it was morning.''

Trevelyan's eyes were wide, his flesh covered in sweat. He was almost out of breath. Chatham gave the merchant prince a moment to compose himself before he said, "How long have you had this dream?''

"Months.'' Trevelyan shook as he replied.

"And it's always the same?''

"Yes, always. But I don't have the dream every night,'' Trevelyan said, attempting to regain the dignity he worried had been lost by his passionate, fear-drenched delivery. "Sometimes it skips a week at a time. Usually not more than a few days.''

"Guard your soul.'' Chatham laughed. "How very quaint. I'm sure you've heard the rumors of the black magic of Rien, and those born without souls?''

"A myth, to frighten children. I've seen the tall men and women with bruised skin, pulsing veins.'' Trevelyan did not add that he felt uncomfortable in their presence. "There are deformed births in every generation.''

"But you *have* heard," Chatham said in a hearty tone that neither confirmed nor denied his own belief in the subjects he had raised. "Well then, perhaps it's in the realm of possibilities that these childish fairy tales have left their mark upon your lower mind, and influenced your dreams."

"What could the hollow men possibly have to do with my *visions*?" Trevelyan said indignantly.

"Ah," Chatham signed. "Visions are they? I thought they were merely dreams."

The young prince pressed his lips together, his patience waning.

"I don't suppose the upcoming anniversary of your great-grandfather's journey to the summit of the wolves would have anything to do with these dreams," Chatham said.

"You're a foolish old man," Trevelyan responded much too quickly. "I don't know why I talk to you."

"Why indeed?" Chatham said. "Look, as one corpse to another—"

Trevelyan lay flat and closed his eyes. "I'm going to get some rest now. I haven't slept in days," he announced in a substantially raised voice. "Whatever I said must be written off to my exhaustion. In truth, it is part of a romantic poem I am composing for my lady, Ariodne."

Chatham's eyes narrowed. He knew the boy was no longer paying any attention to him. The old man looked away and whispered, "Pleasant dreams, young prince. I'll be here if the wolves come to bite you on the backside."

If Trevelyan heard, he made no response. Less than a minute after he closed his eyes, Trevelyan felt himself sinking into a deep, dreamless sleep.

When Trevelyan woke, his exposed skin dry and hard, a few sections already peeling, he found Chatham standing over him, blocking the low, bloated sun. Although the old man was in silhouette, Trevelyan could see that the *menuki* was no longer embedded in the man's chest. Looking about the castle walk, the young prince realized they were alone. All the remaining "casualties" had left the area.

Trevelyan moaned, trying to gather his thoughts. His hands absently brushed over the blades of the *menuki* shaft that still jutted from his chest, solid to the touch until it pierced human flesh.

"What?" Trevelyan hissed, his throat raw. "Have the death counters already been here?"

Chatham shook his head, the expression on his dark face unreadable. "It would seem the Kintarans were tired as well," he said without a trace of sarcasm. The man was relaying facts, nothing more.

An instant later Trevelyan understood. The dark shaft in his chest suddenly faded from existence.

"Stand up and resume the battle. No one has to know that you were wounded," Chatham said.

"That would be a lie."

"I won't tell, and I'll be the only one with the knowledge," Chatham said. "Except for the Kintaran, that is. And who would take the word of a lowly foreigner over yours?"

Trevelyan rose to one knee and hesitated. He could not deny that he was tempted, but there were other, more important considerations than his pride. "Shantow is my friend. He is heir to an empire that dwarfs our continent."

Chatham's head tilted to the left and he scratched the back of his neck furiously. "Then you fear a reprisal?"

Shaking his head, Trevelyan whispered, "The only reprisal I fear is from my own conscience. All men are bound by law."

"But this is not law," Chatham countered. "Merely rules of a game, rules you made up and can change at will."

The prince settled back to the ground, shoving his longbow out of the way. He felt like an imbecile for lying on top of the weapon for so many hours. A slight ache had formed in his lower back.

"Ranseur and I made an agreement. I can't go back on my word now just to escape embarrassment."

"Indeed?" Chatham murmured.

Folding his arms over his chest, Trevelyan said, "A contract is a contract. If nothing else, we Arayncourts know how to honor our pledges."

Chatham stood and walked past Trevelyan, gazing low into the valley. There was silence for a time, then Trevelyan whispered, "I wonder if any of the wolves have been here."

"You of all people should know," Chatham muttered. "Arayncourts are supposed to be sensitive to the presence of the foul creatures, even when they try to hide and observe."

Trevelyan laughed. "A fairy tale. I can no more sense the wolves than the next man."

"Despite the actions of your great-grandfather Lucian, you claim to have no special connection with the wolves," Chatham said absently, his shoulders dropped slightly. If not for Lucian's courage in braving the summit of the wolves in search of his sister, mankind would no longer exist on Autumn. The first wolves had been debating on exterminating the race of man, as they did the plague-carrying rats in Auger. The boy's overwhelming display of love and devotion restored the faith of the wolves in man.

Trevelyan frowned. "Lucian Arayncourt was a stubborn, petulant child without enough sense to bow before his betters. That he saved the race through his actions was a fluke. Read his diaries from his later years. He was the first to admit it."

"You're not jealous of what he achieved, are you?"

The young prince hesitated a moment too long, then said, "If you're going to join the other cowards, you should leave soon. The death counters will be here before long."

Moving so quickly that Trevelyan barely registered the older man's actions, Chatham sank to a crouch, pivoting his head so that the light flushed his face. The long hidden left side of his face was revealed to the young prince, who reacted with a sharp intake of breath at the sight.

A ragged scar began over the man's eye, continuing downward over his cheekbone to end at the edge of his lip. Three deep lines were cut into his flesh. The wounds were of unnatural origin and would never heal.

Chatham had been maimed by the wolves.

"The mark of three claws," Trevelyan cried as he climbed to his feet and snatched his longbow from the ground. Three of the shafts in his pack were crafted by Cynaran weaponsmiths from true wood and steel. "You're a criminal!"

The old man looked away. "I was—once. When I was young. The Adjudicators caught up with me and gave me a choice: serve my time in their rotting prisons or accept the punishment of the wolves. I chose poorly. A decade in captivity would have been far easier to take than a lifetime of reactions like yours. The wolves should kill all their prey. Their concept of mercy is a farce."

"Why don't you go to Rien, with the other outcasts?" Trevelyan said, his bitterness at being deceived coloring his words.

"They're coming," Chatham said softly. "The death counters are approaching from the village.'' Without turning, the old man added, ''If you like, I'll take a position a kilometer or so away from here, on the flatland.''

Trevelyan heard the distant laughter of children. Those too young to fight had been given the task of combing the battle-field and assessing casualties.

''I've paid my debt,'' Chatham growled. ''I've heard you speak in public, about giving those who have erred a second chance. Are your words as hollow as the soulless creatures that plague our world?''

Trevelyan was furious, but he maintained his position. ''We have nothing further to talk about. I want nothing to do with liars or pretenders. If you had come to me honestly—''

''You would have turned away sooner,'' the old man said with a smile as he walked past Trevelyan, toward the flatland that stretched away from the valley.

The young prince made no move to stop him, and within a few minutes the old man turned down a tree-lined path and vanished from the castle walk. As the children's laughter became louder, Trevelyan set his longbow beside him and lay back on the earth, his thoughts dark and troubled.

CHAPTER TWO

At half past three in the morning, Trevelyan managed to slip away from the celebration at Castle Ranseur. The triumph of the Arjunian forces over Trevelyan's Cynaran troops was ac-complished by the most narrow of degrees, but it was a victory nonetheless. Although Fluerte, Grafath, and Arjunia were de-pendent on Cynara's trade overflow for survival, there was a good deal of resentment on the part of the people of the smaller, far-less-prosperous lands. The festival and the staged battle had given the people a safe outlet to vent their frustra-tions. Predictably, Shantow had been insufferable. If there had been any members in attendance who did not hear the tale of the ambush from the Kintaran's lips, they learned of it second-hand that night.

The half moon of Autumn lighting his way, Trevelyan passed through the village, walked across the bridge, and navigated the tree-lined Arjunian hills with ease. His gaze was fixed on the glowing night fires of Cynara, which rimmed the top of the last rise, when he heard the rustle of leaves behind him. Resisting the urge to draw his *kris*, Trevelyan followed his instincts and continued at a leisurely pace.

"You'll be happy to hear that I didn't go around advertising the defeat of *your* entire company at the hands of just two of my men an hour after we left one another."

Ten paces behind the young Cynaran, Shantow cleared his throat and adjusted the backpack holding his weapons.

Soon, Shantow walked beside his friend, the reddish-orange glow of the horizon swelling as they reached the summit and found themselves at the edge of a precipice. The two men looked down at the lights of the city stretched out below.

"Cynara," Trevelyan whispered, a smile flickering across his face in the half-light. Returning to the city of his birth always stirred a passion within him that only his love for Ariodne had rivaled. Every time he viewed his homeland from such a distance, he felt as if he were seeing it for the first time.

The rectangular, walled city was wreathed by a section of land cut into huge arrowhead formations that pointed outward from Cynara in ten separate directions. The arrowheads were carefully constructed docks that jutted into a waterway known as Trader's Haven. Islands following the zigzag formations of the dock broke the waterway into two lanes capable of allowing supply ships careful, regulated access. The maze created by the unusual series of well-guarded cays and bridges made Haven the most secure port in Aranhod.

Behind the fortress walls, the shining towers, massive domes, and exquisite design gave the city distinction even at a distance. At the nexus of Cynara, just north of the Pavilion of Justice, lay the palace known as Arayncourt Hall, with its ornate columns and spacious courtyards. Although the government held its meetings and the adjudicators tried their cases in the Pavilion, Trevelyan's home saw more traffic in a typical day. Several fires and a good deal of activity could be seen in the great outdoor theater built by his father. The theater opened out from the hall's rear gardens like a gigantic shell displaying its fiery pearl. Despite the hour, performances were still going on. Turning his gaze to the far north of the city, Trevelyan could see the pinnacled splendor of the Citadel of the Mavens, where the women of the Forge remained entranced and untouched by time. The wolves' houses were low and squat, difficult to see at night.

Several leagues beyond the outskirts of the city, the hills picked up once more and joined Haven's river in its northeasterly course to the coastline and the Trader's Reach. A single, twisting spire rose above the hills, straining in its efforts to claw its way to the heavens: the summit of the wolves.

"Let's go," Shantow said, and the two men turned to the right and followed the road until it began to weave downward, to the Cynaran valley. They were halfway to the basin when they were forced to step out of the way as a young horseman riding bareback descended from the crest of the hill. He was not alone: the face of a young woman peeked out over his shoulder. She smiled blissfully as she hugged him from behind. In seconds the riders breezed past Trevelyan and his companion and were swallowed up by the winding road the young prince had just traveled. The firm arms of the overhanging branches caught their laughter and tossed it back through the night. Scowling, Trevelyan walked to the top of the hill, the urgency drained from his gait.

Ariodne, Shantow thought. Earlier he had watched Trevelyan answer the steady flow of questions concerning her unexplained absence at the party; he had handled the queries with his usual light touch, but he must have been seething. "I didn't see Ariodne at the castle. Wasn't she invited?"

"She was *invited*," Trevelyan snapped. "Ranseur's wife was upset that she couldn't bother to make an appearance, at least. I suppose it would have killed her to show some support for what I was trying to accomplish. The tension between the four regions has been ridiculous as of late. Now everyone seems to be getting along."

"Ah," Shantow said happily. The Kintaran enjoyed counseling others on matters of romance. He considered himself an expert. "You are not to be upset. Chianjur did not come either, and she is my wife."

"She's also close to nine months pregnant," Trevelyan protested. "I'd say that's a worthwhile excuse."

The green-eyed Kintaran clamped his hand on Trevelyan's

shoulder, forcing the prince to slow his pace. "I and Chianjur knew each other as children and grew up together. It is easy to forget that no one really knows what is happening in the mind of another, unless they open their fool mouths."

They reached the basin and began the long walk to the first guard station, just over a league away. "Ariodne is by no means hesitant to make her desires clear."

"I wait to hear the problem." Shantow laughed. "Is it that she's older than either of us?"

The young prince began to walk faster and said, "I don't know what the problem is, exactly. Perhaps it's with me. I want us to be together. I know she wants that, too. But she doesn't want to be *married*."

"Do you love her?"

Trevelyan did not hesitate. "Yes."

"And you are in your—what? Eighteenth winter?"

Trevelyan stared at his feet as they walked. "You already knew that. You're only a year older—"

Shantow leaped ahead of his friend and forced him to stop. "But I'm not the one that needs to be reminded of my youth. Ten years maybe will pass before I achieve rule of my empire. There will be time to learn, to grow. My friend, you have been given more responsibility than anyone your age should ever be forced to handle. Maybe Ariodne wants the two of you to have a chance to be young before you consider growing old together."

"You and Chianjur were married at my age!"

Shantow let out a deep breath and ran his hand through his wild black hair. "In Kintaro, marriages are sometimes made as early as thirteen winters."

The prince felt utterly defeated. A trio of tiny, white lights detached themselves from the guard station and sped away from the city, toward Shantow and himself.

"Go to her tonight," Shantow said softly. "Tell her you love her. Stay with her."

"You make it sound so simple," Trevelyan said as he watched the pinpricks of light on the road grow brighter.

"It *is* simple," Shantow cried. "There is maybe nothing so simple, or so beautiful."

From the road, both men could hear the sounds that accompanied the light of the wavering lanterns. The trio of horsemen that arrived moments later were members of Trevelyan's royal guard. The leader of the horsemen, a tall, sandy-haired man named Lebel, dismounted and walked forward. "Shantow Yakima? We are for you."

"Explain quickly," Shantow said flatly. From the moment he saw the riders approach, his instincts had warned him that something was terribly wrong.

"Mistress Yakima has gone into labor. Ariodne is with her. We were sent to find the two of you and bring you to the city."

A slight tremor ran through the Kintaran. He felt numb. "This is . . . She's not due for another—"

"The baby is premature," Lebel said as he leaped to his mount and extended a hand to Trevelyan. "We must hurry."

No other words were spoken as Shantow and the prince accepted the help of Lebel and his men. Trevelyan leaped into the saddle behind Lebel. Shantow rode with one of the other horsemen. The riders turned back for the city, driving the mounts forward without mercy.

Ahead lay one of close to a dozen fortified bridges that separated Cynara from the mainland. As they approached the first guard station, Trevelyan recognized one of the men on duty and screamed, "Slow us down, Konigsmark, and you'll be shoveling dung the rest of your tour!"

"It's the prince all right," the guard shouted, "let them pass!"

"But the bridge—" another guard countered.

"Go!" Konigsmark cried as he rushed inside the guard house. "Stop what you're doing and close the bridge!"

As Lebel's mount struck the first board of the bridge he heard the distant shouts of a dozen outraged men and risked a sideways glance to the rippling waters of Trader's Haven. A merchant ship was approaching, with sailors leaning over the deck, their fists raised in the air. The horseman looked back and saw that the two halves of the bridge had separated, and a gap several meters wide had already opened between the sections that rose in opposition. The bridge had been opening to let the ship pass. Lebel ground his heels into the flanks of his mount and pushed ahead as he uttered a soft prayer. The other horsemen followed his lead.

Seconds later, when they were within thirty meters of the midpoint, the bridge groaned and shook. The movement of the opposing flanks had suddenly been arrested. Their shadows lengthened suddenly as a series of bright flashes went off behind them, a signal to the opposing guard station to send a runner to the main gates.

"Good man, Konigsmark!" Trevelyan shouted in Lebel's ear. The mounts leaped over the yawning two-meter gap with ease and raced across the second leg of the bridge, to the opposite shore. Speeding past the remaining checkpoint and entering the short stretch of road that led to the city entrance, each member of the small party watched as the heavy stone doors of the fortress wall slowly opened, revealing a flood of golden, sparkling light.

Without pausing, the riders entered the city and navigated the narrow maze of short, winding streets. The cramped passageways were jammed with revelers who had taken their parties to the street. When news circulated that an Arayncourt was in their midst, the people of the city closed in. They were anxious to indulge in the legendary good cheer of the merchant prince and his friends.

There was no time wasted on pleasantries. Those who did not clear the way for the prince and the future Kintaran emperor were shoved out of the way with the blunt end of the horse hammers Lebel and his men carried.

Miraculously, when Shantow, Trevelyan, and their companions emerged at the far end of the gauntlet of well wishers, only two members of the crowd had sustained injuries of any consequence. Cutting across the city through a series of wet, filth-strewn alleys, the riders made it to the front gates of Arayncourt Hall.

The iron gates had been thrown open, and the courtyard was congested with people. The gatekeepers, who had been informed the moment Shantow's wife went into labor, left their posts and kept the celebrants away from the prince and his company as they rode to the front steps of the palace and dismounted. Lebel ordered his men to see to the mounts as he followed the prince and his friend. Once inside, they were ushered into one of the private hallways used by the servants, to a narrow staircase. Shantow's legs threatened to give out beneath him as he took the stairs three at a time. They rushed to the third floor, where the private and guest quarters were kept and heard the screams of a woman through an open door as they approached the landing. A soft blanket of hushed voices drifted below the screams.

"Chianjur!" Shantow shrieked. The sounds of conversation

ended abruptly as Shantow, Trevelyan, and Lebel climbed the final steps to the landing. The Kintaran stopped as he looked down the immense, beautiful hallway and saw a large group of people gathered outside his wife's chambers, near the end of the hall.

There was another scream from the bedroom and Shantow barreled forward, his hair matted with sweat, his eyes wild. The onlookers gathered their drinks and delicacies and hurried away from the private chamber.

"I'll keep them away," Lebel said as he broke from the side of the prince and rushed toward the men and women at the far end of the hall who tried to appear casual. Trevelyan caught up with the Kintaran, who gripped the doorjambs and stared into the spacious room that had been decorated with artifacts and fineries from his homeland. Against the east wall of the chamber lay the bed he shared with his wife. Through a thin curtain that had been fashioned from white rose petals sewed together with meticulous care, Shantow Yakima saw several figures at his wife's bedside.

It took him a moment to register the dark splotches that had struck the inside of the curtain and soaked through. With the exception of a woman's soft moans, there was silence behind the white curtain. The silence was disturbed by a weak, trembling voice that spoke in his language. Shantow heard the voice with perfect clarity, but he refused to listen to its words. They were the most horrible sounds he had ever heard in his life.

"It's dead. Thank the earth mother it was born dead."

The room began to spin, and Shantow stumbled forward, grasping at the curtains for support. As he fell, his hand struck the delicate white fabric. It ripped apart beneath his weight, and his body sank to the foot on the bed.

A cold stench filled his lungs, reviving him. Shantow raised his head. He was dimly aware of the presence of Trevelyan behind him, and his wife, who lay upon the bed with Maven Ariodne holding her, rocking her the way a mother would comfort her newborn. But his gaze was locked on the white-haired woman who held his son in her arms. The woman was Chianjur's family physician, brought from Kintaro to help ease Shantow's wife through her pregnancy.

There was a look of unfettered disgust on the woman's face as she stared at the dripping, still body of the infant she had just delivered. Shantow forced himself to rise. Trevelyan attempted to help, but the Kintaran shoved him away with surprising strength as he looked at the body of his son.

The creature's flesh was dark and bruised with thick red and green veins. Its bluish-black head was large, malformed, and its body was bloated, as if it had been drowned. Crimson stains covered its hands. The baby had tried to claw its way out, Shantow realized as he took a step closer, one hand pressing against the bed for support.

"It's over," the physician said quietly. Shantow could not remember the woman's name. He looked away from the corpse and stared into the face of his wife. There was an odd mix of fear, shame, and resignation in her beautiful countenance. Chianjur's family had originally been from the most northern territory of Kintaro, and her features were unusual for her people. Her face was long and thin, her eyes only slightly rounded. The woman's perfect blue eyes were unfocused, and her flesh was unnaturally pale. Framing her face was a tangle of soft black hair.

"She's in shock," Ariodne said softly. The Maven was a slender, fair-skinned woman with fiery red hair set in a regal style by a jewel-encrusted headdress. Her eyes were bright green, her lips bloodred since birth. She wore a silk crimson wrap that clung so tightly to her body that it left tiny red marks across the tops of her breasts.

The stains that had seeped through from the bedsheets to Ariodne's gown barely showed. There was a brief look of surprise in her face as her gaze locked with that of the Kintaran's, then it faded and was replaced by a sharp, protective glare.

He blames her, Ariodne thought. On my mother's soul, he blames her for this.

Chianjur began to sob once more.

At the foot of the bed, Shantow closed his eyes and tried to convince himself that he was experiencing a nightmare. The events he was witnessing could not have been taking place. They had no business in his orderly world.

There was a shrill, inhuman cry from behind the Kintaran that shocked him to full awareness. Shantow turned and faced the frightened old woman from his homeland who cradled the now-wriggling monstrosity in her arms. Trevelyan stood beside the woman, and whispered a single word.

"Alive."

From her bed, Chianjur laughed hysterically. The Kintaran ignored her as he stared at his son. The infant's eyes were open and staring. They were red like wine, with catlike slits for pupils. The tiny blue-black hands clawed at the old woman's arms and drew blood. Short, angry hisses came from the monster's lips.

Shantow shrugged off the backpack holding his weapons, and it struck the wood floor with a dull thud. Spreading his arms, the green-eyed Kintaran finally spoke: "Let me . . . hold him."

Snapped out of her trance by the words of the future emperor, the old woman rushed forward and unburdened herself. Shantow took the child, his face emotionless.

The old woman stammered, "The child was born without a soul. It is *hollow.*"

The deformed child writhed in his father's arms, his tiny features contorted in hatred and rage.

Shantow knelt beside his leather traveling pack and cradled the slippery body of his son in one hand as he dug into the bag and withdrew one of the silver shafts.

At the head of the bed, Ariodne understood what was about to happen before anyone else. Chianjur's hands suddenly lashed out and grabbed her arms as she tried to step away from the bed. Ariodne shouted, "Trevelyan—"

The young prince couldn't bring himself to move as he watched his friend grasp the stem of the shaft and drive it toward the monster's exposed throat.

An instant before the steel tip struck home, the child's eyes flashed open wide in fear and comprehension. Its mouth opened and its lips twisted in defiance. Impossibly, a word burst from its lips: "RIEN!"

The arrow plunged into its neck. There was a final hiss, a watery, gurgling sound, and it was over.

No one spoke. There were no cries of protest. No denials.

For a time, the silence in the chamber was complete.

Then the weeping began again, but this time it was Shantow who cried as the body of his son was taken from his stiff, unfeeling arms.

CHAPTER THREE

"How is she?"

Ariodne turned, startled by the presence of her beloved. It was midmorning, and she had left Arayncourt Hall more than an hour before, taking the longest route she knew to the tower of the Ivory Dagger. She had been staying at the small inn for the last year, because of the scandal she had caused in the Citadel of the Mavens.

Scattered about the main chamber, mixed in with the incredible clutter of smoked glass jars, lengths of rope, ornate wooden boxes of every size, rolled-up scrolls, fist-thick texts, and piles of dirty ceremonial clothing, were keepsakes from the brief, shadowy period when both her parents were still alive: stuffed toys in the form of dragons and other beasts of legend, sparkling pearl necklaces, rings with precious stones of every hue, and pale yellow sketchpads filled with portraits of Ariodne and her parents when she was a child.

Her father had been an artist whose reputation was known across the world. Consuming more than half of the east wall was a beautiful tapestry commissioned by Trevelyan as a gift. The artist had used one of her father's sketches as the basis for the portrait of Ariodne's family. In the tapestry they were depicted as she would always remember them: loving and strong. Ariodne was in the portrait as well, an innocent child unaware of the potential horrors of her world.

The other walls were a gallery of her father's paintings, strange, surreal representations of the sleeping gods, their war, and the time before man. Originally planned as a pictorial history of humanity's beginnings, when man was nothing more than the dreams of the sleeping gods made flesh, the series was never completed.

Ariodne had no bedchamber, nor was there a bed in the main room. A few chairs set aside for visitors had been buried beneath white silk bundles. Islands had been cleared throughout the chambers, and only portions of the hardwood floor were visible. Near the single window, directly across from the heavy entrance door, Trevelyan sat upon the pile of blankets, pillows, and sheets that made up Ariodne's sleeping area. He had bathed and changed his clothes. The prince wore a simple red velvet top shirt and a tight-fitting pair of white breeches stuffed into black leather thigh boots. His *kris* lay beside him. He seemed distant, shaken.

Curled up with the merchant prince, Ariodne's roommate lifted his head from Trevelyan's lap and barked twice. The soft black fur of the mastiff had been brushed in a half-dozen directions by the prince, and a tuft of hair rose straight up over his eyes. The animal's beauty did not take away from his formidable size, or the razor-sharp teeth that gleamed in the morning light.

"Lykos," Ariodne scolded as she stared into the hound's kind, expectant face. The dog panted in excitement. "You're supposed to keep the ruffians out."

A small laugh came from the merchant prince. His hand absently caressed the animal's back. Lykos sneezed, shook himself free of Trevelyan's hand, and padded to his mistress. Ariodne bent down and allowed the dog to lick her face as she caressed his flanks. "Yes, my valiant protector." She laughed as she looked back to Trevelyan. "Has he been out?"

"The city's health and safety council may be targeting your roof shortly, but yes," Trevelyan said.

Ariodne patted Lykos on the rump and sent him into one of the other rooms. The animal returned seconds later and hunched down in the doorway, his gaze fixed on the door.

The Maven walked toward Trevelyan. The sensuous, tight-fitting silk wrap of the previous evening still clung to her. She sank to the floor beside the prince, placed her arm around his shoulders, and rested her head against his chest. Despite the breeze from the open window, the sunlight that fell upon her face was almost too hot to bear. Trevelyan eased the headband from her hair, and she threw her head back, allowing her hair to flow free.

"What are you doing here?" she said as she moved her hand over his chest, sliding it inside his open shirt until her fingers spread over his rock-solid breast.

"I have declared this a day of mourning," Trevelyan said. "My business concerns can wait. How is Chianjur?"

Ariodne pressed her head into his neck and closed her eyes as she kissed the pulsing vein beneath his jaw. "She is asleep, finally. Her doctor is with her and will not leave her side. Shantow did not return *once* to check on her."

Trevelyan nodded. "He was busy disposing of the body and conducting the rituals of mourning that follow a Kintaran cremation. I cleared the theater and posted men to keep away the curious. He's still there, with his entourage."

"He recalled the bodyguards?" Ariodne whispered.

"Yes, and he won't talk about what he has done."

They held each other in silence, cherishing the warmth their closeness gave each other. Trevelyan finally spoke. "Will the wolves come for him?"

Ariodne shifted uncomfortably. "One would have to ask the wolves," she said, instantly regretting her feeble attempt at humor. The prince tried to pull away from her, but she held him tight. "I don't know. It *was* murder."

"In the eyes of the Adjudicators, perhaps."

"The baby was alive," Ariodne insisted. "He killed it."

Trevelyan brought his legs under him and stood up. This time Ariodne made no move to stop him. Looking out the window in the direction of the Pavilion, Trevelyan watched the people of his city hurry about the busy streets. Nothing had changed, yet everything had changed.

"That thing was declared dead," Trevelyan said flatly. "It was born without a soul."

Behind the prince, Ariodne pulled her legs up and wrapped her hands around her knees. Her hair fell in streams, touching the floor, as she turned her face away and looked to the portrait of her family.

"You're a Maven, Ariodne. Use your power to merge with the Stream of Life. Let the cards tell us if my friend lives or dies because of his actions."

Ariodne's throat was dry. "But you're a rational man, Trevelyan. You don't believe in our mysticism. Remember?"

Trevelyan crouched down and reached behind a stack of pillows on the floor. His hand closed on a small box he had seen many times, and could describe from memory. As he drew the black box into the light, Ariodne winced. She could see the red, engraved legend on its lid that read "little bear," her mother's name for her hairy, full-bearded husband. The long, thin fingers of the prince opened the simple latch and withdrew the silk-wrapped set of cards before she could mouth an objection.

The Maven stared without making a sound as the prince tore open the silk covering and thumbed quickly through the cards until he found the executioner. Trevelyan held the single card faceup and allowed the others to fall to the floor. On the face of the card was a picture of a ravenous wolf savaging his prey. It was the death card.

"Is this in the future of my friend?"

"In all our futures," she said softly. "Eventually."

Standing before his love, Trevelyan's shoulders fell as he released the hangman's card. "I must know if I have to take special precautions to protect Shantow's life."

Ariodne rose and stood before him, allowing her hands to meet his, their fingers gently encircling each other's.

"What would you do? There is nowhere you can send him where the wolves won't find him. Or would you try to exile the wolves and turn Cynara into a fortress? The rulers of Rien tried the same thing. They even killed the wolves sent to bring them to justice. Then the hand of the Unseen leveled the city, and turned it into a wasteland. It is still that way today, hundreds of years later.

"Besides, I *can't* read the cards now that you've handled them. I'll have to start again, with a new deck. It may take weeks before I can do as you request."

Trevelyan knew she was telling the truth. As had often been the case, his anger had defeated him. Ariodne brought her lips close to his and stopped. "There's something I want to show you. Wait here."

He nodded and settled back against the window frame. As Ariodne left the room, he stared down at the scattered array of cards at his feet. Only three cards had landed faceup. Trevelyan kneeled down and stared at the cards until Ariodne returned. She had taken off the silk wrap and removed her jewelry. A loose-fitting, thin blue robe was draped over her body. She was tying the belt at her waist when Trevelyan noticed the strange black flower in her teeth.

He drew a sharp breath as she took the flower from her teeth and held it before her face. "The black lotus!"

Smiling, Ariodne nodded and pressed the soft black petals to her nose. Inhaling deeply she sighed, "Sweet."

Next to the window, Trevelyan stared at her in shock. In their religion, the lotus signified eternal life. It was the black lotus, however, that the first wolves had used to trap the sleeping gods. The scent of the flower had placed the four gods of the elements in a state from which they would never revive. The flower was incredibly rare on Autumn. Trevelyan had only seen one other in his lifetime, and that flower was preserved in amber.

The young prince watched her carefully, waiting for a sign of weakness, or some indication that she would collapse.

Ariodne waved the flower before her face, then laughed and threw the lotus to the floor.

"You see? I have breathed in its fragrance, but I am no immortal, nor am I trapped in a dream. I will wither and die, just like the lotus." Trevelyan watched as the flower crumpled to fine black dust, then vanished from existence.

"It was a trick," he said. "Its stalk was black. You made the image of the lotus with the Forge. It wasn't real."

She laughed and covered the distance that separated them. "But you believed because you wanted to believe. You were blind to the truth."

Trevelyan closed his eyes as Ariodne took his hands once more. She kissed him lightly on the forehead.

"The legends aren't meant to be taken literally, don't you see? I can't use my powers as a Maven to predict the future. The gift of prophecy is just a myth."

"Then what about the cards, and the Stream of Life?"

She kissed him again, this time on the lips. The prince barely responded. "When we die, our souls go to the Stream of Life, where our knowledge, our memories, are washed away, so that we may enter the Well of Souls pure, and rejoin the world in a new form."

"A child knows that," Trevelyan said as he slipped one hand around her waist. When she moved to kiss him again, he pulled her close and pressed his lips hard against hers.

"The history of all man can be found within the stream," Ariodne said breathlessly as she reached up and caressed the side of his face. "In her trance, a Maven can sift through the knowledge and memories of countless generations, seeking advice on specific questions put to her."

They kissed again, and Ariodne's lips parted slightly. Trevelyan started as her tongue probed his pale lips, then he relaxed and opened his mouth as well. Ariodne pulled away. She was barely able to speak.

"The cards let us . . . ah, communicate what we learn while entranced . . . "

Trevelyan's entire body was shaking. "You're cold," she whispered. "We should close the window."

The red-haired Maven looked past the prince to the window. As she tried to step away, his fingers took hold of the belt at her waist. With a single tug, the belt was released and the robe fell open.

He stared down at her perfect body, then forced himself to look at her brilliant green eyes. "I love you," he said.

"Yes," she whispered, and shrugged off the robe.

Behind them, Lykos began to whine.

Trevelyan pressed his lips together, a smile straining to erupt. Ariodne broke into a grin as the mastiff padded closer, plopped down at her feet, and sneezed. A cascade of laughter filled the room as Trevelyan excused himself and struggled with the dog. He dragged the beast to the private stairwell leading to the roof, shoved the animal up the first few steps, and slammed the door.

When he returned to the main chamber, Ariodne was standing beside the window, the robe held in front of her. She closed the window and started to turn.

"Wait," Trevelyan said, his voice cracking.

Ariodne laughed and looked down at the street. "All right," she said, a wicked edge to her voice.

"So beautiful in this light," the prince whispered as he eased behind her, wrapping his arms around her waist. "We shouldn't," he said as he kissed her neck.

They stared out at the street below, the city alive with activity. "We *should have* a long time ago," she murmured. "Let's get away from the window."

Ariodne spun in his arms, leaving the robe in his hands. She knelt down on the bed of pillows and reached for Trevelyan. He backed away and sat on the window frame as he pulled off his red velvet top shirt, removed his thigh boots and breeches, then dropped to his knees.

A moment later they embraced, Trevelyan's strong arms easing Ariodne to the floor. She felt the cold sting of the Cards on her bare back and ignored them. Their bodies crushed together as they kissed. Ariodne took hold of one of his bold, probing hands and pressed it against her chest.

"Feel my heart?" she breathed. "It's beating for you. Just

for you. I love you, Trevelyan Arayncourt. I will *always* love you."

"Then marry me," Trevelyan said urgently.

A wide smile spread across Ariodne's face. "Perhaps," she said, her voice high and filled with deviltry.

"Perhaps?"

"Sorry, that's all you get," she purred. "For now."

They kissed, and Trevelyan's hand slid past her heart, skimming across her bare flesh until she cried out with pleasure. "Well"—she laughed—"maybe not *all*."

After they made love, Trevelyan lay beside Ariodne, unable to catch his breath. For a time they had taken comfort in the pleasures their bodies had to offer each other, pushing away the horror that was only a few hours in the past. But now, as they lay together on the floor, images of the murder they had witnessed intruded upon his thoughts.

"If the wolves come for Shantow, there's little we can do," Trevelyan said. "But we don't have to tell the Adjudicators anything."

With her free hand, Ariodne wiped the sweat from her face before it dripped into her eyes. "I don't believe you're talking about this now," she said.

"I know," Trevelyan said as he squeezed her hand and brought it to his lips. "Sorry. Being with you was so much more than I had ever dreamed it could be. We two are one, *finally*. But I can't stop thinking about what Shantow did, and what he said later, that he had done it out of love."

They were quiet again. As hard as he tried, he could not banish his thoughts of the grey-bearded man he had met on the castle walk, and the scar the old man bore: the mark of three claws, the punishment for allowing another to die due to one's own selfishness or inaction.

Ariodne swallowed hard. "If it helps you, tell me."

"Don't you see?" he said harshly. "I could have stopped it. I could have prevented Shantow from killing his son."

The Maven considered the implication. By the law of the Unseen, Trevelyan was also a criminal. Ariodne sat up and turned to stare at Trevelyan's peeling, sunburned face. "All the gods!" she whispered, fear overtaking her.

"If the wolves come for Shantow, they'll come for me, too. Please help me, Ariodne, to save Shantow *and* myself."

"The cards are tainted," she said. "Without them—"

Trevelyan cut her off. "When I dropped your cards, only three landed faceup. Could that mean anything?"

The Maven bit her lip. "Describe them."

"Better I show you," Trevelyan said as he turned and searched the floor for the cards he had seen. He found two of them easily. The third had to be peeled from Ariodne's back. She slipped into her robe. Despite the closed window, she felt a terrible chill as she pointed at the first card.

"The Tower," Ariodne said, reciting from texts she had studied from the day she had been apprenticed to the Mavens, just after the death of her parents. "An ambitious structure build on a foundation of false premises, misapprehensions. When knowledge is used for evil purposes, then destruction reigns down from the Unseen."

"*Rien,*" Trevelyan choked. "What that creature said before Shantow killed it."

The red-haired maven shuddered. "One interpretation," she said and moved on to the next card. "The Moon, representing sleep and dreams."

The merchant prince dragged one of the sheets from his feet and covered himself as fear turned the sweat covering his body to ice. He thought of Black Mask, and his dream.

"The Moon's three phases of intuition concern body, mind, and spirit. Through the eye of the Moon, the Unseen watches over the birth of the soul into its next life."

Trevelyan's eyes were growing dark. "And the last?"

"Judgment," Ariodne whispered. "The reawakening of conscience under the influence of the wolves. The mystery of birth in death."

Trevelyan laughed bitterly and gathered his clothing.

"Don't leave," Ariodne pleaded.

"I must," Trevelyan said without emotion as he quickly dressed and attached his swordbreaker to his belt.

Watching her lover with a tired, pained expression, Ariodne wondered how the warm afterglow of their lovemaking could have already turned so cold. Trevelyan was not her first lover; there had been many. But he was the only man who had ever truly received her heart.

She couldn't bear to see the practiced, detached look he now wore on his face. Sensing this, Trevelyan turned away and looked out the window as he buttoned his top shirt. Three streets away, to the south, he saw a squat, red stone building.

Few men had ever visited the house and come away unscathed. Those who left it and still possessed a tongue gave it a name: *the house of judgment.*

In truth, it was the house of the wolves, one of many spread through the city.

"I'm sorry, Ariodne," he said softly. "I don't want to leave you. But it seems Shantow and I have an appointment with the wolves, and it will do neither of us any good to keep them waiting."

Ariodne sat on the floor, hugging herself. "Yes," she said, her voice dry and cold. She did not bother to say that the cards could be wrong. Her instincts said they were true.

At the window Trevelyan stared at the red stone building. If he had looked straight down, to the busy street four stories below, he might have seen the pair of tall, hooded men, who had been staring up at the window for the past quarter of an hour. He might have seen one of the men gesture in his direction, then point at the ground-level entrance to the Ivory Dagger before both men hurried inside.

Instead, he turned away from the window, found Ariodne standing before him, and opened his arms to his beloved for a final embrace. They kissed, but there was no passion, only resignation in the kiss. "You have magic," she said in a small voice. "The Forge is now yours. Our love made it so."

Her words surprised him. The magic of the Forge was the last thing on his mind.

"If your will is great enough, you can create armor that even the wolves can't tear through," she whispered, then pulled away. "Go with my love in your heart. Even the wolves can't take that away from you."

"No one can," Trevelyan whispered. His facade crumbled as he caressed the side of her face, then ran for the door. Seconds later it slammed shut behind him, and she heard his footsteps racing on the wooden stairs. Ariodne went to the window and looked down to the street, waiting to see Trevelyan hurry away from the Ivory Dagger. Long minutes passed, and her tension became unbearable. Trevelyan had not left the building.

"What's keeping you?" She opened the window and suddenly she heard a scream. The glass window of the first floor exploded. She was about to run for the door when she saw the crowd parting at the end of the street.

Her heart nearly exploded in her chest as she saw the pack of wolves that raced toward the Ivory Dagger.

CHAPTER FOUR

Seconds after Trevelyan had closed the door to Ariodne's rooms and started down the stairs, he felt an incredible urge to turn around and go back. His need to be with her nearly overwhelmed him. Then he thought of the wolves.

Trevelyan did not want Ariodne to see the wolves lead him to the house of judgment. There was no telling when they would come, but after the warning Ariodne had found in the cards, he knew their arrival was certain.

Windows at each landing provided the only source of light as Trevelyan ran to the ground-floor landing and stopped to adjust his top shirt. A pleasant, yet thoroughly artificial smile was on his lips as he pushed the service door open and stepped into the first of the smoke-filled back rooms of the Ivory Dagger.

As the merchant prince entered the crowded room, passing tables where men gambled freely, despite government restrictions, he was assaulted by three men whom he had turned away several times at Arayncourt Hall. They were armed with a cartload of crumbling texts, endless reports, and extended proposals for some new moneymaking scheme. The men were young, barely out of university, although one had already gone to balding. Their desperation was obvious.

"Lord Trevelyan, we only need a small amount of funding to continue our research," the balding man groaned.

Trevelyan's stony facade of tolerance was ground to dust within seconds. He cursed the tavern master, whom he had paid a generous amount to ensure that he was not bothered.

"I will not listen to matters of finance today," Trevelyan snarled as he shoved past the balding man, who stumbled back over a chair. The reports the spokesman held in his arms flew into the air as the man struck the floor. His companions rushed forward, grabbing at the cloud of papers. As the sheets that were not caught drifted to the floor, the blond-haired, balding man shook his head and tried to regain his senses.

A few of the gamblers laughed as Trevelyan stormed past. The merchant prince ignored the pleas that issued behind him from the would-be entrepreneurs as he walked briskly through a slightly larger room where a cluster of earnest young men and women indulged in a philosophical dispute over the use of magic in modern art while they smoked some unpleasant new import from Kintaro. A stocky figure cloaked in shadows blocked the entrance to the taproom of the inn.

"You could learn a thing or two about tolerance," a familiar guttural voice said. The man blocking the doorway turned and folded his arms over his chest. Despite the poor light, Trevelyan recognized the shock of curly, white hair and the deep-set eyes that glittered bloodred in the darkness. He strained his eyes and made out the ragged scar below the man's eye. The prince knew he could not be seen with such a man.

"The criminal," Trevelyan spat as he raised his hand to push the grey-bearded man out of his way.

"Wouldn't do that," Chatham sighed.

The prince ignored the old man. His open palm was within an inch of Chatham's armored chest when the man suddenly sprang from the doorway. Snatching the wrist of the prince in a tight, painful grip, Chatham yanked the young man forward with enough force to make his feet leave the ground. Snatching a handful of the prince's top shirt in his free hand, Chatham spun Trevelyan around and deposited him in a chair that almost shattered beneath his weight. Trevelyan had only enough time to blink and question his senses before Chatham sank to the chair directly beside him.

"I have no time for this," Trevelyan said as he tried to rise. The sharp tip of a blade nudged his side. Chatham's powerful hand closed on his shoulder and eased the prince back to the chair. Leaning against the wall at their backs were the old man's skrymir and horse's hammer. His broadsword remained in its hilt.

"Get comfortable, boy," Chatham growled.

Trevelyan scanned the room. Several people had turned in the prince's direction. He was about to demand assistance when he felt the knife prick his bare flesh. Trevelyan smiled warmly and the onlookers went about their business.

"I didn't think you would be this stupid," Trevelyan hissed.

"What is it you want? Money? You are a thief, aren't you? Did you find a sleeping body to steal that dagger from at the game?"

Chatham laughed. "Why are you in such a hurry, boy? Running from the wolves, are you?"

Trevelyan tensed. If the Adjudicators had learned of Shantow's actions the previous night, they might have set a bounty for the prince and his companion. He wondered if Lebel had come back and witnessed the slaying. Or if some other curious party wandered close to the room.

"Or is it running *to* them?" Chatham snarled. "Don't worry, boy. I'm the last person who would advocate that course of action."

The merchant prince closed his eyes. "How did you know?" he whispered.

"It's the fear stink. I can smell it on you. Only one thing in this world brings on that scent. The wolves."

Trevelyan nodded. The blade eased back from his side. Chatham's grip on his shoulder, however, remained firm.

"We should talk, boy," Chatham said softly. "We should talk before you do anything rash. Tracking you wasn't easy."

"My people will take you apart for this," Trevelyan said. The knife poked him once again.

"Be quiet. By all the gods, you just don't know what's good for you, do you?" Chatham didn't wait for a reply. "I came here for a reason. There's something you ought to know. Now shut up for a moment and listen."

The prince nodded slowly. Chatham was about to continue when the trio of men who had attempted to petition Trevelyan appeared before them. The balding man slammed his report on the table.

"In your public addresses you said that a businessman must know when to stand up and take his stab at success."

Trevelyan's shoulders slumped. "Kill me now," he whispered to the grey-bearded man.

"Do you have to listen to this all day?" Chatham said, genuine concern in his voice.

"This is mild compared to the tedium I face."

"What horror," Chatham said.

The balding man cleared his throat. His companions fixed their gazes on a stain marring the floor. "You have said that a businessman never turns away anything that is offered him.

Well, fate has offered us a chance to tell you of our venture, and I insist you listen.''

Chatham growled. A low, throaty rumble built up in the back of his throat and rolled from the cracks between his gritted teeth. The balding man's gaze drifted to Chatham, who lowered his head and eased his lips back in a feral smile. ''If you stay, I'll be forced to tear your hearts out with my teeth and devour them one by one.''

As if to illustrate his point, the grey-bearded man used his free hand to take a wooden jar from the center of the table and place it on top of the balding man's report.

''A touch of black pepper makes it all the more tasty,'' the old man said as he flicked the cover from the jar and spilled the contents on the man's papers.

''Lord Trevelyan, you can't allow this outcast to speak to a citizen in this way. This is an outrage.''

Chatham took another wood jar from the center of the table and slammed it beside the pepper. ''I understand rosemary goes even better, although I haven't had the occasion to try it as yet.''

''You're joking,'' the balding man said. The muscles in his cheeks quivered as he spoke.

''Am I? Who will be the first to test me?''

With trembling hands, the balding man cleared the spices from his report. He dusted the papers carefully, as if they comprised a priceless volume of long-forgotten history, or the last copy of a precious work of literature. Gathering the papers in his hands, the man frowned and motioned for his companions to follow his lead.

''Wolves blood,'' Chatham sighed as the men moved off. ''I'd go mad if I had to face that every day.''

''They're leaving,'' Trevelyan snapped. ''Tell me what's so damned important.''

''A fair question,'' Chatham said as he withdrew the blade. ''Do you see those two sitting at the table across the room, near the door? The hooded ones, dressed as shamans, wearing black and gold robes, boots, and gloves.''

The prince's gaze followed the sullen trio led by the balding man as they walked to the table Chatham had mentioned.

''Yes, I see two men by the window,'' Trevelyan said as he considered running from the grey-bearded madman. Then he thought of the old man's incredible speed and decided to remain. The merchant prince shifted his gaze away from the door and found himself staring down at his sunburned hands.

"They're not men. I've been following them halfway across this city," Chatham said. "They've been stalking you just as I have."

"Assassins?" Trevelyan said, suddenly regretting his decision to allow his bodyguards to pursue other options. "And what do you mean, they're not men?"

"They're not human," Chatham grunted. "And yes, they've been talking about killing you all morning. They seemed very happy at the prospect. I felt you deserved a warning."

Trevelyan glanced back to the doorway just as the young future businessmen left the inn. The table by the window was empty. The prince went back to the study of his hands.

The "assassins" had probably left behind the balding man and his friends, Trevelyan realized. He no longer felt anger for the old man. Chatham obviously belonged in an institution. The strain of going through life with a scar that marked him as an eternal outcast had driven him mad. The prince wondered if that would be his fate, too. Then he heard the sound of the old man's dagger striking the ground.

"Trevelyan!" Chatham shouted, startling the younger man from his thoughts. The prince looked up just in time to see a pair of throwing knives sailing at his face when the table suddenly rose up before his eyes. The sound of the heavy blades striking the wood rang in his ears as he saw the sharp tips emerge from the underside of the table. Chatham's large, powerful hands gripped the closest of the four table legs as he pushed away from his chair, the table rising into the air as he stood. Trevelyan caught a glimpse of the hooded men breaking in opposite directions as the small table was hurled at them. The table flew six feet and crashed into the edge of another table where a young couple was enjoying an early meal. They drew back in shock as their table was upended, their plates skidding to the floor and shattering.

The young prince leaped from his chair and drew his *kris*. The hooded men were back on their feet, and Trevelyan was startled by each man's incredible height. Their faces were obscured by shadows captured within their hoods, but their empty gloved hands opened and closed lazily, like the maws of a wolf savoring his feast. The young couple from the opposing table ran for the exit. A half-dozen groups from the large taproom, including those sitting at the bar, surged forward. Others had appeared at the door from the back room.

"Keep back!" Trevelyan commanded, then turned slightly in Chatham's direction. "I'll take the one on the left."

The hooded man Trevelyan had targeted swept forward and struck the wall as Chatham's hand closed over Trevelyan's wrist and pulled the young prince out of danger. The grey-bearded man wanted to scold Trevelyan on several points: announcing his plan to his enemy, separating from his partner, and refusing the help that had been offered to him from his fellow Cynarans at the inn. Unfortunately, there was no time for lectures. The second attacker was rushing forward, and his companion had taken the horse's hammer the grey-bearded man had left against the wall and was preparing to swing the spiked weapon at the head of the prince.

"Always take whatever help is offered!" Chatham managed to say as he used his left hand to snatch a pepper jar from another table and hurl the container at the face of the hooded man before him. The man dodged the jar with ease and it sailed across the room with surprising velocity. Two men dropped to the floor to avoid the jar as it flashed across the room and struck the front window, shattering the glass.

"Trevelyan's continuing the games!" a drunkard from the bar shouted as he smashed his glass upon the bar.

At the center of the conflict, barely a heartbeat had passed since the hooded man had crouched to avoid the jar Chatham had thrown. The white-haired fighter took advantage of the momentary respite by drawing his broadsword and lunging forward. His victim howled as the blade pierced the robes and met with a thick, tough hide. An inhuman cry sounded in the inn as Chatham forced the blade deeper.

From the doorway to the back rooms a red-haired gambler shouted, "This is no game! Those are real weapons!"

Behind the old man, Trevelyan thought, So nice of you to notice. Gripping his *kris* he turned and looked at his hooded opponent. Light reached into the crevice of the hood's parted folds and Trevelyan saw the dark, snarling face of his attacker. The man's skin was bluish-black, splotchy, and bruised. His eyes were catlike slits. Red and green veins throbbed in his neck and temple. Trevelyan saw all this in the fraction of a second before the monster swung the horse's hammer at his face.

Dropping to his knees, Trevelyan raised his *kris*. The shaft of the hammer was caught in the teeth of his swordbreaker, but the impact of the weapon dragged the prince along with it. The blue-skinned attacker had placed so much force in the blow that he could not stop the arc he had begun. Instants before the head of the hammer buried itself in the wall, Trevelyan released his grip on the *kris* and was thrown into a pile of chairs.

The prince felt a blinding pain as he struck his head on a heavy wood leg. Dazed by the blow, Trevelyan shook his head and brought his legs up under his body. Two meters to his right, he heard a heavy thud as the *kris* dropped to the wood floor, shaken loose from the hammer as the weapon struck the wall and sank into the wood.

Then, directly behind him, came the sound of a blade scraping along wood. The prince was frozen. The monster had found Chatham's discarded knife.

Despite the throbbing in his head, Trevelyan scrambled toward his weapon. His movements were sluggish, his reflexes dulled by the pain. The long, thin fingers of the prince were a meter from his weapon when he felt a slight pressure at the base of his skull and realized the creature had taken hold of his silky tail of hair.

With a sharp, agonizing yank, the attacker dragged Trevelyan to his feet, and slid the cold blade of the dagger against the young man's throat. More than a dozen people had moved forward, weapons drawn, ready to assist the prince.

"I have him!" the attacker screamed. "Try to help him and he's dead!"

Less than three meters behind the prince, Chatham cried out in frustration. He knew that he should have killed both hooded men earlier in the day, when he had the chance. But he had never expected them to be foolish enough to attack in a public place. The grey-bearded man wondered what they hoped to gain by killing Trevelyan here, where the crowd would tear them apart the instant the prince was dead.

Grappling with the hooded giant he had just impaled, Chatham jerked his blade upward, causing another wail of pain. Then the attacker's hand shot out and struck the flat of the blade, shattering it easily, although a section of gore-drenched metal still jutted from his side.

A five-inch, jagged length of steel remained on the hilt of the broken, two-handed sword, and Chatham attempted to drive the makeshift dagger at the throat of the hooded man when his attacker darted to one side. Gripping the old man's wrists from above and below, the hooded man rammed Chatham's face with his elbow in a quick succession of blows.

No one tried to help the white-haired outcast. He was not surprised. Chatham allowed his body to go limp. The hooded man's grip on Chatham's wrists was firm, and the grey-bearded man swung his body against that of his tormentor. As the section of the broken sword that remained imbedded in the hooded man's side loomed before his chest, Chatham prayed that his armor would hold. In a way he would have welcomed death, but not now, not like this.

The hooded man screamed as Chatham's body struck the blade, forcing it all the way through his body until it ripped through the robes at the giant's back. The black-gloved hands of the hooded man sprang open and Chatham sank to his knees, ramming his elbows into the moist wound he had created. His attacker bellowed and doubled over, his chest dropping toward Chatham's back. The old man slid out from under the toppled giant and allowed the hooded man to fall flat on the floor. Then he pounced on the man's back, pulled off the hood, and slid the five inches of steel from the hilt of his broken sword against the throat of the black-haired, blue-black-skinned creature.

"Stalemate," Chatham said as he gazed into the eyes of his attacker's companion, who continued to hold his blade against Trevelyan's throat. "Let him go."

The dark man holding Trevelyan shook his head. His cat's eyes blazed with hatred. "We were born of the hollow. Do you know what that means?"

Chatham was not interested in the ramblings of the creature. Something else had captured his attention. His nose wrinkled as he sniffed the air. There was another scent on the young man, one he had avoided for so long that he had almost forgotten what it meant. Magic, Chatham thought. Trevelyan can use the magic.

The gaze of the prince met the old man's face as Chatham mouthed two words. *The Forge.* Trevelyan closed his eyes slowly and attempted to concentrate.

"Don't ignore me!" the monster said, his blade biting into Trevelyan's throat, drawing blood. He felt his body shaking and he found it impossible to focus past his fear.

"All right," a soft feminine voice said from the crowd of people at the doorway to the back rooms. "Tell us what it means." The merchant prince felt his heart slow and his fear ease away as he saw Ariodne step into the room. She was wearing shining black armors and mails that she must have forged only moments before.

"Maven Ariodne," the dark man hissed. "The prince's whore."

Trevelyan squirmed in the dark man's grasp. "Bastard."

The dark man laughed. "As a Maven, you of all people should know that a man born of the hollow is a man born without a soul."

"You believe you can take his soul to fill your void," Ariodne said gently as she moved closer. The slur meant nothing to her. "And murder is the way to achieve this."

There was a flurry of activity just outside the window. Dark shapes moved back and forth. She forced herself to ignore what she had seen. Fortunately the people inside the inn were too engrossed to notice what was happening outside.

"Only if the soul is great, or *descended* from greatness," the hollow man proclaimed. "Trevelyan's family is blessed by the wolves. His great-grandfather—"

"I know. But *he's* just a boy," Ariodne sighed. "How great can his soul be?"

Trevelyan choked off his own reply and frowned.

"And could it possibly be great enough to fill your need, and the need of your friend?"

The hollow man glanced to his companion on the floor.

"Don't listen," the man cried. "His soul will be more than enough for us both."

Sitting atop the giant, Chatham pressed the blade harder against the monster's throat. "Quiet," he snarled.

Ariodne stepped past Chatham and his prisoner, stopping just a few feet away from the man holding Trevelyan. She crossed her arms and raised an eyebrow.

"You don't believe me?" she said. "But you said it yourself. A Maven should know these things."

The hollow man's gaze sped to his companion, then met the glittering, red eyes of the grey-bearded man. "She's right. Kill him if you must. I'm taking this one with me."

"No!" the giant on the floor shouted as he grabbed Chatham's hand before the old man could cut his throat. The wounded giant rose up on his knees, pitching the grey-bearded man to the floor.

As the giant rushed forward, Ariodne allowed the image she had created in her mind to become reality as she stared at the exposed throat of her lover. There was a hiss and the air turned rancid as a black, steel-plated collar suddenly appeared between the blade and Trevelyan's flesh. Ariodne took Trevelyan's hand and pulled him free of the hollow man's embrace, the creature's blade scraping across the metal collar of the prince.

They were barely free of the hollow man when his screaming companion collided with him, the second man's hands closing over the hollow man's throat. The wounded attacker lifted the hollow man into the air by his neck and threw him back at the wall, where the sharp spike of the horseman's hammer waited.

The hollow man's head struck the wall less than an inch away from the spike. Stunned by the impact, the blue-skinned monster sank to the floor, knocking over Chatham's skrymir. The razor-sharp hook hit the ground an instant before the hollow man, and he halted his descent before the blade could bite into his chest.

"Enough of this," Chatham said as he ripped a sword from the grasp of one of the onlookers and advanced on the wounded giant. The dark man turned and opened his gloved hands.

Everyone in the taproom of the Ivory Dagger froze as a chorus of growls erupted from beyond the shattered window.

"You imbecile," the wounded man of the hollow said as his companion used the staff to get to his feet. "I never should have listened to you."

The wolf pack outside the window began to howl. Their cries were high, piercing, and mournful.

The call of retribution.

The hollow man hefted the skrymir as he looked at his companion. "Better we should die at each other's hands, is that what you're thinking?"

The wounded attacker said nothing as he ripped at the collar of his robe and flung the cloak from his body. The purpose of his disguise had been to hide his deformity. Having stripped himself of all but a fur cloth at his loins, the dark man reveled in his strangeness. The bulging red and green veins throughout his powerful body surged as if they were about to burst. He enjoyed the frightened gasps of his captive audience.

The hollow men knew they wouldn't leave the inn alive. It

didn't matter. They had a statement to deliver. A declaration of hatred and contempt.

"I've been ready to die from the moment I entered this life," the dark man snarled.

The prince stood beside his love and squeezed her hand. "What are they talking about?" Trevelyan whispered. "The punishment for attempted murder is severe, but it's not death. The wolves take only your hands, eyes, and tongue. Don't they understand the law?"

"That's the law for man," she replied quickly. "The hollow are judged by more harsh standards. Trevelyan, you've got to get out of here."

"No," he said as he looked to Chatham and saw the man's reddish scar. "I won't run from my destiny."

Ariodne looked to the window. The wolves were no longer prowling back and forth outside the inn. They had issued a summons and the guilty had not appeared. Now they were preparing to strike.

She suddenly realized that she and her lover were standing within striking distance of the six-foot skrymir the hollow man held in his hands.

The realization came too late.

"I won't die without a soul!" the blue-skinned monster screamed as the skrymir flashed in his hands, the curved blade descending toward Trevelyan's face. Before Ariodne or the prince could move, a figure already in motion surged from the crowd and shoved Trevelyan out of harm's way. As the prince struck the floor he heard a sound behind him that sickened his heart: the skrymir struck home, burying itself in the flesh of his savior.

Trevelyan rolled and saw the disfigured, bloodied face of the young, balding man who had approached him a few minutes ago. For an instant he couldn't understand what he was seeing. The balding man had left the inn. His return had to have been obscured by the confusion of the attack.

The dying man fell forward, a small group of papers stained with his blood held tight to his chest.

"Trevelyan!"

The prince heard Ariodne's scream and raised his arm. He was only dimly aware of the gory red hook of the skrymir as it bore down on him once more. The image of a shield appeared first in his mind, then became a reality as he felt a strain in his chest, a slight film of sweat upon his skin. He heard the sound of wind rushing past him and smelled bitter almonds. His first view of the heavy black weight tied to his arm came as it was battered toward his face. The blade of the skrymir struck and bounced off his shield.

Rising to one knee, Trevelyan heard a scream from the crowd and instinctively turned to the window.

The prince stared at the jagged opening in the center of the window, and the spiderweb pattern of cracks leading away from the damage. The first of a half-dozen wolves had leaped toward the window, its paws striking the fragmented, razor-sharp section of glass below the opening. The window exploded as the first wolf burst through the glass, followed by five of his companions. The wolves flooded through the opening, showering glass in their wake.

The first wolf moved in a grey blur, landing on a table a considerable distance from the window and springing toward the soulless man bearing the skrymir. The blue-skinned creature raised the hook-tipped shaft a moment too late.

The wolf's jaws clamped down on the hollow man's left wrist, biting down hard as the impact of its body forced both creatures to the floor. Just before the wolf and his prey sank out of view, the soulless man screaming in fear and pain, Trevelyan lowered his crude, black iron shield and caught a glimpse of the face of the wolf.

He recognized the strange black pattern surrounding its features and forced himself to hold back his own cry of shock. It was the wolf that had haunted his dreams.

Black Mask.

Two more wolves, one with auburn fur, the other pure white, were already inside, vaulting toward the hollow man's companion. The wounded man raised his hands, curled into claws, in the air as he grimaced and welcomed the attack.

The wolves launched themselves at their prey. The wounded giant barely flinched as he felt the claws of the auburn wolf scrape his arm. His body rocked as its maw closed over this wrist and the full weight of the animal slammed against his chest, its paws raking deep gouges in his flesh as the wolf struggled to find some way to dig in and support its weight. The fur of the wolf was wet. The animal stank. The soulless man felt the cold shock of saliva dripping from his wrist, and looked to see his own blood mixed with the wolf's spit.

The white-furred wolf struck the wrist of the monster's free hand, and the wounded giant toppled, falling back to the hardwood floor as yet another wolf, a white-furred creature with four black paws, leaped at his face.

At the window, the last of the wolves arrived. The pair of wolves moved in unison, and seemed indistinguishable from each other. Salt and pepper fur rippled as the wolves leaped to the aid of the first wolf.

It was over in moments. Trevelyan was surprised to hear the soft, gurgling moans of one of the victims. Ariodne had been wrong. Human justice applied to the hollow.

The moans abruptly stopped.

No one spoke. Only the soft padding of animal paws—tiny sharp clicks of hard claws tapping wood—was audible above the ragged breathing of those who had watched the spectacle of the short battle and the justice of the wolves.

Trevelyan remained on his knees as the leader of the wolves approached, its back paws sliding on one of the slick pools of blood before the prince. No one dared laugh as the animal scrambled to regain its footing. Trevelyan watched the familiar patterns of grey and white fur surge as the animal fought to contain its natural instincts now that the blooding had begun. The turquoise eyes that stared out from the black mask of its face were no longer still. They were wild and fierce.

Trevelyan's hand went to the left side of his face, covering a wound that had not yet been created. He bowed his head as the wolf came within striking distance.

"Not here," he whispered, attempting not to beg. "I will go to the house of justice."

Black Mask snorted and raised its paw. The edge of its sharp claws tapped Trevelyan's face, then withdrew. The prince trembled as he raised his face. He did not understand the gesture. The blood that soaked the paws of the wolf had been transferred to the face of the prince.

Behind Trevelyan, Chatham moved to Ariodne's side. The old man's face bore an expression of contempt as he stared at the shadowy face of the wolf and whispered, "Get on with it."

If the first wolf heard, he did not respond. As Black Mask stared at the prince, the wolf with auburn fur joined him and gestured with its snout at the body of the young, balding man. The reddish-brown fur of the wolf was dark and wet with blood. The animal nuzzled the body's ribs tenderly.

Trevelyan shook his head. A pressure was building up inside him. He was in the presence of a creature whose race was given breath by the Unseen, the creator of the elemental gods who in turn created the world and all mankind. Even more, this particular wolf had plagued his dreams for months.

Anger coursed through him as he recited the words from his dream, "I don't understand, damn you!"

Black Mask stiffened. A low growl sounded from the wolf and the five remaining wolves spread out at either of his flanks, covering the only route of escape for the prince.

To the side of the wolf, Chatham broke from Ariodne and bent beside the body of the young man. "I'll do it," Chatham said. Grabbing the dark green jacket of the balding man, Chatham turned the body over roughly. The man's face was bloody, his eyes rolled up in the back of his head. The wolf with auburn fur snarled.

Chatham snarled back and the wolf retreated a few steps. The white-haired man pried open the fingers of the dead man and handed Trevelyan the blood-soaked pages.

"Here," Chatham said. "They want you to have these, for some reason."

Ariodne crouched beside her lover as Trevelyan did his best to hold the soggy pages together. The prince read the title on the first page aloud. "Prophecy through the elements: Predict the moment of your appointed demise and learn to avoid it!"

There were a few nervous laughs in the taproom.

Black Mask growled and raised his paw, his claws gently brushing the pages without damaging them further.

Trevelyan swallowed and looked at the other pages. He frowned until he came to the last sheet. The dead man's blood had caused the ink on this page to run. He did not read aloud the few words he could make out. For an instant his fear of the punishment of the wolves vanished as he stared at the last page. It said:

". . . liquid fire . . . the preparation and use . . . formula . . ."

A few uninterrupted strings of symbols the prince could not decipher followed the headings. The prince felt as if he had been struck, the wind knocked out of him.

His father had chased the secret of liquid fire until the day of his death. The quest had been passed on to Trevelyan. The prince laid the paper flat and tried to soak up the blood from the sheet with the sleeves of his top shirt. He worked at the task furiously, all else forgotten. If used as a weapon, he knew, liquid fire could change the course of his world.

Trevelyan cursed. The blood had done its damage. The paper was ruined. His thoughts were consumed with the mystery of how this foppish youth could have found the secret, if indeed he had. Trevelyan looked up and scanned the room. The youth's companions were not present. The balding man had returned alone.

Directly before the prince, Black Mask growled.

"Trevelyan," Chatham said as he placed his hand on the man's back, "I think we should take it with us. I neglected to mention that I saw Shantow and his entourage surrender to the wolves before I arrived here."

Trevelyan picked up the single sheet of paper and handed it to Ariodne. "I'm coming, too," she whispered. "Don't try to stop me."

The prince nodded and adjusted his blood-soaked top shirt as Chatham and the wolves turned and walked from the carnage. Treading carefully, the young man walked to the spot where his *kris* lay, close to one of the savaged bodies of the hollow men, and picked up the weapon. Quietly the prince eased his swordbreaker into its sheath. The pair of wolves that appeared to come from the same litter waited for the prince, their salt and pepper fur on end.

Trevelyan ignored the eyes of his fellow Cynarans as he followed the grey-bearded fighter and the wolves. The old man held the door as the animals filed out of the Ivory Dagger, the prince and his lover close behind.

CHAPTER FIVE

The journey to the house of the wolves had taken considerably longer than Trevelyan had expected. His entourage drew a number of curious looks from people on the street who stopped to watch the procession. During the course of the long walk,

Trevelyan had reclaimed his charming and thoughtful veneer. When he was asked to explain the reason for his tour, which had been stopping the flow of human traffic wherever it went, the prince laughed and said, "I wish someone could tell me!"

In truth, the merchant prince could not fathom the motives of the wolves. Had the animals scarred him, *then* paraded him throughout the city, he would understand: the utter humiliation would make his punishment complete. But it was rare for the wolves to take pleasure in their handiwork. They performed their tasks, then went about their lives.

The reaction of the people to Chatham had been severe. Several people threw insults his way; in deference to the wolves and the prince, those moved to violence at the mere sight of the scarred man restrained themselves.

Many put forth the theory that the prince and his lady had assisted the wolves in the capture of the scarred outcast. When the prince neither confirmed nor denied such theories, Black Mask swiped his claw at the young man's ankle. The thick leather of his thigh boots protected his skin and Trevelyan understood the warning.

Maven Ariodne had fared better with the populace. Her title and position as a healer of men's souls had helped her to earn a deep-seated respect that even her most outrageous public acts could not usurp.

The group passed several of the squat stone buildings set aside for the Autumn wolves. By the law of the Unseen, one house had to be erected for every two square kilometers of man's blight on nature, civilization. When they passed the building closest to Arayncourt Hall, Trevelyan turned to Ariodne and said, "Where do you think they're taking us?"

"To wherever they have Shantow," Chatham interrupted. "Why don't you just enjoy the stroll?"

Black Mask sneezed, and Trevelyan looked at the animal, suddenly reminded of Lykos, Ariodne's guard hound. The wolf responded to the look by fixing the prince with a contemptuous glare, the cold intelligence in his turquoise eyes forcing away any further comparisons.

Wagons and horse-drawn carts were driven onto the sidewalks as the wolves plunged directly through the center of the narrow streets. Remnants of the week-long festival were strewn about the city. Banners dangling from shops declared massive savings. Street vendors approached the wolf pack several times, offering fresh meats. The animals did not acknowledge the offerings, and the prince knew why: he had seen the remains of their victims at close range.

The wolves had fed well this day.

More than once during the journey Trevelyan had heard comments about the unusual makeup of the wolf pack led by Black Mask and his auburn-furred mate. Generally the wolves were highly territorial. Each pack knew the limitations of its area. If they chose to leave their home ground for any reason, movement was allowed only at night, through various neutral pathways about the city. Violence between the animals was rare, but not unheard of. Wolves that wandered in from outside the city had a difficult time joining any of the elite houses of Cynara, even though they provided new blood for the packs and helped to cut down on inbreeding.

The prince had no explanation for the hybrid pack that led him through the city, although he learned their social order quickly. Black Mask and his mate were the leaders, their raised tails proclaiming their authority. The pure white wolf and the animal with black paws were lieutenants, the grey and white twins young recruits, anxious to please.

Ahead, the spires of the Citadel of the Mavens could be seen over the high roofs of the artisans' district. Of course, Trevelyan thought. Shantow had come to the Citadel in search of counseling. When the time came to surrender, he chose the closest house he could find.

As they turned the last corner the short grey building came into view. The windowless dwelling was caked with filth that even the heaviest rains could not wash away. As the group approached, a black-furred wolf relieved himself on the side of the building, scent marking the dwelling as a warning to wolves from other packs.

A tall, brown-skinned man stood beside the single entrance, a low archway. The man was wearing the ceremonial robes of an Espiritu healer, a swirl of brilliant colors reflecting the chaos of Enlytome, the sleeping god of wind. His short-cropped, black hair was barely visible beneath his elaborate headdress. The healer was in his late thirties and his handsome features were set in a solemn mask. Only his soft blue eyes betrayed his regret over the duty he would soon perform: the wolves required the assistance of a human physician so that not all their woundings were fatal.

"Come inside," the man said. "I am the healer of the fourth house." Trevelyan nodded. The healers rarely gave their true names. The prince felt Ariodne's hand gripping his arm, tight and unyielding. "Have no concern, Maven. *You* may enter without fear," the healer whispered.

The prince stopped abruptly and turned to look at his city one last time, ignoring the crowd gathered at the opposite corner. Despite the warm afternoon sun caressing his features, the prince felt bitter cold. Black Mask and his pack waited impatiently behind the prince.

At the entrance, the healer nodded. He had seen this many times before. No man emerged from the wolves' house unchanged, and so they attempted to hold on to a piece of their old life for as long as possible. "It is time," the healer said softly. "Your friend is waiting inside."

Trevelyan snapped to attention and bent low to step inside the darkened entrance. Black Mask broke from his pack and slid past the prince, brushing his leg. The healer, Ariodne, and Chatham followed Trevelyan into the shadows. The remaining wolves brought up the rear, preventing escape.

Once inside the wolves' house, the prince was able to stand almost to full height and survey the series of tunnels carved from red clay that stretched before him. Braziers holding lit torches provided the only illumination as the wolf leader hurried to the first juncture and darted out of view, to the right. Trevelyan looked over his shoulder and saw the resigned expression of the healer. The tall man had clamped one hand on his headdress to keep it from scraping along the roof of the tunnel and becoming dislodged.

The prince caught a glimpse of Ariodne's worried face and Chatham's glare of annoyance before he turned back and placed his hand on the cavernous wall for support. The juncture was before him, and the prince started as he followed Black Mask's lead and found the wolf waiting for him. The turquoise eyes of the wolf gleamed in the near darkness, picking up reddish-orange flickers of torch flame. Then the wolf turned and padded a short distance to a second branching tunnel off to the left. An instant after the wolf vanished into the tunnel, Trevelyan heard a short growl and a human cry of surprise erupt in unison.

A red-haired boy of less than sixteen winters backed out of the tunnel, a stream of apologies bursting from his lips. He wore a simple grey tunic and carried a foul-smelling sack in his arms. Trevelyan put up his hands before the boy collided with him. The young man spun, his eyes widening as he saw the face of the merchant prince.

"Lord Trevelyan!" he cried, then stepped out of the way so the small group could pass.

The healer whispered to Trevelyan, "Because of his age, the Adjudicators gave young Parrinder the choice of serving time or serving the wolves. He hasn't quite decided if he made the correct decision."

They passed a dimly lit room where a dozen large stone slabs lay on the straw floor. Bits of meat and bone were strewn across the slabs, along with wooden bowls that had been licked clean: the feeding ground of the wolves.

The tunnel bent to the left once more and Trevelyan's heart lifted as he heard a familiar grousing voice: "You sleep in your own dung. I am supposed to value your wisdom?" The prince could not restrain a smile. Shantow was alive.

For now.

Black Mask entered the den of punishment, the prince close behind. Although the room was vast, it was dimly lit and practically featureless. The floor was exposed earth, with piles of large stones. A series of empty manacles dangled from the bloodstained far wall. A pack of eight black-furred wolves surrounded their prey.

Shantow sat with one hand under his chin, the other resting at his thigh, angry and bored. His red-rimmed, emerald eyes were sharp and alert, although he had not slept, and his wild, stringy black hair had fallen into his eyes.

The prince went to his friend's side, stepping between the black wolves. "Shantow," he said. "You're all right."

The Kintaran seemed to be in a contest of wills with one of the wolves. Their gazes were locked. Trevelyan had seen his friend play this game with members of his entourage. The one who looked away first was the loser.

The black wolf threw his head back and yawned. Shantow slapped his knee in victory. His brief elation faded as he remembered his circumstances.

"They do *nothing*," Shantow said. "They sit. They stare. Occasionally one maybe goes off to pee. They haven't eaten since I've been here. I maybe don't like that."

Trevelyan nodded. That statement was as close as the man would come to admitting the fear they shared.

The black wolves closed ranks around the pair as Ariodne and Chatham entered the Den of Punishment. Black Mask took his place atop the highest pile of stones in the room. His auburn-furred mate padded close and climbed to a niche just below Black Mask. The lieutenants and dog soldiers formed a line at the bottom of the stones. The black wolves lowered their heads and looked in the direction of Black Mask.

Trevelyan stared at the wolf pack that surrounded Shantow and himself: these were the wolves who belonged in the fourth house. Black Mask and his pack had come from somewhere else, and had been welcomed without hesitation.

"Where are your bodyguards?" Trevelyan said softly.

"I sent them back to the hall. I wanted to die with as few witnesses as possible. Perhaps my judgment was rash."

"We'll soon see," Trevelyan said.

Across from the prince, standing near the doorway beside Chatham and the healer, Ariodne tried to steel her nerves as Black Mask and his companions started to howl. In the confined space, the howls of the wolves bounced from every wall. If she had closed her eyes, she would not have been able to tell where they originated. The black wolves joined the now-deafening chorus, and the Maven was forced to cover her ears with her hands. She had never been to a wolves' house before, and her fear caused her to wonder if the howls were a prelude to their attack.

As if sensing her thoughts, the healer said, "No, this is wrong. They are quick and merciful. Never like this."

The intensity of the howls grew. Ariodne barely heard the words of the healer. The red-haired Maven cursed herself. Having promised herself that she would use any means at her disposal to protect the life of her lover and his friend, she suddenly realized how foolish her plan had been. Even armed with the aid of the Forge, she would be lucky if she managed to kill even one of the animals before she and her lover were torn apart.

Chatham rushed forward and snatched up a small rock. The grey-bearded man threw it at the rising stones where Black Mask and his pack stood. The rock struck the flat grey stone at the feet of the wolf leader, inches above the head of the auburn-furred wolf.

The howling stopped. There were a few yips of surprise from the salt-and-pepper-furred wolves, then the entire cadre of wolves bared their fangs and a series of low growls filled the den. The pupils of Black Mask's eyes narrowed.

"Enough, you curs!" Chatham shouted. "You and I know damn well why you've brought these people here. End your mysticism and get on with it!"

Behind Chatham, Ariodne was struck down by a blinding pain in her skull. As she sank to her knees, Trevelyan moved as if to run to her side. Three of the black wolves looked back to the prince, their eyes blazing. Shantow took hold of his friend's arm and held him in place as he shouted her name. The healer was about to kneel beside the red-haired Maven when Chatham spun and drew the shattered hilt of his broadsword in warning. The tall black man backed away, although anger had replaced his expression of concern.

Kneeling in the soft dirt, her black armor ice-cold against her flesh, Ariodne thought she was going insane. Something was trying to pierce the walls of her consciousness. A voice unlike any she had heard before.

Very well.

The eyes of the Maven flashed open and she stared at Black Mask in horror. The women of her order had always been blessed by a special rapport with the wolves. But at most that rapport manifested itself in feelings, instinctive knowledge. What was happening to her now was impossible.

Do not struggle. Will not cause you harm.

Her body quaking, Ariodne forced herself to her feet. Turning her gaze to the pale, frightened face of her lover, Ariodne gasped, "Its thoughts. Its thoughts are in my head."

At the center of the room, surrounded by the black wolves, Shantow released his hold on Trevelyan's arm and took a step forward. "Then ask what it wants."

The Kintaran turned and faced Black Mask before Ariodne could reply. "If we are to be punished, then make it so. If you want to hear a confession first, then fine. I know why I am here. A demon took the place of my son and I killed it." Shantow placed his hand on his chest. "I wept when it was dead, but my tears were for the son it had taken from me, not for the stinking flesh I held in my hands. I know what happened and I will pay for my actions with my life. That is the law of the Unseen. But it was Chianjur who opened the doorway to great darkness, and took the seed of evil inside her body. She nurtured it, made it strong. She allowed her soul to be corrupted—"

"You ignorant, superstitious bastard!" Ariodne screamed. The Kintaran froze, his eyes wild. "Your wife loves you. She'd rather face death than bring shame upon you," Ariodne said. "She's as much a victim as you are. More so."

"Are those the thoughts of the animal or yourself?"

"You can't blame Chianjur for something so totally beyond her control—" The Maven screamed. Pain lanced through her head.

Please listen.

Ariodne clutched her skull. She could not fight the intrusion. *Privacy needed. Healer must go.*

Before Ariodne could speak, two of the black wolves detached from the pack guarding Trevelyan and Shantow. The wolves padded straight to the healer. "I'm not going anywhere," the tall man said. Ariodne felt the pain lessen.

No punishment. No need for healer.

The Maven relayed the thoughts of the wolf. The healer stared at her suspiciously, then left the room with his escort. Still inside the ring of black wolves, Trevelyan shook his head. "Why are we here, if not for punishment?"

Across from the wolf leader, Chatham sank into a crouch. "Tell them, fur face."

Black Mask regarded Chatham, then looked to Trevelyan and Shantow. "Or do you want me to do it?" Chatham added.

Crisis. A war. Our soldiers will not be enough. The Unseen will not help.

The Maven spoke quickly, relaying the words of the wolf leader only seconds after she heard them.

Black Mask turned to face Trevelyan and Shantow. The black wolves backed away, opening a path for the prince and his friend so they could leave the circle and stand before the wolf leader. Trevelyan glanced at the dark, angry face of his companion as they walked closer to Black Mask. The lieutenants and the pair of young soldiers padded out of the way. "What crisis?" Trevelyan said. "Are we pardoned for our crimes?"

Inside her head, the wolf's thoughts were becoming jumbled. Walking closer to the animal, she whispered, "I can't understand."

Black Mask closed his eyes. In Ariodne's mind, his thoughts were once again clear and powerful. She walked past Chatham and stood at Trevelyan's side. Black Mask was on their eye level, his auburn-furred mate just below. The Maven unconsciously reached out to touch the dark fur of the wolf's face when his mate rose up on her haunches and growled. Ariodne withdrew her hand quickly and turned to look at her lover and his friend.

"He says that you have both committed crimes. One killed a child of the hollow, the other allowed it to occur. Soon these will be crimes no longer, they will be articles of war. Fight in this war and your crimes shall be forgiven."

"We are to make war with the hollow," Trevelyan said bitterly. "No. My grandfather fought in the war of the Forge and died in the Trade Wars that followed. My father had me swear never to make a declaration of war. I won't make a mockery of all he represented unless you can make a much better argument than this."

To the side of Trevelyan and his companions, Chatham sprang from his crouch. "The hollow has already made the declaration. Imagine if they had succeeded in killing you today, what a victory that would be for their side."

"That was only two men. Not an entire race," the prince said. "Besides, the hollow have no nation of their own. They are outcasts—"

"Rien," Shantow said bitterly. "The monster that sprang from my wife's belly cried 'Rien' before I killed it. That is where all the outcasts gather."

Ariodne touched her head. "Events that cannot be stopped now move ahead. Soon the hollow will inherit a leader. But the wolves do not know who this will be, and so they cannot stop him from taking power. The *guardian* will explain. He will prepare you," Ariodne flinched. "He will prepare all of us."

Trevelyan felt a shudder run through him. He now understood that his dream had been given to help prepare him for this moment. Staring into the perfect stillness of Black Mask's turquoise eyes, Trevelyan said, "What guardian?"

The throat and tongue of the Maven went dry. "The guardian of the soul. Your soul. The one soul on all of Autumn that must not be corrupted."

"Corrupted by what?" Trevelyan said impatiently. "And just who is this guardian, anyway?" His heavy arms crossed over his chest, Chatham cleared his throat. The prince turned and stared at the scarred face of the grey-bearded man. Then he looked away and regarded Ariodne. "They can't be serious," he said.

The Maven's already pale flesh turned ashen as she gazed into the turquoise eyes of the wolf leader. "They are. You are to accept Chatham as your guardian, and in one month's time, on the anniversary of Lucian Arayncourt's journey, he is to accompany you to the summit of the wolves. There you will be met by the first wolves, those immortals who imprisoned the sleeping gods. The exact nature of the crisis, and what you must do to save the race of man, will be revealed at that time."

Ariodne looked down. "Our audience has ended."

Without another word, the red-haired Maven turned and walked to the arched doorway. Trevelyan was torn between following his love and staying to take issue with Black Mask's incredible proclamation. But without Ariodne to serve as an intermediary, there was no point in arguing with the wolf. He turned and walked to the place where Ariodne waited, her back turned to the conclave of wolves. Shantow followed.

Only Chatham remained. He glanced at Black Mask and said, "Went rather well, fur face. Don't you think?"

Black Mask looked away in contempt. The grey-bearded man laughed and rushed to catch up with his charge. "Come on, boy. We have work to do."

Trevelyan turned to the old man. "I have only one question: Out of all the people in this city, in this *world*, why did the wolves choose you?"

A grin spread across Chatham's face as he looked to Ariodne. "Why don't *you* tell him? I'm sure my friend over there must have mentioned it."

The Maven shook her head. "I'm tired of relaying messages," she said.

The prince stared into the dark eyes of the grey-bearded man. Tiny red slivers floated across Chatham's pupils. "I'll ask you again: Why did the wolves choose you?"

"I should have thought that was obvious by now," Chatham said as he pulled his lips back in a parody of a smile and leaned in close. "You see, I used to be one of them."

Trevelyan stared at the old man. "You're mad."

Chatham laughed. "Not anymore. But I fit that description once, about two hundred and forty-one years ago."

The flesh of the prince seemed to shrivel. It was on that date that the mad wolf shattered the code of justice on Autumn, changing their world forever. But the wolf had been caught and destroyed by the first wolves of Autumn.

Or so the legends told.

"I won't believe it," Trevelyan said.

With a shrug, Chatham gestured back to the wolves. "Ask them. They'll confirm what I have to say." The prince turned and fell silent. His companions looked back to see what had caused the young prince to stop dead.

Black Mask and his pack of wolves were gone, even though Trevelyan and his companions stood beside the only exit.

"Or perhaps not," Chatham said as he shrugged again and walked happily from the Den of Punishment.

PART TWO

A Fire Upon the Ice

CHAPTER
SIX

Kothra sensed betrayal the moment the small crystal ship bearing the messenger and his companion came into view from the south. The afternoon sun created an array of dazzling colors as its light filtered through the clear, honeycombed chambers that made up the ship's hull. The intensity of the light made the frantically waving figures on board look like shadows in the form of men.

Gripping the guardrail of the iron-plated casket the merchants of Knossos had laughingly referred to as "a highly efficient and cost-effective seafaring vessel," Kothra felt a chill settle onto his bare flesh. Until now, the numbing cold of the arctic reaches between Priam and his destination had not affected him in the least.

Concentrating on recent memories of the ancient rituals burnt into his memory by Rhoecus of lower Chiabos, and the deadly, searing heat of that land, Kothra began to sweat, which turned to ice as it fell away from his steaming body.

For an instant Kothra debated on attempting to outrun the small ship. Then he sensed the presence of at least one of his own kind on board, perhaps more. He was approaching the Trader's Reach of northern Aranhod, the last civilized outpost he was likely to see before reaching his goal in Bellerophon. A single question weighed heavily upon him as he prepared to drop anchor and wait for the second ship to come abreast of his boat.

Lifting the anchor above his head with as much effort as a child might display when discarding an unwanted toy, Kothra hesitated as he saw his reflection in the water. His flesh was bare with the exception of a belted wolf's pelt around his waist, a distasteful if not unlawful display in most civilized countries. His skin was bluish-black with dark green splotches. Blood vessels seemed to have burst throughout his body. Bright red and green veins disfigured his gargantuan form. He had arching brows, well-sculptured cheeks, and a solid, square jaw. His face, had it belonged to a human man, might have been considered handsome. There were times when he had yearned to pass as human, but his red eyes with black slits always betrayed him as a man of the hollow.

Kothra cast the anchor into the center of his reflection and turned away from the waters before the likeness could re-form.

As the ship approached, Kothra considered the expert craftsmanship that had gone into the boat's design. Carved from crystal by builders using the power of the Forge and reinforced by silver plating, the forty-foot ship was outfitted with every luxury. As Kothra was given a better view of the two men on board, he realized that the ship must have been stolen.

They were also men of the hollow, both just over two meters, and they wore little more than Kothra. Their physiques were exceptional compared to an average man, but slight in contrast to the giant who suddenly leaped from ship to ship, covering the three-meter gap with ease.

Standing less than a meter from them, Kothra realized that it hadn't been a trick of the light: one man had actually dyed his hair a bright canary-yellow. He did not allow himself a visible reaction to this ludicrous peacock.

For an instant he had hoped that at least one of the men would prove to be older than himself, but they were both considerably younger; it seemed that no one was older than Kothra, whose fifth year was quickly approaching. The peacock opened his mouth to speak, but Kothra cut him off.

"Couldn't this have waited?" the dark man snapped. "The Trader's Reach is only a few hours north, and my supplies are low." The tall man leaned in close, his rancid breath blowing in the peacock's face.

The younger men trembled. The one who had dyed his hair bright yellow stepped forward and said, "The knowledge you carry in your head is far too valuable to risk in a hostile climate." The man hesitated, as if attempting to phrase his question in the most diplomatic way possible. At length he merely sputtered, "You were successful, weren't you? In Chiabos, I mean. You learned their secrets?"

Kothra laughed. "I know how they do it."

The second man shook his head and looked scornfully at his fellow. "He doesn't know anything. You can't make fire out of water—"

Kothra was on the man in an instant, his powerful hands closing on the man's throat and effortlessly lifting him into the air. "Never question my word, you soulless bastard."

"He's young, he doesn't understand!" the peacock cried. Kothra's grip tightened. "Please, he's my brother!"

A vicious smile spread across Kothra's face as he dropped the younger man to the deck and turned to the blond. "Your parents were stupid enough to try again after they had you and they let both of you live?"

"They didn't intend to," the blond said. "They were going to kill him, and I protected him."

"Good," Kothra said, vague memories of the parents who deserted him brushing against the walls of his defenses. Allowing his rage to subside, Kothra said, "Why did you say the Trader's Reach is hostile? Aranhod is neutral."

"Not all of it," the second man said solemnly as he caressed his bright red throat and rose to his feet. "Two men of the hollow tried to assassinate Trevelyan Arayncourt, merchant prince of Cynara. As a result, our kind has been exiled from Cynara and the Trader's Reach."

Kothra's head was swimming. He was becoming numb, detached. His eyes half closed as he struggled to make some connection with his surroundings.

"There's no cause for alarm. We have more than enough supplies to share with you," the peacock stammered.

"Of course," Kothra muttered. Suddenly his pupils narrowed to slits and Kothra felt his lips slide back to show his pure white teeth. They had been sawed into points by the shamans of Chiabos. "Now why are you really here?"

"Branagh sent me," the peacock said softly.

Kothra felt the chill return. But it wasn't fear that brought the comforting wave of cold through his system. He felt the connection once again; he felt more than just half alive. The peacock was silent, waiting. At length Kothra spat, "Well?

What does he want? He can't expect me to surrender the secret to such as you."

"No," the peacock cried, as if the knowledge might burn him. "There is a change you must know about."

Under Kothra's hand, a crystal rail exploded into bright shards. Kothra allowed a sigh to escape him.

"The town of Ithcra has fallen to raiders. It would not be safe to meet there." The peacock smiled.

Kothra wanted to laugh. When did a human worry about the safety of one of his kind. "Go on," Kothra said coldly.

"I was told you're familiar with the Campion outpost," the peacock said. Kothra nodded and the blond felt some of his earlier confidence return. He enjoyed giving orders to the towering devil before him. "You are to proceed there directly, where you will be met by a small party who will take you to Branagh."

Nodding his head, Kothra turned away and stared out at the partially frozen wastes. An idea was forming. Leaning over the rail so that he could be seen in profile, Kothra bit down hard on his lip until a few drops of blood struck the rail and melted the slick sheet of ice that had formed. He heard the sharp intakes of breath from the messenger and his companion and held back any reaction of his own. Blood was sacred to his kind. To willingly part with even a drop marked one as unconcerned with their own mortality, insane.

"Why did Branagh hire two men when one would have done the job? It's not like him to spend a dime more than he has to, or share a secret with anyone who isn't necessary," Kothra whispered. "Or doesn't he know about your brother?"

The peacock ran his hand through his fine yellow hair and grunted noncommittally.

"I thought not. I have a change of plans," Kothra said as he felt the small wound he had inflicted upon his mouth already healing. "You will go to Branagh and inform him."

Once Kothra had given the information to the peacock, the yellow-haired man of the hollow took a step back, allowing Kothra plenty of room to debark from the crystal ship and return to his iron casket. Kothra had toyed with the idea of taking the crystal ship, but he did not want a vessel that announced his presence so readily. He hesitated.

"Is there something else, Lord Kothra?"

Kothra flinched at the reference. Part of his payment from

Branagh was a title. The rest of his payment would have been enough to restore Rien, his homeland, to the glory it had attained before the god of the wolves destroyed it. "What about the supplies you promised me?"

The peacock flushed, a bright red glow infusing his cheeks and spreading to his brow. He looked to his brother. "Help him with the supplies!" the peacock commanded.

Kothra grinned. Although only ten months, or perhaps a year separated the brothers by human reckoning, there was a span of nearly a decade between them by their calculations.

"You're getting your hands dirty, too," Kothra said to the peacock, and the brother of the hollow man smiled. Kothra was taken by the grotesque and out-of-place appearance of any semblance of joy when it arose on the face of a hollow. Even to him, it was unnerving.

He made a note to smile whenever possible.

After transferring the last sack of freeze-wrapped meats to Kothra's ship, the peacock finally put words to the growing alarm that had gripped his brother and himself for the past twenty minutes. "You haven't left enough for our trip to Bellerophon!"

Kothra practiced his smile. The sight put an end to the complaints of the blond. "You're right," Kothra said, "I only left enough for one of you and only one of you will go."

To their credit, the two men stood together, waiting for Kothra to attack. The blond had been warned of his irrational, random bouts of violence. But Kothra merely leaned against the rail and grinned.

"I'm tired of doing all the work on this voyage," Kothra said as he pointed at the messenger's brother. "Besides, I want to make sure my precise words get back to Branagh."

The brothers of the hollow did not move.

"Don't make me come over there and take you," Kothra said softly. The two men looked at each other. With downturned eyes the peacock sighed, "Do as he asks. We'll reunite in Bellerophon."

The second man was safely aboard Kothra's ship when Kothra leaned across the rail and spoke one last time to the peacock. "If you tell Branagh or his men about your brother's presence, I assure you he will die."

The peacock winced in confusion. "Why—"

"Do you have any doubts that I'm serious?" Kothra said as he pulled back his lips, exposing his pointed teeth.

"None," the peacock said.

Kothra laughed as he ordered his new servant to pull up anchor and watched as the peacock set sail on his own. After a time, only an occasional sparkle of light remained to show the initial parallel courses of the ships. Then the crystal ship veered southeast, and quickly vanished from sight.

The journey to Kothra's new destination lasted another two weeks. Abbas Bute, Kothra's new companion, still allowed his body to age. Kothra found the smell of decay quite unappealing. The company of humans, their bodies dying by degrees, also repulsed him.

Kothra touched his chest. One day his heart would burst. He pictured his chest opening like a flower, pushing his heart into the air like a rare delicacy for the gods to feast upon. What strange fruit would emerge from his death, he wondered. Would it be bitter or sweet?

Six days into their journey, when they cleared the final peninsula of Delgeth and moved past the ice regions and into clear waters, the tension between Kothra and Abbas lifted slightly. After four more days at sea, they spoke less as master and servant than as traveling companions thrown together out of necessity, although Abbas never forgot his place when it came to the division of duties.

Thirteen days out, they saw the rocky, treacherous shores of Bellerophon and set anchor a kilometer out to sea. After swimming the freezing waters to shore, a raft filled with weapons and supplies trailing behind their tireless bodies, Abbas and Kothra climbed to a large, flat, pale gray rock and unloaded the raft. The noonday sun had risen directly over their heads and Kothra ordered Abbas to break open their rations and prepare a meal before they moved on. When they finished, Abbas hid what they had not consumed beneath the grey stone and hurried to assist Kothra.

Most of the items they would need fit snugly in the harness Kothra had specially rigged by a weapons maker in the isles of Knossos, the former prison colony west of Rien. Abbas was forced to struggle with all that was left as best he could. The long climb up the craggy, uneven surface of the protective, outer wall that served to hide the bowl-shaped valley of

Telluryde from harsh waters and the prying eyes of man took the rest of the day and half the night.

When they reached the snow-covered summit, Kothra allowed Abbas to sleep for a few hours. The younger man curled up on a snowbank, the heat his body generated already turning the snow to slush. The necessity for rest was long behind Kothra, yet he indulged in the pleasures of allowing his mind to dream at least once a month. Tonight, however, he decided to spend his time reconnoitering the area.

The valley was exactly as he remembered it from the pilgrimage he made nineteen months earlier, the journey that began his association with the government of Bellerophon. Even in the dim light of the half moon, Kothra could see into the strange elliptical formation of the valley, its walls spiraling downward in interlocking tiers to the small, two-hundred-meter stage at its base, where a single opening led out through granite double doors to the narrow valley of the Whispering Earth.

The walls of that valley rose straight up, and were impossible to climb, even to one with Kothra's training. Absolute silence was required during the trek through several stretches of the twenty-kilometer-long valley, as falling rock could be disturbed by even a whisper.

But inside Telluryde itself, the rising, labyrinthine walkways that comprised the bowl-shaped valley concealed entrances to long-forgotten halls of worship and study, and areas where inconceivable tortures once took place on a daily basis. Kothra was familiar with several of these chambers. As he visited a few of the areas he knew the best, careful to follow routes he had once memorized instead of the tantalizing new pathways created by the snow and ice, Kothra felt a great sorrow that Telluryde was now deserted.

The wolves had finally cleaned house, just as they had in Rien, his homeland.

As he walked through an area he could only think of as a grand cathedral of death, inspired works of art were still in evidence, although they had fallen into decay. Fine blue-white moonlight filtered in from the open doorway, allowing Kothra to appreciate at least a part of the hall.

Blown and sculpted from the walls by talented men who wielded the power of the Forge and knew they forestalled their own deaths only by adhering to the wishes of Telluryde's rulers, the unmistakable beauty of the dizzying, twisted works could not be denied. The support pillars were gigantic representations of Telluryde's legendary founding fathers, dead men who had not allowed the end of their lives to interfere with their sacred goals. From the depths of a small chamber at the rear of the hall, Kothra heard heavy panting. Animal noises. Had the wolves left a pack behind?

Staring into the darkness, the man of the hollow caught two bright red pinpricks of light. A glint of white. Fangs. Straining, he could hear the soft padding of close to a dozen paws. Three more sets of bloodred eyes pierced the darkness. From the deepest reaches of the chamber, Kothra heard even more activity.

The pack was getting ready to move against him and he was weaponless. The panting had changed to low growls.

"So you've finally caught up to me," Kothra whispered as he allowed his arms to gently fall to his sides, his hands open, ready. "Come on, then."

Kothra knew that if he turned and ran, he had every chance of escaping the cathedral and shutting the doors on the animals before they could catch him, trapping them in a tomb. Eventually, driven insane by starvation, the predators would turn on one another. The thought pleased Kothra, but it wasn't enough. If these were wolves, he wanted them to pay for the misery their kind had inflicted; even if all the world saw the wolves as protectors, Kothra's vision was clear. Autumn was a prison, the wolves jailors. When the day came that he escaped its confines, he would not leave it unchanged. He had sworn that long ago.

Kothra was pulled back from his thoughts as one of the creatures surged forward, then stopped. The animal was now a murky grey form at the edge of the shadows, but Kothra could tell what had captured its attention: the single piece of clothing he wore, the wolf's pelt tied around his waist.

"That's right," Kothra said, pulling his lips back to reveal his sharpened teeth. "One of yours."

The creature hesitated for a moment, turned to look back at its companions, then, as if sensing their expectations, swiveled toward the dark man and leaped for his throat. Kothra was surprised at how easily he caught the creature, plucking it from midair as if it had been standing still. Even before he sank his razor-sharp teeth into its neck and tore out its throat, Kothra realized that it was not a wolf at all, just a wild dog that had strayed from its home and come across a lair more luxurious than it ever expected.

Enraged, Kothra threw the carcass at the remaining dogs and stormed out of the cathedral before the stunned creatures could move. Slamming the heavy doors together just as he saw the pack advancing to the entrance, Kothra felt only a tinge of satisfaction as he heard the bodies of the animals crashing against the door, then their whimpers.

Kothra rested against one of the doors, listening to the dogs, and thought about the man who had commissioned him to travel to the fire isle and retrieve the secret of the greatest weapon known to man, a weapon devised by savages whose mystery could not be unraveled by the greatest minds in the civilized world. Kothra laughed. It was all so simple. His smile faded as he thought of Erin Branagh, Bellerophon's minister of defense.

Unless Abbas Bute's peacock of a brother had made record time back to Campion, Branagh and his people were still waiting at the outpost, unaware of the new meeting place Kothra had decided upon. Knowing Branagh, Kothra was certain that the defense minister would arrive by the only manageable land route: the winding trail that followed the Croixette River, then through the valley of the Whispering Earth. The defense minister harbored an intense fear of the whims of the sleeping goddess Tsuemetle, who controlled travel by the waterways. Telluryde was just over one hundred and seventy kilometers north of Campion, and the way would not be easy. That gave Kothra several days, maybe even a week, to prepare.

Not that he would need it.

The Telluryde basin had been used as a training ground for the blind assassins of Fenris, the city that was now the capital of Bellerophon. It was considered a holy land by some, a place of unspeakable horrors to others.

As Kothra left the entrance to the grand cathedral he heard a sharp snap beneath his right foot, and looked down to see the chalky remains of a human shoulder blade, crumbled under his weight. The first man of the hollow frowned. Even in death humans presented him with difficulties.

Returning to the summit where he had left Abbas, Kothra found the younger man fast asleep. The snow beneath his body had completely melted leaving a tiny clearing of dead, twisted grass around his exposed form. Icicles had formed at the edge of the indentation and Abbas woke as Kothra found a seven-inch-long stiletto made of ice and snapped it off. The assassin would have to work quickly. It was an effort to keep his body's natural heat from melting the icicle.

"What are you doing?" Abbas said, still groggy.

Kothra moved forward, hefting the icicle like a knife. "You wanted to know what I required of you when Branagh and his men arrived."

The ice dagger glinted in the moonlight. Kothra pulled back his lips and whispered, "I'm about to show you."

CHAPTER
SEVEN

Erin Branagh ignored the cold, sharp sting of the harsh, thin air as he wiped away the last remnants of the clump of displaced slush that struck him in the face moments before. Leading a forty-man contingent into an overdue confrontation with Kothra of Rien, with only his point man, Lon Freyr, ahead on the ride, Branagh made the decision to retire completely from field duties after this mission.

He was a short, stocky man in his forties, with a thick black beard and steel-grey eyes. In his youth he had been a warrior with the strength and disposition of a wild bear; later those qualities had dissolved into a charismatic blend that helped him to achieve the love and respect of his people and the office of foreign defense minister. But now he was a frightened little man who knew that he had made a mistake.

Sending Kothra to the fire isle of Chiabos to secure the knowledge of liquid fire, that country's single, terrible line of coastal defense, had been a masterstroke. Sadly, Branagh had made promises to the dark man that Orrick, leader of all Bellerophon, had decided not to honor.

Shuddering, the bearded man turned his thoughts away from the recent past and concentrated on the narrow white road ahead. The pace of the ride through the valley of the Whispering

Earth had picked up, and Branagh was grateful. Early that morning, just after rations, the men had spent time using the power of the Forge to change their dark, heavy winter coats into shining black armors.

The armor of each man was exactly the same: over the heart was the seal of Fenris, a mighty set of wolf's jaws gently closed on a gloved fist. The headpiece displayed the watchful eyes of the wolf upon the brow and sharp black fangs above the eyes of the soldier and under his jaw. Tight black mesh covered the exposed joints, the hands, and part of the scalp. A black shield was slung over the back. The only diversity was in the style and choice of weapons, ranging from swords and crossbows, to daggers and garrotes.

Only one man refused to Forge the armors, and that was Skuld, the last living assassin of the cult of Telluryde, a foul-smelling old man who wore bright red ceremonial robes and a high leather collar about his neck. Branagh felt uncomfortable in the presence of the aging fanatic who had trained Kothra in the basin of Telluryde. The assassin claimed that he had come out of a sense of duty. As Branagh turned to watch, new wrinkles seemed to form around the old man's eyes and mouth as he laughed and sang to himself in a language Branagh could not even attempt to understand.

The uncompromising cheerful mood of the killer unnerved Branagh as the party he commanded approached the final bend of the narrow road that led to the doors of the Telluryde arena. Praying that Kothra would listen to reason, Branagh allowed his eyes to focus on the tiny gap between the towering slabs of rock and took in a vision of a sleet-grey sky. Several times on the long ride Branagh had imagined that the world had been turned upside down, and he was staring at a great winding river from an impossible height. That image returned to Branagh now, and suddenly changed as his horse rounded the last turn. The sky was swallowed up and the monotonous dead white of the valley was broken as a fist of darkness crashed down upon the party.

Branagh ordered the company to slow to a halt. When it was safe, Branagh dismounted and led his mount farther into the darkness. "No torches," the bearded man said. "You'll only make targets of yourselves."

A few minutes later Branagh jumped as Lon Freyr appeared beside him and whispered, "The doors up ahead have been left only slightly ajar. They seem to be rusted in place. At best we can fit through one man at a time.''

Branagh allowed his eyes to adjust to the darkness. Freyr was a tall man with tightly curled red hair, a thin, wiry build, and a piercing and unforgiving stare. Branagh saw Freyr's cold eyes despite the heavy shadows. A faint sliver of orange was visible up ahead, stretching upward three times the height of an average man. Forcing himself to relax, he spoke soft words of encouragement to his men as they dismounted. Somewhere close, Skuld was giggling.

"Skuld," Branagh hissed, "you go first. If there are any traps, find them.''

From the distinctive and unpleasant smell that rushed at him, Branagh knew Skuld had moved up beside him. The old man now moved without even a whisper to betray his position. A sharp intake of breath came from the assassin, and a throaty sigh sounded in the darkness. The Forge had been summoned.

Skuld took a step forward, toward the orange glow, and Branagh saw the skrymir, a twelve-foot shaft with a razor-sharp hook at its end, in his hands. Slowly weaving the instrument through the darkness, Skuld attempted to locate any trip wires Kothra may have placed in their way. In moments the old man had moved to the door. He motioned for Branagh and his men to follow as he slipped inside.

The aged assassin was waiting just a few feet inside the corridor when Branagh emerged weaponless from the doorway. Several candles had been lit on the ground at the end of the polished walkway, and Branagh's tired legs nearly collapsed beneath him as he took a few steps forward, his mind reeling at the sight that had caused even Skuld to lose his jovial attitude. Beyond the shadowy mouth of the corridor, in the stage that was the core of the arena, a dark man knelt in the grey half-light. The man was not moving. White flakes stuck to his skin. Icicles reached downward from his limbs.

"He's dead," Skuld whispered in genuine surprise.

Branagh's heart was thundering as he shook his head and shouted his denial, "He can't be!''

"We've come all this way to listen to the secrets of a dead man," the assassin hissed, anger replacing his surprise.

Behind Branagh and the assassin, Freyr and two others entered the corridor. The two soldiers were Eisler, a young, black-haired, green-eyed recruit with a constant shadow of a

beard upon his face, and Lanthrop, the soldier assigned to
shadow and train him. Although he was only five years older
than the nineteen-year-old Eisler, five years in the Bellerophon
army had cost Lanthrop dearly. Despite his youth, he carried
the marks of a much older man: hollow cheeks, bloodshot eyes
lined by crow's-feet, and a map of faded scars throughout his
body.

The door suddenly slammed shut. There was a scream that
was cut horribly short, then silence. One of the mercenaries
had been caught between the doors.

"We're trapped in here!" Branagh screamed as he felt the
blood drain from his face. The arena began to spin. Although
he had brought close to forty men with him, only four had
made it inside the arena. Freyr and his companions pounded at
the door and searched for the release mechanism to open it
once again, but Branagh knew their efforts would be wasted.
He whirled on the old man. "You were supposed to check for
any traps that monster left behind!"

On his knees beside Branagh, Skuld appeared to be calling
upon the Forge. When the assassin rose, however, his hands
were empty. "You worthless old man," Branagh croaked.
"Where do you think you are? We'll die in this place if we
can't find another way out. This is a death trap!"

Skuld looked out at the arena with an approving grimace.
"I'm home," the assassin whispered in Branagh's language,
his words tinged with an accent Branagh couldn't place. "Shall
we go?" The assassin gestured toward the lone figure at the
center of the stage. "We must pay our respects."

Branagh turned to Freyr. "Take your men and examine his
body and belongings. He may have written the secret down."

Motioning for Eisler and Lanthrop to follow him, the point
man brushed past Skuld and walked briskly to the side of the
dead man, where he stopped and waited until his companions
caught up. As he crouched beside the body, Freyr examined the
dead man as best he could without actually touching the body.
The blue-skinned man sat with his arms at his sides, his head
hanging forward, his hair falling before his features. Icicles
half the length of spears dripped down to the ground from his
head. Shorter crystalline formations dangled from his arms,
legs, and torso.

"There's nothing," Freyr pronounced as he stood.

Close to the sealed entrance, Branagh and Skuld watched as

Freyr's companions knelt beside the dead man. Freyr had taken four steps when Eisler, the less experienced of the two men, allowed a short, nervous laugh to escape him.

"That's odd," Eisler said. "The ice is melting."

Freyr turned just in time to see the hollow man's eyes flash open as he pulled away from his cold restraints. "Kill him!" Freyr screamed, but his words came too late. The monster sliced at the icicles with one hand and gathered a handful of ice daggers in the other with incredible speed.

Eisler stumbled back as the dark man spun in an arc, the sharp points of the ice daggers biting into the soft flesh of his unprotected face before he was aware of what had happened. Clutching at the steaming, ragged wound, that only seconds before had contained two green eyes, a hooked nose, and generous lips, Eisler fell to his knees. With his single undamaged eye, the soldier stared at the impossible sight of his own rich blood staining the thin coat of snow in the arena. He was dead before his body sank forward, his forehead striking the slick surface with a crack.

Ivor Lanthrop, the second man close to the revived killer, did not stand idle as Eisler was killed. A second after the murderous arc that tore open the younger man's face, Lanthrop saw an opening. Cursing all the gods he could think of because there was no time to draw a weapon, the mercenary improvised, planting a kick he was certain had the power to collapse the rib cage of a packhorse.

The dark man was rocked less than an inch by the blow. He looked down and saw a series of scratches on his ribs that matched the pattern on the sole of the mercenary's boot.

Lanthrop's hand was on the hilt of his sword when he saw the black slits of the killer's eyes expand. Suddenly Eisler's murderer was standing inches away, and Lanthrop hadn't even seen the monster take a step. The warrior felt a huge hand close over his and squeeze down with enough force to crush all the bones in his hand, despite his steel glove. Opening his mouth to scream, Lanthrop saw a dark blur, then felt a second hand close over his throat, lifting him up and turning him with ferocious speed.

In his peripheral vision Lanthrop saw a flash of metal erupt from his chest and heard his chest plate ripping apart. But there was no pain. A second later he was dead.

Behind Lanthrop, Freyr attempted to release his grip on the

sword he had just driven through his ally's back, but he could not force his fingers to release the weapon. Over the shoulder of the dead man, Freyr stared at the face of his enemy. The dark man smiled.

The monster's teeth were flat and perfect, not ground to points as Jevon Bute, the blond-haired hollow messenger, had reported. Freyr had only a moment to digest the information before the dark man shoved the body that separated them back against the point man. The hilt of his own sword caught Freyr square in the stomach, cracking his abdominal armor and knocking the wind from him as he sailed backward, his head impacting on the arena's floor. Then all he knew was darkness.

Abbas Bute stepped away from the bodies and looked at the two men who remained. Branagh and the human assassin had not moved from the door. The entire battle had lasted less than fifteen seconds. Skuld was laughing.

"Damn you!" Branagh shouted at the old man, then turned to face the soulless creature who came within a dozen yards of the bearded man before he stopped. "Kothra, you've proven your point. Let's talk."

"You want to talk to Kothra," the dark man said, anger shading his words. "He's somewhere else. Or do we all look the same to you?"

Branagh took a few steps toward the monster. "Goddess of the earth," he whispered. "Who are you?"

"Abbas Bute," the killer said. "Jevon's brother."

The bearded man seemed to shrink. His shoulders drew up and he swallowed hard, his throat dry. Guilt and fear welled in the man's eyes. Abbas Bute nodded. It was as Kothra said it would be. His brother was dead.

Branagh's hand was shaking as he pointed at the dark man. "Kill him," he commanded the aging assassin, his gaze never leaving the creature standing twenty yards away. There was no reply. He didn't bother to look. The air beside him smelled fresh and clean. Skuld had deserted him.

"We can talk about his," Branagh pleaded as he reached for the dagger beneath his belt at the base of his spine.

"Don't worry." Abbas Bute chuckled as he closed on his prey. "We will."

* * *

In the deserted guard station above the great doors to the coliseum, Kothra smelled a foul odor. A gentle smile came to his lips.

"A bath wouldn't kill you," Kothra said without getting up. He was sitting in a simple stone chair, the operating mechanism for the doors, a series of jagged gears and ropes, in plain view beside him. A brass pipe rose out of the floor beside the mechanism, and by adjusting a series of rings to the side of the pipe, Kothra was able to view the chamber below, outside the double doors, from any angle. A series of spy holes as thin as a man's finger coupled with wafer-thin mirrors provided the means. Several stone desks and cots made up the remainder of the room's modest furnishings.

Kothra glanced at the glass surface of the pipe and saw the bulk of Branagh's men arguing. When he looked back, Skuld was sitting on the desk before him, the old man's thin, goosebumped legs peeking out of his robes. The assassin hadn't made a sound. "Anything can kill you," Skuld said as he hopped down from the desk. "Anything at all."

Kothra stood and embraced the assassin. There was a scream from the arena below. Both men ignored it for the moment. Skuld pulled away and surveyed the hollow man.

"You've grown older, changed considerably. But only a year has passed since we parted," Skuld said in fascination. "All you told me is true. Hollow men age a year for every month they live."

"Until we will the aging process to stop," Kothra said. "I'm forty-seven months, but I could pass for twenty-nine. Unfortunately, the trick only fools humans. We of the hollow are connected in a way I find difficult to explain. There is no way for us to deceive one another on certain matters."

Skuld's eyes were alive with possibilities. "When the Mavens commune with the Stream of Life, they describe something similar."

Turning away from his former teacher, Kothra said, "The Stream of Life is closed to us. The Forge is closed to us. The Well of Souls has none to spare for my race."

Skuld placed his hand on Kothra's shoulder. "I know something of pain."

Looking back at the old man, Kothra felt as if he were seeing Skuld for the first time since the aged assassin arrived in the cramped room. Green and black spots dotted his translucent skin. Legions had appeared and been sawed away. The screaming multitude of visible ailments was enough to deafen the soulless killer.

Skuld unbuttoned his high leather collar, revealing bright red scars that ringed his neck. Rope burns.

"You tried to kill yourself," Kothra gasped. "Why?"

The robed assassin closed his eyes. "Because I'm old. My usefulness to this world passed long ago. But I cannot die. Do you understand? I *cannot* die."

A second scream sounded from the arena.

"You had best get down there, before your apprentice kills him by accident," Skuld said as he drew his scimitar and laid it upon the stone desk at an equal distance from both men. "Before we see whose reflexes are better, you must understand something. When I first trained you, I sensed your potential for a grand destiny. The time to live up to that promise has finally come. I only regret that I cannot stay to see my dream become a reality. I have always believed in you. Now your metamorphosis is at hand."

"What do you mean? What is it I am to become?"

The old man frowned. "A god, of course," Skuld snapped, and reached out for the scimitar with dizzying speed. To his credit, Skuld's hand brushed Kothra's as the dark man snatched up the weapon.

Minutes later, Kothra navigated through the intricate series of passageways that led to the arena's modest stage, the scimitar in one hand, a much heavier burden in the other. As he emerged from the mouth of the last tunnel, Kothra saw Branagh writhing in agony on the ground. Abbas was standing over the defense minister, content to bask in Branagh's cries of torment. Both of the bearded man's legs were twisted at impossible angles, the bones shattered. Daggers had been driven through Branagh's feet, pinning him to the ground. Eisler's and Lanthrop's bodies had been piled nearby and Freyr lay near the door, where he had been dragged, unconscious.

Branagh's face, white with shock, was turned in Kothra's direction. When he registered the object in the dark assassin's hand, he began to scream like a madman.

Kothra grinned and released his burden with a gentle toss. The old man's head struck the ground and rolled to sit beside Branagh's face. There was a peaceful, contented smile upon its features. Branagh tried to look away, but Kothra was upon him, his bluish-black hand forcing the bearded man to stare at the remains of Kothra's teacher.

"He wanted to die," Kothra snarled, "but his religion prohibited taking his own life, or allowing an inferior to kill him. It would have made a mockery of his holy trust. That's why he volunteered to join you."

Branagh's entire body was trembling. Still alive, he reminded himself, I'm still alive for a reason.

"We can negotiate," Branagh whimpered. "It was Orrick who decided you should be denied your title and position. I was just carrying out orders. Please!"

Kothra released the bearded man and took a step back. "No more talk. We're beyond that now." Turning to face Abbas, Kothra nodded. "You've done well. Now it's time to show Branagh the secret of liquid fire."

The dark men turned and started to walk away. For a moment Branagh was able to ignore the pain in his limbs. "You're letting me go," Branagh sighed in amazement.

Both men stopped and looked back at the weeping human.

"No," Kothra said as he pulled his lips back, revealing the sharp points of his teeth. "We're going to see if the flames will take to snow and ice."

Branagh looked around sharply. The entire Telluryde arena was covered in a soft white haze. As understanding grew in Branagh's eyes, the bearded man shouted to Abbas, "It's his fault your brother's dead! Kothra sent Jevon to me knowing what would happen to him."

Kothra's smile faded as he regarded his apprentice. "He's right, you know."

Abbas stood poised between the two men, considering Branagh's words. The bearded man nodded and smiled, his body flapping in the snow like a fish caught on a spear. "The reward we offered stands. I can give it to you from my own fortune. Please, don't let me die here."

The tip of Kothra's scimitar scraped along the ground as the giant said, "He *was* your brother."

Abbas shrugged. "Another day of his whining and I'd have killed him myself."

Branagh felt his heart shrivel in his chest. Opening his hands and bowing his head slightly, Kothra acknowledged the other man's decision. "Let's get started," Abbas said. "I'll get the canisters we brought over on the second trip."

An hour later Kothra stood within the entrance to the escape tunnel that led to the small room above the double doors. A lit torch crackled in his hand. He watched as Freyr came around, Branagh's hoarse wailing finally breaking through the heavy fog of the point man's consciousness. The tall man's senses returned to him with a start and he scrambled to his feet, instinctively looking for a weapon.

"If you have half a brain, you have nothing to fear," Kothra said mildly. "Unless I drop this before my apprentice opens the gate for you."

Freyr hesitated as he looked in the direction of his commander and saw the dark, murky stains that covered the stage of the arena, forming odd, twisting patterns. Black concentric circles led to the place where Branagh lay. All of the dark trails led back to a pool of black liquid just before Kothra's feet. The walls and several of the upper tiers had been splattered as well. The point man stood in a pure white clearing that included the door.

Branagh was screaming once more, barking orders for Freyr to come and set him free. The point man looked to Kothra and his piercing eyes held absolute understanding.

"Good man," Kothra said. "Here are your new orders. Return to Orrick and tell him that I'm going back to Rien. An auction will be held for the secret of liquid fire."

The point man nodded. From the middle of the arena, Branagh was cursing the red-haired soldier. Freyr ignored the man. Kothra laughed and shouted, "Abbas!"

The great doors opened just a crack as Kothra threw the torch and a wall of flames appeared, covering his retreat. Freyr ran for the doors and squeezed between them, ignoring the bloodied remains of the soldier who had been crushed between the doors earlier. The point man found himself pushing at his comrades as they tried to get inside, his cries and the mounting inferno behind him ignored by his fellow soldiers. Easing past two men, Freyr cleared the doors just as they abruptly slammed shut once again, crushing the life from a new pair of victims just as they caught a glimpse of the blazing arena and the screaming man at its heart, sitting up as flames washed over his body.

In one of the middle tiers of the arena, Kothra stopped to watch the fire as it spread across the ice, consuming the arena of the dead. At the center stage he saw Branagh writhing beneath the flames. Then he heard a loud crack, and the floor of the arena broke apart like a brittle piece of glass. The dying man vanished as the stage collapsed.

"There was an underground," Kothra said in surprise. "Skuld never told me—"

Suddenly a cloud of flames raced toward the soulless men from the mouth of the corridor they planned to use as an escape route. Without a word Kothra leaped into the hall and directed all his energies into outracing the flames, into survival. To his surprise, Abbas matched his every stride.

Twenty minutes later they ascended the final stairway and burst out into the clean, cold air. Working together the men shoved a massive stone they had displaced the day before over the mouth of the exit and collapsed as they heard the rush of flames beating against the covering.

"Look at it," Abbas said, and Kothra turned to see all that was left of the Telluryde basin: a massive white mouth, spitting up flames at the steel-grey sky with a venom Kothra had felt many times before. The dark assassin wondered if the god of the wolves was looking down at the sight, and he thought of Skuld's last words.

That night, as they swam back to their ship, Kothra was comforted by the faint orange glow that danced upon the waters, and occasionally he would turn and look at his handiwork, a blaze that seemed to burn the very heavens.

The words of Kothra's teacher returned to the assassin again and again. When Kothra and his apprentice were safely on board his iron ship, the younger man turned and whispered, "You've done well, Lord Kothra."

The soulless man smiled, the faint glow of his handiwork flicking across his razor-sharp teeth.

That night, a god was born in the fires upon the ice.

PART THREE

The Summit of the Wolves

CHAPTER EIGHT

"Trevelyan, you're like a cat who sticks his nose into a fire, then acts surprised when he gets burnt," Chatham said under his breath. They were outside Arayncourt Hall, just beyond the main gates, and the merchant prince had been swallowed up by a crowd of demonstrators.

Trevelyan had spent the morning in the usual fashion: He had slept late with Ariodne, whose snoring could be heard from the hallway, along with their passionate and vigorous lovemaking; injured his hand in his morning practice duel with Shantow, who seemed in as black a mood over the loss of his child as he had ever been; and had spent several hours in the regally appointed audience chamber, listening to more than a dozen petitions from local businessmen and entrepreneurs. When it had become clear that the greatest service Trevelyan was capable of performing had been restraining himself from yawning in the faces of his people, Trevelyan had canceled his remaining appointments and scheduled a goodwill tour of the city. The young prince felt that it was time for his supporters to see that Trevelyan Arayncourt was prepared for any challenge he might encounter tonight at the summit of the wolves.

The moment he had attempted to sneak away from the hall, he had been engulfed by the crowd waiting outside.

Two dozen men and women carried signs that labeled them as part of a fringe group that desired the legal privilege to destroy any child born as one of the hollow. In the past week, legislation had been introduced before the Council to make their desires law.

Three times during the past week, members of the group had gained an audience with him under the pretense of legitimate business, then launched into a tirade. As Trevelyan attempted to push his way through the crowd, Chatham watching the situation carefully to ensure that the younger man was in no real danger, their arguments were once again shouted in his face.

"These are abominations the Unseen permits only to show us our wickedness reflected in their crimson eyes!"

"Your vote carries influence," a dark-haired woman with an oval face and deep-set, grey eyes shouted.

"Trevelyan, if it were your son, what would you do? Would you have a monster carry on your name?"

From the night he stood by and allowed Shantow to murder his child, Trevelyan had been attempting to avoid thought or discussion of this issue. Although he did not openly support the slaughter this group advocated, he was not entirely opposed to the idea of somehow controlling these creatures, of setting up an encampment where they could be raised apart from normal children, their special needs catered to, their dark influence kept under control.

"Lord Arayncourt, these beings are growing in number, their powers are evolving, normal men don't stand a chance against them in the workplace," a sandy-haired man in his mid-forties said in a reasonable tone. The man's face was haggard and worn and his clothing—a coat of black mesh, shiny black boots, and black leggings—had been newly forged.

Trevelyan was surprised by his words and the man's thoughtful and controlled delivery. He raised his hand in a motion to silence the other demonstrators. "I would see this man alone. I find information more desirable when it's not cloaked in histrionics."

The forceful, confident manner of the young prince caused the crowd to move away without question, keeping a safe distance from the scarred, older warrior who strode up to the pair and tilted his head slightly as he grinned at the sandy-haired man. The man glanced at him suspiciously, his gaze fixing on the older man's scar.

"What is this criminal doing at your side?"

"He can be trusted," Trevelyan said.

"I should hope so," Chatham said as he clamped his hand on Trevelyan's shoulder and laughed. "Considering the way

I've kept the wolves from his door. Or is that your window where Black Mask used to wait for you at night?''

To his credit, the prince gave no visible reaction. The old warrior's comments had stirred an angry nest of questions in his mind that would wait until he and Chatham were alone.

"Tell me your name," Trevelyan said to the blond man.

"Kiernan Leggett. I am a soldier under the command of Rolland Storr. Our company has been infested by a trio of the blue-skinned devils. You have faced one of these hollow men in combat, you know their abilities far exceed ours. The reflexes, speed, and strength of their weakest man makes him the superior of our finest warrior.''

Trevelyan considered the man's statement. Rolland Storr was a condottiere whom Trevelyan's father, Oram, had befriended. The last time Trevelyan had seen the mercenary leader was the day of his father's ceremonial cremation.

"I know Rolland Storr," Trevelyan said. "I find it hard to believe that he would employ men of the hollow."

"It is true," Leggett said. "Our commander thinks very highly of you, milord. If you were to talk to him—''

Trevelyan stared at the man's black clothing. "Why aren't you wearing the uniform of the Black Wolf company?''

The soldier looked down in shame. "Storr gave the order that I was to accompany all three men of the hollow on a mission to protect one of the colonies off the mainland of Cynara. I refused the assignment.''

The prince understood. Storr had no choice but to relieve the soldier of his duties for insubordination.

"What you have told me is valuable information," Trevelyan said. "I will discuss this with Rolland. You did well to bring this to my attention.''

"But the larger issue still remains. How are you going to urge your people in the council to vote on our proposal?''

Trevelyan smiled the perfect diplomat's smile. "In a way that will benefit all concerned. Have no worries.''

Leggett took the hand of the prince, surprised at Trevelyan's slight wince of pain at the gesture. "These creatures must be kept down. There's no telling what they will do if we allow them to hold positions of authority.''

"Yes," the formerly silent Chatham said as he leaned in close to the out of work mercenary. "And all those bearing the scars of the wolves should be sent to Rien, where they belong." The strong afternoon sunlight cast deep shadows in the crevices of Chatham's marks of punishment.

"I must be going," Leggett said as he lowered his head to the prince and gave a hateful stare to the old warrior before he departed to rejoin the waiting crowd. Several people were raising their arms, calling out to the prince.

"Quickly now, boy, if we don't get away from here at this moment we will be spending our afternoon listening to this." Chatham took the arm of the young prince and steered him toward a pair of horses that were tethered close to the guard station. Drawing his knife, Chatham sliced the soft leather restraints of the first horse, a pure black stallion, and leaped upon the mount.

"This is theft," Trevelyan said indignantly.

"Nonsense, I purchased the horse myself and paid the guards to keep it here for emergencies. Now get on!"

The crowd was almost upon them. Trevelyan mounted the horse, grabbing hold of Chatham's waist, and in moments they passed the meeting place of the council and turned down the Avenue of Commerce. "I'm not sure that I believe your claim that we did not *steal* this horse," Trevelyan said gravely.

"I'm not sure I care," Chatham responded good-naturedly. They passed several markets, including one run by a merchant who claimed his neighbor was putting him out of business by purchasing untaxed goods and had petitioned Trevelyan for assistance. As the man had reported, his market was suffering greatly from his competitor across the street.

"We should stop and look into that man's claims," Trevelyan said cheerily as he at last eyed a purpose that would keep him from thinking about his meeting with the first wolves at the summit tonight.

Chatham did not slow their pace and they were soon beyond the market. "We are hardly unknown in this city, Lord Arayncourt. If I hadn't allowed myself to be talked into playing the role of your keeper by those intolerable curs at the fourth house, I might be a good choice. But my notoriety has grown since I met you."

"It bothers you that you are treated as a criminal."

"The reactions of men are predictable," Chatham said. "I wish that the Unseen were dealt with so easily."

As they rode on, Trevelyan said, "Has there been any progress in deciphering the notes we found on liquid fire?"

"None. The identity of the man who died at the Ivory Dagger is unknown, as are the whereabouts of his companions."

They stopped and dismounted several blocks away and Chatham found a stable for the mount while Trevelyan busied himself with the practice of greeting merchants by their first names, accepting gifts that he promised to return for later, and fending off advances from young women who should have known better and their parents, who were too old to care about protocol. Once the novelty of Trevelyan's presence wore off, the two men were left alone. Chatham wandered toward the shop of a weaponsmith, and stopped to admire the level of craftsmanship that was displayed in the custom-made swords hanging in the window behind a thick layer of glass.

"I haven't seen work like this in fifty years," Chatham said in admiration. The grey-bearded warrior stared at the intricate designs carved upon the hilts. Each sword told the story, in words and detailed illustrations, of the man who commissioned the weapon. Chatham understood that none of these swords were for sale. They had been willed back to the smith upon the deaths of their owners, a custom that had all but died away recently.

"Chatham," Trevelyan said finally, "what you said earlier, about keeping the wolves from my window . . ."

"What about it? Do you want to know if I'm actually guarding your dreams as well as your life? That would lend credence to my claims, all of which you've beaten down and placed in a box marked 'the fantasies of an old man.'"

"You claim you were the Mad Wolf, that—"

"I must talk to the owner of this shop. Will you excuse me?" Chatham was through the door of the weapons emporium before the prince could voice an objection. Defeated, Trevelyan followed him inside.

The shop was carpeted in sunlight, which reflected off hundreds of weapons on display, many from foreign lands. Each bore the same distinctive signature of the craftsman who owned the shop, Adair Ryton. Trevelyan was instantly struck by the number of empty places along his racks.

"I've heard of this man's work," Chatham said quietly as he admired the cut of an Inness dagger, a long, thin blade designed to pierce the heart from behind.

"Cynara attracts the very best," Trevelyan said.

"You, sir, are living proof of that."

Both men turned and found themselves facing a slender white-haired man in his seventies who was dressed in a brilliant yellow and red topcoat with sky-blue leggings and boots that were made from the skins of fire-lizards from Shantow's homeland. The full ceremony for the creation of a pair of boots such as these culminated with eating the meat from the *arba* that had been skinned, a rare delicacy, when the boots were delivered.

Adair Ryton's wealth had to have been considerable if he could afford such an extravagance, Trevelyan thought. Staring into the man's pleasant face, he noted the arched eyebrows, hawklike nose, cleft chin, high cheekbones, recessed ears, and full, silky hair of the weaponsmith. The man had the look of an artisan who rarely, if ever, had occasion to utilize his creations.

"I am Trevelyan Arayncourt and this is my friend—"

The hawk-nosed old man drew in a sharp gasp when he saw Chatham's face.

"Is something wrong?" The old warrior was instantly aware that the reaction had little to do with his scars.

"I know you," the man said cautiously. "You are the one they call Chatham."

Rubbing ferociously at the underside of his chin, screwing his features into a mask of distaste, the grey-bearded warrior said, "You see, Trevelyan, it is just as I told you. Word of our association has spread."

"I met you once before," Ryton said. "In Labrys."

"That's possible," Chatham said uncomfortably. "I've been to Labrys many times."

"You were a mercenary fighting in the Holy War against the savages in Auger."

Chatham was silent. Sensing his companion's disquiet, Trevelyan looked around the main room of the emporium and said, "The merchants have complained uniformly that their business has suffered as of late. People are keeping to their houses. But you seem to be doing very well."

"Yes," Ryton said, his gaze never wandering from Chatham's face, "the people do not feel safe in their homes with the threat of the hollow men. And with the way the wolves are acting, you would think the Mad Wolf was inspiring them. The people prefer to be well armed."

With a gentleness Trevelyan would usually not associate with the grey-bearded warrior, Chatham put his hand on Trevelyan's arm and whispered, "I think we've seen enough."

"I had thought the same when I viewed your handiwork," the hawk-nosed old man said, his memories becoming all too vivid. "I was a boy. It was almost seventy years ago. You saved my father's company, you saved me."

"You've made a mistake," Chatham said coolly. "Look at me. I'm not old enough to be the man you describe."

"I could never forget you. You butchered two dozen men, savages they might have been, then tore apart their corpses, limb from limb. There were arrows in you. Wounds all over your body. I saw one of them run you through the heart. You should have been dead."

Forcing a smile upon his grizzled face, Chatham nodded and laughed. "I come from a long line of soldiers. My name has been passed down for over two centuries in my family. The man you remember from your childhood may have been my—"

"But he had your scar," the hawk-nosed weaponsmith said.

A moment passed in silence, then the grey-bearded warrior walked slowly to the door and waited for Trevelyan to follow. Trevelyan held out his hand in friendship to the old white-haired man. "Adair Ryton, it was a pleasure—"

The old man took a step back, refusing the offer. The merchant prince lowered his gloved hand.

"Take him and leave," Ryton said, obviously shaken. The memories he had relived were shocking and brutal reminders of the true use of the products of his craft. "Please."

Lowering his eyes, Trevelyan turned and left the weapons emporium with Chatham. They walked back to the stable where they had left their horse, Trevelyan watching the people on the street as if he were seeing them for the first time. The weaponsmith was correct, some of the citizens glanced over their shoulders in fear, others watched the darkened, trash-filled alleyways for attackers, their hands resting on the hilts of partially concealed weapons. Trevelyan felt a terrible wave of depression wash over him.

"You can't feel responsible for this," Chatham said.

"They're more likely to harm one another than to protect themselves from monsters they imagine walk these streets."

"I see there's no sense in arguing the point with you," Chatham said. "As usual, you're determined to pity yourself. That is how it should be. One should do what one does best."

Trevelyan stopped suddenly and placed his hand on the grey-bearded warrior's chest. "It's true, isn't it? What you've been saying from the start. You *are* the Mad Wolf."

Chatham sighed. "If you're ready to accept my story as the truth, then I will tell it to you. The choice is yours."

Trevelyan scanned the street anxiously. "We should go somewhere that offers us privacy."

"If you say," Chatham sighed, then glanced over to the partially open doors of the tavern on the opposite side of the street. A few minutes later they had secured a private table at the rear of the taproom, away from the bar. As they were led to their table by a tall, flaxen-haired serving maid, they passed a table with three solemn-looking men who wore the traditional luminous silver and gold uniforms of the Adjudicators. They regarded the prince with civility as he walked past, Chatham at his side. The old warrior grinned and ran his hand over his scar as he commented below his breath that the one on the right could stand to take off a few pounds, then openly wished them a pleasant day.

After they were seated and their orders were taken— Chatham requesting a Winter Wake, a drink made popular in Bellerophon several decades ago, Trevelyan ordering a mild ginger and rye twist—Chatham began his story.

"I was born two hundred and fifty-nine years ago, I was born a wolf. I had fangs and fur and glaring eyes. For nineteen years I wore the form I was born with, and I fulfilled the task the Unseen has set for all the wolves of Autumn. The scent of those who had broken the law of the Unseen came to me in my sleep, with the knowledge of the proper punishment to be meted out. I was the perfect soldier, the ideal killer. I lived with my pack in the ninth house of wolves in Radella, between northern and southern Aranhod. We were an incestuous brood, but that was common.

"In my nineteenth year, Wildheart, the leader of our pack, was fatally wounded in a skirmish with a pack of wild dogs. The healer of the ninth house was powerless to save him, and my achievements and skills had clearly marked me as his successor. I performed the duty that was expected of me, tearing out his throat to end his suffering. But something about the act unnerved me. I had never harmed another wolf and strange thoughts came to me when I was pack leader.

"I had terrible dreams. Dreams far worse than yours. I saw

the faces of my victims, heard their screams of agony. The dead and the maimed that I had created returned to me even when I was not resting. I began to question my own mortality, and became terrified of death even while I dealt it with impunity. The dreams the Unseen gave to me became unclear, the scents that would lead me to my prey confusing."

The grey-bearded warrior took a long drink, then wiped his mouth and stared at his hand, as if he were disgusted with himself for the all-too-human gesture. "I followed the scents and I inflicted the punishments I believed were proper. I ruined lives while my delirium increased. Soon I began to wander the streets in answer to dreams that did not come from the Unseen, but from my own fevered imagination.

"You know what happened to those who were marked by the wolves in the days before the Adjudicators. They were considered outcasts, their friends and families turned their backs on them, they were forced to leave their homes, live in Rien or other even more hellish places. Many claimed innocence, but the wolves had never been wrong and to question their actions was absurd. My victims were not believed when they claimed they had committed no crimes.

"My violent spree continued, my attacks became more erratic, and my pack chose to exile me. It didn't matter. People fear the wolves. It's in their blood. Finding those who would provide me with shelter and food when I was in my more lucid stages was a simple thing."

Chatham stared at his drink, shards of bloodred glimmering in his eyes. "The Unseen did nothing to stop me. Several years after the first wolves came for me and meted out their punishment, I learned the self-aggrandizing legend man had written to explain how I was stopped.

"They claimed that one of my victims traveled the world over to seek justice. He burrowed beneath the tree of life, whose roots encircle the planet, and where the crypt of the Mercenopy, goddess of the earth, is buried. The wounded man confronted one of the first wolves, who looked within the soul of the man and saw that he told the truth. The error was redressed, and all the victims of the Mad Wolf were returned to their rightful places in society."

"And what really happened?" Trevelyan asked.

"The first wolves got fed up, that's what happened," Chatham said indignantly. "They wanted to rein me in the moment I first harmed one who did not deserve it. But they were bound to act only upon the will of the Unseen, and the Unseen did not seem to care about my actions. After the first wolves could no longer stand to see the system of justice they had helped to implement become bastardized, they took their first action without the orders of their lord and master. It's a good thing they did. I wouldn't have stopped on my own. I had begun to purge myself of my nightmares by killing indiscriminately; I had begun to like it.''

"Chatham, this is a bit too much for me to take all at once. The Unseen would never be so callous."

"Indeed?" Chatham said bitterly. "Ninety-seven years after I went mad and the Adjudicators were given power, the first wolves were ready to order the wolves of Autumn to wipe out the plague of mankind. Was it the Unseen that changed their minds, or a young boy named Arayncourt?"

Trevelyan was silent.

"And what is the Unseen doing about the hollow?"

"This is blasphemous," Trevelyan said. "Besides, the legend says that the Mad Wolf was killed."

"Killing me would have set no example. They did worse than kill me. They turned me into one of you."

From across the tavern, the serving maid who had tended to the merchant prince and his scarred companion issued a terrible scream. The trio of Adjudicators sprang from their table and raced for the door.

Trevelyan rose to his feet and Chatham's hand shot out, grabbing his arm. "This doesn't concern us," Chatham said.

"Come with me or drown yourself in drink," Trevelyan said as he pulled away from the grey-bearded warrior and followed the Adjudicators from the tavern.

On the street, Trevelyan saw two black wolves from the fourth house racing down the street. Those who were on the street stumbled upon one another in their attempts to clear a path for the sleek, powerful creatures. The Adjudicators were running after the wolves, the sedate, proud bearings of the lawgivers turned into a mockery by their flight.

Ahead of the wolves ran a tall, blond-haired man carrying a large sack. Chatham stepped out of the tavern behind Trevelyan and winced. The fear stench of the wolves' prey hung heavily in the air. The smell sickened the grey-bearded warrior. He licked his lips. Mixed with the fear was the unmistakable taste of guilt.

Trevelyan followed the Adjudicators and Chatham called out to him. The merchant prince did not look back.

"This is not our business," Chatham said as he sprang into a dead run, quickly overtaking his charge. Together they saw the blond-haired man running from the wolves dart into an alley-way, the wolves only meters behind.

"Do not touch him!" one of the Adjudicators cried from the mouth of the alley. A small crowd began to gather as Trevelyan and Chatham made their way to the side of the three silver-garbed men. The alley was a dead end. The wolves had the blond-haired man trapped.

A cold, piercing intelligence registered in the eyes of the wolves, along with a ravenous hunger as their bodies trembled. Trevelyan thought he saw movement within the black bag the blond-haired man clutched close to his breast.

"Help me," the man begged. He was thin, with fine, shoulder-length hair, his face was white with exhaustion and terror, his thin lips chewed black, deep blue circles beneath his eyes denoting his lack of sleep. The clothes he wore had been forged recently.

One of the black wolves looked to Chatham. As if he sensed the animal's thoughts, the older warrior nodded and said, "The blooding is upon them. We can do nothing here."

Two of the Adjudicators stepped forward and froze as the wolves turned toward them, the more aggressive of the two unleashing a howl that caused many of the onlookers to run away in horror. Both men were very young, not yet thirty, with short black hair and thick, bushy eyebrows that almost met. Their features were similar enough for them to pass as brothers. The last Adjudicator was out of shape, still panting for breath from the short run, his silk tunic bulging at the wide gold belt. He had a sunburned face, and sparse curly red hair. His body shook as he raised one of his pudgy hands and pointed at the blond-haired man.

"You stand accused by the Unseen," the fat Adjudicator said. "What is your choice of justice? The wolves will be brutal but swift. With us you may spend years or even your life interred, daylight a distant memory."

Trevelyan thought of his last tour of the underground caverns that served as prisons for those judged guilty by the courts of man.

"This is pointless," Chatham said, anxious to leave, the desire of the wolves to gain release from their killing fever beginning to spread to him. His fingers curled and spread over the hilt of his sword.

"Let man's law judge me," he said, the bundle in his arms moving once again.

"You, the accused," Trevelyan said as he stepped forward, unmindful of the wolves even as they growled at him in warning. "What is that you carry?"

Suddenly the piercing cry of an infant erupted from the sack. The wolves paced back and forth, the baby's screams driving them into a frenzy. The blond-haired man glanced down at the wolves, frightened to make eye contact with either of the animals, whose mouths hung open, their fangs exposed, spittle dripping to the filth-laden floor of the alley. He quickly uncovered his burden, and the merchant prince was surprised to see healthy pink flesh.

"Is the child yours?" Trevelyan asked.

The man shook his head. "My child was born of the hollow. He did not live. My wife could not face what had happened. She sits by the window, her arms open as if she were cradling our child. I saw this child sitting unattended in the market and something inside me snapped. I don't know what made me do it. I was desperate."

The wolves were pacing back and forth, cutting off entrance to the alleyway.

"Wolves of the fourth house, I am Trevelyan Arayncourt. Allow this man to step forward and surrender to the justice of man. Let me take the child and find its mother."

One of the wolves bared its fangs and hissed at the merchant prince. Chatham knelt low, pulled his lips back in a grimace, and hissed back at the wolf. The animal backed away, nudging aside its mate.

"They will not let him out," Chatham said, "but they will let you in."

Trevelyan squeezed his eyes shut and drew in a sharp breath. Then he opened his eyes and walked forward as if the wolves did not exist, holding his hands out to the blond-haired man, who held the child tighter against his chest. The baby was still screaming.

"They're going to kill me," the man said, tears falling from his eyes.

"They won't," Trevelyan said softly. "But you must give me the child. That is the first step to leaving here alive."

Reluctantly, the blond-haired man passed the crying child to Trevelyan. The merchant prince turned on his heels, his gaze suddenly locking with Chatham's. The old warrior's eyes were glazed over, red slits forming in the depths of his black eyes. The sound of the rapid breath of the wolves allowed the prince to break away from the hypnotic stare of his guardian and push himself toward the mouth of the alley, just as the Adjudicators screamed in protest and the wolves leaped at their prey.

The prince stood rigid, immobile, as he heard the screams of agony from a few feet behind him. He held the baby close to his breast and closed his eyes as the horrible sounds of ripping flesh echoed from the filthy alley. People were shouting in horror and disgust.

The wolves ended their attack and padded softly from the alleyway, one of the sleek black animals brushing against Trevelyan's legs.

"A healer," the red-haired Adjudicator screamed, "someone find the healer of the fourth house! The man will die from his wounds."

People were pushing past him as he opened his eyes once again and stumbled forward. Chatham led him from the alley.

"Curs!" the Adjudicator hollered in rage. "You are to wait until you have led your victim to the house of punishment! These are not the ancient times, damn you!"

"Are you all right?" Chatham asked.

"Are you?" Trevelyan responded, frightened to look into the older man's eyes. The baby had become silent with Chatham's approach.

"You saw," he said quietly. "When the first wolves turned me into a man, they did not wish for me to be ordinary. I can still feel the call of blood. I have been told it is reflected in my eyes."

"It's true. You have not been lied to."

"Nor was the accused, Trevelyan."

The merchant prince nodded. He told the blond-haired man that he would not be killed. That was true. The punishment for stealing the child of another was crippling, the tendons in the legs eaten away never to re-form, a mark of two claws scratched into his forehead, a line of shame that started at his scalp and ended just between his eyes.

"Let's try to find the mother of this child," Trevelyan said absently, the screams of the wounded man in the alley fading as the pair walked quickly down the street.

CHAPTER NINE

Thunder rose from within Ariodne's chambers at the Ivory Dagger, the thunder of hearts fit to burst as lovers strained to find release. Ariodne lay beneath Trevelyan, her hands tracing the tight musculature of his arms, her sharp fingernails leaving tiny red trails in their wake. Harsh afternoon sunlight had poured through the windows when they began; now, by the orange flames of candles set on a table behind their heads, they catered to each other's desires and needs, taking satisfaction in the tiny flutterings, the gasps and cries, the frantic motions that eased off and became languid indulgences. Soon their rhythms matched, their gazes locked, their bodies strained against one another in quicksilver motions that caused screams as Trevelyan stopped suddenly, a torrent leaving his body. He fought to keep his eyes from closing as Ariodne rode down from her own crest and caressed his face, nodding in loving satisfaction as she allowed him the full pleasure of the moment.

He sank down upon her, still connected, and buried his head in the crook of her neck as he began to weep. The Maven caressed the back of his head, running her hands through his silken black hair. For long moments neither was able to fully catch their breath and speak. Their naked bodies were covered in sweat. Ariodne felt the incredible heat within her finally cool, and her lover rose from her, parting from her body, and wiped the tears from his face.

She sat up and pressed her face against his hard chest. "What's wrong?"

"No," he said as his hands found her bare back and caressed her gently. "Foolish thought."

With a surprisingly effective shove she forced the dark-haired prince to his back and straddled his legs, the flickering candle-light casting half her face in shadow as she held his hands behind his head and allowed her long red hair to dip down and brush against his nipples. Trevelyan cleared his throat and attempted to maintain his composure.

"This isn't fair," he said, fighting off a trembling grin that would not be denied.

"Yes, life is difficult," Ariodne said casually as she leaned down and covered the nipple with her mouth, flicking her tongue over it until it was hard. He gasped as she bit lightly, then leaned up and plunged her tongue into his ear. Kissing her way to his neck she ran her bare teeth over his strong flesh, pausing for a moment. "Do you think your 'royal audience' will pay you the same heed if I give you a small reminder of our affection? A love bite right—"

"You win!" Trevelyan said, and his lover lifted her head and covered his mouth with hers.

"Tell me," she gasped as she released his hands and ran her hand over his face.

"I want you to marry me."

Ariodne was silent, her expression revealing nothing as she lay down beside the prince and whispered, "I will."

Trevelyan rose to one elbow, staring at her beautiful face, the soft orange glow of the candles washing over her like a mist, softening her hard features, granting vibrancy and life to her pale flesh. There was not a trace of pity in her expression, as he had feared that he would find, only love. "Are you sure?" he asked.

His words touched something deep within the red-haired Maven and a wicked smile appeared on her lips. "Not to massage your ego, Mercenopy forbid, but you *are* good in bed. When we have a bed, that is. Even when we don't."

"Perhaps I should change my vocation," Trevelyan said. "With my pretty face I'm sure I could find work."

She laughed. "I've thought about this. I decided that I could live without you, Trevelyan. I could do it easily. I've been alone before. But I *choose* not to. I don't make choices like this lightly, I don't make them out of pity. I love you and I don't want to go on if I'm not carrying a part of you inside myself. I need you."

Trevelyan reached up and brushed the hair from her face.

She blew on a remaining strand and it arced back, gently adhesing itself to her wetted lips. "I need your love. I want you. And I want to always be with you."

He nodded slowly and drew her close.

"Marry me," she whispered.

"Yes," he said in the near darkness, a breeze suddenly wafting into the room, snuffing out the candle, casting them into the waiting arms of night.

"It certainly took the two of you long enough. Wolves don't bother to have long discussions, you know. They mate, they kill. Humans mate and they kill each other!"

Chatham sat at a table with three other soldiers who he had stripped of their week's earnings in a game of chance. Shantow sat beside the grey-bearded old man. The prince and his lover had arrived seconds before through their private entrance to the smoke-filled back rooms.

"He cheats," the Kintaran announced. Trevelyan and Ariodne looked at each other and shrugged.

"It wouldn't surprise me," she said.

"How can I cheat?" Chatham snarled. "Listen, Trevelyan, have you played this game before? I'll explain. It is a simple mental exercise. I write down a word, something off the top of my head, and I try to get you to think of it. You count off in fives, from five to fifty-five, to five hundred and fifty-five, and so on, until you reach five billion—"

"Yes, I understand," Trevelyan said.

"Then when you get to the last number you say the first thing that comes into your mind. If I guessed correctly, then I win. How can I cheat?"

The young prince thought of Chatham's former life as a wolf, the enhanced senses he still carried, his gift of immortality, and concluded that low-level psychic abilities were not an impossible addition to his closet full of tricks.

"Give them back their money," he said, "we have an audience with those who will not be kept waiting."

With a grunt of displeasure Chatham shoved his winnings back to the other men and rose from the table, following the small party through the inn, to the streets. A chill immediately greeted the merchant prince when he stepped outside, and he pulled his topcoat tight.

"It's cold," he said in surprise. The evenings were generally warm at this time of year. Shantow raised his hand and shuddered. Groups of men on either side of the street wore very little, as if they were not affected by the cold.

"It seems this wind is meant for us alone," Chatham said finally. "It begins at our backs, and leads us there."

The old warrior pointed to the twisting spire of the summit of the wolves in the far distance.

"There is no sense denying it," Trevelyan said, then called for a page to bring out their horses. He knew, however, that the shaking of his hands had nothing to do with the unnatural wind. In moments they were riding toward the outskirts of the city, the ice-cold breeze cutting through them, the lights of the city dwindling at their backs.

Shantow had barely spoken since he arrived at the Ivory Dagger. Ariodne rode up beside him and said, "Chianjur, your wife, sends her regards."

"I have no wife," Shantow said, and spat on the ground. "The ceremony of Turning Face has been performed. Within one month our union will be annulled."

Ariodne was stunned. The Kintaran ritual for divorce could be performed with the consent of only one party if hard evidence could be presented of the other partner's infidelities. The young ambassador actually believed that his misshapen progeny had been the result of Chianjur's affair with a man of the hollow. Throughout Cynara and many other cities in Aranhod, the murders of spouses delivering soulless children had increased, along with suicides to circumvent the justice of the wolves.

Putting aside her intolerance of Shantow's ridiculous views, Ariodne attempted to reason with the man. "Your wife is never outside Arayncourt Hall without the escort of one or more of your bodyguards. How could she have betrayed you?"

"It would have maybe taken only one night," he said. "Nine months before the birth, Trevelyan hosted the Masque of the Dead, honoring those who had fallen to protect this land. There were servants, three at least, who were not human."

"Chianjur would not betray you," Ariodne pleaded, "especially not with one of those monstrosities."

"They are rumored to be extraordinary lovers."

"She would not lie with any but you. You know that," Ariodne said. "She would have no desire for them."

"Desire is maybe not at issue here," the Kintaran snarled.

"You mean you think she was raped," Ariodne said slowly, skirting the gossamer line between attempting to understand Shantow's delusions and encouraging his fantasies. "If you're right, that changes everything, doesn't it?"

"It changes nothing. She brought shame upon our families."

Shaking her head in frustration, Ariodne said, "Shantow, the child was *yours*. You know that—"

"You maybe are the one who doesn't know things," the Kintaran said as he gathered up his reins. "You don't know to quiet your stupid mouth and keep your place. In my country a woman would never speak as such to her betters."

"We're not in your country, Shantow. And with the way you're treating your wife, I'll *never* accept you as my better. You have to stop denying the truth—"

"Your truth!" Shantow screamed as he spat in her direction, then pulled ahead to take the point. The red-haired Maven hung back, allowing Trevelyan to catch up with her. She related the conversation to her lover, then added, "He believes she was attacked, raped at the Masque."

"That would explain a great deal," Trevelyan said. "In Kintaran culture, despite the teachings of the Mavens, the laws of the wolves and the Unseen, despite common sense, the woman who is attacked is punished almost as greatly as her assailant. If she is married, her marriage is annulled and she is forbidden to ever share her bed with a husband again."

"Barbaric," Ariodne said in disgust. "They blame the woman for being a victim?"

"For not fighting back hard enough, for not forcing the man to kill her when he had taken his pleasure. That shame is ultimate in their society."

"I suppose they feel she invited the rape?"

"By the same virtues they uphold in a wife, yes. And the husband and his entire clan are shamed, too. At least until he finds the guilty party and brings him to justice. If he doesn't, then he must relinquish his name, his title, and perhaps his life. That is, if he chooses to stay with the woman who is shamed."

In that moment, the reasons for Shantow's obsession with the destruction of the hollow suddenly became frighteningly clear: he knew that Chianjur would not willingly betray him, but the only way that he could stay with her by the doctrines of his country was to find her assailant and dispatch him, even if that meant destroying an entire race.

At the gates of the city they were stopped by an overweight sentry while traffic in the locks was halted and the bridge was lowered.

"The four of you have the look of a war party," the sentry said jovially.

"Indeed," Trevelyan said as he drew his *kris*, "we have the blood of an appropriations committee to spill."

"Not a bad idea, Lord Trevelyan." The fat man watched the bridge move into place and signaled the guard station on the opposing bank to give the travelers free rein. "Perhaps later you can sever the head of the monstrous tax bill that awaits the working class every month."

"I've already tried," Trevelyan said as he replaced his weapon and seized the reins of his mount. "The blasted thing always grows back."

With that the merchant prince ground his heels into the sides of his horse and led his party across the bridge. Passing the second guard station the small group found a trail that ran parallel to the shore, and Trevelyan watched the heavy cargo ships that lumbered into port carrying the cheap raw goods from foreign lands that would leave as high-priced luxury items after they were refined and packaged. The heavy laboring sounds of creaking wood drifted to him, the shimmering waves created by the oarsmen reached out, distorting the mirror image of the golden city of his birth.

As a boy Trevelyan had dreamed of journeying on such a ship, exploring the lands he had read about only in books. His father, Oram, had never allowed this dream to come to pass. The man had feared his enemies and worried that they would take their vengeance upon him by harming his only child. And so Trevelyan had never left northern Aranhod.

You never gave me a chance, Father, Trevelyan thought. As if in reply, a cold gust of wind snapped at the small of his neck, blowing his long black hair into his sullen face. The merchant prince looked away from the harbor and guided his mount toward a trail that snaked off from the shore, leading them deep into the thick woods. Soon they were cutting a pathway through the hills outside Grafath, the twisting spire of their destination always in view, reaching up to claw at the full, bloated moon overhead.

The next two hours passed slowly. When the road widened Trevelyan guided his mount to Ariodne's side and rode with her, Chatham and Shantow behind them. They passed through a sparkling stream, journeyed through a small farming village, then encountered a stretch of deadlands where people had been buried centuries earlier, before the practice of submitting a corpse to the cleansing of the flame became common practice. Beyond the deadlands, they rode through a large, featureless steppe, the craggy summit growing larger every minute, until they were finally at the base of the misshapen monolith.

Trevelyan dismounted and stared at the precarious trail that weaved around the outside of the spire. The others joined him, looking for a place to secure their mounts.

"That won't be necessary," Chatham said gruffly. "Trevelyan must make this part of the journey alone."

"How will he understand the intent of the wolves? I was the one who heard their thoughts!" Ariodne said.

They began to argue and Trevelyan raised his gloved hand. All discussion ended and Trevelyan walked to the side of his lover. "He's right. I have to do this alone." He caressed the side of her face and she gently took his hand, bringing it to her lips, then her chest, above her heart.

"I'll be here for you," she said softly. "I will always be here for you."

Sadness swept over him at those words, although he had no idea why he should feel anything but comfort. Leaning down, he whispered, "I will make you my wife."

"I will hold you to that," she replied.

Then he turned to Shantow, who took his friend's hand. Trevelyan flinched in pain and Shantow suddenly remembered. Lowering his gaze, Shantow said, "I am sorry for this morning."

Trevelyan grasped the man's arm, ignoring the lancing bolt of pain that shot upward from his hand. By Kintaran tradition, apologies were rare. Those who inflicted injury made amends, but words of this type were hardly ever spoken.

Chatham drew his dagger and handed it to the young prince, handle first. "Take this. You will need it."

Reluctantly Trevelyan took the weapon, then turned to the crumbling path that led to the glassy plane at the final rise of the summit and began the long walk to the top.

Once he disappeared from view, Ariodne went to Chatham. "You said there's a reason for our being here. Tell me."

Chatham scratched the back of his neck. "You, Maven

Ariodne Gairloch, and Ambassador Shantow Yakima will have the task of mending the wounds the wolves are about to inflict upon his spirit and his sanity. You must be patient and kind, even when you wish to throttle him. I don't envy you."

Ariodne gazed up at the summit and heard the fall of stones, indicating Trevelyan would soon round the first full turn around the spire.

Above his friends, Trevelyan felt his heart thunder in his chest as heavily as it had hours before, when he had made love to the woman who would be his wife. The climb was far easier than he had expected, and the rumors he had heard that couples sometimes made this journey so they could look out and see the golden spires of Cynara as they satisfied each other seemed perfectly reasonable to him. He would not have been surprised to find a pair of lovers screaming their hearts out instead of a spectral band of wolves when he arrived at the top, but instead, the glassy, marble plane at the tip of the summit was completely deserted.

"Can't be right," Trevelyan said as he stumbled forward, the journey at its end, its result a mockery. Anger seared his mind and he screamed in rage at the fool he had been made into by the wolves and their promises.

Suddenly a sharp wind cut across the back of his neck, and his shadow, visible only in the moonlight, lengthened as an explosion of brilliant blue-white light erupted behind him. A chorus of earsplitting howls cut through the night, the volume and intensity great enough to force the prince to cover his ears to relieve the pressure against his eardrums.

The howling stopped. *Turn and face us,* a voice urged within Trevelyan's mind.

The wind faded, and his shadow once again retreated, but a faint white glow remained as Trevelyan looked in the direction of the light and felt the tension he had been carrying quickly drain from him. He found a grin tracing its way across his features as he stared at the first wolves and realized that he had seen them before, first in his dreams, then in the fourth house of the wolves in Cynara.

If such a thing were possible for a wolf, Black Mask also seemed to be grinning at his private jest.

Welcome, young lord.

Trevelyan reeled at the perfect beauty of Black Mask's voice. The rich, melodious tones seemed to burrow into the deepest regions of his mind. A moment later he understood that he had heard this voice before; the wolf was using the comforting and strong voice of his father, Oram. Or perhaps his brain was simply reinterpreting the messages sent by the first wolf, playing tricks so that Trevelyan would not fall before the weight of such fantastic circumstances.

There was no rocky throne for Black Mask to sit upon this time, lording over his wife and fellow wolves. His auburn-furred mate was at his side, the pure white wolf flanking him yet remaining a respectful distance behind, the wolf with black paws across from him. The salt and pepper dog soldiers completed the inverted V formation of the animals, looking at one another with sad, lonely glances.

"Why the charade?" Trevelyan asked.

Black Mask sneezed, shaking his head in an undignified manner. *You needed time to see that the world is changing. Also, in this time, at this place, we are very strong. Able to see more, tell more.*

The enormity of what was before him filled the young prince with a giddiness he had not expected. "You are the first wolves," he said. "You betrayed the gods, dragged them into the crypts where they lie to this day, tricked them into inhaling the scent of the black lotus so they would sleep an eternity. You were there when mankind leaped from the dreams of the sleeping gods and you threatened to destroy us when we became too much like them."

Warriors of the Unseen. Hand of justice.

"Bloody *paws* of justice," Trevelyan said, throwing his hands into the air. "*Fangs* of truth." He stared at the wolves. They were unmoved by his ridicule. Chatham treated them as if they were too damn solemn for their own good, maybe he was right. The wolves shifted uncomfortably.

"By the Unseen, get to it!" Yes, he thought, get to it before my mind snaps.

Autumn is dying, Black Mask said without emotion.

Trevelyan stopped, his legs threatening to give out beneath him. He wanted to ask Black Mask to repeat the statement, but he didn't feel he could bear to hear it again.

"What do you mean, 'dying'?"

The hollow. The glaive. They are connected.

"The men of the hollow can't use the Forge. What are—"

The glaive is a lie. Created by the Mavens to disguise their sins.

"What sins have the Mavens committed? How could they when your children exist solely to punish the guilty?"

Black Mask growled in frustration. *The Forge. The Forge is their sin.*

"Help me," Trevelyan implored, "help me to understand."

Black Mask's auburn-furred mate moved forward, gently padding to the dark-haired prince, where she stopped and looked at him with intelligent, jade-green eyes. Trevelyan crouched down before her, his body quaking in fear. Claws extended, she raked one of her front paws over the other, drawing a small trickle of blood, then looked back at him.

Your blood is needed, Black Mask whispered in his mind. *Trust Walks With Fire.*

The auburn-furred wolf raised her bloody paw to his wounded hand. Trevelyan shook as he removed the glove, exposing the broken finger secured to its splint, and drew the dagger Chatham had given him. Slicing the blade across his palm he allowed the wolf to rest her wounded paw in his.

There was a blinding light as an aurora burst over the night sky, flooding the summit with illumination. Pain tightened at the back of his head as his mind rebelled at the vision before him: the aurora began to spin, the deep blues and reds swirling and coalescing into a vortex, a tunnel that reached out and overwhelmed the young prince.

Suddenly he no longer had a body made of flesh and blood. He was light, a single pulse racing through the tunnel as nightmarish visions leaped out at him. He saw a deep waiting pool filled with millions of souls, bright, pulsating forms that were vaguely human, that took shape, then relinquished it, forming shining waters.

The Well of Souls, he thought, amazed that conscious thought was still possible. Then he saw the Mavens of the Forge, a dozen women, their hands linked, calling upon forces they knew nothing about. With each incantation, souls were drawn from the well, leaving a bilious noisome substance that pervaded the shining waters, snuffing out their light. In the center of the circle of Mavens, twisted, tortured souls danced in agony and death, their light extinguished, blackened husks left in their place, corpses that the Mavens shaped into tools, weapons, clothes.

Suddenly the vision passed and Trevelyan found himself racing back through the tunnel, facing another explosion of light and sound, then a darkness so absolute he was certain that he had either died or lost his mind.

His eyes flashed open as he smelled the fetid breath of a wolf and felt the pressure of Black Mask's body pinning him down. Walks With Fire was beside him, the other wolves stationed at four points surrounding him. Trevelyan stared into the perfect turquoise of Black Mask's eyes as the wolf pulled back his lips and exposed his fangs.

"The Forge, magic," he said absently, "it's a lie."

Not a lie. Magic is real. Killing.

The first wolf backed down from the prince's chest, allowing him to sit upright. He stared at his hand. The cut in his palm and his broken finger had been healed.

"The Mavens broke down the walls protecting the Well of Souls. Every time we use the Forge we're destroying yet another unborn soul."

Soon there will be none left. That is why the hollow came into being. But there are many wells in Autumn. Not all compromised. That is why some children are born with souls, others without. The hollow cannot procreate, unless it is with a partner who has a soul. Eventually no new children will be born and all mankind will perish.

"The wells that have been tapped, is there any way to save them?" Trevelyan asked breathlessly.

The waters cannot be purified. They must be used up and replaced by fresh waters of life, such as those provided by the tears of the sleeping gods. Any who are without a soul will gain one if the well is replenished.

"The tears of the sleeping gods," Trevelyan whispered.

The only way to bring about the tears of the sleeping gods without waking them is by using the black lotus and the red-white rose. The scent of the lotus will maintain their slumber. The scent of the red-white rose will force them to confront the truth about themselves. The gods, once made to see themselves for what they are, to confront their pointless, wasted existences, must surely weep.

"The lotus, the rose—they are legends, not real."

You will find the lotus in the heart of your greatest enemy.

"In his heart? You're saying that I have to kill him."

How you obtain the lotus is not our concern.

"The rose?"

That must be a secret, until you have secured the lotus.

Confusion seeped through the prince. "Why? Why must we do this? Can't the Unseen force the tears of the gods? Is there no other way to regain the integrity of the wells?"

Black Mask was silent for a time. Then he looked to his mate. Walks With Fire, who closed her eyes and lowered her head. The first wolf turned back to Trevelyan.

We made a promise to your race with Lucian Arayncourt. A promise to protect. Our vow will not be broken, even if it means going against the wishes of the Unseen.

"The Unseen wants us to die?" Trevelyan asked in shock.

Autumn's God has been angered by man's sacrilege and has decided that if mankind is to be saved, it must save itself.

Bitterly, Trevelyan said, "Tell me of this enemy."

Your nemesis will reveal himself shortly. The threat, as your friend Shantow surmised, will come from Rien. Now you must go, and tell Chatham we desire an audience.

Trevelyan got to his feet. "That's it? Go tell the world that our greatest discovery is truly our worst folly? That we are destroying ourselves by using the Forge?"

Tell no one. They would brand you as mad. Your empire would be lost. Your value to us, and to them, diminished. Carry the secret within.

"But if they stopped using the Forge—" he pleaded.

They will never stop. Not until the wells run dry.

Trevelyan pulled the top knot of his shirt closed. The cloak he had forged was gone. The air had turned cold. "The souls that have been destroyed—they will never live again."

Never.

"What of my father? Has his soul been destroyed?"

Black Mask hesitated. *The Unseen does not allow us to look that closely. Oram may live. For how long we cannot say. Your audience is at an end, young lord. For now.*

Trevelyan half expected the wolves to vanish in a brilliant flash of light, but they remained, milling about, playing with one another as if he were no longer their concern. When Trevelyan reached the base of the spire, he relayed the desires of the wolves to Chatham, who swore and started up the pathway.

"You're shaking," Ariodne said as she ran her hands over Trevelyan's arms. "You're like ice." With a smile she called upon the Forge. Trevelyan's eyes grew wide at the accompanying hiss as he identified the sound as the final breath of a soul meeting its destruction. Ariodne slipped the black shawl she had created around his shoulders, and he felt as if he were wearing the skin of his ancestor's soul.

At the glassy plane atop the summit, Chatham approached the first wolves. "You pitiful curs. You didn't tell him that while the lotus will be found in the heart of his greatest enemy, the rose will be found only in the heart of his greatest love. Both must be sacrificed for the world to be saved. Ariodne has to die at his hands and you disgusting creatures didn't have the courage to tell him."

Chatham spat on the ground before the wolves.

"When this is over, I may not want to be a wolf again."

We both lied to the boy and withheld information to get him to do what must be done. Are our methods so different?

"You have always received a thrill by circumventing the Unseen, haven't you? Answer me honestly, you smelly bastard, do you really care if mankind is wiped from Autumn, or is it the pleasure of the quest that moves you?"

The turquoise eyes of the first wolf blazed, their intensity becoming overwhelming, until their blue-white fire seared the plane of the summit, leaving Chatham alone. He looked at the lights of Cynara in the distance. For a moment the golden glow of Trevelyan's homeland seemed to flicker and die, the beautiful spires of the city vanishing into ruin. Then the brilliant light returned, the city untouched.

"Show me no more of the future," he whispered, "and I'll do whatever you want."

The wind sailed past him, a rogue gust that dissipated quickly, leaving a message from its creator.

You would have anyway, Black Mask said, a tinge of amusement in his voice.

PART FOUR

The Forge

CHAPTER
TEN

"No, my liege, the stockades of Fenris were not to my liking," Lon Freyr said quietly. The tall, red-haired man had turned his cold and merciless stare upon the leader of all Bellerophon, Searle Orrick. Freyr stood in Orrick's private chambers, dressed in a simple white frock. Weeks of imprisonment had made him drawn and haggard-looking, although his eyes continued to burn with defiance.

When the guards came early that morning to the dark and stinking pit where he had been thrown with five other prisoners, he sensed that his suffering would soon be over, one way or the other. He was led above ground, where he was offered a succulent feast, a bath, and an intensely beautiful and sensual woman with hair the color of straw and eyes the perfect blue of the Autumn sky. The food and the chance to bathe he accepted, the woman he did not. He had been repulsed by the gesture. Freyr was married and the custom Orrick had started of sharing partners had never struck him as particularly civilized.

The journey to Orrick's palace had consumed several hours in the freezing cold and the soldier had been bundled tight. When they arrived at the nation's capital, he was taken to a modestly appointed red room where servants forged a steady supply of coals for the furnace.

Freyr was stripped of his clothing, dressed in the white frock, then given an audience with a court-appointed storyteller who kept him entertained until Orrick made his appearance. In the past, the former point man had only seen the ruler from a distance. He was amazed by the power and vitality the man exuded in close quarters. Orrick was close to forty and his body was in perfect condition; Freyr was reminded of the men of the hollow, with their heavily muscled physiques. The ruler had thick black hair brushed back to expose his imposing brow, arched black eyebrows and dark eyes, a solid square nose and jaw, and Cupid lips that spoke not only of solidarity and strength, but of compassion and tolerance. He wore a white frock identical to the one given to Freyr. His words snapped Freyr out of his reverie.

"Then you will help?"

"It would be my honor and privilege," Freyr said, and wondered exactly what he was agreeing to. Up to this point, Orrick had merely reminded him of Branagh's failure to retrieve the secret of liquid fire from Kothra of Rien and the message Kothra had forced the soldier to relay to Orrick. Once he had made the journey back to his homeland, Freyr had passed along Kothra's words to Orrick's second in command, Wolfram Hilliard. For his efforts he had been stripped of his position and thrown in prison.

A servant entered the quarters, bearing a tray with a flask of a rare, imported red wine and two glasses. Orrick dismissed the short woman, then served Freyr and himself. Taking a moment to savor the drink, Orrick grinned at Freyr.

"Do you know what sets us apart from those blue-skinned devils? Beyond the obvious, of course."

Freyr was silent. He could tell when his commander was asking a question for the sole purpose of answering it himself. "Yes, they are monstrous, they don't look like us, our natural inclination is to be afraid of them. But the differences run deeper than the color of their flesh. We envy and despise them their strength, power, and cunning. But are these qualities that make them rise above the level of the beast? I don't believe so.

"A hollow man has no soul. He walks upright, he speaks, he gives the appearance of personality and free thought, but in the end, he is but a pale imitation of a man. His intelligence is that of an animal that spends time among his betters and soon believes himself to be their equal. Kothra is confused, willful—that makes him dangerous. Branagh did not show that creature his proper place among true men."

Freyr was sickened by the torrent of unreasoning prejudice Orrick was spitting out. The time he had spent with hollow men had convinced him that they should be treated with the respect one gave a capable enemy, not the scorn reserved for an undisciplined child.

"Kothra was able to do what human agents have failed to accomplish for several decades," Freyr noted.

Orrick waved his hand impatiently. "Naturally he was able to secure the formula for liquid fire from the savages of Chiabos; he is a savage himself. I should not indulge myself at your expense. It all comes down to this," he said as he held his hand out and drew a breath, his muscles tightening as he summoned the power of the Forge. The rancid smell of magic filled the room, accompanied by a harsh whisper, like a gasp for breath, and a seven-foot, smoked black glass statue appeared. Freyr was startled by the statue's resemblance to Kothra of Rien, including the teeth that had been sharpened to points, exposed by an evil smile.

"The Unseen grants the power of the Forge to men, not devils. With this power the poorest of men can obtain shelter from the storm, clothing for their family, tools to build a better life, and weapons to protect those he loves. But he must be clean of spirit. He must have a soul."

Orrick turned to the imposing statue beside him and lashed out with a powerful, close-fisted blow to the exposed stomach of the statue, smashing the midsection into a rain of glass shards, causing the upper half of the figure to tumble forward, the arms and head splintering into dark fragments as they struck the floor. The jaw, with its sharpened teeth, scittered across the floor and landed at Freyr's bare feet. Orrick stepped over the broken glass, the jagged pieces passing harmlessly through the soles of his feet.

"Without a soul, no matter their outward appearance, the men of the hollow are fragile and weak," the ruler said, then laughed. "As you can see, they shatter easily."

"Yes," Freyr said, attempting to avoid the grinning glass mouth at his feet. "I see that."

But if they have no souls, the soldier wondered, how can they exist at all? What fills the void in their hearts?

Orrick's expression had changed, his indulgent smile replaced by the stern look of a commander prepared to address his men. Freyr caught the look and came to attention.

"Let me come to the most pertinent facts: A search party recently came back from Telluryde. Their report substantiates your claims of what occurred. I am pleased to tell you that your period of holding is at an end."

"My period of holding," Lon Freyr repeated dully.

"Or so it will reflect in the official record. We do not countenance failure, *Lieutenant*," Orrick said stiffly. "Your family, by the way, has already been notified of your return. They know nothing of your adventures in Telluryde. If you are wise, it will remain that way. They are preparing for your visit tonight. In the morning you will depart."

Freyr was about to speak when the full impact of Orrick's statement struck him. He had just been lifted from ranks of the vanished men, returned to active duty, and granted a substantial promotion. If he was to return at all from the mission Orrick had yet to outline, he would have to bring news of his success, or his family would suffer along with him when the time for punishment and discipline came.

Ruthless, he thought. "What would you have me do?"

Orrick finished his glass of wine, then poured another, making note that Freyr had not yet touched his. "Your thirst seems limited to a taste for knowledge. That's fair. I received a communication from Rien yesterday. Kothra has been granted asylum there."

"Not surprising," Freyr commented.

"Indeed not. He claims that he has had time to consider his actions, and that perhaps he was rash in his declaration that he would sell the secret of liquid fire to the highest bidder due to our betrayal. After all, we sponsored his journey, and a man of the hollow could hardly expect a post in a government such as ours. He wishes for us to send a small negotiating party to Rien, for the purpose of establishing a fair price."

"Of course, he's lying."

"Of course. That is what men of the hollow do. We must assume that he has another reason for dragging our representatives to that wasteland he calls a home," Orrick said as he took a seat on the edge of a small red cot.

"Perhaps he wishes to stall any military attempts to take back what is rightfully ours. Rien was a fortress city. He already has liquid fire. Given time he could rebuild—"

"He would also need resources that are beyond him: money, equipment, supplies. The hand of the Unseen destroyed that place. Who would dare sponsor its restoration?"

Freyr was silent. He had seen Kothra destroy a monument

that had withstood nature's attempts to bury it for decades and had stood close enough to see the hatred in his eyes. There was very little he put beyond the hollow man.

"A diplomatic envoy has already been prepared, along with a full military escort. You will command this mission. You have seen Kothra, you can tell the men what to expect."

"Is there anything else, sir?"

"Yes. Get as close to that monster as you can. Learn his secrets. Find his weakness so that we might exploit it. Then report back to me. If that is not possible, your family will receive the full benefits payable to one who lost his life in my service."

The red-haired lieutenant felt weak suddenly, and fought to stand at attention. His mind flashed forward to the evening he would spend with his wife and child, and to his farewell to them in the morning. They could not be allowed to know that he would never see them again. He prayed they would not be able to sense the overwhelming finality that now marred his every thought. The task Orrick had set for him would be impossible to achieve.

Suddenly another option occurred to him. He could take his family and try to escape. Criminals had often lost themselves in the outer colonies beyond the northern region. One day they could book passage to Aranhod, where they would live without the threat of Orrick and his insane plans.

"One other thing," Orrick said mildly. "I've taken the liberty of posting sentries at your home. They will be at your disposal the entire evening, no more than a shout away."

In his mind, the lieutenant's fantasy crumbled and fell, exactly the way the city of Rien had fallen almost two hundred years before. He averted his eyes in deference to his commander, forgetting for an instant the grinning, razor-sharp set of smoky black teeth that rested on the floor, tilted upward slightly, as if Kothra were smiling in welcome.

Walking through the narrow streets that led to the Citadel of the Mavens, Trevelyan was filled with unreasoning dread. Chatham had elected to accompany the young prince to the citadel. A fine mist clung to the black stone streets that curved to the right. Three-story buildings with tall, arched windows rose up on either side, monolithic sentinels bearing their shadow-laden stone faces to the street. Ahead, beyond the next turn, intense orange sunlight washed over the partially visible University of Sciences.

The street opened up into a wide five-cornered junction, a stone island bearing a series of iron rods, many of which had mounts tied to them, lay in the middle of the far road, the final stretch that would take them to the citadel. The building was visible at the end of the long street, pure white sunlight washing over it, making the spires appear insubstantial. The streets were slowly filling with people.

Chatham seemed absolutely delighted with life this morning; his charge, however, wished that he were still asleep. Stifling a terrible yawn, Trevelyan shook his head and tried to wipe the sleep from his eyes.

"I feel horrible," Trevelyan moaned.

"Good," Chatham said brightly. "You look that way, you might as well feel that way."

"I don't want to do this," Trevelyan muttered.

"We all have to do things we don't want to do. Remember, whining doesn't become a prince."

Waving his hand in the air to dismiss Chatham's words, Trevelyan kept his head low as they approached the citadel. In a solemn voice, Trevelyan asked, "What did they say to you last night? You said that we would talk this morning."

Chatham shrugged. "The wolves told me the same thing they told you. Magic may wipe out the race of man."

"You don't seem very worried."

"I'm a wolf that walks upright, not a man. I'll shed this skin somehow." The grey-bearded warrior threw his head back and exulted in the bright morning sunlight. "Perhaps if there are no more men, my penance will be at an end. Unless they let me live, the last man on the planet. That would be a hellish fate, wouldn't it? Ah well, I suppose we'll just have to work especially hard at this savior of mankind business after all."

Trevelyan grunted.

"Work on your sense of humor, boy. You might as well laugh at yourself. The Unseen knows, others will be only too happy to pick up your slack."

The prince shot a glare at his guardian. "Are you saying people are laughing at me?"

"No," Chatham said with a grin. "I'm just saying that your tight-rumped behavior is hardly what is required now. You must laugh at death, ridicule tragedy, stare boldly into the pool of your own suffering, and give what you see there a wink. You shouldn't make life harder than it needs to be."

The old warrior stopped suddenly. "Look, we're here. Now isn't *that* exciting?"

They stood before the Citadel of the Mavens. The black stone building consumed a city block, its gold-trimmed spires reaching higher than those of any other building in Cynara, threatening to impale the clouds. The design was a simple square, each plane interrupted at its center by protruding towers, topped by a dome covered with dagger-shaped observation towers. The materials that had been used in the construction of its beautiful facades were gold, silver, steel, and stone; at its core, however, the citadel had been forged. Trevelyan stared at the building, wondering how many souls had been sacrificed to construct and then maintain the solidity of the temple.

The doors and outer walls bore intricately sculpted faces and figures of soldiers and saviors of the Mavens' cause. The entrance Trevelyan had chosen displayed the proud, stern face of his grandfather. The doorway was guarded by female sentries wearing shining black armors similar to those Ariodne had manifested at the Silver Dagger. Only women were allowed to serve at the citadel as students, healers, providers, and soldiers. Ariodne had been trained in every capacity. The woman who stood before the prince and his companion had the look of those who had devoted themselves solely to the cause of protecting the citadel at any cost. Their training and their willingness to take a life or lay down their own if necessary was widely known and respected, although they sometimes met with derisive remarks in the less-refined areas of the city in their off hours.

Mesh skull caps concealed the women's hair, plates with steel grills obscured their faces, leaving only their heavily shadowed eyes to give them any distinction. The woman on the left had deep blue eyes, the one on the right soft brown. They carried weapons that had not been the products of the Forge: short swords, daggers, axes, bludgeons, wire nets. Both women were very tall, with trim, athletic builds.

As Trevelyan and Chatham approached, the blue-eyed protector drew her short sword and aimed the tip in the pair's direction. "We cannot let you pass."

"What's wrong? Is there trouble in the citadel?"

"No," the blue-eyed woman said coldly.

Trevelyan considered moving past them—after all, they wouldn't dare to lay a hand on him—but recent events had made him cautious. "Do you know who I am?"

"Yes, Lord Arayncourt. But as long as you traffic with such as *that*," she said bitterly as she pointed her short sword at the scarred, grey-bearded warrior beside him, "we cannot allow you to enter our citadel. Renounce your association with the criminal and all will be forgiven."

"You're stepping beyond your authority," Trevelyan said heatedly. "Chatham is my personal guard."

The blue-eyed sentry looked sharply at the old warrior for a moment, then returned her full attention to the young prince. "You have no need for a guard within our walls. Dismiss him and you may enter."

"Chatham, you're fired," Trevelyan said in a level tone.

"Yes," the old man sighed. "I knew it would happen one day. Perhaps I'll just wait around out here until you're done, that way you can accompany me to a fat old tree in the woods and bear witness as I hang myself in grief."

"A fine idea," Trevelyan said.

"Good," Chatham replied brightly.

"You're a pair of fools," the brown-eyed sentry said harshly. "Circus clowns."

The affront was more than Trevelyan was willing to accept gracefully. He spun and addressed the brown-eyed guard and said, "Did you know what they do to those who botch their suicides in Rien?"

The sentry's brown eyes widened in fear at the mention of the dark land beyond Aranhod's northern border.

"They nurse them back to health, allow them to regain their strength and will to live, then execute them for their crime." Trevelyan watched through the front grill of the sentry's black steel mask as she screwed her face up tight. "Life is precious. Blood is precious. Now move out of my way before I decide that yours is less worthy of my respect and spill some of it in my frustration."

Without another word, the sentries backed away and opened the heavy double doors of the citadel. "I won't be long," Trevelyan said without looking over his shoulder. The doors were slammed shut behind him.

Outside the citadel, Chatham found himself thinking about

the story Trevelyan had told of Rien's laws. His instincts told him that the prince truly believed that he was making up a fairy tale to unnerve the sentries. A childish thing to do, of course, but Trevelyan was little more than a boy himself. What Chatham found disturbing was the accuracy of Trevelyan's tale, considering he had no earthly means of having gathered the information. Any who would have attempted to tell that story would have unwillingly swallowed their own tongues before they could say more than a few words, and paper upon which the secrets of the city were written would instantly burst into flame once Rien's borders were crossed. But somehow Trevelyan had *known*.

"You're a bad influence on the prince," the blue-eyed guard said quietly.

"On everyone, it seems," the old warrior said with a winning smile. "We have time to pass. Would either of you be interested in a game of chance? The odds would be against me, and all we need to play is some paper and ink."

"Bugger yourself," the brown-eyed guard spat. Chatham slowly turned away.

"Wait," the blue-eyed guard called. "I think I might be in the mood to dish out a little humiliation to this flea-ridden criminal."

Chatham smiled, then assumed a solemn, cowed expression as he turned on his heels. "So be it," he said. "By the way, how much money do you have on you?"

The sentries regarded each other, then dug for their money pouches.

Inside the grand hall of the citadel, Trevelyan felt a pang of guilt at his behavior with the sentries.

The hallway was awash with bright sunlight from arched windows behind him. Torches lit the corridor ahead. Great stone pillars rose on either side of him, a dozen such pillars lining each side of the hallway ahead. Archways were carved between each set of columns, and behind the archways were small receiving areas devoid of privacy, then a series of locked doors. Statues, paintings, and glass-enclosed display cases with remnants of the Mavens' former lives were left outside the chambers. The ceiling was also curved, a golden honeycomb reaching down to the high observation level, the Mavens' walk, on the second floor. Although he appeared to be alone in the north wing of the grand hall, several guards patrolled above, each of them armed with bolos and crossbows. Trevelyan could understand why the sentries were remanded to the second floor: if they patrolled on the ground level the sanctuary would have the feel of an armed encampment.

A sudden breeze whipped before his face and the bolt from a crossbow bounced from a nearby pillar, clattering to his feet. The prince looked up sharply to see a total of six guards with crossbows aimed in his direction.

"Surrender your weapons!" one of them called.

Trevelyan's hand absently brushed the hilt of his *kris* and he realized that the sentries had been too shaken to issue the standard command that he leave his only means of protection at the door.

"I beg your pardon," he said with practiced humility. "Your sisters at the door neglected to make the request—"

A second shaft sailed through the air, brushing against the hair of his ponytail. Too many words, he thought as he slowly untied the scabbard at his waist and let it fall to the ground. Then he bent and removed the dagger that was secured to his thigh, dropping it to the stone floor.

A new voice called. "Ruzena and Deile are at their posts, talking with a man who bears the mark of three claws."

"Trevelyan Arayncourt," the sentry who appeared to be in command said triumphantly. "The prophecies were true. We were told you would visit your mother today."

The young prince tried not to appear startled. He had only made up his mind last night.

"Do you know the way?" she called.

"Naturally," he responded, although he was certain that he would be lost when he reached the end of the corridor.

"Your mother is in her quarters in the east quadrant," a second guard called, then gave him directions. As he walked through the citadel's winding corridors, occasionally hearing voices raised in chants, Trevelyan passed a group of young women, Mavens in training, who wore black, hooded robes and did not look up at him when he walked past them.

Although the citadel was resplendent, he felt as if he were walking through a hollowed-out corpse, the elegant design and trappings serving as cosmetics. One of the many doorways was open, and he caught a glimpse of a beautiful cathedral, where several dozen women sat cross-legged, wearing short, black-petaled skirts and armless blouses of heavy mail. They seemed entranced. A black smoking tray sat to one side of them. One of the Mavens turned as he walked by and addressed him in a thick, dream-laden voice, her eyes heavy with sleep, her long black hair falling into her pretty face. "The bleeding won't last," she said before she turned away, then softly repeated the statement.

He nearly stopped dead in the hallway, but he had smelled the odd, burning roots before, in Ariodne's quarters, and knew they were used to open the minds of the women to visions from the Unseen, and to help them release their physical inhibitions and allow total communion with the Stream of Life. Attempting to converse with the Mavens while they were in such a vulnerable state, without their permission, would have been a terrible blunder of etiquette.

Nevertheless, the Maven's statement had left him deeply disturbed. The last time he had heard those exact words had been a year earlier, when his father lay dying.

When he came to the final stretch of the grand hall, one of the guards on the second tier announced his presence. He turned a corner and found a black wall barring his way. Suddenly the wall vanished and he entered the east quadrant, an area devoted to a dormitory for the Mavens in residence. Two Mavens sat in black, wooden chairs, constructs forged with ease, and nodded to each other. There was a stench and the sound of displaced air. Then the whispering breath of souls in torment faded and the wall reappeared.

Trevelyan was sickened when he considered the wasting of souls each time their door was re-created, but he understood their caution. From here he would be able to access the gateway to the depths, the labyrinth below ground where the first Mavens of the Forge were sequestered. There was a slight vibration below his feet, like the thunder of hooves from far away. The power that radiated from below stung like the charged air in a field after lightning had struck.

Four armed sentries escorted him through the bare-walled hallways. The funds from private donations that the Mavens received had not been used to augment the black walls, ceilings, and floors. Above the evenly spaced black doorways the walls receded, allowing for ledges upon which sat the family arms of each Maven quartered here.

Finally they came to the black stone doorway of his mother's quarters. "Lady Arayncourt," one of the sentries called as she rapped at the door. "Your son is here."

"I'm well aware," a rich if tired voice said. There was no visible lock. From the other side of the door Trevelyan heard the muffled hiss of the Forge. "Enter."

The sentry pushed at the door and it swung open, revealing a practically bare black chamber. There was a small cot at the rear of the chamber with a red sheet, a desk in the far corner with paper and quill, and a bookshelf beside the desk filled with crumbling texts and scrolls. Six identical long black gowns hung on a rack. On the wall he saw a sand painting encased in glass. The painting was of a beautiful field with two lovers lying in each other's arms, looking up at the soft clouds, the man pointing with a sly grin, the woman smiling but obviously ready to slap him.

Trevelyan's mother stood in a long black gown, her back turned to him. He entered the room. The sentries waited in the doorway. "Please leave us," she said. The first guard nodded, then pulled the door closed from the hallway.

Lyris Arundel spun and called on the Forge to create a lock that fused the door shut. "Now we won't be disturbed."

Trevelyan wasn't sure what to expect when he saw his mother's face, but the vibrant, beautiful visage that greeted him was hardly what he had anticipated. Lyris was almost forty-five, but she could easily pass for ten years younger. Her long black hair fell to her shoulders and was cut in a sweeping line just above her eyebrows. She had hypnotic green eyes and her full red lips were weighty and sensual. Her slashing black eyebrows dipped before meeting and led downward to a sleek, well-sculptured nose bracketed by high cheekbones. The long, sensual V of her throat ended in a hollow between her subtly displayed collarbones. Her generous breasts were partially revealed by her gown.

"I was beginning to think you would never come."

Surprise registered in Trevelyan's voice as he said, "You asked me not to come."

"What does *that* have to do with anything," she said bitterly, then walked to her son and placed her hand on the side of his face. "Poor Trevelyan. You still don't know much about women, do you?"

The merchant prince signed heavily. "Mother, there are issues we must discuss that go deeper than our personal feelings. There will be a war. I need an ally within the ranks of the Mavens. I need you.''

"And what of your lady friend?" Lyris said as she walked to her bookshelf and ran her hand across the collected scrolls on the top shelf, frowning at the thin layer of grey dust she found on her finger. "She should be your confidante."

"You know the way Ariodne is regarded within the order of the Mavens," Trevelyan said. His mother frowned as he went on. "The importance of what I have to tell you can barely be measured. It will impact on our entire world—"

Lyris tried not to laugh. "Trevelyan, you were talking in grandiose terms when you were eight years old. You're even worse than your father was, and that's saying a lot."

"Father's dead. I'd prefer if we don't speak of him. That's not the purpose of this visit."

"Well it damn well should be," his mother said.

Trevelyan's anger strained for release. "You're the one who left. No one drove you from Arayncourt Hall!"

The dark-haired woman, a few inches shorter than her son, crossed the length of the small room and stood before him, pointing a lean finger in his face. "You don't understand, do you? You honestly think that I was running out on you, that I was abandoning you because you reminded me of your father and I couldn't cope with his loss?"

"That is not important," Trevelyan said, struggling to contain his rage.

"I'd say that it is."

"Fine," he shouted. "Then why did you leave? It wasn't the loss of one parent I suffered, it was the loss of two."

Lyris shuddered, as if she had been struck, and her expression suddenly grew dark. "When is the last time you went to the Pavilion and met with the representatives of the ruling families? There are threats from within, threats that you seem unaware of, that are constantly at our door."

"The men at the Pavilion are the men my father put there. He trusted them."

She rubbed at her temples with both hands. "Your father trusted far too easily, that's what led to his problems in the first place. Do you remember when you were, what, three or four and we were in exile?"

"The people rose up in protest," Trevelyan said.

"Yes," she said wearily. "Your father helped to depose the

old government and install one that he could control. But do you think those people have enjoyed being under our control for the last fifteen years? This past year they have tasted freedom. They might have loved your father, but they don't even *know* you.''

Her words were beginning to affect him and he said nervously, ''What are you talking about?''

''I'm talking about the five houses, you fool, of which we are but one. The other four are the house of Radomil, the overseers of the shipping lanes; the house of Zelenka, the masters of the foreign exchange; the house of Melantha, your agricultural supervisors; the house of Sancia, whose family began the Adjudicators and continue to dispense justice apart from the commandments of the Unseen and the wolves. Together with your father they formed a shadow cabinet to run this trading *enterprise* we know as Cynara.

''I went into exile because my life and yours may one day be forfeit. There's an assassin's blade that is being honed even now by your neglect.'' Her features softened. ''I left so that I could keep track of what the other families were doing. The time is coming. There's perhaps six months, a year, maybe less. They already have ways of tarnishing your image. Your involvement with Ariodne Gairloch, for one.''

''Leave her out of it. Don't bring her into this.''

''She's already into it. How blind are you? How stupid? By the Unseen, that I have raised such an ignorant son. Trevelyan, I don't know what you came here expecting me to say. Though I was soon going to—''

''Ariodne and I are going to be married.''

His mother stopped and stared at him in disbelief. ''Then I'm glad you've waited no longer to come and see me.''

''This point is not up for negotiation. I love Ariodne.''

''I'm sure you think you do. But you're just a child. Move slowly. Marry when the time is correct.''

''The time is correct,'' Trevelyan said. ''There is a war approaching and I may die. Ariodne will be an Arayncourt.''

Her eyes were moist with tears when she slowly raised her hands and said, ''Please, I'm sorry if my words seem harsh or cruel, but I have been in this place, I have been pretending to be the grief-stricken widow for nearly a year.''

''You do not miss Father?''

''The Unseen knows that I grieve for Oram. I sleep at night

and I dream of him, I am cold in my bed for want of his body beside me. The pain is great but I won't wallow in it. I loved him and he is gone. I won't lose you. Do you know how resentful he was that his death was due to a sickness eating him up from the inside? Probably brought on by the stress of the position he loved so much.

"I was there when he coughed up blood. I watched as he denied all that was wrong with him. Seeing a physician, getting better was always something he would do later, when he had the time. Well, that killed him. Truth be known, as much as I miss him, as much as I love him still, I am angry with him for his shortsightedness, his stupidity. If he had cared as much about his family as he did about the people of this enterprise, he might have been with us now.

"That is why I'm asking you to concentrate on the threats that face you here in Cynara. You'll do yourself and those you profess to love no good at all if you are dead." She turned to stare at the sand painting of the lovers. Trevelyan joined her, placing his hand on her shoulder as he stared at the portrait. The man in the painting looked identical to the merchant prince.

"It's you and Father. I've never seen this before."

"Ariodne's father created this portrait long ago, when we were young. The four of us were friends, Oram and me, Gowen and Chaney. I want you to know that I have no reason to bear ill feelings against your union to Ariodne Gairloch, other than the one I have been trying to make you see. There is a danger at Arayncourt Hall that you must face. If you don't, it will destroy all of us, Ariodne included."

Trevelyan considered his original purpose for this visit, to try to enlist his mother's aid in convincing the first Mavens of the Forge that they must disband, that the magic they discovered was slowly erasing mankind from the planet. The threat she had described was one that he would have to investigate, when there was time, but the matter of the Forge could not wait. The dark-haired prince told his mother everything that had occurred, starting with his dreams of Black Mask and his meeting with Chatham at the tournament, concluding with the commandments of the first wolves on the summit. "Do you believe me?"

She glanced back at him as if he had suddenly become simpleminded. "Of course I believe you."

Trevelyan was shocked by her reaction. He wondered if she were humoring him. She seemed to sense his disbelief and so she shrugged and explained, "Your father had a dream like yours the night he died. He woke and told it to me. That was before I noticed the blood. There was no time after that for him to have told the dream to anyone else."

"Then I was not the first choice of the wolves," Trevelyan said dully.

"Apparently not," she said, gazing at the door with rising apprehension. "But you are your father's son, his heir in every way. I only wish you weren't so damn young."

"Eighteen winters is old enough," Trevelyan said.

"I'm not talking about how many years you've tucked under your belt," she said softly. "You've got a lot of living to do, that's all, and your father always kept you protected, sheltered from the world because he feared the reprisals of his enemies."

"That was his reason?" Trevelyan said in astonishment.

"What other could there be?" she said.

"You've given me much to think about, Mother. Is there anything I should have sent to you?"

Lyris shook her head, her rich green eyes clouding over as the seal she had created on the heavy black door vanished. Trevelyan walked to the door, pulled it open slowly, then peered into the hallway. There was no one in sight.

"Odd," he said as he took a step into the hall and gasped as his boot slid. Grabbing hold of the jamb he steadied himself, then looked down to see a glistening red smear on the stone floor. His first impulse was to kneel and dip his fingers into the substance. Instinct caused him to draw back suddenly and look up.

A figure was perched on the ledge above the doorway. At first Trevelyan thought it was one of the Mavens in training, a woman wearing the black, hooded gown. Then he saw the bright red eyes with catlike slits, flaring, dark nostrils, and the perfect white teeth of the face beneath the hood. Beside the grinning hollow man on the small ledge were the carefully laid-out bodies of two of the sentries who had guided him to his mother's chamber.

"I was beginning to think I would miss you," the blue-skinned creature said as it leaped from its perch and landed before the young prince. There was no time for Trevelyan to react as the soulless man lightly brushed the side of Trevelyan's face and whispered, "Follow me."

Inside the chamber, Lyris was on her feet, screaming, "Trevelyan, it will kill you!"

Slamming the door shut, Trevelyan called upon the power of the Forge and sealed the door from the outside. The hollow man was halfway down the twisting hallway, laughing as he ran to the entrance to the underground.

Trevelyan cursed and followed the creature. By the time he reached the top of the stairs leading downward, the monster had vanished. A single thought went through Trevelyan's head as he descended into the darkness: The war against the hollow had begun.

CHAPTER ELEVEN

Trevelyan followed the soulless man.

The first Mavens of the Forge waited in the maze of catacombs ahead, entranced, hands linked, helpless. The air became heavy as waves of force from the lair of those who had been considered immortal rose from the darkness. The floor of the tunnel carried the telltale cast of the Forge. The black sand radiated a heat he felt through his boots.

Ahead, the tunnel curved to the left. From the flickering orange glow at the mouth of the tunnel, he surmised that a lit torch hung in a brazier beyond the curve, just out of view. When he touched the hard stone of the wall he could feel the vibrations caused by the first Mavens' powerful worship. The waves of force came from the absolute black of the receding tunnel behind him.

He turned and allowed the power of the Mavens to wash over him, a host of invisible fingers caressing his body. The heavy, highly charged winds from the tunnel would act as a beacon, guiding the hollow man directly to their lair. The killer had snuffed out the light behind him.

Then the lean-muscled prince thought of the red eyes with

catlike slits the assassin displayed and considered that the hollow man may not have needed light. He looked to the gleaming fire in the other direction and decided that a torch would make him a perfect target, he would have to go into the tunnels blind. Trevelyan moved forward into the darkness, his hand on the hot, drumming stone to keep him steady with the constant twists and turns of the catacombs.

The tunnels were silent and the slight crush of his boots upon the sand seemed to become louder as he followed the inviting breeze given off by the Mavens' power. The sound of his own breath intensified, becoming sharp, ragged gasps as the winds grew heavier and started to push at him.

After a few minutes of groping through the darkness, the prince froze as his boot struck something heavy and large. Reaching out with his left hand he felt nothing in the air before him, although he half expected a sword wielded by the assassin to swing down and sever his hand. Kneeling, he felt the cold, dead weight of butchered flesh. Sentries had also been posted in the catacombs. Running his hand along the woman's bare arm, tracing his fingers along her collarbone until he found her neck, he verified that she was dead. The bones beneath the flesh of her throat had been crushed. Her armor had faded with her passing.

The temple's defenses stand for decades, then all it takes is one man of the hollow to bring it all down, Trevelyan thought. Perhaps that's the point.

Trevelyan was about to rise when he considered the weapons of the sentries; they were not forged. Searching on his knees, Trevelyan found a pair of *tallos* stars, razor-sharp steel weapons the size of a large hand, with a round hole in the center and five pointed blades radiating outward. Shantow had taught him that most people used the weapons as throwing stars, but they had a more deadly use.

Fitting his thumbs in the center holes of each *tallos*, Trevelyan closed his fingers over the dulled notches between the cutting blades and swiped at the air before him. He silently gave thanks to the dead woman at his feet. At least now he had a chance against the killer.

Continuing on along the dark tunnel, his back brushing against the catacomb wall, Trevelyan held his hands before him as weapons. There was no sound, no hint of movement from the tunnel. The shuddering walls at his back indicated he was getting close to the Mavens. The harsh force of the silent winds from the tunnel buffeted the exposed side of his face and he was afraid to stare full into the harsh gusts.

The wall at his back suddenly gave out. The intensity of the dark winds faded to a mild breeze that seemed to emanate from several different sources. He had reached some type of juncture. Feeling his way with the backs of his hands, Trevelyan discovered five separate tunnels leading off from the main trunk. The vibrations in the walls were identical, the force of the power-charged winds equally distributed. Suddenly the back of his hand found something dark and cold, chiseled like marble, but alive.

"Where do I go from here?" the hollow man said.

Fear closed over the young prince. Before Trevelyan could thrust his hand upward, plunging the razor-sharp points of the *tallos* into the exposed throat of the hollow man, he was lifted from his feet and thrown against the wall. There was a hollow crack as his back struck the wall, and his hand raked across his own thigh, opening a thin wound.

"I asked you a question. Answer it and I might let you live." The soft crush of sand beneath his massive feet and his rich baritone voice revealed the hollow man's position.

Trevelyan had threats to hurl and pronouncements to make. For once he kept his mouth shut. Death was coming and it had assumed the grinning shape of the hollow assassin. He reached out with the weapons, locking his upper arms straight into place, then bent his arms at the elbow, crossed one arm over the other in the attack position Shantow had taught him.

"I'm as blind as you are, but I can smell you. I can smell your fear. And your blood."

Trevelyan could not control his shaking as the hollow man stopped directly before him. Apparently the assassin was unaware of the weapons Trevelyan held.

"You're like an old man with palsy," the towering killer said as he laughed. "I can hear your teeth chattering—"

Trevelyan struck, lashing out with one hand closely following the other in an upward arc. The *tallos* blades bit deeply into the monster's flesh, carving an X in his chest as he roared in pain and surprise. Trevelyan's hands were on either side of the murderer's throat, about to cross and tear open his bluish-black neck with the piercing double blades, when the killer punched him hard in the ribs, cracking one of them with the blow. The prince was bounced against the wall by the force of the blow. The assassin's massive hand caught the side of Trevelyan's head with an openhanded slap that left his ear ringing and upset his equilibrium. The prince stumbled, then fell to the ground, the dark cloak of the world spinning above his head. He heard a faint dripping.

A heavy, bare foot connected with Trevelyan's shoulder. It was a glancing blow, obviously aimed at his head. As he had been trained, Trevelyan spun with the force of the kick, and rolled twice in the black sand. His right arm was numb.

"You made me bleed," the assassin said in disbelief. "I am Nayati of Rien, follower of Kothra. I claim your soul—"

Before the Kothrite could finish, Trevelyan rose to trembling knees and swung the gore-drenched *tallos* blades in an angry swipe. He was amazed when the weapons caught the thick flesh of the creature's upper thigh and severed an artery. Blood spurted into Trevelyan's face and the monster hopped backward, holding one hand over his wound to stem the bleeding. Suddenly an icy wind picked up at his back and blew toward the left tunnel. He heard the soft crush of sand. Nayati was coming for him, favoring one leg.

The footsteps stopped.

"Yes, lord," the Kothrite whispered. "I will follow." The hollow man turned and hobbled off in the other direction.

Trevelyan felt a horrible desperation. Gathering his will, the prince visualized a wire-mesh net weighted at four corners and called upon the Forge. The shriek of a dying soul sounded in his one good ear and he heard the net fall.

The mesh had the consistency of a spider's web. The hollow man brushed it off without slowing.

"Father, forgive me," Trevelyan whispered as he attempted to forge a wall that would trap the hollow man. Again, the scream and the gentle kiss of displaced air.

The Kothrite tore through the light canvas barrier that had been erected. Trevelyan listened in frustration as the footsteps grew softer, then faded altogether. The monster had gone into the tunnel the rogue wind had indicated.

Trevelyan dragged himself to his feet, stumbled a few meters, then fell. He crawled toward the mouth of the tunnel, heard his ears pop, then rose and hugged the wall as he followed the monster toward the lair of the first Mavens.

Practically delirious with pain, Trevelyan moved through the tunnel. With every step he could feel his injured rib scratching against something inside of him and a boiling hot liquid in his mouth that he swallowed, praying to the Unseen that it wasn't his own blood. He was no longer frightened or angry, he was simply determined to stop the Kothrite.

Ahead he saw a pale orange glow steal across the glistening stone wall. Then the harsh winds of force reached around the curving tunnel and plowed into him, striking him like a balled fist. He fell against the wall and held on. A terrible scream of pain pierced the heavy winds; the voice belonged to the Kothrite. Trevelyan heard a triumphant female shout. One of the sentries was confronting the hollow man. The *tallos* still gripped in his bloody hands, Trevelyan pushed against the winds and went for the light. Hold on, he thought. Together we'll take him.

There was a terrible, bone-splintering crack, then silence. His heart fell when he rounded the curve. Bright light splashed the stone walls of the tunnel, revealing an open doorway, one of the ornate double doors torn from its hinges and lying on the black sand. Torrents of blinding white light flooded outward from the room. A guard wearing black armor lay before the doorway, shuddering as she tried to crawl toward the lair of the Mavens. The light made her appear ethereal, but her wounds revealed her mortality.

A ragged, bloody cut had been made in her helm, and her own broken sword lay beside her. The hilt of a dagger protruded from the back of her neck. Both of her legs had been broken, white bones sticking out from her night-black armor. Her face was covered in blood. That she was alive and able to move was miraculous enough, he thought. But when she saw him approach she did not beg for his aid, or ask him to end her suffering. She turned back to the doorway and continued to struggle toward the blinding white light ahead.

Trevelyan stepped past her, resting his palm on the jamb of the white doorway, shielding his eyes from the glare with his free hand. The waves of force no longer felt like a lover's caress; now they were the raking talons of a demon.

Trevelyan stepped into the room, his eyes adjusting to the harsh light. The lair of the Mavens did not appear to exist solely on the material plane. The twelve women of the Forge were at the core of the swirling mass of confusion, a dozen ordinary-looking women in black dresses sitting cross-legged in a circle, hands linked. A column of swirling bluish-white light rose up at the apex of the circle, leading up to a cyclone that grew in diameter until it filled the sky far above: the walls, floors, and ceiling were gone.

All around the Mavens were constantly shifting images that seemed to be ripped from the memories of a multitude of people. Men and women made love, others murdered each other, children were born, people wept in disappointment over love or money—portraits of envy and greed were matched by scenes of unbelievable kindness and charity. The images were contained on large cubes that had been pressed together to form a surface for the Maven to sit upon. Beneath the first layer were a half dozen more, all receding in size, until they vanished. Beneath them lay an endless white abyss. Trevelyan looked down and saw that he was standing on one of the soul traps. When he instinctively stepped from it, another formed beneath him.

"Arayncourt!"

The prince looked up and saw the Kothrite standing behind one of the first Mavens of the Forge. The blue-skinned man wore a wolf's pelt and nothing else. A tangle of black hair flowed from his left hand. He was holding one of the Mavens up by the hair, a knife to her throat. At first he thought that Nayati had already harmed the woman, as her face was splattered with blood, then he saw the wounds he had opened upon the hollow man's flesh.

The Maven's head lolled from side to side, but her eyes were closed. Her hands firmly gripped those of the Mavens on either side of her, as they had for the past forty-two years. They had not aged in that time, the magics they had released tending to their physical requirements.

The red eyes of the Kothrite burned in triumph. He had a shock of white hair that peaked in the center of his forehead. His physique was typical for his kind, his anatomy exaggerated as if by the brush of a painter, grotesque veins pulsing just under his bluish-black flesh.

Tentatively, Trevelyan walked to the circle of Mavens, the soul traps winking in and out of existence to create a bridge for him to cross.

"Look at you," the hollow man said. "You're covered in blood. Hardly a state that befits royalty."

"How do you know me?" Trevelyan called.

The Kothrite's grip on the Maven's hair tightened and he nodded in her direction, his gaze never drifting from the face of the merchant prince. "Touch one of them and all things are known. Now I won't have to send for you."

Trevelyan stopped a meter before one of the Mavens. The Kothrite was a quarter of the way around the circle. There was no chance that he could reach the monster before it murdered the dark-haired woman.

"Remove the blades," the hollow man commanded.

"When you release the Maven," Trevelyan countered.

The blue-skinned Kothrite hesitated, his gaze wandering for a moment; the pain and loss of blood from his wounds was affecting his concentration. "I have heard the voice of the one true god. Not the Unseen. He who came before."

"Blasphemy," Trevelyan whispered.

The black slits in the monster's red eyes narrowed. "Drop the weapons or I will cut her. Not enough to kill her. Not this time."

Trevelyan knew there was no point in arguing. Sliding the *tallos* stars from his hands, the prince allowed them to drop into the perfect white abyss below. The blood-drenched weapons spun and fell from view instantly. "So now you've gotten what you asked for. Let her go."

Nayati laughed. "I haven't begun to get what I want."

"The Mavens cannot grant you a soul."

"I know that," the Kothrite said, his features twisting in contempt. "Those fools who attacked you had not listened when the summons was given. If they had, they would have known better than to surrender their hopes to superstitious rumors. Our god has promised us souls, but only when we have proven ourselves worthy."

The prince watched Nayati's face. The hollow man was young and frightened, despite his bravado. They had that much in common, anyway. He knew with startling certainty that this man was not the enemy the wolves foretold, but he might be his gateway to the keeper of the lotus.

"You said that you are a follower of Kothra of Rien. I'm not familiar with the name."

"You will be soon. I am Nayati, follower of Kothra, he who holds the secret of liquid fire," he said proudly.

"Liquid fire? That's impossible," Trevelyan said.

"Send word to Orrick of Bellerophon. He will confirm what

I have said. I am the chosen ambassador of the newly re-formed nation of Rien. Full rights and trade with our country must be established immediately. You will carry this message to the world. That is all." The Kothrite shook his head once as if to underline his statement.

"If the world refuses to comply, you would kill the Mavens? That would be tantamount to a declaration of war."

The hollow man nodded. "Of course. But for now we wish to negotiate peacefully." Nayati removed the knife from the throat of the Maven. "This display was only a warning. If our demands are not met, the next time will be worse."

The hollow man looked down in surprise as the Maven below him moaned slightly, then began to whisper in a language he had never heard before. His gaze moved upward sharply and he explored Trevelyan's face for some indication that the prince understood what was happening. He had been told that the Mavens never moved or spoke. The young prince was equally disturbed by the sounds coming from the woman.

Trevelyan decided to take advantage of the hollow man's disquiet. "You know that you won't leave this place alive?"

The Kothrite shook his head. "I must return to Kothra with your decision. You will grant me immunity."

"From the Adjudicators, perhaps. But no one can control the will of the Autumn wolves."

Nayati ground the hair of the Maven between his fingers nervously. "You can. Your family is rumored—"

"Rumors only," Trevelyan said sharply. "The wolves will stop you. You have killed in a sacred place."

"Kothra must be told of your decision."

"And so he will be, if I have to take the message to him myself. Come away from this place with me." Trevelyan offered his bloody hand. Nayati did not move. "The wolves can be quick and merciful or they drag your death out over a period of weeks. I've seen it done."

The merchant prince took a step forward and the hollow man drew back, yanking on the hair of the Maven. There was a startled gasp from the woman as her hands slid away from those of the Mavens on either side of her and she screamed, "The horror of what we have done!"

Her eyes were wide with terror as she reached for the hands of her sisters, then stiffened as if a knife had been thrust into the back of her neck, although both the hollow man's hands were in view, his blade hanging at his side. She spasmed, suffering from an attack that originated inside her own body. Then she fell forward, her hair sliding from between the fingers of the hollow man, and was pitched into the column of swirling light, where her body was reduced to ashes in seconds. The column changed color from a soft bluish-white to a bloodred fire mixed with black gore.

From somewhere far off, Trevelyan heard a rumble.

"What happened?" Nayati asked.

"I don't know." Trevelyan watched the vibrant flesh of the remaining Mavens grow pale. He had guessed that the sudden shock of awareness had been too much for the woman.

A grim look of finality replaced the fear the Kothrite had allowed Trevelyan to see. As much as death terrified him, the thought of returning to his holy land with news of this disaster seemed infinitely worse. He raised the blade he still clutched and closed both hands over the hilt.

"This is not what Kothra wished to occur. I have failed him. Now I must return to dust, with no soul to carry on."

"Nayati, wait!" Trevelyan said, but it was too late. The Kothrite plunged the dagger into his own throat, then danced backward, flailing in agony as his blood spurted from the wound. Shaking in his death throes, he glanced at the fire pillar and made a leap into the column, his flesh consumed by the flames in seconds.

From somewhere close a black door appeared. Trevelyan raced toward the passageway, the soul traps springing into existence beneath his feet. He glanced over his shoulder at the Mavens and saw that where the circle had been broken, the women on either side were straining to rejoin their hands. The reddish-black column was becoming wider. The sky was on fire and quickly descending.

Trevelyan leaped through the doorway as he heard a chorus of screams.

CHAPTER
TWELVE

In the borderlands between northern and southern Aranhod, Aldoesse Tessier labored in silence. He was a tall, stout man with thick black hair that flowed to his shoulders. Tessier was a master builder and he was old enough to remember the days before the Forge, when the task of a master builder was very different. Then he would watch his father supervise a crew of fifty men, and the construction of a building such as this one would have taken months rather than days. The Mavens had requested a new temple—their order had grown, the quarters they had been given were not enough.

The rulers of Volney, the closest city, had refused to pay for a new temple. Instead they had suggested a compromise: Dormitories would be built to house their new members. The buildings would be plain, unlike the opulent dwelling that had nearly drained the city's finances twenty years earlier. From the sly grins of the Maven Ulrica, an attractive woman close to Aldoesse's age, Tessier suspected that the end result that had been achieved had in truth been the Maven's goal all along.

One of Tessier's sons had been with him on the construction site; the other was off using the skills he had learned from his father to gain employment in the deep south. Nine men had been employed by the builder, contract laborers who had considerable talent with the Forge.

The first two dormitories were practically complete. The dry walls were needed in the first, the interiors and sealing from the elements were still necessary on the second. Construction on the last building had been neglected due to last-minute haggling between Tessier and the financiers. But now all conflicts had been resolved and the builders had come to the stone quarry that the Mavens had acquired the rights to for their new buildings. The material they needed would be cut in a single swift motion by the casters. Then they would forge winches to transport the stone from the quarry and wagons to cart it back to the site. Maven Ulrica stood off to the sidelines, watching anxiously.

Just before he gave the command for the men to begin, Tessier glanced at the Maven and thought of how similar Ulrica was to his wife, who had died seven years earlier. She gave him a slight smile of encouragement. Elated, he closed his eyes and shouted the command.

A terrible red flash cut across the sky as the Forge was called. The quarry exploded in a hail of stone, a sound of displaced air echoing in its cry across the small valley.

Maven Ulrica watched in horror as eleven men went down at once, blood leaking from their ears.

In Labrys, a country that disdained the order of the Mavens but took full advantage of the Forge, three men sat on the dock of the Eastern Rea, arguing over the outcome of a local tournament. The first man, Elki, grabbed a large fishing hook and brought it down toward the face of another grizzled sailor, whose eyes flashed open in fear as he called upon the Forge to create a shield to absorb the blow. The sky became red and a scream hung in the air as the hook came down, bouncing from the shield that had appeared on the second man's arm. Despite this, the older sailor fell back, his eyes blank and staring, blood dripping from his ear.

A third of the way across the world, on the island of Aiyana, off the shores of Kintaro, two young lovers scrambled from the bed that belonged to the girl's parents. They had just heard a door from the first floor, a voice calling out, footsteps upon the stairs. There was no time to dress before they were discovered. Grinning at each other, they called upon the Forge. Outside their window, the sky flared red.

Olanko Twen, the girl's mother, pushed open the door to her bedroom and screamed when she saw the bodies of her daughter and her male friend sprawled across the floor, the boy dressed in a black tunic with leggings and boots, and the daughter a simple black gown.

In the frozen wastes of Modren, a fisherman testing for signs of thaw was startled when the ice broke and he fell through, into the frigid waters. The fisherman's companion found him instants later, dragging him up through the rip in the ice. He tore his friend's soaked clothing off, then forged dry garments as the sky flashed red.

The shivering man watched in horror as his companion collapsed. His friend was dead and he would soon join him if he did not move quickly. He scrambled into the clothing that had been created for him then clung to the body of his friend until help arrived.

In Cynara, outside the Citadel of the Mavens, the blue-eyed guard who had been losing consistently in the game of chance Chatham had proposed, considered using the Forge to create a staff the equal of the grey-bearded warrior's skrymir so that she could challenge him in a match she knew she would win. She hesitated a moment, saving her own life.

The sky flashed red and from deep within the Citadel of the Mavens came an explosion. Chatham and the two sentries spun in time to see the largest building created by the power of the Forge, one that was systematically rebuilt, each stone replaced daily by the first Mavens, begin to disintegrate. Hairline fractures appeared along the surface, spreading across the heavy black forms of the temple as if borne on the legs of a hundred spiders racing in different directions, tearing deep gashes into the support structures. The damage became more severe and the central dome shuddered, causing the gold-trimmed spires to rock back and forth dangerously.

The elegant facades that had been fashioned from gold, silver, and steel buckled under the intense pressures buffeting the citadel from within. A huge gold beam fell from the second story of the temple, crashing to the ground five meters from where Chatham and the sentries stood, its base digging a meter-deep hole in the stone walk before it tipped over and crashed to the ground. The brown-eyed guard broke from her paralysis and reached for the door. The figures that had been sculpted into the surface of the door writhed in agony as the door lost its consistency and became a boiling hot slab of featureless metal, fusing the entrance shut. The sentry cried out in frustration.

Chatham recalled his vision of the lights of Cynara fading and thought, Not now, the boy is still inside!

People flooded from their homes and businesses to witness the destruction of the citadel. Far above, an observation tower teetered, then broke away from the dome with a snap, falling toward the wall of the citadel where it shattered into a dozen shards, the smallest nearly seven meters in length. The remains of the tower showered down upon the street and Chatham watched helplessly, screaming for people to scatter as one of the largest chunks struck the crowd.

The stone towers had been forged, and matter created by the Forge could not harm living creatures. But the heavy steel reinforcements that clung to the stone surfaces operated under no such restrictions, and they sliced at the crowd with deadly force, as if guided by a malevolent hand.

The razor-sharp pinnacle of the tower fell point first, striking the ground harmlessly in an area devoid of onlookers. Then the final section of the tower fell, and from its trajectory, Chatham guessed that it would strike the blue-eyed guard at any moment. Flinging himself at the woman, he knocked her out of the way and tripped on a piece of rubble before he could get clear of the massive chunk of debris. Chatham turned in time to see the heavy black stone and razor-sharp steel consume his vision with its descent.

The blue-eyed sentry rose on one arm, about to curse the old man, when she saw the man's jaws open in a scream and felt a shower of blood splash her face-plate as the steel-reinforced section of the tower fell upon the scarred outcast, dissolving into a cloudlike multitude of smaller stones, as it crushed him utterly.

The sentry stared at the pile of debris in shock. Her name was Ruzena Danya, and she had been raised to look upon those who bore the scars of the wolves with loathing. Chatham bore the mark of three claws, the sign of one who had allowed another to die through their own inaction. But he had sacrificed his life for hers. As they had played his foolish guessing game outside the citadel, he had been cheerful and confident, despite the derisive remarks of her sister in arms, the brown-eyed sentry Kiele. From the first moment she saw him he had carried himself with a bearing more befitting royalty than his nasty, swaggering charge had been able to muster. There was a mystery here, a secret she vowed to uncover. The man who had saved her life may have been a criminal, but he was certainly not a common one.

Kiele knelt beside Ruzena and gripped the woman's arm. Before them the citadel was being torn asunder. The walls bulged outward, the gold supports straining to retain the building's original shape. Towers fell throughout the city block the citadel consumed, raining down stone and steel debris upon all neighboring buildings. People in the streets screamed, some in death, others in loss. Suddenly the central dome of the citadel exploded, a reddish-black column of fire twisting upward, stealing toward the sky, sending blocks of rubble as far as four city blocks away. Windows shattered, adjoining buildings were crushed. Suddenly the reddish-black fires were absorbed by the clouds and the column of flame vanished, the citadel collapsing inward upon itself with a deafening roar in the twisting fire's wake.

Ruzena stared at the destruction in shock. The streets were silent for a time as the survivors looked at one another in amazement that they had lived through the raging storm of stone and steel that had destroyed so many others. Then the screams began, the cries of pain from those who had been injured, the wails of grief from those whose loved ones had been reduced to ravaged, bloody shells devoid of souls.

The blue-eyed sentry thought of her sisters in calling, the Mavens who had worshiped peacefully within the walls of the citadel, and wondered if any of them were still alive. It seemed impossible that anyone could have survived the horrible assault that had leveled the greatest building on all of Autumn, but so much of what she had witnessed could be described in no other terms, and so she decided to learn for herself if the first Mavens of the Forge, hidden beneath the ruins of the citadel, or any of their followers, still lived.

The walls before the sentry had been reduced to piles of stone no more than a few meters high with twisted and shattered columns rising from the smoking wreck. Ruzena reached up to her faceplate, releasing the hooks that kept the heavy metal grille attached to her armors, and dropped the mask to the ground. Kiele was standing beside her, worry marring her deep brown eyes. "What are you doing?"

Peeling the mesh skull cap from her head, Ruzena allowed her flowing honey-blond hair to fall to her shoulders. It was knotty and tangled, but its appearance upon the night-black armors was startling.

"We've got to try to help," Ruzena said softly.

"There's no one alive in there. Our duty is to those on the street who are crying for assistance."

"The healers will arrive. The wolves will smell the blood soon enough."

Kiele stared at her fellow sentry in disbelief, then turned and walked in the direction of the wounded. The tall, wiry blond-haired sentry took a few steps toward the ruins of the citadel, then heard the shifting of rocks, the fall of pebbles from somewhere close. She turned to the spot where Chatham had been buried and gasped as she saw movement. Racing to the pile of stones she dug into the mass of rocks and steel with both hands, quickly unearthing the top layer of blood-splattered debris.

With a moan she dragged away the heavy steel beam that had fallen upon the warrior and gasped when she saw the shattered gore of the old man's chest. But it wasn't the damage he had sustained that startled her: it was the impossible, steady movement of his chest. As she watched, the flow of blood was stemmed. His ribs reached outward, snapping into place, his organs expanded, remaking themselves, and his flesh slowly crawled across the wound, knitting a pale covering over his chest.

Ruzena tore into the pile of stones that covered the grey-bearded warrior's head. His features had been reduced to a red, pulpy mass with bits of shuddering white bone staring through. The miracle she had witnessed moments ago was repeating itself now: his crushed cheekbones were moving into place, his eyes rising into their sockets, his pure white teeth growing into the shattered remains of his jaws as stringy muscles grew and stretched across his quivering head. Flesh was soon to follow, and she was surprised to see how young and handsome the warrior had been in his prime, with thick black hair and arched eyebrows, full lips that curled at the edges in a wicked smile, and strong, regal features. Then streaks of grey flowed through his hair and lines were etched over his face. A heavy growth of thick grey hair appeared upon his grizzled face and soon he was once again the image of the old warrior with one notable exception: the scar upon his face had not reappeared.

His eyes were focused and he stared at her in confusion. If it hadn't been for her deep blue eyes, he wouldn't have recognized the honey-blond-haired woman at all. Her features were pleasing, though not extraordinary. Her smile, however, was dazzling as she said, "Your sins are forgiven."

A brief light of hope shined in his eyes, then the three marks ripped across the side of his face. In a solemn tone he said, "The decision is not yours to make."

"I don't understand what I've just seen," she said.

He smiled at the wonder he saw in her expression. "You're

not meant to,'' he said slowly. ''It will be easier for you if you try to forget.''

''No,'' she said sternly. ''The one thing I will not do in this life is take the route that is easiest. I owe you, and I'm going to stand with you.''

Chatham tried to move, although the attempt brought him numbing pain. ''Then help me get up,'' he said, ''Trevelyan's in there. He survived. I can smell it. And there are others. Many others. I can help you find them.''

''Then we must hurry,'' she said, deciding to ignore the temple's restriction on outcasts entering the holy ground. There might be repercussions against her later, but in this time of emergency, she would take her chances. She cleared the rest of the stones away and helped him to his feet.

Trevelyan slowly returned to consciousness. He recalled the doorway opening before him and his escape from the lair of the first Mavens. As he had passed through the doorway, something had struck the back of his head and his mind had fallen into a black void before his body struck the ground.

Lying on the soft black sand, Trevelyan dreamed, or thought he had dreamed. Voices came to him. Women arguing.

It must not continue.

Don't be an idiot. We have no choice.

We can follow Alcara's example and go into the flames, where this nightmare will finally be at an end and our souls may leap from the cliffs of Nyssa and take flight.

After what we have done, we would fall to the Waiting Pool of Souls. The waters are poisoned, tainted. Only the Unseen can grant us release and pardon us for our crimes.

A new voice joined the argument, frantically pleading, *There is no more time, we must form the barrier.*

Our worshipers—

Have always claimed they would give their lives for us. Now is their chance to prove it.

The voices ceased abruptly. Sometime later Trevelyan struggled upward from the darkness, and awoke.

A soft blue glow lit the area before him, revealing large pieces of fallen, natural stone beside him on the soft black sand of the catacombs and the body of the sentry who the Kothrite had murdered. The doorway of the Mavens' vast chamber had been melted to slag, but a jagged, man-sized opening remained. The blue glow came from the sanctuary of the first Mavens.

The merchant prince smelled the thick, dank air. The catacombs were collapsed and buried under rock on his left and a light breeze came from the tunnel off to his right. Air was getting in; that meant there was a passageway to the outside. He wasn't trapped, he wasn't going to suffocate.

There had to be a reason why his life had been saved. As he struggled to his feet, his ribs scratched against one another, causing a blinding explosion of pain that sent him to the ground once more. Once again he heard the voices of the women play from his memory:

The chosen is outside our door. He is in danger.

Protect him. In return he will carry our words back to the world of man

The pain subsided, the voices of the first Mavens fading with the wrenching agony. Trevelyan crawled forward, to the soft blue glow, dragging himself through what had been the doorway to the first Mavens' lair. The floor was black and polished, like marble, and slick walls were visible for a few meters on either side of the merchant prince.

Directly ahead lay the curved surface of a glowing blue dome. Only a small section was visible. Trevelyan knew that the Mavens had sealed themselves within the enclosure. Behind him, the prince heard voices. Chatham and two others calling his name. The wolflike senses of the old warrior would have tracked the prince through his scent.

"Trevelyan, it's your mother, are you all right?"

They were far enough away that Trevelyan knew he would have enough time to fulfill his debt. He raised his hand to the surface of the dome and pressed his flesh against the polished, unbreakable glass wall.

The Forge will continue. The Mavens will continue. The people have nothing to fear.

Trevelyan lowered his hand, the pain in his ribs growing unbearable as he thought, for that very reason, the people should know fear beyond any they had ever imagined.

The merchant prince heard footsteps crunch in black sand outside the passageway and the ring of an anguished cry as he collapsed beneath the onslaught of pain.

PART
FIVE

The War
Against
the Hollow

CHAPTER THIRTEEN

Ariodne looked out at the sun setting on the horizon, a bloated red orb sliced neatly in two as it sat upon the calm waters in the distance, its lower half shredded and trembling upon the waves. Her lover stood beside her on the deck of the *Adventure*, a trading vessel that had been heavily armed and prepared for the long journey to Rien. In the morning they would dock at the Trader's Reach, where their new supplies were being readied.

Over a hundred men and women served aboard the *Adventure*, and Trevelyan had handpicked many of them. The ship's captain had relinquished his quarters for Trevelyan and Ariodne, the first mate was sleeping above deck to make room for Chatham. Although the grey-bearded warrior would have gladly traded places with the tall, brown-haired young man with a hooked nose, sloping forehead, and small, piercing eyes, his duty was to serve as bodyguard to the prince.

Only a skeleton crew was above deck as Trevelyan and Ariodne wrapped their arms around each other and stared out at the dying sun. Ariodne kissed, then ran her tongue over the pulsing vein in the prince's throat, allowing her teeth to lightly scrape his flesh. He rested his face in her hair, his gaze locked on the sinking orb of light.

Ariodne sighed and tried not to squeeze at his bandaged ribs as she said, "This was your fantasy, wasn't it? You're allowed to relax and enjoy it. There is time."

"I love you," he said softly and knew that she was right. On this journey there was nothing but time, time to rest and to heal, time to contemplate the uncertain future that lay ahead of him at their shadowy destination, and most of all, time to *remember*.

After Chatham, Ruzena, and Lyris had carried the young prince from the ruins of the citadel, he returned to consciousness lying in the street, surrounded by a small crowd of onlookers and the healer from the fourth house. Delirious from pain he repeated the final message that the first Mavens had left for the people. Word spread quickly, those within earshot carrying the proclamation to all who would listen. The Mavens had chosen their words carefully and had known that the people would cling to anything that would allow them comfort in this tragic moment. The prince had not told them about the earlier, more callous conversation he had overheard between the women of the Forge.

Soon Ariodne was beside him with a wet cloth, dabbing the caked blood from his face. She explained that Chatham and the sentry had gone back into the debris to help in the rescue efforts. All the wolves from the city had congregated in this place, their animal senses an invaluable aid in locating the survivors of the citadel's collapse. Lyris was helping those who had been wounded in the street, her twenty-year-old skills as a battlefield healer coming into play.

The healer from the fourth house had moved on to another victim of the disaster. The tall, brown-skinned man was kneeling three meters away, over the quaking form of an obese man whose top shirt had been cut away to reveal his bloody chest. A wiry, silver-haired woman in her twenties knelt beside the man, tears streaming down her face.

"The bleeding won't last," the healer said as he placed his hand on the woman's shoulder, reassuringly, then set to work bandaging the man's wound.

Trevelyan's memories flashed upon the dream-laden eyes of the Maven he had encountered on his way to his mother's chamber, the one who had spoken the same words less than an hour before the tragedy. Sensing his disquiet, Ariodne assured the young prince that his personal physician, Wardell Regan, had been called and would arrive shortly.

Two of the Autumn wolves appeared, motioning with their snouts for Ariodne to move off. Her services were needed elsewhere, she knew, but she was reluctant to leave his side.

"They will stay," the young dark-haired prince said.

Ariodne curled her hand in a fist and stared into the dark, intelligent eyes of the wolf that remained closest to her lover, a grey wolf with two black front paws. The second wolf was black with striking golden eyes. The usual rivalry between packs had been forgotten in the crisis. The fiery-haired Maven kissed Trevelyan full on the lips and promised to return. His consciousness faded as he looked into the golden eyes of the second wolf and observed a sadness he could not explain. The look filled him with anxiety.

When he opened his eyes again he was in his bed at Arayncourt Hall. Lyris was sitting on the edge of the bed, speaking with two men, one with a thick neck and red hair, the other younger and thin, with dark hair. Chatham stood in the back of the room, obviously not welcome in the conversation. Sabin Lot, Trevelyan's appointment master, rushed to the side of the merchant prince.

"Sign this," Lot said, proffering an ink-dipped quill. The young prince scribbled his signature.

Lyris turned to him and gently placed her hand on his leg. "Loans to businesses that were crippled, relief to families whose providers were slain in the destruction of the temple," she explained warmly.

"How many?" Trevelyan croaked.

His mother leaned over and kissed him on the cheek. "Don't trouble yourself. We have matters under control."

"The Forge?"

Lyris turned, her pure green eyes suddenly veiled by her silky black hair. "Time enough to answer all your questions later. Try not to worry yourself."

Trevelyan became anxious. "Mother, don't you remember what I told you?"

Wardell Regan squinted at the young prince as he crossed his heavy arms and said, "Your mother's right, you need rest. Everyone must leave now."

Lyris and Sabin Lot left the room together, the physician stopping before Chatham. "I said everyone."

Chatham tried not to laugh in the man's face when he said, "Do your skills as a healer extend to working miracles upon yourself after you've had your arms ripped off and stuffed down your throat?"

Regan turned pale and left the room.

"I thought not," Chatham said and locked the door behind the red-haired man. He walked to the bed and looked down at the prince. "Trevelyan, the situation is serious. Your mother has been to the Pavilion, and she has said that the hollow men are responsible for the citadel's destruction. Tell me all you remember. A panic has begun in the streets. A meeting has been called at the Pavilion for three days from now. Adeben Nowles of southern Aranhod will be present."

Trevelyan was filled with unease at the mention of the name, and he forced dark memories from his childhood to remain buried. "Then I must be there. Nothing would please that man more than to help start another war."

"And so you will," Chatham assured him. "But that is not what you will tell *them*." He nodded to the door.

"Chatham, I'm sure that my mother had planned to tell me of this when she felt I was strong enough to hear it."

"Perhaps you're right. But for the sake of argument, keep quiet about what I have told you and see what transpires over the next few days."

The following days proved Chatham's words correct. Lyris had kept a tight watch on the visitors Trevelyan was allowed, and had refused to admit Ariodne to the hall on several occasions, telling Trevelyan that she had expressed no interest in his condition. On the second day, Trevelyan had looked out his window and saw his lover stalking away from the palace angrily. Chatham was beside him as he went to his desk and drafted a letter for the grey-bearded man to smuggle from the hall that had become his prison.

"We need someone whom we can trust who will deliver this letter without question," Trevelyan said. "Do you have someone up to the task?"

With a boyish smile Chatham said, "I do indeed."

For the next two days, Lyris said nothing of the meeting at the Pavilion or the disquiet in the streets. Outwardly, Trevelyan contented himself with composing a fresh ballad and devising the entertainment for the upcoming Masque of the Dead. He did not leave his room, nor did he ask about Ariodne. Lyris seemed quite pleased. When he was alone, he put such foolishness aside and composed the speech he would use to address the Cynaran council and its visitors.

On the day of the meeting, Trevelyan waited until twenty minutes after he saw his mother and her newly formed entourage leave for the Pavilion before he turned to Chatham and nodded. Together they walked the corridors of Arayncourt Hall.

Many tried to talk the young prince into returning to his bed, but no one had the audacity to stand in his way.

There was a hush in the vast receiving chamber of the Pavilion of Justice as Trevelyan and Chatham made their appearance, interrupting the first few lines of his mother's carefully scripted speech. As Chatham had predicted, Lyris was claiming that the statement she read had come from Trevelyan. The young prince could guess the content. Nothing would reunite the troubled factions of the Cynaran government and the discontented rulers of the five houses better than a war, no matter the cost in lives.

"Trevelyan," she said nervously.

"Thank you, Mother. I will continue from here," he said as he approached the stone platform where she stood.

Lyris stared at him in disbelief that gave way to a cold, angry glare. "Of course," she said, and backed away.

By Trevelyan's estimate, more than a thousand people were gathered, including Shantow, dressed regally for his formal duty as ambassador from Kintaro. Four heavily built Kintarans stood behind Shantow. The expressions on all four of the men were identical displays of stoicism. An empty seat was beside Shantow, Chianjur was nowhere to be found.

Trevelyan did not see Ariodne in the crowd, but he could sense that she was close. For the moment he was content to see Chatham take his position beside Lyris, smiling pleasantly at the dark-haired woman, who regarded him with distaste. Sabin Lot stood next to her.

"The hollow have banded together under the leadership of one they call Kothra. Through my investigations I have learned that Kothra was a mercenary who in his later period performed tasks primarily for Orrick of Bellerophon. One of these tasks involved journeying to the fire islands of Chiabos, where it is rumored he brought back the secret of liquid fire. He is using this knowledge to bargain with us for the right to once again proclaim Rien a city recognized by this council and by the world, awarded full treaties and trade agreements. That is the threat we face."

Trevelyan waited, allowing the voices that had suddenly been raised in alarm to die away. "I have come here to tell you that declaring war against the hollow should be our last alternative. I believe that we should send a small reconnaissance party to Rien, which I will lead."

"Ridiculous!" Shantow said, rising to his feet. "My father

will back us with a full invasion force from Kintaro. We must take Rien, level the city. I will personally take the head of this Kothra back to my homeland, where it will be tied in a sack and used in our tournaments."

Cheers rang out from the crowd. Every person in the room had been to the remains of the citadel or had lost a friend or loved one in the destruction or the Hour of the Red Sky, when all who were in communion with the Forge died.

"Enough!" Trevelyan shouted, the word shattering the discord that had engulfed the room. "I was in the lair of the first Mavens. I will tell you all that occurred."

Trevelyan recounted his battle with the Kothrite, as the Maven Alcara fell into the twisting column of flame and was consumed, the soulless man taking his own life, racing into the fire after her.

Adeben Nowles of southern Aranhod stood up. He had been the regent to Coman Degula, the five-year-old heir to the leadership of Ronalda, the seat of the southern Aranhod throne. Then the boy drowned in an accident and Nowles was voted into office, where he had remained for thirty years.

Nowles was a short man, in his late sixties, with a startling girth and a red, sunburned face. "Trevelyan, even if we were to accept that the destruction of the citadel was an accident, what of those who were slain by the devil as he entered the citadel?"

Nowles gestured to his wife, a beautiful blond woman half his age who appeared thoroughly cowed by her husband. She handed him a three-page document from a stack of papers she held on her lap and he read off an account of the atrocities Nyati had committed to gain access to the Mavens of the Forge. "Nineteen women in all," he concluded, "including nine superbly trained guardswomen outfitted with every weapon conceivable and the Forge. The behavior of this one hollow man was an obscenity that must not go unpunished by those who sent him."

Shantow led the cries of approval for this plan. Again, Trevelyan was forced to quiet the crowd. "Yes, that was the work of one hollow man. Only one. And you propose that we wage war against a unified army of those monsters when there are other avenues open to us?"

Nowles gave the young prince the same look he had possessed a decade earlier, when he had asked the boy to accompany him to the deserted theater in the rear of the hall to hear a soliloquy he had written. Trevelyan had run from the man in blind, unreasoning fear. The same unease filled him as Nowles said, "Your fears are not shared by the majority. Those who have died must be avenged!"

Trevelyan knew that his cause was losing whatever advantage his presence may have gained it. Suddenly the doors to the receiving hall opened and the former sentry Ruzena entered and stood to the side as an old, white-haired woman dressed in a flowing red gown entered the room.

"Children," she said with reproach. "Children who weren't even *alive* when the last true war was fought, and so they cannot even comprehend the nature of the blood-soaked tapestry they wish to create." The old woman turned her gaze to Nowles. "Or those who did not have the stomach to fight, and sent others to die in their place." Nowles looked away in humiliation. The old woman took a moment to savor this victory as she scanned the faces of the crowd and settled on the narrow-eyed gaze of Lyris Arundel. The beautiful, dark-haired woman mouthed a single word, a name, and the old woman nodded. Resignation clouded Lyris's features.

The old woman was in her seventies and small-boned, but she was not frail. Her hair was pulled back and piled high beneath an elegant black headdress. Pure green eyes peered out from behind a red lace veil that did little to hide her identity. Her cheekbones were high, her nose small and thin, her lips glistening with a tasteful shade of red. A necklace that hung at the base of her throat bore the symbol of their city-state, a lone wolf upon a summit.

"For those of you who require an introduction, my name is Mayra Coinneach-Arayncourt. Years ago I ran this city with an iron fist, while my husband fought and died in the Trade Wars. The banks of the Arayncourt empire hold the note on nearly every person in this room." She smiled grimly. "But I hold the note on the Arayncourt fortune. My grandson was almost killed fighting this creature. If he finds it in his heart to try to reason with these inhuman beings, once again risking his life to do so, then he shall leave Cynara with my full and unconditional support."

"No one returns from Rien," Cathar Radomil, a well-built man in his thirties, said as he rose. Radomil had soft blue eyes, a thick jaw, tight, curly blond hair, and a perpetually annoyed expression. "My family has overseen the shipping lanes for many years. I can think of no one who has made the journey to Rien and returned to tell of it. If we go there it must be in a show of force."

"There is another issue," Sabin Lot said as he stepped forward. "If Trevelyan is off attempting to make peace with these killers, who will run the empire in his stead?"

In her seat, Lyris smiled and began to rise. Chatham dropped to a crouch beside her, grasping her arm with enough strength to make her hiss in pain and surprise as he shoved her back down and whispered in her ear, "Lyris, my dear, do you remember that paper you had Trevelyan sign, the one you told him would authorize relief to those stricken during the fall of the citadel? The paper that *actually* signed over all control of the Arayncourt family business to you?"

"I don't—"

"Don't bother denying it," Chatham said pleasantly. "I believe, however, that you should make damn sure that your document has not been fed into the flames before you embarrass yourself in front of those you wish to impress."

Lyris studied the red flecks floating in the dark eyes of the outcast. "There will be a reckoning," she promised.

"I've survived many," he said and released her arm.

From the rear of the audience chamber, Mayra walked through the central path to the stone podium where Trevelyan waited. "I will undertake the task of running the city's banking empire, if my grandson so desires."

"I do, Grandmother," Trevelyan said, glancing at his mother with a genuine expression of sadness. She would not meet his gaze.

"I believe the time has come to put this matter to a vote," Mayra pronounced.

The margin was close, but with Mayra's support, Trevelyan's proposal was pushed through, with the understanding that several hundred soldiers and mercenaries would head out a few days later, taking the land route. Thousands would follow, backed by troops from Kintaro. The decision to go to war would rest solely with Trevelyan. Searching the crowd, the young prince finally saw the shock of brilliant red hair that could belong to only one person.

"I would like the Maven Ariodne Gairloch to stand," Trevelyan said. From the left flank of the audience, Ariodne rose. Her expression was cold and distant. "There is an announcement I would like to make." She shook her head in a single, violent motion. Trevelyan was stunned. He wasn't sure what to say and so he rattled, "On behalf of my family, I would like to formally issue my sympathy for the loss of your sisters at the temple, and extend any means of assistance you might require."

"Thank you, Lord Arayncourt," she said, then turned and left the receiving hall as the meeting collapsed into a loud, spirited reunion for the many visitors.

In the days that followed, Trevelyan was kept busy by Chatham and Mayra as they poured over the family's accounts, refamiliarizing themselves with the current state of the local and regional banks they owned, and their interests on foreign soil. Ariodne was not in her rooms at the Ivory Dagger. Even her mastiff, Lykos, had vanished. Trevelyan spent his every available moment trying to find her, but his efforts met with failure.

Shantow had sent Chianjur back to Kintaro with her nurse and a messenger who would petition his father to send troops to Rien. Trevelyan's friend had reasoned, "If they are not needed, we will maybe turn them back, don't you think?"

Trevelyan learned days later that Ariodne had met Chianjur's vessel before it left, and said her farewells. Lykos was with her. He was relieved to learn that she was all right, and angered that she had been avoiding him. Finally a message came. "I need more time," the note said simply.

"You need more time for what!?" Trevelyan had shouted as he considered tearing the note to shreds and found that he could not bring himself to do it.

Lyris had barely spoken to Trevelyan or Mayra. Sabin Lot had resigned as Trevelyan's appointment minister and had been promptly rehired by Lyris to be her personal assistant.

Mayra had brought her own entourage, including a private staff and a half-dozen bodyguards. She had spent the last ten years in the township of Tenfellow, content to remain in retirement until she was once again called to serve.

After word had spread of Trevelyan's upcoming mission to Rien, Rolland Storr and his entire Black Wolf company had made an appearance at Arayncourt Hall. Rolland was the tallest man Trevelyan had ever met, outside of those born of the hollow, and the musculature of his incredible physique was apparent even through his formidable armor and mail. His eyes were dark, like smoked glass, his hair full and black, with the soft luster of a panther's flank. He wore a full mustache on his upper lip, his jaw was covered in the same stubble Trevelyan had remembered from their last meeting, a year earlier, at his father's cremation. He was not a handsome man, but he was straightforward, direct, and loyal.

Storr admitted that he had employed three hollow men, then explained his reasoning. "How better to study one who may one day be an enemy, then to open your arms and take him close as a friend?"

The condottiere volunteered himself and a ten-man contingent from the Black Wolves for the journey.

Ruzena had assumed the position left vacant by Sabin Lot. An odd friendship had developed between Ruzena and Chatham. They were clearly not romantically entwined, at times they barely seemed to notice each other in a room, but a delicate cord of respect and closeness had been spun between them, and Chatham's spirits had become even more buoyant than usual.

The investigation into the accusations made by the merchant of Riordan Street had led to the seizure of the trading vessel Trevelyan rechristened the *Adventure*.

The night before the journey was to begin, Mayra had asked Trevelyan to explain his melancholy. "After all, you're on the verge of a grand adventure. Abelard would be quite proud of you, Trevelyan. What's troubling you?"

It was Ariodne, he explained, and told his grandmother of their relationship and his fear that he would have to leave the next day without saying good-bye. Mayra listened patiently as Trevelyan spoke for hours about his lover.

That night, Ariodne was waiting in his bed. He was startled to discover her in the room, and filled with countless questions. Motioning for silence, she shrugged off the pale robe she had worn to protect herself from the bite of cold in the room. They made love without uttering a word, and when he tried to speak afterward she silently persuaded him that the conversation could wait.

In the morning, when he woke, he was alone.

On the docks, where the *Adventure* was ready to set sail, Trevelyan was startled by the sudden appearance of the first wolves. Black Mask, Walks With Fire, and the other four wolves appeared nonchalant as they moved past him and boarded the vessel. Another heavily furred animal brushed against his leg, and Trevelyan was surprised to see the wide jaws of Lykos, Ariodne's mastiff. Then he saw the owner's slender legs beneath her short, petaled skirt and looked up to find Ariodne fixing him with a direct and unflinching stare. "I'm coming along," she said. "If for no other reason, you'll need help with those curs."

Black Mask turned suddenly at the slight, sneezed in the cold morning breeze, then turned away, his turquoise eyes shrouded with disinterest.

"If you had stayed in one place long enough I would have *invited* you," Trevelyan said.

Ariodne surrendered custody of Lykos to a short, curly-haired woman who wore a simple black dress and avoided Trevelyan's eyes as she led the dog away.

Shantow and two of his guards were the last on board.

Hours later, when they were deeply immersed in the trading channels, Ariodne explained that she had been angered by her refusal at the hall and felt betrayed when she learned of his reaction to his mother's tale that the Maven had turned away from him.

"You must never believe that I an unwilling to see you unless you hear it from me. Promise me that you will never again have so little faith in me and in my love for you." That evening, as they watched the sunset, he promised.

On the mainland of northern Aranhod, in the receiving chamber of Arayncourt Hall, Mayra Coinneach-Arayncourt studied the darkness that filled every corner of the room but one. The flickering torchlight had been positioned carefully to make the old woman appear even more formidable than usual. The knock she had been waiting for finally arrived.

"Enter, Lyris, and leave your dog outside in the hall."

The door opened and Lyris closed the door on Sabin as she stepped into the room. His eyes closed partially, he seemed lost without her. "You wished to see me?" she said.

"Lyris, there is an understanding we must come to. Although we disagree and always have on most issues, there is one area of interest upon which I believe our views will coincide. This *woman* that Trevelyan is taken with," Mayra said the word sourly, "she is of questionable morals and a union with her will not benefit our already shaky position with the other four houses."

The younger, dark-haired woman eased into a stone chair before her mother-in-law. "What do you propose?"

"That, my dear Lyris, is where you and your considerable talents come into play. Now come close. What I have to say is for no other ears but your own...."

CHAPTER FOURTEEN

The Trader's Reach was the largest single port in Aranhod, with over ten kilometers of access for ships. As late morning approached, the *Adventure* passed through a very narrow opening surrounded by towering cliffs, upon which were several tiers of guard stations and all forms of man-made defenses to augment the natural protection offered by the shape of the land, including catapults filled with stones, broken glass, and razor-sharp spikes, platoons of archers and swordsmen waiting to ward off an invasion, machines that could fire hundreds of staves at once with deadly accuracy, and forgers who would create jagged obstructions in the path of rogue ships, gutting them instantly.

Trevelyan signaled the ground station with bright, shining mirrors from a distance, then with his already aching throat when they were in hearing range. Once they were through the small opening between the rocks, the Reach opened up immediately, revealing the vast pear-shaped design of the port. Hundreds of vessels swarmed in the waters, some arriving, others departing, many stationary and receiving or unloading goods. Navigators using the Forge sailed through the still blue waters in light-refracting crystal ships, casting small black obelisks in the water that sparkled due to their many-faceted designs and laid out a path for the *Adventure* to follow.

Trevelyan was exuberant as the ship docked and the crew prepared the vessel for the massive cranes that waited to swing across the slight gap between the ship and the dock, depositing their supplies with huge spidery black arms that were forged on demand, skeletal hands lowered over crates, then pulled tight by cables to grip the packages and raise them into the air. All who were not necessary to the loading process were given leave to depart the ship for three hours. They would be ready to leave again at that time.

At one of the dozens of markets situated on the boardwalk that snaked around the full length of the Reach, warehouses several stories high looming in the maze of streets from the enclosed city behind the shipping lane, Ariodne and Chatham browsed through an open-air shop that specialized in brilliant handmade scarfs and sheer, layered clothing from Labrys.

After successfully haggling a reasonable price for an armful of items from the tired merchant who spoke with a thick Labrysian accent only when customers were nearby, Ariodne turned to the grey-bearded man and asked, "Where's Ruzena?"

"She's off somewhere, enjoying herself, I'm sure. She has never been out of Cynara before," he explained.

"And Trevelyan? I thought you had officially been granted employment as his bodyguard?"

"Then I suppose I'm being frightfully lax in my duties," Chatham said with a winning smile that was wasted on the Maven. "Or perhaps I am *here* to look after his interests."

After paying for the scarfs, top shirts, gowns, and skirts, the red-haired Maven deposited the spoils of her shopping into Chatham's thick, barrellike arms, then merged with the flowing crowd. Chatham followed the woman by her scent and caught up with her in a glass blower's tent.

The glass caster was a red-haired young man, seventeen at the outermost, Ariodne guessed, who wore a ruffled amber smock and bloodred leggings. The crowd surrounding the boy was entranced by his artistry and enchanted by his self-effacing but charming smile as he displayed his showmanship. He concentrated grimly with a furrowed brow, then stole glances at the enraptured children and available women, giving them winks or knowing grins. Ariodne was instantly won over by his level of achievement and self-confident manner. Busts of actors and military leaders, the likenesses captured perfectly, were strewn among glass sculptures of graceful jungle animals, birds in flight, wise yet playful cats, and a series of Autumn wolves that were proud and majestic.

The caster was creating a wolf when he noticed Ariodne and almost faltered in his concentration. His gaze seemed to burn into her and she gasped inadvertently.

You may have what you desire, a thick, guttural voice said in her mind. *He has never seen one such as you. His heart is already yours. Surrender yourself—*

"No!" Ariodne shouted, spinning to look at the grey-bearded old man in complete horror. Chatham was in her mind, trying to influence her judgment and behavior. Employing the skills she had been given by her teachers at the citadel when she was just a girl, Ariodne located the gossamer bond that linked their conscious minds and severed it brutally. She felt violated by his actions.

His expression was complex, difficult to read, as if he were attempting to play a part while needing desperately to allow his true feelings to reign. A kaleidoscope of emotions reached out from the old man: anger, jealousy, and fear mixed with a terrible sadness and a desire to protect. But who was he trying to protect, she wondered. And from what?

The Maven's outburst had drawn the attention of the crowd. Embarrassed and filled with rage she turned and left the small tent, ignoring the plea of the red-haired caster who begged for her to stay, tears suddenly welling in his eyes. Chatham's power had been worked upon the boy, too.

The grey-bearded man watched Ariodne disappear into the crowd. This time he made no move to follow her. An overwhelming sadness filled him as he thought of the destiny he had just attempted to override. To find the rose, Trevelyan would have to take the heart of his deepest love. The boy was emotionally fragile. If he were to lose Ariodne to another, his feelings would turn to hatred, then vanish altogether in time. Another way would have to be found for Trevelyan to secure the rose, and perhaps one day, when this was over, the lovers could be reunited.

Nevertheless, what he had done was wrong for many reasons, not the least of which that he had just exposed one of his many secrets to one who would gladly reveal him to the young prince. Suddenly he smelled Ariodne's familiar scent. He turned to face her as she snatched the clothing she had purchased from his arms.

"If you ever touch me in that way again, I will kill you," she said flatly.

As she walked away from him a second time, Chatham whispered, "If only that were possible." She hesitated for a moment and he wondered if she had heard his comment. Then she was gone.

In the late afternoon, the *Adventure* was far from the Trader's

Reach, running a course parallel to the contour of the northern Aranhod coast, when they spotted what appeared to be a derelict vessel in the distance. Trevelyan had climbed to the crow's nest with a spyglass and he reported that the sloop was disabled, its topsail fallen into the waters, the ship heeled over slightly. The people on board waved frantically, the gold and silver robes of the Adjudicators flapping in the sharp winds. Returning from the crow's nest, Trevelyan met the captain and Chatham on the fo'c'sle deck. "What would Adjudicators be doing out here?"

"There's only one way to find out," Trevelyan said.

The *Adventure* cruised to within a kilometer of the vessel when the impossible occurred: the large wooden column holding the fallen topsail was suddenly shoved upward, jammed back into place by two of the robed men. As they labored, the wind caught the corner of one of the men's costumes and whipped it back, revealing heavily thewed bluish-black legs and arms. The hollow man turned and grinned as the sail caught the wind and the ship righted itself. Four more blue-skinned men climbed on board from the other side of the sloop and Trevelyan understood that they had been in the water, helping to push the boat upright.

"Veer off," Trevelyan ordered. "They won't be able to catch us in that ship."

The captain, a tall, rugged man with thinning blond hair, ignored Trevelyan, shoving past the young prince to order his hook-nosed first mate to prepare battle stations.

"Hold on, you can't—" Trevelyan began.

The order was given and the tension that had enveloped the crew suddenly broke. The drills they had performed daily were now called into play as the master of arms distributed weapons and the drummers beat the quarter. Groups formed on the deck, calling upon the Forge to create the catapults and the deadly ammunition they would require.

"We're not at war," Trevelyan shouted. "This is a blatant act of aggression."

"Yes, it is," the captain agreed. "But while you're on this ship you're under my command, and this is *my* decision."

Trevelyan felt the familiar ache in his ribs as he thought of his encounter with the hollow assassin in the citadel. There were at least eight of the soulless men in the sloop, creatures who had certainly been denied access to the Trader's Reach and now wished to pirate the supplies they required. He stared at the sloop, thankful that the hollow men's ship was downwind. The *Adventure* had every advantage and a full frontal assault, such as the captain was preparing, actually had a chance for success, provided the soulless men did not gain access to the Cynaran vessel.

"What if they have liquid fire?" Trevelyan asked. The captain had no reply, although he blanched at the thought of burning at sea.

Rolland Storr and his men readied the second line of attack against the hollow, nocking arrows against their bows, loading crossbows with bolts, sharpening their edged weapons. Trevelyan saw Shantow and his bodyguards speaking with an artist who sketched furiously as he tried to keep up with the Kintaran. Finally Shantow nodded in approval and gestured for his bodyguards to study the drawing. They discussed it briefly as the young flat-nosed Kintaran pointed outward, to the sloop, and all four men raised their clenched fists and shouted an oath in their native language.

Ariodne approached the young prince, ignoring Chatham, who had been unusually quiet. "Why are you allowing this?"

"I couldn't stop it if I tried," Trevelyan confessed. "And if I did, I would lose the respect of the men."

"What respect?" she asked. "You're their liege and they ignore your commands. You may have their allegiance in Cynara, but you haven't yet earned it here. Do something, Trevelyan! Do *anything*. But don't just stand here."

"She's right," Chatham said grudgingly.

The merchant prince looked over to the captain, who was bellowing orders through a horn he had forged. The tall, shirtless man with thinning hair and a sunburned scalp was ordering the crew to bring the *Adventure* as close as possible to the hollow men's sloop. Trevelyan suddenly found himself moving on the captain, snatching the black metal horn from the man's hand as he drew his *kris* and swept the captain's legs out from under him with the weapon's flat. The rugged man dropped like a dead weight. Before he could recover, Trevelyan was kneeling beside him, the sharp edge of the swordbreaker against the man's throat.

The captain was about to reach up and force the weapon away in annoyance when he realized that the *kris* was not a product of the Forge. The man with the thinning, blond hair remained still. Chatham sprang to Trevelyan's side as the hook-nosed first mate rushed to the observation deck. The younger man froze on the small rise of steps when he saw the reddish glare in the eyes of the scarred old man.

Trevelyan leaned into the captain's face. "You, sir, are my employee. *You* bend to *my* will. Is that clear?"

The captain nodded slowly, aware of the heavy weight pressed against his throat, his eyes widening whenever he swallowed. Two of the Autumn wolves leaped onto the fo'c'sle deck. They were Black Mask's salt and pepper dog soldiers. The other wolves circulated through the crew, observing the preparations for battle. The soldier wolves each placed a paw on the captain's shoulder.

"We're turning this ship back," Trevelyan said.

"We can't turn back now," Chatham said. "The hollow are too close. If we go back to our original heading they'll be upwind and upon us within the hour. We must stay and fight."

Trevelyan cursed under his breath. "This is what I want you to do," Trevelyan said, then gave the captain his orders.

Moments later the wolves backed away and allowed the captain to stand on watery legs and address the crew, first ordering them to bring the *Adventure* to a full stop, then shouting, "By the order of our liege, Lord Trevelyan, we will take these devils from a distance. Their strength comes from their abilities in tight quarters. We now have them at an advantage and we will keep it that way."

Trevelyan circulated through the crew, quickly learning their assigned tasks. The wolves kept the captain occupied.

The sloop was still advancing on the *Adventure*, half a kilometer off the starboard bow, when Trevelyan gave the order for Shantow and his men to call upon the Forge. The Kintarans lowered their heads and shuddered as a wrenching cry sounded and a sharp breeze cut across the deck. From the waters came an explosion of displaced water, a sudden, frothing geyser that leaped into the air and quickly lost its power. Floating before the hollow men's sloop was a small black stone island topped with jagged growths that shot out at precise angles. The island was five meters in length, with spikes that rose upward to three meters in height.

The hollow men tried to turn their boat, but a collision was inevitable. The scream of wood bending and cracking as the ship was impaled drifted across the waters, diminished by the howling wind. Huge wounds opened in the side of the vessel commandeered by the soulless men. Struts snapped and wood beams were ground into splinters. The ship collapsed onto the island, heeling over into the waters, the sudden shock of the impact spilling half the crew into the waters.

"Now we must drive the vessel closer and finish this," the captain said.

"Their ship is disabled," Trevelyan said. "They pose no threat to us. The mainland is close enough. Let them swim there and we'll have nothing more to do with it."

"Trevelyan," Ariodne said breathlessly, "they are swimming. The last of them just abandoned the ship. But they're swimming directly *for us*."

"Bastards," Trevelyan said as he considered the damage that even one of the hollow men could perform if they were allowed to board the *Adventure*.

"We're not going to run," the captain hissed. The Autumn wolves growled behind the tall, sunburned man, allowing him to feel their hot breath.

"Yes, we are," Trevelyan said. Moments later the order was given. Despite a general murmur of disagreement over the decision, the crew turned the ship and headed back for their original course. The hollow men changed direction, following the vessel, their arms pumping wildly as they strained to close the distance between them and the escaping ship.

Ariodne gripped Trevelyan's arm. Six of the hollow men were gaining on the *Adventure*. "Impossible," he said. "Wait until they're within range, then fire everything we have!"

Trevelyan turned his gaze to the waters. The hollow men did not stay together, presenting a simple target. They swam furiously toward the *Adventure* with as much distance between them as they could achieve. The image was at once absurd and yet frightening.

When the first of the blue-skinned giants swam to within one hundred meters of the ship, the captain issued orders for the second attack. The catapults launched their deadly cargo, sending a hailstorm of razor-sharp flechettes toward the closest of the soulless men, a black-haired creature with a silver band around his upper right arm. The hollow man hollered in fear, then ducked beneath the waters as the metal shards sliced through the waters. He did not resurface.

On the *Adventure*, Storr ordered the warriors to forge new loads of flechettes as the catapults were reset. His men had stationed themselves near the rail, bows drawn and nocked, waiting for some sign of the hollow men.

Two more were swimming ahead of their fellows. One of the hollow men who had been in the rear of the formation abruptly stopped in the waters and changed direction, heading for dry land. The catapults were launched a second time, each aiming for a separate target. The four remaining soulless men went below the water before the rain of daggerlike shards fell upon the choppy waters. One of the pair who had taken the lead floated to the surface in a cloud of blood, his body torn to shreds by the attack. The hollow man who had been beside him resurfaced immediately after the top of the waters cleared. Swimming toward his fallen comrade, he grasped the man's hair and dragged him along as he swam with renewed determination to overtake the *Adventure*. The final pair of soulless men broke through the surface of the waters and followed him at a distance.

The winds kicked up and filled the sails of the *Adventure*, dragging the vessel farther ahead of the laboring soulless men. The catapults were filled and launched twice more. One of the two men in the rear was killed. That left only two of the creatures in the waters.

The closest of the hollow men was wounded, although he used the body of the dead ally as a shield. The other man dove below the waters to confuse his attackers, resurfacing in unexpected positions.

Ten minutes later the archers began to fire on the closest of the hollow men. Trevelyan noted the blue-skinned creature's shaved head and gold-plated collar as the soulless man heaved the body of the dead hollow man over his head, allowing the arrows to mass in its dead flesh.

"He's to the side of the ship, climbing aboard," the captain screamed.

The soulless man threw the body of the dead hollow man toward the row of archers, knocking a half dozen of them from their feet as he climbed the last rungs with blinding speed. The second man was still in the waters, closing fast.

Ariodne called upon the Forge, casting her black armors, creating a *nilki*, a two-meter staff with a spike and a hooked blade at either end.

The bald hollow man leaped onto the main deck of the *Adventure*, a swarm of fifty men and women closing over him instantly. The first wolves, Black Mask, his mate, and his lieutenants padded away from the crowd, the black-faced leader of the Autumn wolves glancing up at Chatham with a contemp-

tuous expression. Swords and daggers ripped into the dark flesh
of the soulless man and he howled in horror and frustration as
he ripped through the crowd in a murderous frenzy, ignoring his
many wounds. His hands curled into claws, the soulless creature tore into exposed throats, leaving spraying red geysers of
blood to splatter those gathered to kill the monster. One of
Shantow's bodyguards came within range of the hollow man and
screamed as a deep gash was driven into the tender meat of his
shoulder, his now-useless arm dangling by blood-soaked tendons.

"The second man," Trevelyan said. "He'll be coming over
the side any moment."

"You have more to worry about than that," a voice called
out from behind the prince. Perched on the far rail was the first
hollow man they had fired upon, his flesh covered in ragged
wounds, the silver armband glinting in the afternoon sun. "We
only wished to bargain with you for supplies," he snarled.
"We heard the call, knew we had to return to Rien. Those who
die this day by our hands could have lived."

The captain of the *Adventure* screamed in defiance as he
rushed toward the blue-skinned man, forging a stave that he
gripped with both hands. The weapon had a Kintaran design,
the sharp blades of the head prepared to spring open
once inside the chest of their victim. The hollow man laughed as he
gripped the rail with one hand, easing his massive body out of
the way of the awkward thrust of the balding captain as he
grasped the main cylinder of the shaft and twisted it violently,
sweeping the body of the weapon into the captain's stomach
and running him toward the rail, where he pitched over the
side, into the waters.

Ariodne had already thrown her stave at the creature, refusing to give him the advantage of time. He spun suddenly,
raising his arm to ward off the shaft that had been aimed at his
head. There was a sickening thump of metal piercing flesh as
the stave was driven through his lower arm, the razor-sharp
cutting hook slicing through the tough, gristled muscles, opening several of the pulsing, oversize veins of the creature as the
sharp head pierced his chest, pinning his ruined arm to his
body. At the same moment, Trevelyan had leaped forward,
driving his *kris* into the base of the creature's stomach with
such force that they were both nearly swept over the side. The
monster screamed as Trevelyan brought the blade straight up,
the tip scraping the creature's spine from within, the jagged,

perfectly spaced hooks catching the coils of the intestines, then twisted and yanked the blade back, bringing an explosion of gore that caused the young prince to gag, his mind reeling from the horror of what he had just done. Chatham delivered the final blow with his sword, severing the creature's head and kicking the body back over the side while the head struck the rail with the soft squish of butchered meat, the eyes still darting back and forth, the tongue still moving, the mouth trying to form a word. Then the ship rocked and the head fell over the side, with the rest of the monster.

Trevelyan teetered, felt as if he were going to fall to his knees, and groped for Ariodne's shoulder. She was shaking, too. The first mate had witnessed the entire event, and a change had occurred in the way he looked at Trevelyan. The young prince knew that he would have to go on now and act as if what he had just done was something less than the dark, shattering experience he knew it to be.

The pair of young Autumn wolves sat on their haunches, their jaws hanging open slightly, appearing quite entertained by the display. Chatham looked to Trevelyan. The younger man was covered in blood, a barely contained madness playing behind his eyes. Then he turned to the wolves.

"So why didn't you two curs do something?" the grey-bearded man hollered. One of the wolves cocked his head quizzically, the other turned to look at the main deck, where the other hollow man had finally fallen. Shantow was above his quivering corpse, hacking away with a wide-bodied blade while a circle of men and women stood nearby, the bodies of nine men and two women, some dead, others maimed and wounded, lay around them. The healer from the fourth house and several others tried to help those who had been hurt. The crew members who remained stared at the tableau before them in shocked disbelief.

Near the ladder, where the first hollow man had climbed aboard, the last of the soulless creatures was perched, unnoticed by the crowd, staring at the remains of his comrade. Before anyone saw him, the creature leaped back into the waters and swam toward shore.

CHAPTER FIFTEEN

The dead were buried at sea, the wounded cared for to the best of the healer's abilities. The *Adventure*'s captain had been rescued, his injuries slight. The change in the way Trevelyan was treated by the remaining crew members was startling. Even Captain Gower treated him with respect.

Only Ariodne was present that evening when Trevelyan allowed his fear, disgust, and guilt over claiming a life, even one of the hollow, to overtake him. He shuddered and held her, then made love to her with alarming passion and violent release. In the morning they made love gently and slowly, the cool white light of morning washing over their chamber, burning away the madness of the previous day.

For the next week, the *Adventure* sailed farther north. The temperature fell and the wind tapered off. The *Adventure* had been fitted with sails and oars. The death of the heavy winds had forced the crew below decks to man the oars. Trevelyan and Shantow were on the fo'c'sle deck, the warm sun making an unusual appearance. The past few days had been cold, bleak, and grey. Trevelyan explained that he felt ill at ease with the attentions he had received since he had killed the hollow.

"Hmmmph," Shantow said. "At first I was jealous, you understand. It was me that gave the killing blow to the other hollow, the one that took so many of our—"

One of the crewmen slowed as he approached, eyes lowered, and said in a tight low and respectful voice, "Lord Trevelyan," before he walked past the prince and his friend.

"Now I am maybe not so sure I would want what you have been given," Shantow said in his lilting voice.

Suddenly a call came from the crow's nest: a ship had been spotted running a parallel course with the *Adventure*. Trevelyan, Shantow, and the captain arrived at the fo'c'sle deck. The captain surrendered his spyglass to Trevelyan.

"Thank you, Captain Gower," Trevelyan said respectfully. He studied the vessel through the glass, then handed the black cylinder to the captain. "A ship with black sails."

"They come from Bellerophon. You don't seem surprised. Were you expecting one of the black ships?"

Trevelyan ran his hand over his face. He hadn't shaved for days and a light beard had begun to grow. "The possibility was anticipated. We will ignore them for now. In time they will come to us and they will signal. Your men will return their signal with the message that this is the *Adventure*, bearing Arayncourt of Cynara. If they wish further communication, an audience will be granted."

Shantow smiled in approval.

Shortly before nightfall, intense yellow and orange streaks of sunlight shuddering on the darkened water, Trevelyan, Ariodne, Chatham, and Shantow were summoned to the captain's post, where they looked out and saw that a new signal flared from the black ship and the captain translated the series of pulsating lights for the prince.

The black ship signaled that they would adjust their course and meet the *Adventure* in the waters ahead. As they sailed for another three quarters of an hour, the distance between the ships narrowing, Trevelyan attempted to keep his fear and suspicion of the men from Bellerophon at bay.

The ships met by flickering torchlight. The black ship of Bellerophon was larger than the *Adventure*, with a crew of nearly two hundred members of that country's royal navy, a strong sampling of which assembled on the upper decks. The flames reflected off their black armors, but their ebony sails absorbed and snuffed out the light.

A walkway was forged between the two ships. Trevelyan started on one end of the metal plank, a tall, red-haired man who had removed his helmet out of deference on the other. The dark-haired prince was dressed in black armors with red trim— the colors of his ancestors. He had decided not to shave the darkening stubble from his face after Ariodne told him it added a few years and an aloofness to his appearance.

They met in the center of the walkway, over the dark waters sparkling with torchlight. Trevelyan had been well versed in the iron nation's protocol by their ambassador, and so he unsheathed his weapon, raising the *kris* to show that it had been blooded.

The red-haired man's face was drawn, but his eyes burned with a defiance Trevelyan appreciated.

"My name is Trevelyan Arayncourt, Merchant Prince of Cynara," the dark-haired young man said.

"You are known to me, by name if nothing else," the red-haired man said. "My name is Lieutenant Lon Freyr. I represent Searle Orrick. Why are you here?"

Trevelyan forced back a smile. He had been warned to be direct with these people. "We journey to Rien in response to a request from the leader of that re-formed country, a hollow man named Kothra. I believe he is known to Searle Orrick."

The muscles in the red-haired man's face tightened as he recalled his near escape from the hollow man in the bowl-shaped arena of Telluryde. "And to me."

"Kothra claims to possess the secret of liquid fire," Trevelyan continued, and detailed Kothra's threats if his country was not recognized and awarded full rights. The two men shared full knowledge of their respective encounters with the men of the hollow and agreed to meet again in Rien.

As the red-haired man turned to go back to his ship, Trevelyan said, "Lieutenant Freyr, it may have better served your personal interests *not* to have told me any of this. I'm certain that you won't endear yourself to Orrick if he learns that you have spoken so freely. Why did you?"

An angry laugh escaped the red-haired man as he turned and approached the merchant prince once again, moving in close enough to be heard at a whisper. "Have you ever been to my country, Lord Arayncourt? Perhaps if you had, you wouldn't ask. I'm one of those who believes that the head sitting upon our throne may outlive the body of our nation if something isn't done. Perhaps if we achieve victory here, the secret of liquid fire could be utilized to serve the people of my country, not Searle Orrick."

Trevelyan was silent as Freyr returned to his ship.

Much later, after the two vessels returned to their parallel courses, Trevelyan dined with Chatham, Shantow, and Ariodne in his quarters and discussed his meeting with Freyr.

"I suppose that Orrick was going to share the secret of liquid fire with the world," Shantow said sarcastically. "I don't expect that he was maybe going to use it to upset the balance between the three powers."

"Of course that was the plan," Trevelyan said, "but it went badly for them and now we're all in the same position. But there was no need to antagonize the lieutenant. He seems to hate Orrick as much as our informant, Ambassador Obert.''

Ariodne glanced up from the table at Chatham, then back to her lover. ''You trust too easily, Trevelyan. That's always been one of your faults.''

The grey-bearded man lowered his eyes and said nothing.

''At least Freyr has a soul,'' Trevelyan said. ''If I have to trust a man, I want him to be one of *us*.''

Chatham winked at Shantow. ''This is very good. He used to whine for hours before he came to the point.''

''You noticed,'' the Kintaran said.

Trevelyan's appetite had been waning. He set down a sweet roll and said, ''I can only tell you this: If my child was born of the hollow, I'm no longer certain that I would allow it to leave its place of birth alive.''

Ariodne stared at him in surprise that quickly gave way to anger, images of Shantow murdering his son burning in her memory. She tried, but she could not force them away.

''You would have no problem,'' the Kintaran said. ''The woman you love is not a whore who would lay with monsters.''

''I've had enough,'' Ariodne said as she set the white flask that had been in her hand to the table and walked to the door of the cabin without another word.

''Ariodne, wait,'' Trevelyan said imploringly, but his lover was already slamming the door behind her. The trio of men continued to talk for the entire evening.

It was the middle of the night before she returned. Trevelyan had found it practically impossible to sleep without her presence. He pretended that he had been in a deep sleep when she climbed into bed with him, curling one arm around his chest while wrapping one of her long legs over his thighs. ''I love you,'' she whispered.

''I love you,'' he replied softly. Then sleep engulfed him in a comforting wave.

Two days later the captain announced landfall. The black ship under the command of Lon Freyr had once again closed the gap between the two vessels and they approached the craggy grey shore together. Chatham had been here before and he had given the captain the location that would place the *Adventure* closest to the walled city that the outcast nation had been named after.

''From here it's half a day, perhaps less,'' Chatham had told the captain. As the ships anchored well off the foreboding shores, small exploration vessels were being forged. Trevelyan looked out to the land of fear, as he had heard so many of the crew members refer to the hollow land. The temperature had dropped severely and in a month a fine covering of snow would lay upon the vast, uneven vista.

Deadwood fallen from petrified trees floated close to the shore. Twisted grey rocks rose from the waters as if they had been the product of a lava flow. Beyond the rows of white skeletal trees that had born no fruit in hundreds of years the prince could see unnatural black forms.

"The land suffered greatly for Tarrant Vega's excesses," Chatham explained. "The hand of the Unseen ruined this land when it first destroyed Vega's palace. For a time, nothing could grow here, and life was impossible. If it hadn't been for the villagers whom the wolves had saved, the land would have remained barren. But the Unseen showed mercy to the people. There is a stretch of land near the ruins of the fortress city where planting can be done, where the streams provide fresh water, and livestock can thrive."

A woman called Chatham's name and he spun to face Ruzena. The blue-eyed former sentry to the Mavens wore a heavy black cloak over her silver mail, hugging herself as she approached the grey-bearded man.

"Are you cold?" he asked gently as he reached up and welcomed her into a comforting embrace. She lowered her face into the crook between his grizzled, bearded jaw and the rise of his massive chest, nodding in response to his question.

"Would you like to stay with the ship?" he said tenderly, indicating that there would be no shame if she did not accompany him to the ruins of the fortress city.

"No," she said. "My place is with you."

"As you will," he said. Her body shuddered in his arms.

Ariodne wandered toward them. "The first of the landing vessels has been forged. It's time for us to go."

The young prince nodded, forcing his thoughts away from the souls that were dying to create the black sculls. Shifting his gaze to Lon Freyr's black ship five hundred meters across the waters, he saw that the Bellerophon soldiers had manufactured their landing craft in their homeland and now lowered the vessels over the side. Although their economy was always a factor, the military planners did not want their men to drain themselves of any energy they might need when they were about to enter a strange and unfriendly climate. Trevelyan had already decided that once this nightmare with the hollow was over and he returned to Cynara he would subtly implement many of the changes that he had been considering: cutting back gradually on the use of the Forge and rewarding manufacturers who labored by hand with fire and steel as they had fifty years ago. He believed the day would come when the Well of Souls was refilled and the Forge destroyed. On that day men would have to recall their old skills if they were to survive.

Harnesses were forged to lower Black Mask and his pack into one of the waiting sculls. The wolves seemed to enjoy the attention that was paid to their special needs. The first wolf was enjoying the cool sea breeze as he was hauled down over the side of the ship, closing his eyes to allow himself the pleasure of the smooth drop, when Chatham suddenly appeared on the rail, shouting, "You look like a show pup who's sniffed too many black posies, you mangy cur!"

The wolf snapped to attention, suddenly struggling in its harness. The power of Black Mask's exertions caused him to swing back and forth over the waiting ship until his razor-sharp claws cut through the cloth harness. The animal suddenly yelped and plunged to the waters below, missing the scull completely as he splashed in the waters. He vanished below the surface for an instant before angrily resurfacing and swimming to the boat.

Above, Chatham laughed until he felt his ribs ache, Ruzena shaking her head in amusement. The two men who were already in the scull laughed until the wolf climbed aboard, nearly taking their hands from their wrists as they tried to help the creature.

Soon half a dozen sculls were heading for the shore, their thin black rows scissoring in the cold waters. "The current fights us," Trevelyan said, unable to put much force into his rowing due to his injured ribs. The prince's craft took the point, attaining land ten minutes later. The white, skeletal forest lay before them, thicker and more menacing than it had appeared from the ship.

Lon Freyr and one hundred of his men reached the shore as the last of the Cynaran vessels approached, depositing another forty men and women accompanying Trevelyan. "Arayncourt of Cynara," Freyr said as he nodded to the young prince, his black wolf's helm firmly in place.

"Lieutenant," Trevelyan replied. "We face a journey of several hours. My men are fed and rested, anxious to begin."

"And mine have fasted. Such is our way before battle," he said. "If it is battle we go to face."

"Gentlemen," Chatham said warmly, wishing to break the tension between the two men. He pointed to the white forest. "The road is that way. I suggest we begin walking."

"He's our point man," Trevelyan explained.

Freyr finally smiled, the lines around his dark eyes bunching into crow's-feet. "A task I'm quite familiar with," he said. "Lead on."

Black Mask and his pack acted strangely when they arrived on the shore. Walks With Fire raised her head in alarm and broke into a run, vanishing into the woods. Her mate and his followers looked to the gathering warriors on the shores, then ran after her.

Few words were spoken as the troops from Bellerophon merged with the fighters from Cynara and together they approached the white forest, moving past a thicket to an opening large enough to allow three men at a time to pass. The air was heavy and stale. The sounds of boots were muted. The ground beneath them was hard as stone, with fissures and rises snaking across the path where vibrant roots once lay.

Trevelyan removed his glove and ran his hand over one of the thick tree trunks. "Turned to stone," he muttered.

Suddenly a large man with ivory skin stepped out from behind the tree. Trevelyan leaped back in surprise. The white-skinned man stood before the merchant prince, his open hands resting at his sides.

"One of the hollow," Freyr said in astonishment. The giant's flesh was white, but his natural blue-black coloring had begun to show through beneath the camouflaging paint. He looked down at Trevelyan and Freyr with a bemused expression. A second hollow man who had been painted white stood on a heavy bough just ahead.

The creature standing before Trevelyan had a single stalk of white hair rising from his head, held in place with a silver band. The other was bald with white stubble already growing on his skull and a massive scar that began at the crown of his head and continued to his jaw. Both men were naked. Trevelyan heard the nocking of arrows and turned with his hand upraised. "Don't fire!" he shouted.

Lon Freyr was just behind him. Biting his lip in frustration, his gaze cutting between Trevelyan and the pair of ivory-skinned soulless men standing weaponless and vulnerable before them. He turned and signaled his men to hold their fire.

The soldiers gathered in a circle around the hollow man. His partner leaped effortlessly from his perch and walked to Trevelyan and Freyr. Chatham had found Ruzena and placed a comforting hand upon her shoulder. Ariodne was joined by Shantow. The Kintaran reached for his crossbow, a *menuki* shaft loaded and waiting to be fired. Akako, Shantow's guardian, placed his hand over Shantow's as he stared into the faces of the hollow men, reading their expressions well.

"The time will come," he promised, a terrible sadness in his voice.

"You have come for an audience with our savior, the great Kothra of Rien," the scarred hollow man said. "On his behalf we welcome you."

"Lead on," Trevelyan said. "We will follow."

With Trevelyan and Freyr's assent, the crowd parted to let the hollow men pass.

CHAPTER
SIXTEEN

The hollow men walked briskly as the groups from Cynara and Bellerophon passed through the twisted, barren landscape of the white forest. The tired and angry members of the companies were forced to rush through the blinding white forest in their attempt to keep up.

The group leading the movement consisted of Trevelyan, Chatham, Ariodne, Shantow, Ruzena, Rolland Storr, Lon Freyr, and two of the red-haired lieutenant's men. The hollow men were far ahead in the lead. Chatham had identified their scent and had assured Trevelyan not to become concerned if they lost sight of the ivory-skinned giants.

Shantow moved through the small group and clamped his hand on Trevelyan's shoulder as he asked, "Have you ever felt like livestock being marched to the slaughter?"

"Encounters with these soulless bastards lead to nothing but slaughter,'' Trevelyan said bitterly as he thought of their battle at sea. "They are insane."

Rolland Storr, the tall, black-haired condottiere with dark, impenetrable eyes, a thick mustache, and a heavy covering of quickly massing stubble over his jaw, said, "No, but in many ways, the hollow *are* like children. They need approval desperately. And they need a function. Without a chore to perform they become melancholy or fall victim to sudden shifts in their temperament. I've seen them tear-filled and suicidal one moment and ready to cut the heart from an imagined enemy the next."

"We have to find a way to gain control," Trevelyan said. "We need an advantage over them."

"We have something they want," Freyr said. "Our respect. Our allegiance to their cause."

Trevelyan took a moment to consider this, then moved to Chatham's side and whispered, "What happened to the wolves?"

"Black Mask and his lot have always had their own agenda. They're not like their brethren, who leap at the call of the Unseen. They will come when they are ready."

The group was silent as the white forest thinned and they approached the environs of outer Rien. Shantow's almond-shaped eyes narrowed when he saw the glimmering white backs of their guides. He had sworn that before they left Rien, he would find the hollow man that he believed raped his wife. Only when he was soaked in that man's blood would his honor and the virtue of his wife be restored.

They reached the edge of the ivory woods and passed into a black plateau that was marked by deep gashes and rivulets that could have been made by streams of lava. In the distance were mountains that appeared to have been wax that had dripped and cooled into large, globular surfaces and sharp stalactite overhangs. The land reeked of devastation. Clouds once again drifted over the sun.

Close to an hour passed before the group encountered remnants of a man-made dwelling. Five buildings rose out of the side of a large hill, their rectangular doorways gaping and black. The design was simple but elegant, a first floor with a high ceiling, columns rising over the second story leading to widow's walks and further rises buried back deeper into the rock. The buildings looked like facades created for a play and only one was completely exposed, the others shattered or overrun with shiny fingers of rock. Trevelyan guessed that the guards of the forest were sequestered here.

Beyond the next hill they saw cylindrical towers and square observation posts occasionally checked with tiny black windows jutting from a mountain. The remains of a castle, Trevelyan surmised. A village lay at the base of the mountain, a dozen huddled houses and tents. The blue-black flesh of hollow men circulating through their domain was visible even at a distance.

They were led past the village, through shattered stone archways that no longer supported buildings or bridges and past gigantic stone columns that lay in huge fragments beside the road or rose into the sky, a proud series of lonely, colossal sentries overseeing a wretched black road.

Weird black trees with clawlike branches rose beyond a twisting series of hillsides. The high, majestic archways of an abandoned temple jutted from the earth, the walls they had supported long since shattered as if by an angry hand. The young prince was reminded of the deadlands.

As the hour grew late they reached what Trevelyan had assumed to be the ruins of Tarrant Vega's fortress city. He saw a cluster of buildings swarming with hollow men. The structures appeared to have been thrown together in a nonsensical design: dozens of domed towers, steeples, and turrets were squeezed next to squat meeting halls. The pattern was occasionally broken by huge archways strung between bunched-up edifices. No two buildings seemed to have the same height and many were leaning forward at odd angles, threatening to fall onto the road, as if the residents had run out of space and continued to build anyway. Immense curving stone structures reached out from the high base of the unnatural fortress as if they were roots from a tree. Many of the buildings were damaged. Glaring white statues of men holding staffs and lovers dancing at their feet stood on marble podiums near a ruined iron gate.

The hollow men did not stop.

"Chatham, I thought this place was the fortress of Rien," Trevelyan said.

"This failed attempt at a masterwork was the inspiration for Tarrant Vega's city," Chatham explained as they were led through another village, this one populated by hundreds of the blue-skinned monsters who gave only passing nods of interest to the travelers. There were a good number of women of the hollow in the village and the warriors gaped openly at them. Despite their exaggerated and muscular physiques many of the soulless women were quite beautiful. They shared the men's disdain for clothing, wearing only the barest of leathers or mails. A few of the women laughed at the open-mouthed expressions of the visiting soldiers.

Trevelyan was becoming noticeably edgy.

"We are close, boy. Have patience," Chatham urged.

The young prince studied the faces of the hollow men as the group passed through the village in tight ranks. Upon close inspection there were subtle differences in the features and manner of dress of the hollow, but on the whole, they were all perfect physical specimens. Storr had explained that their unique physiology molded them into killing machines from an early age despite their practice of avoiding meat whenever possible and relying on vegetables and fresh catch from the sea.

At first Trevelyan could not guess the purpose of the hollow men's efforts in the village, then he slowly realized that they worked with the tools of builders, tearing apart the foundations of the small community for raw material. When he looked back to Tarrant Vega's first home, he understood that the same process was under way there.

Large transport wagons and carts were hauled in their direction from the road ahead, some pulled by oxen, others by hollow men. The procession of visitors from Cynara and Bellerophon was forced to step from the road to allow room for dozens of the vehicles. As the wagons moved past, Trevelyan saw that they were empty.

The sky was becoming dark when they climbed a final rise and were confronted with a sight that caused the members of the first group of travelers to bring the entire procession to a halt. The warriors spread out behind Trevelyan, Freyr, and their companions, lining the ridge as they each took in the capital city of the hollow land.

Rien may have been built on the foundations of a fallen city, but it was hardly a mass of ruins anymore. A fortress with four smaller adjoining buildings could be seen in the center of the complex. This building had been Tarrant Vega's "walled city" of legend. Now it was only a small part of a sprawling city-state that rivaled Cynara in size and consumed much of the horizon. The solid-looking fortress walls surrounding the city rose four stories into the sky of Rien's twilight. Watchfires were already burning in many of the towers. Dark blue shapes moved through the city. Hundreds of simple buildings had been erected. Beyond the city, tracts of land had been set aside for the growing of food. Underground well springs had been tapped to provide fresh waters and irrigation channels were being cut. From what Trevelyan could see, there was only one way in or out of the city. The amount of industry that had taken place in such a short time was startling.

"Chatham, when did you last visit this place?"

"About fifty years ago."

"All this in fifty years," Trevelyan said softly. He had not noticed the return of the white-skinned hollow men until one of them laughed.

"Fifty years? This has occurred in the last *two* years," he said with pride. "In fifty years we will have a city like this in each of Autumn's nations."

In fifty years, Trevelyan thought, mankind could be dead and the world will be yours. But without those who have souls creating children, your kind will die soon after.

"That is something I'm sure we'll discuss with your ruler," Trevelyan said. "Take us into the city."

"As you will," the hollow man with the fount of white hair said as he turned and gestured for the party to follow. The city was farther away than Trevelyan had thought and the silence of the journey was broken suddenly by the howls of a pack of Autumn wolves. The sounds cut through the sluggish air of early evening, causing the tired travelers to snap to attention. Chatham sighed heavily, painfully, at the noise. Trevelyan spotted Black Mask and his pack first, camped near the massive gateway into the city. The butchered bodies of twenty of the first wolves' brethren had been hung outside the walls. The wolves had to have traveled north from Aranhod and the borderlands to meet their deaths here.

"The legends are true," Freyr said, suddenly terrified at the display. "Kothra is a wolf killer after all."

"And the wolves hold no dominion over the hollow," Ariodne said softly. "That's why we're here."

As they approached the gate, the first wolves growled at the white-skinned hollow men who called to the nearest guard station for orders. Trevelyan, Freyr, and Shantow identified themselves as ambassadors from the three nations Kothra had petitioned, Aranhod, Kintaro, and Bellerophon. Each of the ambassadors was allowed two guards. Trevelyan chose Chatham and Ariodne, Shantow selected Akako Michi, a heavy, even-tempered man who had been his main guard since childhood, and Rolland Storr, and Freyr took only one man from his crew on the black ship: Zared Anstice, a tall, black-skinned man whose head was partially shaved on the top with a thick black growth on the sides. The rest of the troops were given permission to make camp outside the city. Food and fresh water would be provided for them.

Chatham embraced Ruzena, then returned to his charge.

As the gates were opened, Trevelyan turned to the Autumn wolves. He gazed into the turquoise eyes of the wolf that had haunted his dreams for months and said, "Will you just wait there, doing nothing?"

Black Mask pulled his lips back in a mad grimace, spittle dripping from his fangs. Chatham stood beside the young prince and took his arm. "Trevelyan, you know who and what he is. Should he wish to enter the city, mere walls will not stop him. I can feel his thirst for vengeance." The reddish specks of the grey-bearded warrior's black eyes began to dance as he gazed at the carcasses of the fallen wolves dangling over the walls. "I share their desire for blood. But a conflict must be avoided."

The white-skinned guides turned and walked from the gate as a platoon of hollow men arrived to take the diplomatic envoy into the city. The leader of the blue-skinned pack approached Trevelyan, his lips pulled back in a grotesque parody of a smile as he spread his arms wide. He seemed quite unremarkable. His features would have been pleasing if he had been human and his physique was almost identical to that of his fellows. Only his clothing set him apart: around his waist he wore a wolf's pelt, and over his shoulders lay the skulls of animals that might have been wolves or wild dogs, the lower jaws removed, the bone polished and radiant in the soft orange torchlight. The other hollow men stood clear of him, attempting not to look at him directly, paying him a respect Trevelyan believed was normally reserved for religious leaders.

The red eyes with black, catlike slits of the hollow man wearing the wolves' skulls burned in the near darkness as he said, "I am Abbas Bute. We have no need of weapons, but you may keep yours."

A sudden loathing overcame Trevelyan. He wished to hurt this man. "Your envoy, Nayati, was killed in his assault on the Citadel of the Mavens. He died without honor."

"Whimpering like a dog, I'm certain," Abbas said good-naturedly. "Shall we go? Kothra waits for us."

Freyr glanced at Trevelyan. "I have no wish to prolong this," the lieutenant said in a warning tone. The young prince gestured for the hollow men to lead; he would follow.

As they passed through the city, Trevelyan studied the crude buildings the hollow had raised in only two years, according to their claims, and wondered how the task has been accomplished without the use of the Forge. The designs were inelegant but functional. Thousands of hollow men and women surged through the streets, each with some unfathomable purpose. There seemed to be no places of commerce in Rien. The young prince inquired about their absence.

"Our needs are few and we have the means to provide for the masses," Abbas said. "Those who are hungry know where to find food. Clothing is hardly a requirement. Shelter is plentiful and status, with the exception of Kothra and his chosen few, is an irrelevant concept. Everyone here has a task. We are constantly growing, expanding."

"Your system operates without money?" Trevelyan said, aghast.

"We have no need for currency among ourselves. What we have amassed will be used in dealing with your countries."

They continued in silence for a time. Trevelyan saw that many of the newer, plainer buildings had been built upon the ruins of centuries old, finely designed structures. The foundations for towers, steeples, archways, and columns were hidden at the bases of the simple dormitories, warehouses, and meeting halls. The roads were uneven, splatters of crystalline rock causing the hard and well-packed earth to suddenly become as slippery as glass. Huge globs of the now-solid lava they had seen earlier, which perhaps once poured from the mountains and reached over the buildings in the outlying townships, were occasionally glimpsed; hollow men worked furiously to chip away at them.

Blackened images, silhouettes, were burned into the older stones: men and women with gaping mouths, hands thrown up as if to ward off blows, some on their knees, others captured in restful poses, their ends coming as complete surprises. Faces and hands sometimes pushed away from the petrified flows of stone, hands curled into claws, mouths opening to swallow burning liquid.

Chatham broke the silence. "What happened outside?"

"You mean the wolves?" Abbas Bute said. "They massed against us. We have committed no crimes, and if we had, we are not answerable to their justice. Many of our number were killed by the wolves. The animals fought valiantly, if that is a comfort to you."

"Where are the outcasts?" Chatham said. "What happened to the men that came here in exile?"

"There are no outcasts here," the blue-black-skinned man said. "The last was driven off years ago. They go to Knossos for their penance, not here. This is our domain."

"How do you prevent anarchy?" Lon Freyr asked. "Do you have laws? Punishments and prisons?"

"Common sense rules," Abbas said with a wide sweep of his hand, dismissing the subject. His nostrils wrinkled at the smell of decaying meat. Now that he had stopped his own aging process, the presence of men disgusted him.

"Surely not everyone is so devoid of emotion," Ariodne said. The red-haired Maven sensed a presence nearby. Her throat tightened and she felt faint. There was another Maven within the city. The Stream of Life was being sifted, glimmers of the future—the possible and probable futures— struck at her mind. She saw chaos and fire. The forces of the humans devastated. Trevelyan standing alone, his soul shattered. Then the visions were gone and the green-eyed woman ran her hand over her throat, brushing against the black plating of her armors as she strained to recover from the momentary assault of images. "Are there none here with ambition? With desire and jealousy?"

"Our time on this world is short," Abbas explained. "If we were left to create a purpose for ourselves, all that you have mentioned would surely come to pass. But we have been given a task by the one true god, and Kothra, born of Kumuda, a woman who had lain with no man, is His son."

"Kothra is the offspring of the Unseen?" she said, forcing back a contemptuous laugh.

"No," Abbas said, his mood suddenly growing dark. "Not the Unseen—the one *true* god."

The Maven shook her head and decided not to press the hollow man any further. She had wondered if the hollow would adopt the philosophies and religions of man, or if they would create a deity of their own. Now she had her answer. Their world had a history of savages denying the truth of the Unseen and creating their own religions, along with those who worshiped the sleeping gods.

As if sensing her thoughts, Abbas said, "We do not discount the existence of the cruel one, the Unseen, who gave birth to the gods and from which sprang mankind— their dreams made flesh. But where did the Unseen come from?''

''The Unseen is infinity,'' Ariodne said, ''a single speck of light in the darkness, a single shadow among the fires of eternity.''

''Pretty words,'' Abbas said. ''But infinity cannot have a single will or a personality capable of anger and regret and the pettiness the Unseen has displayed. That is how we first knew that the Unseen was not alone. Once we opened our minds to the concept of another, His words came to us.''

''And does your god have a name?'' Chatham said.

The soulless man shouted at the humans, his words stinging pellets fired from the depths of his being: ''To hear His name pronounced on your tongues would be a sacrilege.'' He took a breath and composed himself. ''You people may delude yourselves for as long as you wish. Your beliefs are of no consequence to us. In any case, we have arrived.''

The party had just turned a corner and come within view of the fortress they had glimpsed from the hillside. Trevelyan had expected an ornate and foreboding mansion. Instead, like every other edifice in Rien, Kothra's fortress was of a simple design, with a central palace and four smaller houses linked by covered walkways. Vestiges of Tarrant Vega's excesses were occasionally glimpsed through the design: portions of statues, ornate latticeworks, heavy columns, oversized portals, hand-sculpted archways—but on the whole a simple rectangular structure had emerged with a fortified main entrance.

Once inside the fortress, the ambassadors and their guards were led through a labyrinth of corridors, light chambers, cramped entrances through which they were forced to walk single file, darkened hallways, and audience chambers teaming with hollow men. As his frustration mounted, Trevelyan began to wonder if Abbas was lost in the maze. The journey seemed to take forever. After a time, Trevelyan realized that he had discounted this structure too easily. The intricate series of walkways would make the fortress a death trap to invaders who did not understand its design.

Finally they were led into a wide-open courtyard in the center of the fortress where Kothra of Rien was seated upon a simple white marble throne. A woman stood beside him. Braziers were lit on either side of them, bathing the blue-black-skinned couple in a flickering, reddish-orange light. Kothra's appearance had changed since the time of his return from the Telluryde basin with the secret of liquid fire. He wore a wolf pelt and the skulls of three wolves, one upon each shoulder, the other carved into a crown with sparkling red jewels crammed in the eye sockets. Silver and gold bands encircled his massive upper arms and thighs. Fingerless white gloves made of steel that had been molded to the contours of his hands led to several glistening rings. The short bones of wolves had been embedded in his flesh, sharp cuts made and then sewn over once the visible ivory bones were firmly in place. He smiled, drawing back his lips to reveal his razor-sharp teeth, carved to points, as the ambassadors were assembled before him. A general murmur of disquiet sounded from the group. The first man of the hollow winked in recognition at Lon Freyr.

Abbas Bute took his place on the other side of Kothra's throne. The platoon of guardsmen lined up against the back wall, blending with the shadows.

"Kothra of Rien, Lady Brynna Celosia, I present to you the ambassadors from Aranhod, Kintaro, and Bellerophon," Abbas Bute said. "I will allow each of them to give their own introductions."

As the group of humans dutifully gave their names and titles, Trevelyan's attention drifted to the woman at Kothra's side. She was one of the hollow, tall with the most desirable body the young prince had ever seen. Her face was intensely beautiful, her cheekbones high, lips full and rich. Haunting eyes, dark with thin red slits, were roofed by pencil-thin eyebrows and housed within an oval face with a thin nose. The woman's head was shaved and smooth, with the exception of a single stalk of pure white hair that rose from the top of her head and was secured by a thick gold band that allowed her hair to rise up like water from a fountain and stream downward to the sides of her face. She wore a thin, translucent black wrap that heightened her shapely figure.

In the courtyard, Akako Michi, Shantow's bodyguard, took a step forward and introduced himself. Trevelyan had been half aware of the other's clipped, pointed speeches. Shantow had displayed restraint in Kothra's presence. Ariodne had also fixated on the hollow woman, Brynna, for reasons the young prince could not even guess.

For a moment the only sound in the courtyard was the crackling fires in the high braziers.

Resting one foot upon the marble slab Kothra used for a

throne, Brynna casually ran her hands down the length of one of her long, exposed legs, murmuring to herself as she admired the firm, sensuous lines. Then she smiled to Trevelyan. "Don't stare, pup. It's not polite," she said.

Kothra began to laugh, a rich, hearty laugh that bubbled up from deep inside him and spilled out in generous measure. Brynna rested her hand on his massive thigh and shook her head as she looked to Abbas Bute, who was also smiling.

The first man of the hollow raised his hand, palm exposed, in a sweeping gesture. "May you be fulfilled in the city of the hollow," he said, his voice tinged with humor, his words caked in irony. "I offer you comfort and reassurance in the *land of fear.*"

Trevelyan looked to Chatham. The grey-bearded man shrugged as he considered his options. If the hollow men attempted to take the young prince and his companions hostage until his demands were met, Chatham would launch himself at the blue-skinned giant seated upon the throne. He would not succeed, of course. The attack would be a ruse and he would allow the hollow men to kill him. Then, when his body had regenerated, as it always had, he would be free of whatever imprisonment the others shared, free to find them and rescue them from their prison.

Kothra smiled warmly, forcing his lips shut to spare the humans the spectacle of his razor-sharp teeth. He seemed to sense Chatham's distrust, and he rose from his throne and stepped down to walk before those gathered. "Good ambassadors, you have no reason to fear. You have journeyed far. Tonight, you may explore the city at will. Every kindness and hospitality will be extended to you. If you do not wish to sleep within our walls, we will escort you back to your parties waiting outside our gates. The choice is yours. In the morning we will begin our discussions."

Kothra slapped his hands together, the crack echoing in the courtyard. The platoon of hollow guardsmen reappeared from the shadows. "Gentlemen and ladies," Kothra said, "a pleasant evening to you all."

With that the hollow man turned and strode to an archway at the rear of the courtyard. Abbas Bute followed him.

Brynna sat casually on the arm of the throne and leaned back in a seductive pose. "Tomorrow night we will have a formal banquet in your honor. Tonight, however, our kitchen will prepare whatever you so desire. Do not be shy to ask for whatever you wish,'' she said, and ran her tongue over her lips as she gazed at Trevelyan, who could not bring himself to look away. "*Good ambassadors*, I am at your command. . . .''

CHAPTER SEVENTEEN

Kothra sat alone in his chamber high above the festival hall where the banquet was being prepared for the visiting ambassadors. Abbas Bute had left him and he had been brooding, staring out the window at the city that had welcomed him as their leader and savior. Brynna would be returning shortly, he knew, and they would have a discussion regarding how well his performance had gone. His wife would be pleased; of this he was certain. She would dance for him and they would make love, all the while knowing that their union could never bear them children. Sadness and anger would overtake them both, adding fire to the coupling.

He was uncomfortable with the role that had been thrust upon him. When he had first returned to Rien's shores after an absence of nearly two years, he had been stunned to discover the wealth of changes that had occurred when he was away. The reaction of the people to his sudden appearance had been nothing short of a revelation: they treated him with a reverence he did not believe possible for men and women of the hollow. His coming and the gift he brought had been foretold by the seer, Lady Brynna Celosia. She had told them that they could rebuild the city with the skills they had learned in the outer world. The ruins from the former city and the outlying districts could be salvaged to provide the raw materials. All their efforts would be an homage to their new lord and master—Kothra.

The first man of the hollow did not argue with the will of the people. That first night, Brynna had escorted him to the fortress where he would be made lord and to the chamber they would share. The seduction had been savage, quick, and complete. Brynna offered her magnificent body and her unconditional support. A pressure inside his brain, a trembling vessel of blood that he knew instinctively she could explode at any moment, would not have allowed him to refuse. The threat was unnecessary. Kothra had dreamed of the power she had presented to him; however, he had always believed that he would be granted the thrill of taking it by force, of slowly rallying his people behind him.

"You have so little time," Brynna had told him as they had lain together that first night, bodies entwined. "And so much to accomplish."

The human outcasts had already been driven from Rien. The siege against the newly rebuilt walled city by the wolf pack from Aranhod had been his first true test as a leader and tactician. A dozen men caught outside the walls, tracked down one at a time, had fallen before the creatures. When the wolves massed against Rien, Kothra knew that he had them. Arrows wrapped in swatches of cloth, dipped in liquid fire, had rained down upon the animals. They died in agony. Their pain-wracked howls delighted the hollow man.

Kothra found no shortage of volunteers for the mission to Cynara. Nayati was chosen at random. The young hollow man actually believed that he would be coming back to Rien. The spies he had sent to accompany the assassin had reported back immediately. Kothra was impressed by Nayati's achievement and amazed that a full-scale declaration of war had not been levied against the hollow. He thought of the hatred he had seen on the faces of the ambassadors, particularly the dark-haired young man from Kintaro. His almond-shaped eyes had burned with the need for retribution. The hollow man sensed that the others were holding the Kintaran back and so he had sent Abbas Bute to visit the young man and learn what would trigger his wrath.

Staring into the night sky that had settled upon his city, Kothra felt a momentary weakness. His entire right side became numb, his breath short. Closing his eyes, Kothra forced the inner workings of his body to realign themselves and deal with the threat of decay that wormed through him. As his thick, heavy veins pumped fresh blood through his system, Kothra was assaulted by memories from his past, images of his true parents. A terrible need settled over him: the need for a soul, the desire to live out his days as a man, capable of love, blessed with the gift of leaving the world a son, an heir to the empire he would forge.

In the darkness of his chamber Kothra waited for the moment to pass, suppressing a scream of terror that would have brought the guardsmen from outside his door to help him. But then they would have seen him as less than a god. No, he realized, better that they believe the lies, the myth. Brynna had been correct all along.

The fear left him, but the longing remained.

In the courtyard in the center of the fortress, Shantow Yakima fought a duel with his bodyguard, Akako Michi. Weapons, even those of the Forge, did not come into play, although they had used the power to create a black practice mat beneath them. The older, heavier man crumbled under a series of blows to his face and ribs, falling to the mat with a thud. Shantow stood over the man, his bare chest heaving. They each wore black leggings cut off midway down the thigh. The bodyguard, who was trying to brush the matted hair from his eyes as he struggled to a sitting position, had forged a thick black wrap to cover his ribs, Shantow's favorite target. One of his teeth was loose and he considered the indignity of spitting it out before his student; better to wait until he was alone, he decided.

"You let me win!" Shantow hollered in his native language. "You are not supposed to do that! How will I learn anything from you when all you do is let me win!?"

In truth, Akako hadn't allowed Shantow to win a match in several months. He was pleased to see the amount of skill and control the young ambassador had not only retained but honed despite his overly indulged passions and hatreds. Even the frustration he had felt in believing that Akako was humoring him and throwing their matches had not dulled his edge. The older man looked up as Abbas Bute and two of his men entered the courtyard.

"Shantow, my foster son, we have visitors."

The young Kintaran looked up in anger at the hollow men. The fever for battle was still upon him and he had to turn away quickly, squeezing his eyes shut as he said a prayer for self-control. Remember the old way, he chided himself. Balance. A warrior must not feel too much or too little.

"We were leaving," Shantow said as he opened his eyes and reached out to help his teacher to his feet.

"A pity," Abbas said with genuine regret in his voice. He

spoke Kintaran with ease. "Do you see that window above, on the upper tier?"

Shantow looked in the direction Abbas had pointed, trying not to be impressed with the hollow man's command of his language. In the darkened wings above the courtyard lay a booth with a glass window. "You have been spying on us?"

"You're an artist. We were admiring the display," Abbas said, adding a closemouthed smile. "A few of my men would like to test their skills against you. I explained to them that you are a guest here and said that I would ask if you had any interest in a friendly bout. Have you?"

Visions of hollow men bleeding and writhing at his feet threatened to consume Shantow. "Only a coward sends his men where he himself is maybe not willing to tread."

Abbas smiled. Human responses were so easy to predict. As Kothra had surmised, Shantow harbored an unnatural hatred of their race. The hollow man released the leather straps that secured the wolf skulls to his shoulders and presented them to his men. "As you wish. So long as you can differentiate between harmless sport and a blood duel."

Akako placed his hand on Shantow's back. "Don't do this," he warned.

"You're maybe beginning to sound like an old woman," Shantow said, shrugging off the comforting hand of his body-guard. The hollow men laughed and Shantow smiled with them. "Perhaps this one can offer me a true challenge."

"I have no doubt," the towering giant said politely.

Akako retreated, the image of a pair of crossbows loaded with *menuki* shafts poised at the front of his thoughts, waiting for the summons of the Forge to become real.

"Your rules?" Shantow asked.

"I'd say death, disembowelment, and dismemberment are out of the question. After all, we barely know each other."

"Agreed," Shantow said with a grin. For a moment he had almost forgotten that he was dealing with a man of the hollow. "Until one of us cries 'yield,' then?"

"A wonderful compromise," Abbas said as he raised his hands and wriggled his fingers. "Master Yakima, have at me—"

Shantow struck with incredible speed, carefully avoiding the movements he had used against his teacher. The hollow man reeled from the first blow, a closed-fisted strike at Abbas Bute's liver. Anchoring one leg just behind that of the hollow man, Shantow gripped the man's shoulder and brought his knee into the giant's midsection. Abbas doubled over. The young Kintaran stepped behind him, gripping the hollow man's wrist, and prepared to wrench the soulless man's arm from its socket when Abbas Bute's massive hand closed over Shantow's arm and he suddenly lifted the dark-haired human high into the air, allowing him the indignity of dangling helplessly over his head like a child's toy, before he threw Shantow down to the mat. The ambassador landed in the manner he had been taught, relaxing his body to avoid injury. Before he could twist out of the way, the hollow giant fell upon him. Shantow brought his legs up over his chest, his bare feet absorbing the shock of the incredible weight of the hollow man as they connected with his chest. He tried to straighten his legs and force Abbas from him, but the soulless warrior only smiled.

"You honestly believe you have the strength to move me?"

Shantow wasn't about to talk. The hollow man had made the mistake of not pinning Shantow's arm. The dark-haired Kintaran brought his hands together on either side of the hollow man's head, closing over his ears in a powerful slap. Abbas Bute sprang upward, clutching at his ringing ears, his equilibrium disrupted, and Shantow escaped. He would recover quickly, the young ambassador knew from one of Rolland's brief lectures. He would have to end this quickly, he thought. Then another idea came to him.

Abbas struggled to his feet and Shantow struck him repeatedly in the face and upper body. A wide sweep of the hollow man's thick arm brushed Shantow away as if he were an annoyance. "You fight like a gnat!"

At the edge of the practice mat, Akako watched with concern. His young student was not employing strategy or skill. Shantow was throwing himself at his enemy like an inexperienced child. Akako was saddened to think that all of the training he had given the future emperor was forgotten now that the youth was facing a true enemy.

Abbas Bute had fully recovered from Shantow's attempts to disorient him. From his expression, Shantow judged that the man's festive mood had fled. The hollow man drew his fist back in anger, prepared to deliver a blow that would have caved in several of Shantow's ribs. Then he considered his actions. With a grimace he telegraphed the punch and held back his strength, so that if it connected, the young ambassador would not be seriously injured.

Shantow ducked the blow with ease. "I knew your heart wasn't in this," he said, dangling his arms loosely at his side, making no move to protect himself. The soulless monster took a step forward, then planted his feet, his huge hands closed into fists, one poised to strike. "Come for me. Come for me in earnest," Shantow taunted.

Abbas Bute swallowed. "I'd kill you. Whether I meant to or not. That is not something that could be allowed."

"You maybe want my respect, do you not? Do as I say."

"No," Abbas said, lowering his fist.

The young Kintaran's expression became unreadable. "You've insulted me. You were maybe going to let me win, just to give me a false sense of power over you. That way tomorrow, I would not see the hollow as a true threat. That means that you do not consider me an honest danger," he said, his thick black hair falling over his brow in sweaty tangles as all the muscles in his face tightened and he summoned the Forge. A heavy black stone, a meter across, materialized well over the head of the hollow warrior and dropped upon him, tearing a deep gash in his forehead as it struck him. Abbas collapsed to his knees. Shantow drew back his hand and once again lifted magic from its secret place. Four long daggerlike pieces of steel materialized between his fingers and he threw them toward the face of the hollow man. Abbas raised his arm and hollered as the black metal shards sliced into his arm and were embedded deep into his flesh.

Shantow circled the hollow man. "How do *you* like it?"

One of the two guards who had accompanied Abbas moved forward. Akako called upon the Forge and created the dual crossbows, lifting each in the direction of the guards.

"Stay back!" Abbas screamed as he sprang to his feet and leaped with abandon at his tormentor. Shantow reached out and tapped into the Forge a third and final time, creating a black staff with razor-sharp blades at either end. He gripped the weapon tightly and swung it as he sidestepped the behemoth's advance. Digging the staff into the practice mat, anchoring it so that he caught Abbas Bute in the midsection with the flat of the weapon, Shantow caused the creature to flip over the shaft onto his back. The young Kintaran yanked the weapon from its mooring, spun it with a flourish so that the blade flashed brightly as it caught the torchlight, then raked the blade over Abbas's throat before he could react.

It took Kothra's second in command a moment to realize that his head was still attached to his body.

"That edge was dulled," Shantow explained as he flipped the weapon over, the sharp edge suddenly wedged against the hollow man's throat. "I could still have your head. What do you wish to do?"

Abbas closed his eyes and dropped his head back in shame. "I yield."

Shantow smiled and the weapon faded from existence. He backed away so that the hollow man could rise. The metal shards in his arm disappeared, but the damage they had inflicted remained. The Kintaran forged a black cloth for Abbas to wrap around his wound, stanching the flow of blood.

"In my country, the loser of a bout maybe owes the victor a boon," Shantow said.

Nodding impassively, the hollow man said, "For that and the insult I bore you, you shall have it."

"There were three men of the hollow who attended the Masque of the Dead in Cynara almost a year ago. I have learned their names and I have every reason to believe that they have come to the city."

"What do you want with them?" said Abbas mildly, although he could tell just what the young Kintaran desired.

"The right to deal with them with impunity. At least one of them has committed crimes upon the royal personage of Kintaro. For this I would see them punished," Shantow said.

Abbas agreed to Shantow's terms and took the names of the hollow men who had committed the real or imagined wrong.

"They will be brought to you," Abbas promised. "With the hope that you will not hold the crimes of a chosen few against our entire race. We desire peace between our nations and we will do what is needed to bring that about."

The soulless man and the young Kintaran clasped hands in agreement, unaware that in the darkened theater high above the courtyard, Lady Brynna Celosia sat listening to their every word, shaking her head. Silently she planned her own response to Shantow's request.

Trevelyan swam in and out of awareness, fighting his way through a black haze. He had been immersed in dark dreams orchestrated by an even darker dreamer. Ripping across the normally placid horizon of his dreams were nightmares of the Autumn wolves enthralled by the hollow men, turning on mankind. In his dreams, everyone he had ever known or cared about was dead and he was swimming from the shores of Rien while blazing fires raced across the water, reaching out for him with fiery claws.

Suddenly the room came into sharp focus and Trevelyan sat up, gasping for breath. He was in Ariodne's chamber and it was the middle of the night. The red-haired Maven gripped his hand and helped to calm him. Within moments he was breathing normally again.

"I didn't hear you come in last night," she said softly. "Did your explorations with Chatham prove helpful?"

Trevelyan nodded.

"The nightmares have returned?"

He shuddered, squeezing his eyes shut. Softly he said, "In my dreams you are dead. And the last time I had dreams such as this, they were of Black Mask and the first wolves."

Ariodne drew back.

"Don't leave me," Trevelyan said.

"I won't," she promised and took him in her embrace. He suddenly realized that the robe she wore had been created by her father for Ariodne's mother, it had not been forged. The intricate designs of the embroidery told the story of a soul's passage through the Stream of Life and ascension to the cliffs of Nyssa, where it would either plunge to the Waiting Pool of Souls, merging once more with the multitude in the wells, or take flight and travel to a place of perfect harmony the Mavens called Cyrilla, the end of all journeys. The Mavens had destroyed this natural cycle, and he was the only one who could restore it.

Several hours later, Ariodne woke, her eyes wide with concern, her voice high and muddled like that of a child. "Was I snoring? Was I keeping you awake?"

"The sounds you make are the sweetest music to me."

"Politician," she murmured, then added a desperate, "I love you," before she drifted back to sleep. After a time, Trevelyan sank into a dark, dreamless sleep.

CHAPTER
EIGHTEEN

The next morning, Trevelyan was seated across from Kothra in the open courtyard. A high, regal throne had been salvaged from one of the unused wings of the fortress and brought out for Kothra's visitors. Chatham and Ariodne were at the side of the merchant prince, the first man of the hollow was flanked by Lady Brynna Celosia and Abbas Bute.

"Before this meeting is begun in earnest," Ariodne said, "I have a request from Lord Arayncourt."

Trevelyan twisted uncomfortably in his chair. He had no idea what Ariodne was about to do.

"The four of us should depart and allow our lieges the privacy to talk freely," she said.

"Why doesn't young Arayncourt make this demand himself?" Abbas Bute said. Lady Brynna regarded Ariodne coolly.

"Cynaran custom. If you are offended by the request you may take your retribution on me, not him."

"Have no fear of retaliation," Kothra said. "I am not insulted. You may all leave. Trevelyan?"

The young prince nodded slowly. He had wished for the presence of his friends during the proceeding and would have words with Ariodne after he had left Kothra's presence. But for now he could not contradict her and appear to be weak.

As Ariodne and Chatham neared Kothra's wife, she felt a surge of satisfaction from the white-haired hollow woman's expression of loathing. The Maven had not wanted to allow Celosia the opportunity to shape the thoughts of either man.

Once the first man of the hollow and the Cynaran ambassador were alone, Kothra smiled. His razor-sharp teeth, carved to points and polished like ivory, glinted in the soft light of morning that filtered through from above. "Now that we have the formalities out of the way, we should get to the heart of these discussions. You know what I desire?"

"Nayati performed his duties, yes." Trevelyan could not erase the edge from his voice.

Kothra laughed. "You're not going to give at all. I like that. Do you know why I wish Rien to be recognized by the three powers? Why a trade agreement is necessary?"

Trevelyan was silent. Finally he said, "It was a mystery until last night. You grow what you need for food, you have raw materials from all the outlying districts from which you can build. I went exploring and discovered what your people have called the pleasure pits. What you need is the marmion root and all the other substances you people thrive on in the pit, including the hard-to-find liquors. Even literature is scarce. You don't have poets. You don't have artists or storytellers. What you have is a growing population hungry for stimuli that are not to be found here."

"This is what I like about you, Trevelyan. You have a hunger for knowledge. I appreciate that. As you so eloquently stated, we have hungers, too. But there is more. My Father, the almighty that rules beyond the realm of the Unseen, wishes for us to prove ourselves worthy of souls. For that reason we must become the fourth power of Autumn."

The dark-haired prince nodded. "If we provide what you desire, what do you have to offer in return?"

"Our services," Kothra said.

"As thralls?" Trevelyan was startled.

"As workers, not slaves. You have seen what we were able to create here. There is no end to what we can accomplish in the outer world."

"But the people don't want you in their countries."

"That is unfortunate but true," Kothra said. "Rien could be an asylum for my people, a place where they will not be persecuted and will have the chance to build new lives."

"What you seek is a bribe for your absence."

Kothra shrugged. "You have that option. Bellerophon has welcomed our presence. A goodwill tour has already been planned. Kintaro has maintained that they will provide what we need if we stay away. They understand the repercussions of a lengthy, drawn-out conflict and want no part of it. That leaves only you, Trevelyan Arayncourt. Heir to greatness, as I understand your lineage."

"I have a few questions. What happens when there is no room left in Rien? Will the nation be forced to expand its borders? And if so, will it use liquid fire not only in defense, as you have stated, but as a tool to eventually conquer Aranhod and take control of the world trade network?''

Kothra stared at the young ambassador, his lips pressed together, the blue-black flesh of his lips trembling until he could no longer restrain a tide of giggles. ''Forgive me,'' he said between racking sobs of laughter. Tears were coming to his eyes. ''I have an image in my head of you practicing that speech before a mirror for hours on end.''

His amusement suddenly faded. ''Dealt with many power-mad world conquerors, have you?''

''No,'' Trevelyan said. ''You're my first.''

Kothra's smile returned. ''What exactly do you think my people would do with this world once they had it?''

''I didn't expect you would think that far in advance.''

The blue-black-skinned man leaned forward. Sunlight reflected off the bones sewn into his flesh. ''We live very short lives and we cannot bear children. Death will serve to allay your fears and keep our numbers down.''

''What of the death of the first Maven at the hands of your emissary? The destruction of the Citadel of the Mavens? The Hour of the Red Sky?'' Trevelyan asked. ''This was a serious blow, felt the world over.''

''A regrettable occurrence that is over and done with.''

''Not for those who were left behind, those whose loved ones died for no reason other than your desire to be taken seriously as a threat. Their blood is on your hands.''

Both men were silent for a time.

''You wish me to make some recompense?''

''I do. If peace between our races is what you want, then you must make an offering to prove your sincerity.''

''What do you want? A sacrifice? A thousand of our heads to line the ruins of your lost citadel? How *barbaric*.''

Trevelyan finally smiled. ''Give me the secret of liquid fire and I will see that it is shared with the world.''

''We would be defenseless,'' Kothra said. ''Our knowledge is the only thing that will keep your nations from taking us as slaves. You have the advantage of numbers.''

''Your people could *never* be made docile. Give to me the secret of liquid fire and all you ask for will be awarded you. My position is very clear on this point.''

''Mine as well,'' Kothra said quietly.

Trevelyan scratched his newly bearded chin. "You may not possess liquid fire at all. And if you do, you may not have the means to mass-produce it."

"A demonstration will be arranged."

The young prince sighed and opened his hands. "Kothra, eventually another will make the discovery. Then you will have nothing of value to offer and your nation will be overrun by those seeking vengeance for your actions. If we come to an understanding now, all thoughts of war will be put aside and Rien will be protected by Cynara of Aranhod."

"Perhaps you are not aware that I have already met with the ambassadors of Bellerophon and Kintaro."

"With disastrous results, I would imagine." He pictured Shantow trying to restrain himself in Kothra's presence.

"Both meetings went quite well," Kothra said, "surprisingly enough. Both men accept that Nayati acted far beyond his authority."

Trevelyan wondered if he was still dreaming. "What of those he killed? The destruction of the Citadel of the Mavens? The murder of one of the first Mavens?"

The hollow man shrugged. "My emissary was supposed to enter the citadel by stealth, not by murder, then call for you. Your friends have accepted this explanation and are now working out agreements with me."

"Insanity," Trevelyan said. "Even if this is true, they are only two men, each with millions who will brand them traitors and cowards for their decision to comply with your wishes."

The young prince rose and stood before Kothra. "I convey the will of my people. And of the Autumn wolves."

The hollow man raised a single eyebrow at this. "Then tell me why the wolves are camped outside our walls, frightened to come in despite our invitation."

"You're a wolf killer. They could not control themselves if they were in your presence."

Although Kothra's face was impassive, his hand closed over the arm of his marble throne, squeezing tight enough to cause a hairline fracture to appear in the stone.

"They'll walk through fire if they must to deliver this justice of the Unseen."

"We are not bound by your laws," Kothra said. "We serve a higher power."

"So you say. Kothra of Rien, you know my terms. I will need a decision by this time tomorrow."

The young prince turned and walked toward the door where Abbas Bute had led the others.

"Arayncourt!" Kothra bellowed.

Trevelyan stopped but did not turn.

"Don't forget the banquet tonight," Kothra said evenly.

"Lord Kothra," Trevelyan said politely. Then he left the courtyard.

Long moments passed as Kothra sat alone, carefully weighing Trevelyan's comments. Then Lady Brynna Celosia entered the courtyard, demanding to know all that had transpired. He was already beginning to feel odd and detached, his body demanding to be released to the inevitable onslaught of decay and death. Brynna sensed this and added her strength to his. In seconds the moment had passed and Kothra told her what had happened.

"It was the prince's little whore, that bitch Ariodne," Brynna said in anger. "She knew what we had planned. A few gentle pushes and Trevelyan would have agreed to our terms without hesitation. Nor would he have felt the compulsion that Yakima struggled against. Arayncourt wants peace. He actually believes it is possible."

"It *is* possible," Kothra said dully. "What he said made sense. A war would serve no one."

Brynna closed her eyes and wrapped her arms around the back of Kothra's head, pressing his face to her breasts. There was one who not only desired war, but needed it if its freedom was to be attained. She concentrated and allowed the presence of her god to wash over her, fill her with its spirit, offer its commands to her.

All she had told Kothra was a lie. There was no deity whose power could rival that of the Unseen. Not yet, anyway.

Her master was older than the race of man. Sleeping and entombed, waiting to harness the power that a war between the races would bring. Waiting to be freed from its slumber.

The Mavens had broken through the walls of the Unseen's kingdom when they shattered the first Well of Souls and took its power. The Unseen's cry of rage at the violation had been loud enough to reach the senses of one of the four sleeping gods who had been entombed by the first wolves. From that god came the force that empowered the soulless to live and breathe, although they had no right to do so. From its many aspects and dreams came each of their personalities.

They were all the sons and daughters of the slowly waking god. Kothra had been the firstborn son; that had not been a lie. Lady Brynna Celosia had been its first daughter. Their union would someday give to their god what it most desired: freedom and the power to take vengeance on the wolves and the Unseen. Brynna leaned down and kissed the hair of her lover.

He shuddered at the inner torments of his decaying body, his death slowed once more, delayed as it had always been.

"It will be over soon," she whispered, but it was a lie. The pain and suffering had only just begun.

CHAPTER NINETEEN

The festival hall was filled with activity when Trevelyan, Ariodne, Chatham, and Rolland Storr arrived. The room was modestly appointed and could not compare with the grandeur of the smallest dining room in Arayncourt Hall, but it was an improvement over the drab surroundings that marred the rest of the fortress. Great stone pillars encompassed the vast room, leading upward to wide arches that were topped off by the flat horizon of the first floor. A second tier of matching archways flickered with orange light. The ceiling was concave. Hundreds of tall metal candlesticks lined the room in carefully set patterns, creating pathways and islands through the hall with their bright glowing light. The main table was set with gold chalices, silver plates, and silk napkins. Bread, wine, and cheese were carefully laid out. More than a dozen hollow men and women were present, dressed in gold lamé tunics or wraps, many standing beneath the archways, waiting to be of service, others performing last-minute checks on the arrangements. The smells of succulent meats drifted from the darkened alcoves behind the archways along with the crackling of cooking fires.

The young prince and his companions were led through the labyrinth of candles to the wide table where they learned that they were the first to arrive. He found it difficult to reconcile the sedate, dispassionate hollow servants with the out-of-control, sweating, and mad participants he had encountered in the pits. Over the course of the day he had told Ariodne all that he had witnessed in the chambers below the fortress.

Later, Trevelyan had attempted to gain an audience with Shantow and Lon Freyr, but they refused to see him, preferring the solitude of their quarters. Chatham and Rolland had spent several hours together exchanging war stories while Trevelyan and Ariodne enjoyed a few quiet moments alone, taking advantage of the lull in activities.

Seated in the festival hall, Rolland leaned back in his seat to avoid the heavy frame of the grey-bearded warrior. "Young lord, you must tell me where you found this one. He's a walking encyclopedia of battles. From the way he describes these century-old conflicts, you'd think he'd been there!"

"I keep telling you, I was!" Chatham said in his guttural voice. He grunted and tasted the wine that had been provided. He found it strange that after a few tankards of spiced ale earlier in the day he seemed to be on the way to becoming drunk, although for the past two hundred years liquors had not affected him.

"Yes," Rolland said jovially as he looked at Chatham, "one hundred and ninety years ago you fought for southern Aranhod in their war against Labrys."

"And I was forced to marry an Espiritu princess," Chatham said. "Let's not forget that!"

"What happened to her?" Ariodne asked.

The old warrior's shoulders sagged and the joy drained from him. "She became old and died. I went on unchanged."

Rolland slapped his back and laughed. "And took a dozen more wives, I imagine."

Chatham grunted as he ran his hand over his scar. "No. There are not a dozen women in the world who would take an outcast for a husband. Manon was unique."

"I thought you said she was forced into the union," Ariodne said playfully.

"Oh, no," he said. "I was the one at swordpoint—at her request. She found me irresistible for some reason."

"An unfathomable mystery," Ariodne said. "A princess can have anyone she desires."

"Manon was young," Chatham said. "Very young."

"Like Ruzena," the Maven countered.

The grey-bearded man was silent.

"Wait now," Trevelyan said. "You married into royalty?"

"Only once," Chatham said. "Our kingdom was small and plagued with conflicts. One of her father's enemies seized control, slaughtered her family. I escaped with her to the hill country, where we lived in peace for thirty years, until her death. When we needed money I sold my arm and my reputation in dealing with local battles. It got to the point where I would ride with a company to a castle to lay siege and the ruler would negotiate a price greater than what we had already been paid so that we would leave him alone and go back and attack his enemy, the one who hired us in the first place. Then we'd go back and negotiate with the first party for even more money not to destroy their palace, then back to his enemy, back to the first one—in just five years we cleaned out both their treasuries!"

"And I thought I invented that pastime," Rolland said with an appreciative laugh.

Chatham shrugged. "But I doubt that my claim to the title would be taken seriously now."

A weighty sigh escaped Rolland Storr as he said, "We could be laughing and dining with these monsters one moment, fighting for our lives the next. I do not trust them."

"Nonsense," a voice interrupted. Trevelyan looked up to see Lon Freyr and Zared Anstice arrive at the table, taking their places on the bench across from Trevelyan and his friends. "The hollow have been most generous with their hospitality. They have provided shelter, food, and drink—"

"And an invasion force armed with liquid fire to help you take the throne of Searle Orrick," Trevelyan said flatly.

The red-haired lieutenant flinched. "Kothra told you."

"He mentioned a goodwill tour. The rest was obvious."

No one spoke. The tension between the two leaders was palpable. Lon Freyr's cold and merciless eyes narrowed as he asked, "What do you plan to do?"

Trevelyan raised his gold chalice. "For tonight, Cynara is neutral. In the morning I expect an answer from the lord of the soulless to my terms for peace. I will deal with you in accordance to how I must deal with him. I would wager, however, that your crew has no idea of what you plan. If I were you, I'd be afraid to tell them. At least until the hollow were on board, prepared to press them into service."

"Searle Orrick will drive our nation into bankruptcy and ruin," Freyr growled.

"I know," Trevelyan said as he smiled and leaned forward. "I'm the one who holds the note, remember?"

Freyr's chest heaved in barely restrained anger.

"I'm a reasonable man, open to reasonable solutions for bailing your country out of the hole Searle Orrick has kicked it into. The Unseen knows, my father approached him with solutions for years and met with nothing but rejection of his proposals." Trevelyan took a sip of wine and savored it for a moment. "If you succeed," he said, "if you *somehow* succeed in your plan to depose Searle Orrick, I will be the second man that you must deal with. If you *dare* come at me with a force of arms, I will drive you back into the fiery realm of Candlesar whether your allies are the hollow with their liquid fire or even the gods themselves, and your widow will grow old, weeping for your loss. Am I understood?"

"Perfectly," Freyr said, his voice betraying no emotion.

"Good," Trevelyan answered. "I've always preferred a civil conversation to the cacophony of discussion with steel. But in our business, both have their place."

The red-haired lieutenant nodded.

Shantow and Akako arrived, the grinning young Kintaran and his bodyguard sitting in the two vacant seats beside the men from Bellerophon. "Trevelyan, you look so serious. Have you maybe been touting your own importance again?"

"Merely engaging in speculation," the young prince said.

"Well, don't try any of that on me," Shantow said with a wink. "I would expect that you are maybe *pissed* over my decision to recommend a peaceful settlement with the hollow. But remember, my country values privacy and isolation. If there is a way to secure that without bloodshed—such as sending the heir to the throne off to a heathen land such as Cynara to become friends with its people and its young merchant prince—we are not above it. Proceed with these monsters as your conscience tells you, I will do the same."

Kothra and his entourage arrived and took their seats at the head of the table. The first man of the hollow seemed dazed and confused, hardly the charismatic leader he had presented himself as earlier in the day.

"I trust we haven't kept you waiting too long?" Brynna said, carefully avoiding Ariodne's gaze.

"Not at all," Trevelyan said, speaking for the entire party. "Besides, the time was put to good use."

Abbas Bute and Shantow exchanged looks. The hollow second in command smiled and nodded slightly, then looked away. Lady Brynna Celosia raised her hands to signal the servers to begin. The meats that had been sizzling above grills hidden within the shadowed archways were placed on large metal trays, sliced and garnished.

Within moments the servers were swarming around the table, offering their various dishes to the ambassadors. Conversation was brief and Kothra managed a few pleasant words in response to the compliments over the meal.

"Generally we do not feast on meat," Brynna explained, "but we were willing to sacrifice a few of our dumb animals for your pleasure. The islands of flame, the candles you see before you, were Kothra's idea."

"Yes," the first man of the hollow said as he rose from his stupor, his eyes suddenly focusing, his body uncoiling like that of a serpent raising its hood before a strike. "From your poem, Trevelyan."

The young prince had completely forgotten. In one of his earliest works he had told the story of a lowly candlestick maker's attempts to romance a wealthy lady of society. The islands of candles had led to the bed where he at last made love to her.

It will take more than this to seduce me into giving you my allegiance, he thought, the words of the first wolves returning to him as they had many times since their arrival in Rien. He could not yet be sure that Kothra was the enemy he had to slay, the one that harbored the lotus within his heart. Perhaps in the morning, when he received Kothra's answer to his demands, he would know.

"I'm flattered that you know my work," Trevelyan said. All those who died in the citadel and during the Hour of the Red Sky know yours.

The meal proceeded with pleasant talk of other lands and cultures that riveted Kothra. The food was tasty and well prepared. Brynna explained that their chef had spent time working for humans in southern Aranhod. Near the end of the feast three hollow men arrived, each carrying a large silver-covered dish. Shantow stared at the three men as they walked around the table and stopped just behind him. His pleasant mood faded as he examined their faces for the slightest trace of guilt or fear. To his surprise, not one of the soulless giants registered either.

They don't know why they're here, Shantow realized. They haven't yet been formally accused.

Lady Brynna Celosia rose and called for the attention of her guests. Conversation was immediately stilled and she turned to the young Kintaran ambassador. "Shantow Yakima, we have prepared a special dish for you, one best served cold."

Akako glanced at Shantow, who nodded in response. The thick-bodied older Kintaran stepped back from the table and drew his sword. Abbas Brute sprang to his feet as Brynna laughed and cried, "I give you vengeance!"

By her signal, all three hollow men removed the silver lids from their plates, revealing the severed heads of three soulless men on the serving trays. Each man seemed to have been caught by surprise, their red eyes with black slits wide and staring, jaws open in horror. Trevelyan and Ariodne registered protests as the servers placed the dishes on the table before Shantow, who stared at them in disbelief.

Brynna said, "May I represent to you Elsu, Caldaur, and Mauli. They are the hollow men who were present at the Masque of the Dead in Cynara last year."

Looking away from the staring, severed heads, Shantow glared at Abbas Bute. From his expression, Shantow knew that the hollow second in command was as surprised by this turn of events as he had been. "You don't understand," Shantow said. "I needed to question them, to witness their confession."

"Ah, but they would have lied, they would have said anything to save their worthless necks," Brynna said. "As you can see, that is no longer a consideration."

Stepping away from the table, Shantow pointed at the heads on the table. "Take this offering away and with it maybe my only hope of restoring the honor of my family."

The hollow men covered the heads and removed them from the table. Shantow turned to Kothra. There was no guilt, surprise, or repentance in his expression. "This is how you hold to your promises?"

"It would appear so," Kothra said.

Moving past Lon Freyr and Zared Anstice, who watched the proceedings in stunned silence, Shantow pushed Brynna out of his way and leaned down to spit in Kothra's wineglass. The first man of the hollow laughed as Shantow and Akako walked toward the path created by the rows of candles. "You must stay. There is another surprise and you must see it."

The Kintarans did not stop.

"Shantow!" Trevelyan called. His friend glanced up at the ceiling, then turned to face him. The young prince did not even attempt to mask the suspicion in his voice as he wiped his fingers in the silk napkin, then dropped it to the table. "The feast is over. We should stay together."

There was no mistaking the command for a request. "As you say," Shantow replied.

Trevelyan turned to Lon Freyr. "Are you with me?"

"I go where the party is," the red-haired lieutenant said smugly. He was still angry over their earlier exchange.

"Lord Kothra, what is it you wish to show us?"

"A demonstration that you requested," Kothra said as he stood away from the table and gestured for his servants to attend to the remains of their banquet. "Follow me, please."

The first man of the hollow led the party through one of the darkened alcoves to a winding staircase that he took three steps at a time. Lady Brynna Celosia held one of the candlesticks before her as she and Abbas Bute followed their liege at a more leisurely pace, Trevelyan and his companions close behind the blue-black-skinned giants. Abbas occasionally looked over his shoulder to Shantow; the hulking second in command appeared completely mystified.

After climbing four flights, they were taken to Kothra's private chamber, a large room decorated solely with a handful of mementos from the mercenary's campaigns. Kothra stood at the wide-open window with his back turned to the door, a sword he had pried from the stiffening fingers of a dead enemy clutched in his hand. A trio of two-meter-long metal spikes tipped with razor-sharp blades hung from a wooden rack beside the stone slab he used for a bed.

"Trevelyan Arayncourt," Kothra said with a trace of his former lethargy, "come see what your desires have caused. Bring the other ambassadors."

The young prince stepped to the window, Shantow and Lon Freyr falling in beside him. Lady Brynna Celosia handed the candle to her husband, crossed her arms over her heavy breasts, and blended into the shadows at the far corner of the room. Mystified, Abbas Bute anxiously joined the others.

Rien stretched beneath them with hundreds of dimly lit buildings leading to the city walls and the watchfires in the towers. The hills they had crossed to arrive at the city of the hollow were tinged with moonlight and the ivory forest glowed eerily in the far distance. "I don't understand," Trevelyan said. "There's nothing to see."

Kothra set his sword on the floor and ran his heavy hand over the dust-covered stone of the windowsill. Suddenly he threw a handful of dust into the air and shoved the lit candle forward. An explosion of crackling, blinding light caused the watchers to draw back from the window.

"Bastard!" Trevelyan shouted, covering his eyes.

"Don't be alarmed. A simple magician's trick," Kothra said as the ambassadors took their hands from their faces. "A harmless chemical reaction the wizard priests of Chiabos shared with me before they gave me the secret of liquid fire. But in answer to your statement, I am a bastard. The bastard son of a god whose power dwarfs that of the Unseen."

Trevelyan saw pinwheels and tiny stars of green and red light imprinted on his slowly clearing vision. Kothra had retrieved his sword and was using it as a pointer, aiming it beyond the twisted hills, to the forest. A flash of light was returned from the distance, a brief shower of white flame that momentarily lit a stretch of the skeletal trees.

"This is what you wished to show us?" Shantow said.

"Of course not," Kothra replied. "This was merely an after-dinner amusement. The true spectacle is about to begin. Look there."

Trevelyan's gaze followed the path indicated by Kothra's sword. A sharp luminescence sprang up at the base of the white forest, steadily growing brighter and more intense.

"You've set the woods on fire," Chatham said, confused.

"But they were stone," Lon Freyr countered.

"Look closer and think," Kothra snarled. "What lies beyond the forest?"

Bright yellow and blue flames exploded beyond the woods, the intense light casting the trees in silhouette.

"The waters off your coastline," Trevelyan said slowly. "You used liquid fire to turn them into an inferno!"

"So I have," Kothra said.

Lon Freyr trembled in rage as he said, "But we had ships out there with hundreds of men on them."

"You still have them if they are quick enough to outrace the flames." The hollow man frowned. "Of course, they do seem to be spreading rather quickly. I suppose now it's in the hands of your god." Kothra grinned at Trevelyan and pulled back his lips to show his razor-sharp teeth. "Perhaps the Unseen will take this opportunity to show you the amount of interest the deity has in man's affairs."

"All your talk of peace," Trevelyan said bitterly.

Was real, Kothra thought, then he felt the crushing weight of Brynna's desires as she cut through his consciousness with a psychic blade and forced her will upon him. Let them leave, she urged, but let them carry a message of blood and terror back to their countries.

No, Kothra thought. We will all be destroyed in a war.

Kill the Maven. Kill her slowly and make her lover watch as she pleads for mercy. Take her and allow—

A shrill scream erupted from the corner of the room and the voice in Kothra's head suddenly vanished. He picked up the candlestick and aimed its light in the direction of the scream. Lady Brynna Celosia was lying in an ever-expanding pool of her own blood, her eyes shut, her lips slightly parted. Ariodne stood over her, one of the two-meter-long metal spikes from the wall gripped in her hands. The arrow point of the weapon was still buried in the beautiful, white-haired soulless woman's ribs.

"Ariodne," Trevelyan cried hoarsely, Kothra standing beside him in shock.

"She was controlling him," the red-haired Maven said as she set the weapon down and approached her lover and the leader of the hollow men. "Against his will, she was ordering him to rape and murder me. I had to defend myself."

Ariodne, Kothra, and Trevelyan stood before the open window, the flickering light of the burning sea in the distance casting highlights upon their faces.

"I would have defended you," Kothra said as he attempted not to look at the body of his wife. His voice was choked with emotion. "I have forced her down many times before."

"Not this time," Ariodne said in measured tones. "I felt her power. No man could have resisted. She wanted to start a war between our races."

"Where she would have failed, you have succeeded. Your kind will fall before me. Your deaths will be sweet. Then we will take what we desire, starting with your beloved Cynara."

Kothra shuddered. "You say that no man could have resisted her. But as you might have already realized, Maven Ariodne Gairloch, I am *not* a man." The slits of his eyes narrowed as his muscular frame tightened, his hands closing into fists. "I am the son of a god!"

With a backhanded slap across her face that echoed through the room, Kothra swept Ariodne toward the window, where she stumbled against the sill, reaching out desperately for the wall, her fingers missing it by inches as she fell through the wide opening and plummeted through the air to the ground five stories below.

Trevelyan did not allow himself the luxury of panic. He visualized a heavy rope tied around Ariodne's wrist with a grappling hook on the other end and called upon the Forge. The black hook appeared, digging into the heavy stone below the window ledge as the rope suddenly tightened. He heard a second sharp crack and a heavy thud from two stories below as his lover's body struck the side of the fortress and dangled there. He could not tell if she was dead or alive.

From the corner of the room, Lady Brynna Celosia moaned and Kothra barrelled through the humans to kneel at her side.

Lon Freyr saw his plans crumbling. "Kothra, we made an agreement. Vengeance on Searle Orrick. Endless supplies of all you desire. Don't you remember?"

"I let you live once, point man," Kothra said as he snapped the shaft protruding from his wife's body just below the wound. "Do not expect the same mercy twice. All of you will die. All of mankind will die, leaving only us."

At the window, Trevelyan, Chatham, and Rolland worked together to haul Ariodne up to the room before the quickly forged rope vanished. They briefly discussed escaping through the window, forging ropes and climbing down over the side, but a company of hollow men was gathering below in the street. Shantow and Akako stood before Abbas Bute, blocking him from leaving the room and sounding an alarm.

"A harness wrapped around her waist would have been a more humane means of rescue." Rolland Storr grunted as Ariodne's lolling head came into view just below the window. Chatham gripped her arm as the rope Trevelyan had forged disappeared. He lifted her the rest of the way through the window and gently cradled her in his arms as Trevelyan anxiously leaned close to feel her breath upon his cheek.

"He's right," Chatham said. "She won't be using this arm for much in quite some time."

"At least she's alive," Trevelyan said as he glanced to Kothra. The first man of the hollow was muttering a litany of incoherent threats as he rocked his wife in his arms. He looked to the doorway and saw the standoff between Shantow and Abbas Bute.

The hollow man wearing a wolf's skull on either shoulder looked to his lord, then squeezed his eyes shut. "I'll take you out of here. Trust me, it's the only way. If you try to fight your way out of this place you'll never make it."

Trevelyan addressed Shantow, who obviously had some private dealing with Abbas. "Do you believe him?"

"As if we maybe have a choice?" Shantow said, his almond-shaped eyes widening in the near darkness.

Trevelyan took one last look out the window at the fiery waters on the horizon, then ordered the company to follow Abbas Bute from Kothra's chamber.

CHAPTER TWENTY

The Kothrite was as good as his word. Abbas Bute led the small party of humans through the hollow city, his presence assuring their safe conduct. They were within two hundred meters of the main gate when a group of soulless warriors approached. The leader called out to Abbas and requested an audience before he went any farther.

Abbas yelled for the gates to be opened, then turned to Trevelyan. "I'll keep them back as best I can. Walk with a purpose. You won't be safe until you top the rise and get with your men. Even then I'd suggest a fast retreat. Kothra's moods are unpredictable. His strength is in this fortress city, but in his grief, and without Lady Brynna advising him, there's no way of predicting what he will do."

"Our men will have seen the fires on the waters by now," Trevelyan said. "They're going to be hungry for vengeance."

"All they'll find is the stale taste of death if they try to fight us," Abbas said. "Go in peace."

Before Trevelyan could thank the blue-black-skinned giant, Abbas Bute turned and walked toward the delegation of soldiers. Shantow chased after him and placed his hand on the soulless man's shoulder. "You act with honor. Your leader could maybe learn something from you."

"Perhaps," Abbas said as he gently squeezed the Kintaran's upper arm. "But I doubt he'd sit still for the lesson. Lord Yakima, I pray you find the honor you seek."

Shantow stiffened. "That is maybe lost for all time."

"Maybe," Abbas called out as he retreated from the group, "and maybe not!"

The young Kintaran ambassador looked to his party and saw that they were another ten meters closer to the high gates. "Come on," Trevelyan was calling, and Shantow hurried to rejoin the group.

They proceeded at a quick but measured pace. Chatham was carrying the unconscious Ariodne. Trevelyan glanced at his lover anxiously, his gaze fixing on the jagged scar at the top of her head, her bright red hair stained a darker shade of crimson near the wound she had received when her body had struck the wall. Rolland, Akako, Lon Freyr, and Zared Anstice walked with their hands open at their sides, images of various weapons at the forefront of their minds. With a thought each could arm themselves with the Forge.

The guardsmen at the gate seemed confused at the sight of the entire human delegation leaving at once and without an escort, but they said nothing; Abbas Bute's orders were not to be questioned. Behind the party, the hollow man who had given them passage was now engaged in what appeared to be an argument with a pack of roving soldiers whose job it was to patrol the city and ensure that its perimeters were safe. The task was actually a punishment for the unruly along with a fortnight of refused access to the pits.

Trevelyan and his party were within one hundred meters of the gates when an alarm rang out from Kothra's fortress. The young prince cursed as he saw the gatesmen react according to their training, closing the gates and sealing the city at the first sign of trouble. The wrought-iron gates swung shut and a dozen hollow men used their inhuman strength to shove a pair of massive stones over the entrance from within. Each stone was cut in the shape of the arched doorway, but together they were just oversized enough that the process of forcing them into place caused their edges to grind smooth, creating a seal that could only be broken when the stones were destroyed.

The city had become an impregnable fortress from without, an inescapable prison from within. The members of the human delegation looked at one another.

"Do you wish to surrender to them?" Chatham said with a good cheer that Trevelyan had come to dread from the man. Surrender was not an option. The merchant prince was certain that in Kothra's present state, the first man of the hollow was looking for enemies to kill, not hostages to ransom. They stood at the end of a wide street in full view of the guards in the towers above. Behind them, Abbas was leading the pack of soulless men back down the boulevard in the direction of Kothra's fortress.

"I don't think we can expect mercy," Trevelyan said.

"Then might I suggest we find a warren where the hollow won't think to look for us?"

"Is there such a place?" Trevelyan muttered, looking around at the long street that paralleled the high outer wall of the city. Every building looked the same. The streets were unnamed, the businesses carried no markings. Although the hollow longed for the means to express their individual natures, their city was organized in a way that squelched their personal freedoms in the name of the common good. Kothra wanted his subjects working together, not competing against one another.

"The hell with it," Trevelyan said, looking back to the main gates. "We'll go over the wall."

"You're mad," Lon Freyr said.

"You can stay here with your new allies if you choose," Trevelyan said. "I'll take my chances there." He turned. Akako and Rolland Storr were staring at the dark stone of the fortress, attempting to guess Trevelyan's plan. Shantow and Chatham grinned at each other. "Rolland, have you ever forged a siege tower?"

"With a small army of casters," the soldier said, laughing. He stared into Trevelyan's face and suddenly realized that the young prince was serious. "*That's* your plan? I thought you were going to suggest that we cast grappling hooks and scale the wall."

"They'd cut us down when we were halfway up," Trevelyan said flatly.

"I didn't say it would work, I just thought that's what you were going to say." He shook his head. "A tower *inside* a fortress."

"We don't have time for a discussion. Can it be done with the five of us?"

"Four of us," Chatham interrupted. "I'm an outcast. The power of the Forge has never been for me."

Rolland crossed his arms and shot a look at Lon Freyer. "What about the lieutenant?"

A series of alarms echoed from all parts of the city. The streets filled with hollow men who raced toward the center of Rien, where Kothra's fortress lay. They had been under orders to ignore the humans and they barely noticed Trevelyan and his companions. The former point man blanched at the sheer numbers of soulless warriors that flooded the street. Kothra had admitted that he did not have a precise count of how many hollow men and women had come to Rien but he had guessed there were several thousand. Freyr would not have been surprised if there were at least that number crowding the central boulevard, racing to answer the call of their resident god.

The red-haired ambassador grasped Trevelyan's arm. "If we have to die, it's best we do it with style. I'll be damned if I'll hide like an animal while they pick this city apart looking for us."

"Rolland?" Trevelyan said urgently.

He nodded at the unconscious Maven. "I'd prefer we had her working with us, but yes. There's no saying the blasted thing will stay in existence long enough for us to get to the top, but I agree with Lon on this one."

"Then describe your tower."

"I will," Rolland said, then muttered, "Thank the Unseen these monsters don't believe in crossbows."

"And, Lieutenant Freyr, try not to be such a fatalist," Trevelyan said as he felt the old familiar tremors of fear.

Freyr smiled weakly, visions of the mouth of spitting flames that Kothra had created at Telluryde slicing through his thoughts. He thought of his wife and son, then cleared his mind and prepared to receive the image of the tower.

"It should be a simple affair," Rolland began, "four landings, corresponding with the height of the fortress walls, four square meters at base and head. The stairs will be steep, a standard zigzag. Forget windows. Best we see what's waiting for us when we arrive. Surround the top with pikes. They can be willed away when we get up there and they may deter our enemy from leaping on while we're climbing up. Set the thing directly between the guard posts at either side of the gate. That's it. Oh, and a door at the base and at the roof, of course.''

Trevelyan grinned. Even Rolland was nervous. That made him feel a little better.

There were murmurs of agreement and the men locked hands as Chatham backed away, keeping watch in case the tide of soulless men surging toward Kothra's fortress suddenly turned and came back for them.

Trevelyan silently begged his father's forgiveness, then gave the order for the casters to begin. The young prince suddenly felt as if his own soul was being torn from him as he heard the familiar screams and the harsh, final breath of the souls they had destroyed. He imagined names and faces, men and women laughing, fighting, making love, and dying. Because of him, they would never have that opportunity again.

The young prince opened his eyes and saw the black tower its pinnacles reflecting the moonlight. Chatham was at his side, Ariodne carefully placed over his shoulder. A deep, ragged snore was coming from her slightly parted lips. The sound filled the young prince with relief. Then he looked up and saw the reactions of the hollow men above on the fortress walls. They were signaling for their comrades at the other towers to come their way. There would be at least ten, Trevelyan guessed. Possibly more. Until now they had not faced more than a few at one time.

"Move!" Trevelyan shouted to his dazed companions. "A delay will cost us our lives."

The company ran to the tower. Trevelyan entered first through a narrow doorway at its base. Chatham, still hauling Ariodne, was directly behind him. The prince shouted for the last man through the door to forge it sealed.

"Remember, Trevelyan, there's only one way to win this thing," Chatham said. "And there are no rules to this tournament."

"Has there ever been with these bastards?" Trevelyan asked as he turned and led the charge up the rickety steps of the newly forged siege tower.

The young prince made it to the second landing when he felt the tower shudder as if a boulder had been thrown against it. Then he heard a shriek. One of the hollow men had been impaled on the spikes at the head of the tower. The creature was screaming in agony and frustration and the black siege tower shook under its struggling. Trevelyan drew his *kris* and in moments he was climbing the final stairs, plunging ahead without regard for whatever challengers might be waiting on the moonlit roof of the tower.

His face was covered in cold sweat, his hands were numb, and his heart thundered painfully as he burst onto the roof and saw the hollow man who had been impaled on the spikes. The soulless man was dead. Two others stood on the stone ridge of the fortress walls, the sweat on their blue-black skin glistening in the moonlight. When they saw Trevelyan, one braced himself as if he were about to leap over the meter-and-a-half-wide chasm separating them, but the other stopped him. There was no sense risking the spikes, the humans would come to them soon enough.

Chatham and the others massed behind Trevelyan as the entire tower lurched backward. Trevelyan grasped one of the spikes and looked down to see three hollow men attempting to pitch the tower over. The tower leaned back and Trevelyan ordered his men to throw themselves on the opposite side of the roof. Their combined weight righted the tower, then sent it crashing toward the fortress wall.

"Rolland, release the spikes," Trevelyan hollered. Suddenly his handhold vanished. Trevelyan rose to his feet and leaped seconds before the tower struck, his feet striking the heavy stone ledge of the fortress wall. He was almost a meter above the pair of hollow men who had patiently waited for their victims to arrive. Without slowing, Trevelyan leaped off the ledge, onto the two-meter-wide walkway, the sharp blade of his sword biting through the throat of the closest soulless guard. A geyser of blood flew up toward the bloated full moon as the man stumbled back, clutching at his throat. Trevelyan spun to face the second warrior and was struck in the right shoulder by a terrific force that knocked him from his feet and caused his right arm to go numb. His head struck the stone floor of the walkway as the hollow man who hit the young prince reached down for Trevelyan's sword.

The reaction of the young merchant prince was swift and brutal. He called upon the Forge, heard a sharp scream in his ear, a cool breath at the back of his neck. Suddenly a thick, black, gelatinous mud covered the hollow warrior's face and hardened in contact with the open air. The gatesman clawed at his face, his eyes, nose, and mouth completely sealed, his chest heaving as he struggled for breath, the mask on his face slowly asphyxiating him. He cupped his hands together and brought them crashing down as Trevelyan rolled out of the way and snatched his *kris* with his left hand. Feeling was returning to his right arm.

Trevelyan stood over the man and brought his sword down for a killing strike, the blade cutting halfway into the monster's neck with a sound similar to an axe chopping into a tree. The hollow man shook as if he were having a seizure and Trevelyan found that his blade was stuck between the creature's vertebrae. Placing his boot on the monster's back, Trevelyan wrenched the blade free and turned in time to see his companions climbing over the ledge. Sliding his gore-drenched *kris* back in its scabbard, Trevelyan went to the ledge and helped Chatham haul Ariodne over the grey stone rise to safety. At least three more hollow guardsmen were approaching from either side of the walk.

The black tower was slipping beneath the company. On the ground, the hastily erected building's front end had dug into the ground and the soulless men were trying to shove it forward, away from the wall. The top end was slowly creeping downward, scraping against the wall as the remaining humans scrambled over the ledge, onto the walk where Trevelyan and Chatham waited.

Trevelyan barked out commands to Shantow and Akako, positioning one at either side of the party, each armed with newly forged crossbows loaded with *menuki* shafts. As the hollow men approached, the Kintarans fired on them. The shafts pierced their chests, the razor-sharp, wire-thin wings opening to slice their flesh from the inside. Shantow and Akako forged new shafts every time they fired, maintaining a steady barrage that slowed but did not stop the approach of the hollow men. One of the guardsmen who had been struck dug his hand into the stone wall, bringing out a large, heavy stone, which he threw at Shantow. The young Kintaran was struck on the side of the face with the rock, his head snapping back as a thin stream of blood splattered the wall beside him and he sunk down to a crouch, raising his bow unsteadily to fire yet another shaft. Guided by luck or the Kintaran's rage, the shaft entered the hollow man's open, screaming mouth with a soft, liquid thud, its wings flying open to cut through and shatter the lower half of his face. The guardsman fell to his knees, clutching at his lower jaw that hung to his chest by a thin flap of red, bleeding meat.

Rolland Storr and the ambassadors from Bellerophon followed Trevelyan's lead, forging plasterlike mud that covered the heads of their prey, suffocating them.

"Trevelyan, have you thought of how we're getting down from here?" Chatham said, joining the young prince at the opposite ledge of the guard wall.

"Scale down," Trevelyan said. "There's no other way. Even if we could forge something soft enough for us to land upon there on the ground, the fall is too great."

"And what's to stop these men from cutting the ropes as soon as we're over the side?"

"Nothing," Trevelyan said. "At least two of us will have to stay behind to hold them off."

Chatham nodded. "Then I'll be one of them."

"Don't be an idiot. I need you alive."

"You forget, I can't be killed. The wolves made me immortal. Even if they hack me to pieces and throw me on a fire I'll come back to haunt them. I'll be here when you storm the city, working from the inside to help you."

A horrible panic overtook Trevelyan suddenly. He did not want to face the coming days without Chatham at his side. Nevertheless, he knew that what the grey-bearded man had said was true. There was no other way.

"Freyr, bring your man. I need your help!"

Trevelyan quickly explained what he needed and the men from Bellerophon began to forge the ropes the company would use. On either side of the small party, the hollow men were closing the distance. Trevelyan unsheathed his weapon and prepared to fight. Chatham wished that he had his skrymir, and resolved to make do with the two-handed broadsword he had taken for the journey to the fortress city.

Ariodne had been set down at their feet. Unnoticed by all, her eyes slowly opened and she brought her left hand to her head, moaning softly. Her eyes would not focus at first. Pain stabbed at her from her right arm, which hung uselessly at her side. Suddenly her vision returned and she saw the red-haired lieutenant and his black-skinned second in command calling upon the Forge. As she struggled to her feet she startled Zared

Anstice, who grasped her hand and turned her to face him, exchanging positions with him as if they had performed a dance step, his dagger suddenly in his free hand, poised to strike. Then he realized that he was not facing an enemy and his momentary fright and disorientation faded.

"Are you well enough to help us forge these ropes?" he asked, pointing to the black hooks with cord they had created over the far ledge. "We need at least—"

His head exploded in a shower of blood, brains, and gory bone. Something heavy struck the Maven in the chest and she fell, the headless, blood-spurting corpse pinning her to the ground as the stone that had been thrown by one of the hollow men rolled to her side. *We exchanged places,* she thought suddenly, and forced the dead man from her.

Rising to her knees she finally took in the carnage that surrounded her and saw her lover and Chatham fighting one of the hollow men who was using the body of one of his fellow soldiers as a shield. Rolland, Shantow, and Akako were busy with a pair of soldiers who had similarly bridged the space between them. Shantow's face had been wounded, white bone showed through beneath the torn flesh of his jaw. He was in shock, but that hadn't stopped him from lashing out wildly at his enemy. His teacher was screaming at him to use the Forge, but he was too dazed.

Off to her right, Ariodne saw the guard strike Trevelyan and knock him against the wall. Her lover nearly tumbled over the side, then regained his balance at the last second. A second blow, this one to the head, drove the merchant prince to the ground. The hollow man started forward, anxious to finish the task he had begun, and Chatham leaped between the two, protecting Trevelyan by drawing the soulless man's wrath. There was no time for the grey-bearded man to hack at the monster with his sword. With blinding speed the creature curled its hands into claws and ripped into the body of the old warrior, tearing apart the mails covering his chest with such force that a cloud of blood burst from the wound. Chatham stumbled back, eyes wide with fear, surprise, and pain as he closed his arms over his chest and was attacked a second time, the monster's hand ripping into the flesh of his upper arm, tearing away a meaty section of well-honed muscle. Chatham screamed like a wounded animal.

"Damn you!" Ariodne cried, and called upon the Forge in

her rage to create five sharp metal flats *within* the body of the hollow man, one in each of his shoulders and thighs, one in his neck. He stopped suddenly, his decapitated head falling forward, his arms and torso dropping in different directions, his legs finally bending at the knee and sagging to the ground.

"By the Unseen," Lon Freyr said as he forged the last of the ropes, "I didn't know that could be done!"

"Neither did I," Ariodne said. She felt weak. A hot trickle of blood raced across her neck from her own wound.

The red-haired lieutenant saw the Kintarans and Rolland Storr struggling with one of the remaining hollow men. Drawing his dagger, Freyr flung the weapon at the creature, striking it from behind in the fleshy meat above its left collarbone. He had been aiming for the base of the skull but the creature had moved too quickly. The hollow man's rage was increased by his wound and he struck Shantow in the chest, sending the young Kintaran ambassador from his feet. The back of his head struck the low wall and one of the stones wobbled and fell away, revealing a wooden cask hidden behind the stone. As Rolland and Akako kept the hollow man occupied, Shantow dragged the small barrel from its hiding place and tore off the lid. A foul stench greeted him.

"Yes," he whispered, "yes, I knew you'd maybe keep some of it here!"

Rising to uncertain knees, Shantow splashed the contents of the barrel on the hollow man's chest, then screamed for a flame. Lon Freyr ran to the closest guard station, snatched a torch from one of the braziers above the watchfires and returned in time to see the hollow man throw off Akako and Rolland, leaving himself wide open for the torch the red-haired lieutenant thrust against his chest. The hollow man faltered and dropped away from the warriors as he was suddenly engulfed in flames. He screamed, a stumbling fireball, and Rolland forged a staff to sweep the dying creature from the guard walks. The gatesman was flung over the wall, onto the black siege tower. Dozens were climbing through the tower, intent on reaching the ledge the same way the humans had. The fiery body of their brother set the roof of the tower on fire as a dozen or more sprang from the final stairway onto the landing.

Rolland knew that he could wait no longer. He released his hold on the tower and it vanished, sending at least thirty hollow men to the waiting crowd and the ground below. The neck of the burning man snapped when he hit.

Trevelyan had come around and was crouched beside Chatham. The old man was quivering with the pain from his wounds. Something was wrong, Trevelyan knew, but what it was he could not say.

"I'm hurt," Chatham said in his low, guttural voice.

"I can see that," Trevelyan said.

"Not like I've ever been. Different. Shouldn't have been able to get drunk, should have realized—" He stopped, his face a twisted mask of agony. *"Dying."*

Ariodne went to the side of her lover. He had not realized that she was conscious. With a strangled cry he embraced her and looked out at the fortress walk. More hollow men were coming. "Get over the side," he barked as he raised his *kris*.

"*You* get over the side," she said, forging her black armors, her right arm dangling uselessly. "You're the important one here and I can't climb with this arm anyway. You've got to organize the others and level this damned place!" She looked down at Chatham. "I'll stay with him."

He looked at the walk and saw Rolland and Akako still standing. Shantow had collapsed, still clutching the barrel that had contained liquid fire. Lon Freyr had forged heavy black gloves and was climbing over the wall, calling out for Trevelyan to join him as he slipped over the side and disappeared from view.

Trevelyan raised his sword and pointed it at Rolland. "You go," he commanded. "I charge you with the task of returning to this place and burning Kothra in a sea of his own liquid fire."

Rolland hesitated.

"You have your orders. Go!"

The warrior turned and went over the side as Trevelyan smiled weakly at his lover. Ariodne forged a short shaft with blades at either side and whispered, "This was not a good decision."

"I love you," Trevelyan said. The hollow men were almost upon them.

"Damn fool reason to throw your life away," Ariodne said as she braced herself and stood ready to fight.

Akako eyed the waiting ropes and looked away with sadness. He stood over his surrogate son. "The only one."

Trevelyan was about to call on the Forge to suffocate yet another of the hollow men when the advance of his enemy was brought to a halt by the flash of lightning, the roar of thunder, and an unmistakable ear-piercing sound.

The howling cry of the wolves. The call for blood.

For vengeance.

The young prince looked up at the fortress walls and was stunned to see Black Mask and his pack leaping from the grey stone ledge, flanking the small group of bleeding, all but defeated humans. Trevelyan heard the voice of the first wolf in his mind:

Forge slings for wounded. Carry them down.

The hollow men slowly drew closer.

We will tend to these.

Chatham raised his head and stared into the turquoise eyes of the first wolf. "Brother, I am *dying*. In this place we are mortal. My service is at an end."

We will not let you die.

"You can hardly stop it," Chatham said with a smile. Then his expression faltered as he glanced up at Trevelyan. Fear moved through him. For the first time in over two centuries Chatham had hope of release from his penance. He thought of his first mate and her death, then Manon. The grey-bearded man had been unable to sire children, either as a wolf or a man. Staring into Trevelyan's bloodied face, he was shocked to realize that he did not *want* to die; not yet, anyway.

Move quickly.

Without another word the wolves broke off into two companies, Black Mask leading the first that ran to protect Trevelyan's right flank, Walks With Fire commanding the second group that raced to attack the hollow warriors approaching Shantow and Akako.

The wolves leaped at the hollow men, tearing into their throats with abandon.

As the Autumn wolves fought to protect Trevelyan and his companions, the young prince worked with Akako and Ariodne to forge the harnesses. Shantow was lowered over the side and Trevelyan saw that the troops they had left on the ridge were now flooding toward the fortress wall. Lon Freyr and Rolland Storr were waiting below to meet them. The screams of the butchered hollow men reached his ears but he ignored them as he worked to set the Kintaran down gently. Freyr signaled that all was well and Trevelyan threw the rope over the side. Chatham was shivering and babbling incoherently as they loaded him into the second harness. Akako carried the grey-bearded man to the ledge as if he were carting an infant and set him down, stepping back to help Trevelyan get a grip on the rope as they worked together to nudge him over the side. His incredible weight nearly dragged them over the side, too, and Ariodne helped to anchor them.

By the time Chatham was safely on the ground, the wolves had amassed a pile of blue-black-skinned corpses at either guard station. They were growling in warning at the hollow men who cautiously approached. Trevelyan was throwing a harness around his lover when he turned and saw one of the hollow men break apart a section of the wall and hurl it at one of Black Masks' lieutenants, the pure white wolf. The animal tried to leap out of the way but its paw was suddenly caught by the hand of one of the men it had savaged and left for dead. The rock struck the white wolf full on and there was an agonizing wail from Black Mask and the other lieutenant as the wolf's neck snapped and its eyes clouded over in death.

"That can't be," Trevelyan said and Chatham's words to the first wolf came to him again.

In this place we are mortal.

That's why they wouldn't enter the city, Trevelyan thought.

The hollow men raised a cry of victory and surged at the Autumn wolves. In his grief and torment, Black Mask leaped at the first of them, the man who threw the stone, tearing off the monster's head with his incredibly strong jaws.

"There's no time for this," Ariodne said as she pushed the harness from her and allowed her armors to vanish, leaving only a heavy black glove on her one good hand. She vaulted over the side as Trevelyan screamed at her to stop. The red-haired Maven grabbed one of the ropes and slid halfway down before she swung close to the wall. This time she was prepared, bringing her feet up to her chest and allowing them to harmlessly absorb the impact. In moments she was on the ground. "Hurry up," she cried.

Trevelyan needed no further urging. He and Akako hurried over the side, sliding down the ropes and reaching the ground fast enough to give them rope burns despite their gloves. He put his arm around Ariodne and kissed her deeply. His entire body was trembling.

The sharp hiss of arrows volleying sounded. He saw the troops firing blindly at the hollow men massing atop the walls and ordered the casters of the ropes to release them before the hollow could take advantage of them and come in pursuit. From behind the sealed gates he could hear a hundred men trying to move the stone barricade.

"Full retreat!" Trevelyan ordered.

Suddenly there was a burst of lightning and the sky seemed to crack as a swirling blue vortex appeared over the fortress walls. The first wolves leaped from the walls, into the vortex, and vanished as it quickly faded.

Trevelyan ran to his men, repeating his command as the hollow men gathered at the wall.

"You'll be back!" a familiar voice called.

Trevelyan turned to see Abbas Bute on the wall, holding the body of the slain first wolf high above his head, acting out the role he would have to play if he were to survive the coming days at his master's court. Although the young prince could not see the hollow man's expression at the distance and Bute's tone was mocking, the weary manner in which he held himself betrayed his sadness.

"And take this cur with you!" he screamed as he hurled the body of the slain wolf over the side. It fell with a thud at Trevelyan's feet. A chorus of laughter echoed in the darkness from the hollow men above.

Trevelyan hesitated, wishing that he could thank Abbas Bute for sparing the body of the slain first wolf the indignities that his fellow soulless men surely would have inflicted upon it; but to do so would have been a betrayal of the trust Abbas had displayed and so he screamed, "Bastard!" at the hulking figure on the wall. He crouched down with Lon Freyr to pick up the body of the white wolf and haul it from the fortress city as his troops finally turned and went back to the rise where they had been encamped.

CHAPTER
TWENTY-ONE

Even surrounded by a hundred men, Trevelyan felt vulnerable as the group retraced the route the white-painted hollow men had taken when leading them to the city. The injuries he had received on the fortress wall pained him; the side of his face was bruised and swollen and his arm ached as if it had been wrenched from its socket. Ariodne had pleasantly told him that he looked like something Lykos, her mastiff, would have chewed upon and quickly tired of. He told her again that he loved her and tried not to look at the scar on the top of her head or her useless, dangling arm.

As they walked, the Autumn wolves appeared from nowhere, flanking the men who had been assigned the duty of carrying the body of their slain comrade. Moments after their arrival, Ariodne was struck down with a sickness she had felt only once before, when Lady Brynna Celosia had accessed the Stream of Life and gathered portents of their possible and probable futures. Three visions came to the Maven as Trevelyan bent beside her, alarmed. She saw herself running across a vast, snow-covered wasteland set ablaze with liquid fire. The vision altered and she was within a large empty room; Trevelyan, bearded, scarred, and insane, leaped at her with a blade that was poised to be thrust into her heart. The final vision was the most disturbing. She saw her lover standing alone in a large, ornately decorated chamber. Black Mask, the oldest of the first wolves, leaped at him.

The visions faded as abruptly as they had appeared.

Lon Freyr had signaled for the procession to stop. He looked back in the direction of the fortress city. "Why aren't they coming after us?"

"Brynna," Ariodne gasped. "She's well enough to enter the Stream of Life. I failed. She's once again in control."

"They have troops gathered at the shore and guards in the

223

Forest of Bone. Kothra could signal them to come for us," Freyr said nervously. "What is he waiting for?"

Ariodne was helped to her feet by her lover. Before he could order the march to resume, the healer from the fourth house approached. "Do you have a good grip on her?"

In his confusion, Trevelyan answered that he did. The healer took Ariodne's arm and popped the bone of her dislocated shoulder back into its socket. She screamed once from the searing pain and wobbled on her feet, but Trevelyan held her tightly. "You could have given me some warning," she said. The Maven felt faint.

"You would have tensed up, made it worse," the healer said. "The pain will leave you eventually, and now you will be able to use your arm." He turned and went back to those carrying Shantow and Chatham as Trevelyan called for the warriors to advance.

They had passed the village and the ruins of Tarrant Vega's first home without spotting any soulless. Trevelyan considered sending in a troop to forage for supplies and food, then thought better of his plan. Although he believed the hollow men and women returned to the city at night after their labors were complete, a small group may have been left behind and even a handful could decimate their ranks if they had the advantage of a battlefield of their own choosing.

Nevertheless, by morning the group would be tired of walking and unable to outrace the soulless if they approached in force. He did not want to speculate on the price he would pay for a few dozen horses.

Animals of any kind were scarce in the hollow land, as the only fertile tracts of land were the fields behind the rebuilt fortress city. He thought of the first pack of wolves that had attempted to attack Rien and had been slain for their trouble, wondering how they survived the long journey from upper Aranhod. More importantly, he speculated on how his men and the troops from Bellerophon would manage to live outside the city walls with no means to access the stores aboard the black ship and the *Adventure*—provided those ships had not been destroyed on Rien's fiery shores.

If Lon Freyr was correct and soulless men were gathered at the shore and the Forest of Bone, as the hollow had referred to it, there was only one place the humans could go. Risk was involved in Trevelyan's plan, but Lon Freyr and Rolland Storr agreed it was their best chance for survival.

The company proceeded across outer Rien in silence. They passed the deadlands, staring at the twisted black trees and shattered cathedral walls, and continued south. Soon they passed the odd mountain with its protruding castle and low-lying village, and finally arrived before the hillside retreat that the guardians of the Forest of Bone had turned into their barracks. The glowing moonlight bathed the exposed columns, the guard walks, and the wide, ground-level steps that jutted from the hill while casting the recessed doorways in deep, impenetrable shadows. The globular, softly molded stone that surrounded the barely visible facades seemed to glow a soft bluish-white.

The company was halted eight hundred meters before their destination and hidden in a large depression in the craggy landscape. Trevelyan stood with Rolland Storr and Lon Freyr at the edge of the pocket of land, surveying the barracks. Ariodne had gone to help Akako and the healer of the fourth house with Chatham and Shantow.

"Rolland, I want you to take a few men from your Black Wolf company and scout the perimeter. If there is any way of getting inside that place other than barreling through the front door, I want to know about it."

"Agreed," Rolland said with a somber tone. "We've lost enough men as it is."

The black-haired mercenary signaled for his men to join him and led them away from the party leaders. Lon Freyr stared at the far left building intently; it was the only one that was not overrun with clawlike stone stalactites.

"There are no fires inside that we can see. Do you honestly believe no one is there?" he asked.

"If there is, we'll have to face them," Trevelyan said simply. "The land is barren for another two hundred kilometers. If we try to get back to Aranhod without food and water we'll die before we're halfway there."

The red-haired lieutenant seemed lost in contemplation.

"It's too late to salvage your plans to form an alliance with the hollow," Trevelyan said harshly. "If you wish to dispose of Searle Orrick you'll have to find another way. For now we are united in a single cause, and that is our own survival. Are you with me?"

Freyr looked up, his cold eyes glaring at the young leader.

"I will grant you my unconditional support and full authority over my men under one condition: If I die and you live, you will use your resources to find my wife and son. They will be living as exiles in the wastelands high above Fenris in Bellerophon with the other dissidents," Freyr explained. "Find them and secure their safe passage to Cynara, to the freedom and prosperity I could not give them."

Trevelyan thought about it for a moment, then agreed. The young prince heard his name called and turned to see Rolland approach with a large group of warriors. "There is no other way inside."

Unfolding his legs from beneath him, Trevelyan rose. A crowd was forming around Trevelyan, Rolland, and the red-haired lieutenant. Trevelyan placed his hand on Rolland's shoulder and said, "Kill them quickly, Rolland. Be as silent, swift, and all-encompassing as death's shadow."

The oath had first been given by his father during the war of the Forge, many years ago. The mercenary understood its significance, as did the Cynarans in the crowd. The heir to the Arayncourt legacy had at last accepted his destiny.

The crowd converged on the young prince. While he was occupied, Rolland and Lon Freyr selected their men. Without delay they advanced to the first of the five buildings peeking out from the mighty stone overhang, approached the doors from either side, glanced within, then slipped inside.

Anxious moments passed as Trevelyan and the crowd waited for Rolland's men to reappear. To keep them occupied, the merchant prince told the full account of his battle with the hollow above the gate at the fortress city.

Across the small camp, the healer from the fourth house sat with Akako, changing the dressings on Shantow's face. The stone had ripped through his flesh and chipped the bone. His disfigurement would be permanent. Ten meters away, the first wolves guarded the body of their fallen comrade. They had not approached the young prince and he had stayed clear of them, although their assistance would have been valuable. Their presence assured him that if the time came, they would go to his aid. Short of that, he knew to keep away.

In an isolated depression far from the others, Ariodne and Ruzena sat on either side of Chatham. The old warrior was unconscious, the heavy lines and creases of his strong face smoothed out. The red-haired Maven could picture him as a young man and realized that he must have been very handsome.

"The healer said that the wounds were superficial—the blood made it look worse than it was," the blond-haired, blue-eyed, tall and lithe young woman said urgently, pleading for reassurance from the Maven. She had said the same thing five times since Ariodne arrived.

"He looks like he'll be well," Ariodne said with a warm smile, which faltered slightly as she felt something brush at the outer fringes of her mind. She looked down and realized that it was Chatham. He was making such a frail and pitiful attempt to claw at the walls of her consciousness that she did not fear to allow him to move a little deeper, so that she could understand the message he was trying to convey.

Ariodne nodded and looked past Ruzena, in the direction of the group that had engulfed her lover. "Ruzena, do me a favor. Go over to Trevelyan and find out what's happened."

Ruzena hesitated. As a guard at the citadel she had become used to following the commands of a Maven without question. But she did not want to leave Chatham's side now that he truly needed her and there was a chance for her to repay the debt she owed him. The strange magic that restored him outside the citadel was not working here. Nevertheless, the healer had told her that Chatham's condition was stable. Besides, Ariodne Gairloch was not only a Maven but also the lover of the party's commander, Trevelyan Arayncourt.

After agonizing over the decision for a few moments longer, Ruzena stood and took a final glance at Chatham before she turned and walked in the direction of the crowd.

Ariodne felt Chatham's presence in her thoughts once more.

Is she gone yet?

Yes, you old faker.

The dark eyes of the grey-bearded old man flickered, then opened wide. He tried to get to his elbows but Ariodne gently forced him back, her hand upon his unbandaged shoulder. He was too weak to resist.

"The medicine that butcher gave me tastes like grease," he said, "and makes me smell like dung."

"I hadn't noticed anything out of the ordinary," Ariodne said with a smile.

Chatham groaned happily. "For the first time in two centuries I'm actually glad to be alive."

"Not that nonsense again," the red-haired woman said. "Your tales of immortality are wearing thin."

"You still think I lied to Trevelyan about my past?"

"No, I honestly *believe* you're the Mad Wolf of Autumn," she said with a sarcasm she generally reserved for her lover.

The old warrior frowned. "How could an outcast have the powers you know I possess?"

"How does a hollow woman call upon the Stream of Life? I have no idea. That doesn't make you an immortal or her a part of the sisterhood."

Closing his eyes he settled back. "Enter my thoughts. Go as deep as you will. I won't fight you."

"It could be a trick," she murmured.

Chatham growled impatiently. "Girl, I'm tired and drained. If either of us is vulnerable, it's me. Now hurry up before Ruzena comes back."

Ariodne found the request too compelling to resist. She had seen Chatham take the brunt of an attack meant for Trevelyan and understood in that moment that he was willing to die for his young ward. The same selflessness was apparent in this request, too.

Placing her hand over the scar that marked him as an outcast, Ariodne closed her eyes and slowly forced her consciousness into the mind of the grey-bearded warrior. The tide of information that rushed at her nearly overwhelmed the young Maven. Forcing herself to sift through the images one at a time, Ariodne plunged deeper and deeper still into the endless abyss of Chatham's life, searching for its beginning. Decades stretched before her, then centuries, until finally she knew that what he had told her was true. As she withdrew from his thoughts, she paid careful attention to the most recent memories, studying them in detail. She could not believe the truth of what she found there as she experienced the summons of the first wolves and listened to their explanation of the Forge and their revelations concerning the hollow. Soon she knew the intricate details of the true quest they had sent Chatham and Trevelyan upon. The knowledge of the lotus her lover had kept from her threatened to overwhelm her. Then she discovered the secret the wolves and Chatham had kept from Trevelyan, the location of the red-white rose. Before she could probe any deeper, fear gripped her and she fled from his mind.

"Insane," she said, opening her eyes. "You tricked me, made me see what you wanted me to see."

"No, it's true," he pleaded.

Her trembling hand covered her face. "Shut up," she said, scrambling away from him.

Chatham's meaty hand closed over her arm. The tenderness of his touch held her in place more firmly than all his strength would have. "For all our sakes, Ariodne, on your love for the boy, you can't deny the *truth*."

The Maven's reaction startled even her. She sank to her knees, her body limp, and began to cry all the tears she had been holding back. Weeping for her lost mother and father, for the terror and loneliness of her childhood, and for the uncertainty and lack of faith she had in Trevelyan's ability to love her and be with her always, Ariodne cried. Her harsh, racking sobs tore through her entire body. Chatham reached up and touched the side of her face with compassion. She violently shoved his hand away, her fingers clawing at the empty air where his hand had been. Finally she allowed her hand to fall limply at her side.

"I'd damn you but it's already been done for me," she whispered. "Why didn't Trevelyan take Kothra's heart and retrieve the lotus while we were in the city?"

"I believe he wasn't sure that Kothra was the one. And he knew that he would never make it out of the city alive."

"And he has no idea about the rose?" she asked as she placed her hand over her chest. "Or that it resides in—" She broke off suddenly with a choke. Tightening her one good arm over her breasts, Ariodne hugged herself and rocked slightly as if she had been subjected to an icy wind that cut across her soul. In a low, haunted voice she said, "He must kill me to save Autumn. He must take my heart."

"The heart of his greatest love," Chatham said. "Yes. That is why I tried to spare you in the Trader's Reach."

"By driving me into the arms of another?"

His throat was becoming dry. "I'm sorry," he said.

"I'm sorry, too." Ariodne wiped the tears from her eyes. "Lady Brynna Celosia knows *everything* about the Forge and the Well of Souls. If she hadn't moved so quickly I'd have driven that spike through her heart and ended this madness. Kothra's nothing without her."

A guttural laugh escaped Chatham. "Kothra's a *madman*

without her. She's the only thing that controls his deadly shifts of temperament.''

The red-haired Maven looked down and thought of the images that had assaulted her hours before, when she felt Brynna sifting through the Stream of Life. There had been a momentary flash of Trevelyan trying to kill her, his blade aimed at her heart. Her lover was still very young, but his eyes were old and tired and he was consumed with hatred and madness. She suddenly knew that this is what would become of him if she fled and he was forced to come after her.

''Ariodne, you have a decision to make. I have done what I can. Now if you choose to continue, your final fate is in your own hands.''

The red-haired woman laughed bitterly. ''I won't run from my destiny. In a way, it's really quite liberating to know the manner of your own death, if not the time and place. There's very little I have to be afraid of anymore— except for the man I have consented to marry.''

''Trevelyan loves you,'' Chatham said.

''And you love him as if he were your son,'' she replied.

The old warrior hesitated. ''I don't know what to say.''

''There's nothing *to* say.'' Ariodne saw Ruzena break from the crowd that had gathered around Trevelyan and hurry in their direction. ''There's something else. When you were a wolf, what drove you mad?''

''I was plagued by my conscience after I was forced to kill our pack leader to end his suffering. Every human life I destroyed from that moment on haunted me and drove me to—''

''No. The Autumn wolves do not *have* consciences. If they did many of them *would* go mad. Your mind was tampered with. Someone drove you to insanity and murder.''

''Ridiculous,'' Chatham said. He had reconciled himself to accepting guilt for his crimes hundreds of years before. The Maven's words disturbed him deeply.

Ruzena appeared and dropped to her knees beside Chatham, overjoyed that he was conscious. There was only a trace of jealousy in her eyes when she glanced to Ariodne and realized that the first face he saw was that of the Maven, not her own, then she chided herself for behaving like a jealous schoolgirl. She owed Chatham a debt of honor, she reminded herself. There was nothing else.

Now if only I could convince myself of that, she thought as

her honey-blond hair fell into her face and she gazed into his dark eyes with a warm and loving smile. "I'm glad to see you're awake, you old sod. You almost missed the best part of the evening."

"What are you talking about?" Chatham said hoarsely.

"Rolland Storr has just returned from the stronghold. His men and those from Bellerophon rooted out five hollow men, slaying all but one of them, whom they've secured for questioning. All the supplies we'll need for the journey home are within. Lord Arayncourt said that we will rest inside for a few hours while lookouts watch over us. Then we will resume our trek from this blighted land and return when we have the strength to level this city with even more force than the Unseen used when it was first destroyed!"

Ariodne's legs were rubbery beneath her as she struggled to her feet. "That sounds like something he'd say," the red-haired Maven spat as Ruzena leaped up and steadied her. "I'll be all right. I must go to him and see if some common sense can penetrate his swollen head."

Once Ariodne was gone, the blue-eyed women knelt beside Chatham and reached down to caress the coarse flesh of his face as she stared at him. He touched her hand, bringing it to his lips. Feeling the heat of his lips upon her skin, Ruzena made a decision.

"What do you see?" he asked.

"A man," she said. "Like any other."

"Not an outcast? A criminal?"

She bent low and kissed the scar he bore. "A mystery. And mysteries are meant to be explored."

He thought of nothing else as she leaned down and kissed him hard on the mouth. Ruzena drew back and giggled.

"What?" he asked, feelings returning to him that he thought were buried and forgotten. He thought of Ariodne's words and wondered if it was possible that he could have a life with honor and love. As Trevelyan would have said, there was only one way to find out. Reaching up to the back of her head, Chatham pulled Ruzena down for another kiss.

She pulled away quickly and he felt his heart catch. Then he saw that she was grinning. "Your lips are very full," she said. "Don't pucker the way you do."

Chatham made a conscious decision not to become insulted.

They kissed again and she threw her head back with laughter. "It has been a long time for you, hasn't it?"

This time he kissed her in the way she desired and she murmured in approval.

"Longer than you know," he said, kissing her lips, her delicate throat, and the hollow between her breasts. Suddenly they were interrupted by one of the Cynarans that Trevelyan had sent to bring all the stragglers into the safety of the stronghold.

CHAPTER
TWENTY-TWO

Soon the contingent of warriors was safely inside the hillside barracks with sentries posted outside the main door, on the guard walk, and in the hills above. From their high vantage, the guards could see the flames on the shores, but they could not spot any sign of either ship.

The task Trevelyan had set for Rolland had been made childishly simple by the design of inner chambers, which had been carved from solidified lava that had flowed down over the buildings, destroying everything but their facades. There was a single large room on the first floor that was used for preparing, storing, and dispensing food. Several long tables with chairs were in evidence, with a kitchen in the back and all the stores the humans would need for their escape lined up against the wall. A stairway led to the second floor, where the hollow men slept in a series of individual rooms. The assassins had verified that there were no other soulless in the complex except for the five asleep in their private chambers. The group was positioned in the long main corridor with two men facing each doorway. Rolland gave the command for every other man to call upon the Forge. Four of the five hollow men woke to find their noses and mouths covered with mud that quickly solidified to asphyxiate them. As the soulless men began to struggle, the second group of casters swung the chamber doors shut and fused them to prevent their dying victims from launching themselves at their slayers. Heavy shackles were cast for the fifth victim who was taken prisoner. The monster had been secured to the stone slab he had used for a bed and was still there when Trevelyan and Ariodne were led to the chamber. Below, the tables were moved out of the way and almost all the torches were extinguished so that the warriors could lay down and rest, though few would be able to sleep soundly until they were out of the hollow land.

In the guard's chamber, Rolland Storr and Lon Freyr stood beside the young prince. Ariodne had barely spoken to him since she returned from her audience with Chatham.

"What is your name?" Trevelyan asked dispassionately.

"You've killed us all?" the creature responded, struggling in vain to escape the dozens of heavy, linked chains that bit into his flesh. A single stalk of white hair rose from his head, held in place with a silver band.

"Yes," Trevelyan said. "As you would have killed us."

The hollow man was silent.

"He's got nothing to say." Trevelyan sounded bored. "Kill him, but use a sword. The Forge should be reserved for when we really need it. I don't want the men tired and drained if we have to fight our way out of Rien."

Rolland stepped forward and brought his weapon up over his head, poised to strike the monster's head from his neck. The young prince waited for the soulless man to cry out for his executioner to wait, but he was silent. The sword flashed in the dimly lit chamber, its tip scraping against the wall as the cutting edge was stopped centimeters over the soulless man's throat. Rolland cursed and yanked the blade free of the niche it had dug into.

"Just use a dagger," Trevelyan said. The hollow man's composure was lost and his eyes danced back and forth. The dark-haired prince shoved Rolland out of the way and said with impatience and disgust, "I'll do it."

His hand sank beneath the hollow man's head, grasped his hair, and yanked him back to expose his throat. The dagger's edge pressed against the man's deeply bruised, blue-black skin and the oversize veins in his temple and neck pulsed wildly. Trevelyan stopped before slitting his throat and said, "Unless you have something to tell me?"

The hollow man smiled. He had waited out the prince's theatrics, gambled, and won. "Release the chains first."

Trevelyan sheathed his dagger, then clasped one hand over the man's mouth while he squeezed his nostrils shut with the other. The soulless guardsman struggled, bucking against the prince, panic returning to his eyes as he slowly suffocated.

The young prince grimaced. "Don't think we're on equal footing, you murderous bastard."

As the hollow man's eyes rolled back in their sockets, Trevelyan released his grip and allowed the creature to gasp for breath. Ariodne was startled. She had never seen him behave with such calculated savagery.

"I have questions. You will answer them," Trevelyan snarled. The soulless man shook his head violently in agreement. Staring into the hollow man's black-slitted red eyes, Trevelyan said, "Why didn't you have a guard posted outside? Your brothers were down at the shore, preparing to commit an aggressive act against us. Didn't you consider repercussions? Answer!"

"We never thought you'd get this far," the guard said.

"That's a lie," Trevelyan replied. "Why weren't you sleeping in shifts? One of you should have been on duty."

"We don't do it that way. We all sleep at the same time," the hollow man said in a quiet voice, studying Trevelyan's face for any sign that the prince believed him.

Trevelyan slapped the man with the back of his hand. "Blood is precious to your kind," he snarled. "Answer me with something other than the well-rehearsed lines you have been fed and I won't cut you and leave you slowly bleeding to death in this room."

"It's the truth," the guard said more defiantly, although his fear was genuine.

"And you leave your provisions lying about in the open, unprotected? Answer!" Trevelyan said. He was close to the truth but there was something he hadn't considered yet.

"We weren't expecting you!"

"No," Trevelyan said, mulling over the image he held in his thoughts of the stores of food waiting below. There was enough to feed an army. His army, specifically. The skin of the young prince went cold. "Why do you have so much food here?" Trevelyan wondered out loud. "Most of it would rot and spoil before you could get to it."

"We keep well stocked," the man said nervously.

The merchant prince spun and shouted, "The food stores are poisoned. The hollow *meant* for us to come here. Get downstairs and make sure no one touches any of it! If they have already, make them go outside and put their fingers down their throats. Hurry!''

Rolland and Lon Freyr raced from the room, leaving Trevelyan and Ariodne alone with the soulless man. ''Where are the untainted supplies?''

''If any of us survived we were to return to the Forest of Bone to feast with our brothers. There is nothing here.''

For the first time, Trevelyan believed the hollow man.

In desperation, the guard cried, ''You won't bleed me to death, will you?''

Trevelyan drew his dagger once again. Placing the cold blade against the Kothrite's throat, he was not surprised to hear the man's final plea for mercy. ''Don't,'' the guard cried. ''There is something I can tell you. Something that is worth my life.''

''You would say anything,'' Trevelyan said, forcing the point into the man's neck.

''It concerns liquid fire!''

Trevelyan withdrew his knife. ''Be quick about this.''

''When you were in the city, you saw nothing that would reveal where they manufactured liquid fire, or how.''

''Go on,'' Trevelyan said impatiently.

''That's why you doubted that they were doing it at all.''

''Yes, they were working outside the city—''

''There is a labyrinth *beneath* the city,'' the frightened guard said urgently. ''They mine for the materials needed to produce liquid fire, drilling deep into the earth for a black liquid that has no name, procuring limestone and other soft red clays that I only saw a few times when I worked below.''

''I was in the pleasure pits, I saw none of this.''

''The pits are only one small section of the underground. Kothra has designed war machines that will spit liquid fire over vast distances, throwing the flames from the walls, the ground, or from the decks of ships. Only he knows the manner in which the materials are blended. If you can get into the underground you can set the city on fire from its foundations. Rien will burn and be destroyed.''

Trevelyan scanned the monster's face. He believed the hollow man. ''Is there anything else?''

''Isn't that enough?'' the soulless man begged.

''It would have been.'' Trevelyan brought the knife back to his prisoner's throat. ''If we had made a deal first.''

The hollow man saw the terrible satisfaction in Trevelyan's

eyes and knew that he was a dead man. "*You* are the one without a soul, Trevelyan Arayncourt!"

In his rage, Trevelyan grabbed the guard's white stalk of hair and served up the man's throat to his blade.

"Wait!" Ariodne screamed. The hollow man had squeezed his eyes shut, prepared for his own execution. "Keep your eyes closed," Ariodne said softly as she placed her hand on the side of the soulless man's face. "Where do you want to go?"

"The fields," he said without hesitation. "The beautiful fields where I was raised. We were farmers."

With a gentle push into his mind, Ariodne brought down the walls between the past and present for the man. The foul-smelling, torchlit chamber was gone and he was a child again, running with abandon beneath a luscious blue sky. In a trancelike state, she described in whispers what she was witnessing in the mind of the hollow man.

Ariodne took her hand away and saw a peaceful, contented smile on the guard's face. "Now do what you must," she said to Trevelyan and turned her back. Trevelyan prepared to cut the man's throat in the manner Rolland had taught him on the voyage, the knife poised for several long seconds as he recalled his conversations with Freyr. The man insisted that while the hollow did not have souls as the humans understood them, they had free will, individual natures, and the ability, as Abbas Bute had demonstrated, to act with honor and self-sacrifice.

After long moments of struggle, Trevelyan dropped the blade. "We'll have guards placed around him."

Ariodne grasped his hand as she felt a surge of relief that Trevelyan had not surrendered to the madness she had seen in his eyes during her vision. Unnoticed behind them, the chains that had been forged to keep the hollow man on the slab suddenly faded as below the castor died from the poisoned food. The prisoner's will had been powerful enough to force away the vision of his childhood and he rose, snatching the dagger Trevelyan had dropped. Though he did not *need* the weapon, he felt there was a certain irony in using it to dispatch his tormentors. With surprise on his side he was certain that he could escape the fortress and warn his people.

Trevelyan and Ariodne were at the door when Rolland appeared before them. He saw the threat before they did, yanked Trevelyan out of the way with one hand as he called upon the Forge and materialized a loaded crossbow in the other.

The hollow man was about to strike when Rolland fired the weapon, the shaft slamming into the right eye of the soulless man, sending him to the ground, where he died.

Downstairs, Shantow slowly fought his way upward to awareness. The last thing he remembered was the battle on the fortress wall. Now he was in a large single room carved from stone, surrounded by at least a hundred men and women. Akako was standing over him, his back turned as he spoke with Rolland Storr and Lon Freyr. They spoke in whispers.

"We'll take the supplies out and bury them," Rolland said. "That way when the hollow come they'll think we've succumbed to their trap and they won't follow us."

"But what are we going to do for food? There's no game, the land is dead." Lon Freyr seemed anxious not to give in to the mounting desperation all three men radiated.

"What do we tell the ones who have already eaten of this?" Akako said.

"The truth," Rolland said. "They have a right to know."

"What are you talking about?" Shantow sat up and lightly ran his hand over the black bandage that covered a third of his jaw. Akako dropped to the side of his foster son.

"Lay back," Akako said. "Rest."

"I've maybe had enough of that," the young Kintaran said. "Tell me where we are and what is going on."

Trevelyan appeared from the stairway, looking worn and haggard. Before the warriors gathered in the main room could anxiously surround him, one of the sentries appeared beside the wide-open door at the other side of the room.

"Lord Arayncourt, there's an army approaching!"

Ruzena helped Chatham to his feet in another corner of the room. "And here we are, trapped like rats," he snarled.

"You don't understand," the sentry pleaded. "The army is from the south. They are human and there are thousands."

"My people have arrived to save us," Shantow announced.

"*They are not Kintarans*," the sentry said. Trevelyan stood beside Lon Freyr as the man at the door finished his announcement. "They bear the colors of Fenris's elite. They are the warriors of Searle Orrick."

Lon Freyr felt his heart sink. Trevelyan had been correct: his plans to depose the leader of Bellerophon were destined to meet with failure. He walked to the entrance, then out into the night to greet his fellow warriors.

The soldiers from Bellerophon had seen the fires on the shore of Rien, near the Forest of Bone, and had taken their fleet of ships south, to a dangerous reef where they were forced to lay anchor far from shore. The warriors rowed to land, then marched north, in the direction of the city, where they met and formed an alliance with a five-hundred-man land force that had ridden from northern Aranhod.

Lon Freyr's relief that Searle Orrick was not with the troops was short-lived as the commander appeared. "Wolfram Hilliard," Freyr said as he greeted the older man in surprise, smiling at the man who had betrayed him when he returned from Telluryde with Kothra's proclamation.

Staring into the heavily lined, humorless face of the short, practically bald man, Lon Freyr forced himself to clasp the upper arms of his superior in a warrior's greeting. Hilliard had been a professor in his youth, and his clear blue eyes, hawklike nose, strong cheekbones, chiseled jaw, and thin but proud lips gave the impression that he was a hard but fair man, interested in honor and truth. His looks served to disguise his true nature, that of a power-obsessed career military man who was happier to stand beside the throne and influence through whispers rather than take the responsibility of office.

A small delegation had been sent from the barracks to greet the soldiers. The red-haired lieutenant was flanked by Trevelyan, Rolland, and Ariodne. Akako had convinced Shantow to stay behind, threatening to pin him to the ground if necessary. Chatham and Ruzena agreed to stay and help maintain order. A panic was spreading concerning the poisoned food stores. Over thirty people had eaten of the tainted fruits and meats and purged their stomachs.

Outside, in full view of the hillside facades, Trevelyan asked Hilliard if he had seen any trace of the black ship or the *Adventure* when his fleet approached the burning waters.

"We were at a considerable distance," Hilliard said. "We saw something that might have been wreckage, but there was no way of telling without revealing ourselves and risking the flames. Now, if you will excuse me, Lieutenant Freyr and I have much to discuss."

Hilliard led Freyr away. A short, stocky man with thin black hair and the smile and demeanor of a salesman introduced himself as Kenholm Goel, the leader of the horsemen from Joachim, a training facility for swordsmen and mercenaries located midway between Cynara and the outer Rien border. Rolland glanced at Trevelyan in warning, explaining later that he was not impressed by the man or his soldiers, who mulled about or broke into small groups. The deployment of troops from Bellerophon was another matter entirely. They stood in formation, five lines of men dressed in black armors stretching back against the pale moonlit landscape.

Standing beside Kenholm was one of the two young men who had accompanied the balding, blond-haired youth in the Ivory Dagger, the student who had claimed to have unlocked the secret formula for mixing liquid fire. The boy was tall and lanky, his thick brown hair falling into his eyes. He explained his sudden disappearance and that of his companion after their friend sacrificed himself to save Trevelyan.

"All we knew was that Raimi insisted on going back to the inn to hound you some more and that he was killed," he said. "We didn't learn how or why until after we had fled the city and gone to my parents' home in southern Aranhod."

"You thought I had him executed because he annoyed me?"

"*We* thought about doing it all the time," the boy muttered. "Raimi was brilliant but he never knew when to quit. We were his friends, so we stayed with him. He always said he was going to make us all rich."

"Go on," Trevelyan urged. "What became of that mountain of papers and journals you were carting around for him?"

"They're now with your chemists in Cynara," Kenholm interrupted. "Although the notes are incomplete and the formula Raimi had devised for creating liquid fire was lost, our men of science were able to piece together instructions for creating a fabric that resists flames."

"Can it be forged?" Trevelyan said in his excitement.

"It can, but there is an art to it. We had five men who understood the process when we left, twenty-five now."

"Let me work with them," Ariodne suggested. "I'll teach our people." Trevelyan agreed without hesitation.

"Jedrek here will take you," Kenholm said, indicating the boy. The red-haired Maven left with him and Kenholm sighed. "Now we must devise our strategy for taking this Kothra and his little band of outcasts and barbarians."

"What are you talking about?" Trevelyan said. "Rien is a

fortress. There are no humans left, only soldiers of the hollow. More than five thousand, I would guess."

Kenholm blanched, turned his face away, and coughed. "Well," he said, quickly recovering, "we have the might of the Unseen on our side. We have the Forge."

"I'm not giving the order to attack Rien," Trevelyan said, looking out at the troops from Bellerophon. "Even this number of men is not enough. We can't make a stand against Rien until we have at least *ten times* this number."

Kenholm hesitated. "Lord Trevelyan, with every respect, what makes you think the decision is yours to make?"

The young prince turned and watched as Lon Freyr and Wolfram Hilliard argued. Finally, the red-haired lieutenant stormed away and Hilliard raised his fist to his men. Two thousand warriors raised their voices in an ancient battle chant. Even the Cynarans joined in. With a heavy heart, Trevelyan walked away from Kenholm, who added his voice to the growing cacophony.

Near the fortress, Black Mask spat and padded away from the gathering, his turquoise eyes clouded over in disgust.

CHAPTER TWENTY-THREE

Two hundred hollow men worked the field behind the fortress city, ignoring the approach of Wolfram Hilliard's army. The rear gate to the city was open and many of the soulless carted their yield away with indifference to the soldiers who tore through their fragile farmland, trampling their handiwork beneath heavy boots. Trevelyan, his companions, and the troops from Cynara waited behind with Kenholm and his horsemen. There had been no rainfall in the four days after Trevelyan's escape from the city, but the skies were steel-gray and a biting chill had descended on the land, threatening the crops. The hollow had been covering their future harvest with canvas in an effort to protect it from the cold when the army had descended into their fields.

Hilliard led the attack, his pike men flanking him. Their first order of business was to cut off the hollow's food supply and take it for themselves. The unexpected sight of the open rear gates of the city had stirred them into a frenzy, the men rushing forward, shouting battle cries. Though Hilliard had no intention of storming the walls, he was encouraged by the thrown-open gates, certain that the hollow men would be driven away from their farmlands into the city by the sight of his army. A thousand men in black armor and mail surged through the straw-colored field, a tightly formed phalanx one hundred men across, ten rows deep.

Their presence had been anticipated.

Small puddles formed on the ground and soon the irrigation channels that had been cut throughout the farmland filled with water. The fields soon became damp and muddy.

As the soldiers covered the distance separating them from their enemy, the soulless men abruptly threw down their farming tools and dug into the newly packed earth to withdraw weapons that had accumulated in Rien for the past two hundred years. Crossbows freshly loaded with bolts seemed to fly into their hands, the dirt shaken from them and brushed away. The apathy faded from the eyes of the hollow as their archers pulled their bows and satchels from the ground and nocked their arrows. Carts carrying thin layers of corn and wheat were overturned, revealing swords and maces. The soulless fell back to positions that would put them on either side of the advancing unit from Bellerophon.

Hilliard ground the charge to a halt.

Directly before his men, two large war machines were wheeled out of the rear gates. They were shaped like carts and armored with lead on the sides and front. A long nozzle with a firing slit protruded from each. Two oxen were mounted inside each of the machines and drivers sat on the back with turning wheels. The weapons were advanced thirty meters from the walls, aimed at opposite directions. Suddenly flames shot out from their nozzles and fell to the earth, where they struck meter-wide gullies filled with water. The fires raced across the perimeter of the fortress, branching outward as they connected with irrigation channels cut into the ground. Dozens of bright yellow fingers of flame reached out to the warriors from Bellerophon as the hollow men in the field opened fire on them.

The warriors on the side flanks of the formation raised and interlocked their shields. There were screams as the shafts pierced their newly forged defenses. Many of the hollow aimed lower, skewering the legs of Hilliard's men, causing them to fall and leave openings for the blue-black-skinned archers to launch volleys that brought down a handful of men at a time before new shields could be forged.

The barrage continued as the flames raced closer, splitting off into intricate patterns that had been carefully designed to turn the farmlands into a raging inferno before they were done. The hollow men closed behind the warriors, blocking their only route to escape.

Trevelyan gave the order and the horsemen charged into the fields, dividing into two equal divisions. Their mounts were terrified of the flames, but the riders, wearing cloaks and hoods made of the black, foul-smelling cloth that they had been taught to forge, forced them on. Long black sections of the material were draped and tied over the bodies of the horses, thick black harnesses made of the heavy cloth guarding their heads. To their credit, the riders maintained their calm as they rode into the smoking field, firing their own bolts and arrows into the unprotected bodies of the hollow men who had gathered around the flanks of Hilliard's men, punching several holes through the lines of the hollow. The limited supplies of the soulless dwindled and they were forced to throw down their distance weapons and charge at the humans with their swords, maces, and lances.

Some of the hollow men chased the humans on horseback, attempting to run their mounts through before the blue-black-skinned giants could be brought down by arrows. One of the soulless warriors launched himself at a rider and kicked the man from his horse into a burning ditch. Then he raced with the horse toward the rapidly growing curtain of flames that ran parallel to the fortress wall and drove the beast to leap through the fires, where he led the animal through the still-open gates. One of the war machines was driven back to the city, and before it reached the wide-open doorway, another half-dozen stolen horses were forced through the flames to the safety of the city.

On the ground, the man who had been kicked into the burning ditch kept his hood closed over him tightly as he attempted to claw his way from the fiery trap. In his panic he accidentally released the tenuous bond that kept his flame-resistant cloak, leggings, and boots from vanishing. He screamed as the fires scorched his armors and roasted his flesh within the metal.

Near the rear gates, the second machine was driven to the

center of the space between the two flanking arms of the flame and aimed downward. A burst of fire from its nozzle ignited two wide lanes of water that raced directly at Hilliard's group, scattering their tight formation. The bald commander pulled his cloak over his head and shouted for his men to stay calm as they retreated. His boot struck a soft, muddy patch of earth and he cursed as he felt heat at his back and glanced over his shoulder at a two-meter-high scythe of flame that was rushing toward him.

Shoving against the backs of his men, Hilliard covered his head. He lost his footing and shouted as the flames reached the spot where he fell and washed over him. Half the pikemen were consumed. The intense heat scorched the men's bodies. Their hair smoked, their lips shriveled, and their skin dried out as they became parched and desperate for relief, but they were not killed. The men crawled forward, through the flames, a few of them lifting themselves to their feet as they pressed on, their boots sloshing through the mud beneath them, the soles of their feet bringing fresh agonies to them with every step. At their backs were Hilliard's muffled curses and screams, barely audible over the roar and crackle of the flames and the harsh winds that accompanied them.

On the field, the fires were spreading, and the remainder of the troops from Bellerophon took the battleground under the command of Lon Freyr, rushing into the wall of grey and black smoke that now obscured their commander and his primary forces. Hints of movement within the inferno could have been new trenches of flames, platoons of men surging forward to escape their fiery deaths, or horsemen skirmishing with the soldiers of the hollow. The warriors moved in cautiously, a heavy vibration from the ground causing them to stop suddenly as dozens of riders broke from the clouds of smoke and scattered the formation of the soldiers from Fenris.

"Too late, too late," the horsemen were screaming as they plowed into Freyr's lines. He watched helplessly as several of his men were trampled in the confusion, his order to fall back unnecessary. A fireball of incredible size was racing toward them, curling and growing in power. Hundreds of horsemen and foot soldiers escaped from the fires as the rolling thunder-cloud of flame suddenly burst and covered the field in a blinding display of white light and deafening sound. The men behind Freyr turned and looked over their shoulders to see the flash of light as bright as the eye of the sun followed by a huge cloud of grey-white smoke. Shrapnel shot forward, the remains of armors and weapons belonging to men caught in the heart of the explosion. The fields turned black in an instant and dozens of warriors were lifted by a horrible boom that threw them across the field like dolls.

Freyr was on the ground, shaking his head, when he looked down to see that his boots were gone. The bodies of men flew past him, their arms flailing almost comically in the air before they struck the moist, pungent earth. He had been deafened by the blast, and he screamed as he pulled himself from the earth, his legs watery, threatening to collapse. He didn't know if his screams could be heard, or if he was actually making sounds, but he had to order his men to escape from the fields before the fires covered every acre of the hollow men's only source of food. Dead men surrounded him, their chests ripped open, their heads torn from their shoulders. He scrambled back in the direction where Trevelyan and his companions waited, running like a madman as he stared back at the huge black cloud that was marked by flickerings of yellow and red flame, wondering if anything could have survived the devastation. With a rush of sound his hearing returned and the sound of laughter came to him. Turning suddenly he dug his foot into the earth and stopped himself before his momentum carried him into the heavily muscled, blue-black chest of one of the hollow men.

The soulless warrior was unarmed. Freyr reached for his sword, then started as his flesh touched the red-hot metal. The Kothrite laughed and struck him in his ribs, the blow lifting Freyr from the ground, his arms flying outward. Suddenly his back struck the ground and the hollow man was above him, reaching down for his sword. Again, the pungent odor of cooked meat filtered through the stink from the fires raging behind them and the soulless man gasped as he grabbed the hilt of Freyr's sword and yanked it from its scabbard.

"Die by your own devices," the hollow man shouted as he plunged the sword at the chest of the red-haired lieutenant. What happened next surprised Freyr. A black, smoking figure hurled itself at the hollow man, knocking the creature away before the fatal thrust could be finished.

The hollow man writhed in agony as the dark figure closed his hands over the monster's throat, pressing down hard. Incredible heat radiated from the cloaked man. The throat of the soulless warrior baked and fumed until the strong grip of the dark man burned through its tender flesh and crushed its larynx. With a maddened cry, the smoking, black-garbed warrior dug his hands in deeper, ripping out muscle and gobs of tissue, tearing open the monster's artery to cause a torrent of blood to bathe his cloak and finally his face as he tore the hood back and revealed his identity.

Wolfram Hilliard forced the shooting blood to spray into his wide-open eyes as he screamed the traditional vow of vengeance and terror from a language that his people had long since abandoned. Freyr dragged himself to his elbows, watching the red, terribly burned face of his commander. He considered that now, despite this terrible defeat, Hilliard would be more determined than ever to pursue his plans to somehow level the fortress city of Rien.

The red-haired lieutenant still had his dagger.

The back of the older man's head was exposed, the point at the base of his skull vulnerable and waiting. Rolling white clouds surrounded them and no one else was in sight.

He hesitated. In that moment, the opportunity was lost forever. Hilliard spun, laughing, and pointing down at the corpse at his feet. "That'll show these bastards!"

"Yes," Freyr said, helping his commander to stand. The two men supported each other on the long walk back.

From their camp, Trevelyan had watched in horror as the trap the hollow men had set for the soldiers had been set off so simply and methodically. Kothra had anticipated the movements of Hilliard and Freyr and had defended himself expertly; his former life as a mercenary and assassin for Searle Orrick had also proved to be an education.

The remaining Autumn wolves had disappeared for two days with the corpse of their companion. This morning they had returned alone. Presently, the wolves flanked Trevelyan and Ariodne, looking out at the burning field, waiting for the fires to fade and the cloud of smoke to dissipate so they could ferret out the survivors and tend to the wounded.

The majority of Freyr's contingent had survived and at least half of the horsemen and their mounts had escaped, outracing the flames, which seemed to be slowing in their advance. The shouts of men fighting and dying within the blaze rose to the young prince. The survivors were enmeshed in a series of smaller hand-to-hand battles.

"I'm going down there," Trevelyan said as he slipped the

black cloth robes Ariodne had forged for him over his clothing. Rolland, Chatham, and Ruzena volunteered to join him. This time Akako could not rein in Shantow. Trevelyan turned to his friend and said, "You stay here. Someone has to protect our supplies. Besides, with any luck the men your father has sent will arrive soon, and someone of royal bearing must be here to greet them."

"I don't like this," Shantow said. "But I will stay."

Ariodne picked up the cloak she had made for herself and said, "I'm coming with you."

From the fields, the prince could hear the clangs and scrapes of steel against steel. "No!"

"I'm as good a fighter as you," she said defiantly. "Better."

"Your arm's unpredictable. You were bested in single combat seven times because of it in the past few days."

"But I won the other eight matches," she argued, then turned her attentions to the scarred, old warrior. "And I'm certainly in better shape than that lumbering wreck."

"Your kindness overwhelms me," Chatham said. His wounds brought pain with every step and Ruzena studied his face nervously. He whispered, "Surely you don't expect me to let a few scratches keep me from the fun."

She grinned and squeezed his hand.

Ariodne rushed after Trevelyan, calling his name. The young prince spun and shouted at the wolves, "Keep her here. You stinking curs have done little enough in the battle, you owe me that much at least."

As you wish, Black Mask's voice sounded in his mind, then the wolves closed around Ariodne, forcing her to remain, despite the curses she hurled at them and at her lover.

"Rolland, take your men and round up mounts for us all," Trevelyan ordered. "If you find Kenholm alive, tell him he did a fine job and relieve him immediately."

The tall, dark-haired condottiere nodded solemnly and shouted orders to his warriors. Trevelyan turned and faced the Cynarans who were grouped behind him. "Relieve the horsemen who have escaped the field. Take their mounts. I'll lead us in and we'll retrieve the survivors before the hollow can kill them all. Grab the men and take them out if you can, don't engage those monsters unless you have to. Once our men are out we'll let the flames finish them off."

The frustrated Cynarans, anxious to strike out against the hollow, swarmed down the slight hillside to the dazed and injured horsemen who had gathered before the wall of smoke that drifted lazily outward. Few protested as the fresh soldiers from Aranhod's capital took their mounts.

Rolland and his men appeared with rides for Trevelyan and his companions. Chatham placed his hand on the shoulder of the young prince. "Ariodne was right about me," he leaned in close to whisper. "Not only the wounds but the frailties of this shell's age have slowed me down. I'm not sure how much good I'll be to you."

"They're mortal," Trevelyan said as he nodded to the men and women under his command. "You don't see them worrying like old women."

"I don't foresee many of them being alive long enough to have the wisdom of old women," Chatham said sourly as he allowed Ruzena to help him onto a mount.

As Trevelyan swung onto his horse, he was startled to hear shouts from the warriors still waiting on his order to go into the fields. The Autumn wolves, Black Mask, Walks With Fire, and his soldiers were racing past the horsemen, into the field. Ariodne, staff raised, galloped behind them on a stolen horse into the cloud of black smoke. In seconds they were devoured by the choking wall of flame and smoke.

Trevelyan's response was immediate. "Follow them!" he screamed, kicking the sides of his mount and holding on as he was propelled into the battlefield. Chatham and Ruzena rode close behind. Rolland Storr and his Black Wolf company rallied the Cynaran forces, leading them through the curtain of smoke, into the blood-drenched field.

Beyond the walls of fire, the Autumn wolves used their unique gifts granted them by the Unseen to lead Ariodne and the horsemen directly to the survivors, breaking off into five separate paths around and beyond the curling rivulets of fire that turned the earth black and held men captive.

Hilliard and Freyr were close to the edge of the chaos when the troops poured in and two horsemen escorted them to the outer regions of the battleground.

Walks With Fire brought Ariodne to a group of twenty humans who were besieged by a trio of horribly burned soulless fighters who refused to die despite their injuries. Patches of exposed muscle and bone could be seen through their black, ragged wounds. Arrows protruded from their arms, legs, and torsos, and the hilt of a sword was broken off in one of their sides.

Their eyes were bright with madness and they fought with an abandon the red-haired Maven guessed they had found in the opiates from the pleasure pits. These men understood that they were being sacrificed. They had been given the stimulants to make their final moments easier and to give them a reckless edge as they waded through the survivors of the human army.

Ariodne circled behind the hollow men, catching the attention of one of the monsters who turned in time to see a flash of cold steel as his head was separated from his shoulders by the razor-sharp scythe at the end of her staff. The headless corpse wandered a few steps, hands reaching out before it, then collapsed into a flaming ditch. The auburn-furred wolf launched herself at the throat of one of the two remaining soulless men, who fell back, his scream silenced before it reached completion. She had torn out his throat before they hit the ground. The body twitched several times as the Autumn wolf disengaged herself and was struck an unexpected blow that sent her spiraling into unconsciousness.

Ariodne was turning her staff, looking for the final hollow soldier, when her horse made a sound of absolute, mindless fear and she felt a sharp tug. In horror she saw the charred, blue-black hand of the hollow man closing over her horse's reins. Before she could stop him, the soulless man yanked hard enough to snap the neck of her mount. The animal's legs collapsed beneath it and Ariodne was pitched over the side of the horse as it fell. She rolled on the ground before its heavy body could fall upon her, the staff pressed close to her body, stopping when she saw the still form of the fallen Autumn wolf beside her.

Suddenly the hollow man was above her and she swung with her staff. There was a twinge of pain in her shoulder and her arm responded by jerking nearly an inch to the right, forcing her to miss the burned and maniacally giggling soldier. The hollow man grabbed the shaft, pulling it from her hands, and turned it around to bring the weapon down upon her. Ariodne was not aware of making a conscious decision to call upon the Forge, but she heard the scream of souls meeting their ends and felt their breath upon her face as a heavy shield suddenly weighed over her. The scythe struck the thick metal shield, the blade sparking and shattering. The soulless man thrust the broken end of the shaft into her shield, pinning the red-haired Maven in place as he dropped down beside her and reached for her throat.

The humans who had been fighting the hollow warriors

suddenly launched forward, swarming over the remaining burnt man. The soldiers from Bellerophon tore into the monster, ripping its arms and legs from its body and finally pitching its still-flailing torso into the nearby wall of flame.

Ariodne crawled toward Walks With Fire. The wolf was breathing, and as the Maven tried to pick up the animal, the Autumn wolf shook herself and opened her eyes. For the second time Ariodne heard the wolf's thoughts in her mind.

"Yes," Ariodne said, "a very good showing, sister. Now let's find the others."

Beyond several curtains of flame, Chatham and Ruzena had been ambushed by a pair of hollow riders wearing stolen black cloaks. They had lost sight of the salt and pepper dog soldier they had been following and soon found themselves in a small clearing with smoky grey walls rising up on every side. Figures had exploded from the gently rolling cover of smoke and flame just ahead. They were not surprised to see a sword in the hand of one hooded rider, a mace in the other. Before Chatham could call out to them in greeting they were charging forward, weapons poised. In seconds the riders were upon them. Shifting in his saddle to avoid the arc of the mace, Chatham slid over the side of his mount, one boot caught in the leather foothold.

Ruzena had raised the *kris* Trevelyan had taught her to wield, catching the sword of her opponent in its arrowhead-shaped notches and twisting suddenly to snap the weapon in half. The hollow rider lashed out with his bare foot, striking her mount in the side with a solid kick, startling the animal. The hood of the soulless warrior fell back, revealing a creature whose face had been burnt, muscle and sinew hanging on to bone in blackened flaps. Ruzena's stomach tightened as the soulless man swung at her with the shattered sword, opening a bloody gash along her arm.

Chatham heard her shriek of pain as he tried to gain control of his mount, which was racing toward a wall of fire. Freeing his dagger, Chatham cut himself loose and plummeted to the ground seconds before the horse leaped across a flaming threshold, its high screams reaching out to him as he brought himself to his feet. Suddenly he smelled the stink of burnt flesh and sidestepped the attack of the hollow rider who had circled around for him. The monster's weapon had swung in a low arc, snapping at the old warrior's head. Except for his dagger, he was weaponless, his skrymir facing the same end as his horse.

The heavy, spiked metal ball of the mace once again struck

before him and Chatham leaped back, trying to catch a glimpse of Ruzena. The mace slapped at the air repeatedly, herding the grey-bearded warrior closer to the spitting fire behind him. "This is not very sporting of you," Chatham said with a disarming smile.

He had only a passing glance at the red eyes of his attacker as the hollow man laughed and came at him again.

Only ten meters away, separated by a rolling cloud cover of choking black fumes, Ruzena forced away a scream as her opponent reached out and grabbed at the flank of her mount, his bony, charred fingers digging deep into the meat of the animal's side as he dragged their horses close until the heads of their mounts were pressed together, their eyes blazing with fear. The blond-haired, lithe woman jammed the swordbreaker into the monster's stomach as he reached for her. The hollow man laughed as he closed his free hand over Ruzena's armored throat and pressed his ruined face against hers. Suddenly he shifted his grip on the mount, snatching a section of hide just behind the small of Ruzena's back. She sawed at his guts with the weapon and he slowly forced her back, her spine only partially anchored by his arm. With a dull, horrible realization, she understood that he was attempting to shatter her spine.

Close to the wall of flame, Chatham feinted into the path of the mace, then darted away, cursing himself for allowing the rider to get so close. All he could think about was Ruzena; she was facing one of these monsters alone. His concern should have been for Trevelyan, but he had sensed no real danger to the young prince in the burning field. The old man cursed again, this time out loud. He was human here, once again a mortal. His *senses* could no longer be trusted.

Stop beating on yourself and end this, he thought. With the next swing of the mace, Chatham avoided the initial, forceful snap of the weapon, then launched himself forward, seizing the chain and dragging the rider from his mount. Before the surprised soulless man struck the ground, Chatham had pulled the weapon from his hands, flung the metal ball back in the air, and brought it crashing down on the warrior's head, shattering his face and driving the cartridge from the bridge of his nose into his brain. A second swing of the mace and the soulless man's head exploded. Chatham's eyes were flecked with red and he had to force away his animal bloodlust.

The grey-bearded man looked down at the gory mess of

broken white bone and bloody brains and tried to catch his breath. Then from across the clearing he heard the harsh, unremitting snap of bone. Rushing through the smoke he arrived in time to see Ruzena and her adversary fall from their mounts. They dropped in a heap, her swordbreaker protruding from the hollow man's back.

"Ruzena!" he screamed in horror, covering the distance between them in leaden strides, slowing as he came within a few paces of her. He had been around death enough times to know it even from a distance. A single, pain-wracked sob reached up impossibly from his chest and he felt tears welling in his eyes. The old warrior had not wept in more than one hundred years.

"Get . . . this *thing* . . . off of me."

Shocked from his grief, Chatham looked down to see Ruzena weakly attempting to force the body of the dead hollow soldier from her. The grey-bearded man bent down and examined the dead man's back. His spine had been broken in two by the *kris*, bloodstained vertebrae poking out at either side of the weapon's point. Chatham tore the body of the dead man away from Ruzena and pulled her into a tight embrace. Her arms encircled his body and she buried her face in his shoulder, one hand reaching up to touch his soft, white fleece hair.

"We can't win this war," she said softly, the crackle of nearby flames almost drowning out her words.

"Not like this we can't," Chatham agreed as he surveyed the burning field. "Not like this. Can you stand? We have to find the survivors, get them out of here."

She smiled and suddenly her expression faltered, her flesh becoming pale as her fingers dug into his heavy shoulders. "Chatham," she said hoarsely. "I can't feel my *legs*."

Far from the clearing where Chatham and Ruzena clung to each other, Trevelyan followed Black Mask to his final destination, close to the rear doors of the fortress city. He had been led past isolated pockets of fighting, forced to ignore the wounded who stumbled or crawled away from the burning devastation of the fields, riding past his friends who were busy shepherding the survivors from the field, protecting them from the hollow who had survived.

Beyond a wall of flames he could see the guard towers above the closed and locked rear doors. A figure stood there, waiting. Despite the distance, Trevelyan knew that it was Kothra standing

on the parapet, surveying his handiwork. The young prince had
formed a desperate plan. After seeing the carnage the soulless had
so effortlessly wrought, he knew that unless the humans out-
numbered the hollow one hundred to one, the fortress could never
be taken. If he didn't act quickly, those numbers would be rallied,
and the percentage of casualties the humans would sustain would
be higher than it had been in any previous war.

"Kothra!" he shouted. "I come to you not as Arayncourt of
Cynara, but as the will of the Unseen. Our god speaks and acts
through *me*!"

Black Mask turned to Trevelyan in alarm, then looked up at
the fortress.

Suddenly the walls filled with hollow warriors, dozens armed
with bows. "Then your god can be felled with one well-placed
arrow," Kothra yelled in return. The laughter of his men drifted
down, over the flames.

"The Unseen offers a challenge to your weak and pitiful
god," Trevelyan screamed, bringing the laughter to an abrupt
end. "Face the emissary of the Unseen in single combat. Let
no more of our number or yours be sacrificed foolishly."

"It's your little red-haired bitch that I want," Kothra called
out. "Give her to me, then we'll talk."

"All others are immaterial. The battle is between the two of
us, the chosen of our gods. If you run from my challenge, the
Unseen will have no choice but to level this city in such a
manner that no one will ever be able to build here again."
Trevelyan waited for the reaction of the Kothrites. The integrity
of the religion Lady Brynna had formed around Kothra was
now at stake, and the soldiers were worried and expectant.

Kothra grinned. "What are the terms?"

"If you win, full access to the Trader's Reach and Rien
declared a power."

"And if I lose?"

"I'll discuss it with your successor," Trevelyan shouted. He
watched as the hollow man's face seemed to cloud over, as if
he were losing interest and his attention was drifting from the
exchange. The first man of the hollow squeezed his eyes shut,
then shuddered. When he looked down at the young prince, he
seemed contented and amused.

"When and where, young lord?"

"A week from now in the valley outside your main gate.
Your men will stay behind, in the city, and observe from the

walls. Mine will remain on the rise. Your advantage of liquid fire will be of no value, and my people will be too far away to use the Forge against you.''

"A week? I prefer my enemies to be strong and well fed. In a week half your number will have dropped in starvation. The others will be feeding from their corpses.''

Trevelyan said nothing.

"Are you surprised, young lord?'' Kothra called. "As you are suddenly almighty and all knowing, it should come as no surprise to you that by now the troops we had left at the shore, beyond the Forest of Bone, will have attacked your rear flank, killing your companions and destroying your food. I'll give you two days, Arayncourt. I'll even leave some crumbs outside our walls so you don't starve first. Or perhaps your *god* will see fit to provide for you.''

Trevelyan grimaced as he slowly turned, the laughter of the Kothrites quickly joined by their master. Looking down at the Autumn wolf, Trevelyan said, ''Take me back through. We left him back there. We've got to save my friend.''

The turquoise eyes of the wolf narrowed. Together they looked at the smoking field. They could not see the hillside where they had made camp.

"*Shantow,*'' Trevelyan said, kicking the sides of his mount as Black Mask raced ahead.

CHAPTER
TWENTY-FOUR

Ten minutes earlier Shantow had been cursing his friend for leaving him behind. Bandages covered part of his face and he had removed them to see the awful scars that the fight on the wall had left. He was no longer the young, handsome heir to the Kintaran throne. People would turn away from him in disgust, their reaction instinctive and unavoidable.

For the past few days he had been forced to allow his body to recover from the trauma he had received during the attack. He had been given the opportunity to think and that was the last thing he had desired.

As he had watched the wolves lead Ariodne, Trevelyan, and the others into the field of battle, he was once again confronted by his own thoughts. Unwelcome images of his previous life flooded into his mind, moments that he had tried to suppress since the night when Chianjur delivered a monstrosity of a son. He recalled the first time he was introduced to his future wife, when they were children. They hated each other instantly. For years they found ways to torment each other with outlandish pranks and deeply refined insults. Then, one day in the shadows of his father's study, Shantow sneaked a kiss. He expected her to be furious; he had not anticipated that both of them would like it, or that they would be so anxious to continue exploring the pleasures each other's young bodies could provide. Memories of falling in love, supporting her through her many trials, having her strength and her love to hold him up even when there seemed to be nothing else for him in the world, played out before him. He recalled their separation of two years when he was sent to Aranhod, and his delight at the changes that had been wrought in her feminine body when she was finally allowed to join him. They made love for the first time the night she arrived and both were virgins.

There is maybe nothing so simple, or so beautiful, he had told Trevelyan. Or as awkward and traumatic. After they had been together for several nights, Chianjur grew to enjoy their lovemaking as much as her betrothed, and by their wedding night she had surpassed him in her drive to discover new and more exhausting ways of satisfying them both.

A woman gasped from somewhere close, a noise dangerously similar to the sounds Chianjur would make when he first entered her. Nevertheless, the sound brought him out of his reverie and forced him to take in his surroundings.

Shantow and Akako were stationed at a hastily erected camp. Tents and bedrolls had been forged. Occasionally one of the enclosures would wink out of existence, possibly with the death of the caster. A low, squat, stone building had been forged as a repository for their supplies. The roof was the highest point in the camp and that is where Shantow and his bodyguard sat, looking out at the overcast sky that threatened to sink down over the camp and choke it with its gloom. Torches burned in each corner.

"Did you hear that?" Shantow asked. "A woman's cry?"

"It sounded like Delhia Jenorotte, our chef's assistant," the older Kintaran said. "Her child was born of the hollow and her dreams are haunted by its birth. She must have fallen asleep, despite what occurs out there."

Did she sleep with monsters? Shantow wondered. Then Ariodne's words intruded on his thoughts, "Come on, Shantow, do you really believe Chianjur would betray you? You saw her face, she was as shocked as you were when the baby was born without a soul. The only thing more appalling than the tragedy of your child's birth was your reaction to it, and to your wife when she needed you most."

No, he thought, there was evil in her womb, the hollow men took her and she *liked* it. He squeezed his eyes shut. She betrayed me, he chanted inside his head.

Do you *really* believe that? he asked himself.

With a deep, ragged sigh he sent Akako to fetch Delhia. There were just over twenty men from Bellerophon left in the camp as guards. A few hundred soldiers, the riders of Kenholm who had been relieved of their mounts, mulled about at the base of the farmlands, outside the wall of flame, waiting for survivors to stream out in need of assistance. They were too far away to respond to a cry from the camp.

He heard the scrape of heels on the ladder that had been forged on the side of the supply house and was not surprised to see the black hair of the young chef's assistant as the thin woman with a childlike body climbed over the side and sat before Shantow, emulating his cross-legged position. Akako waited below.

"Have I displeased you, milord?" Her eyes were downcast.

"Look at me," Shantow said.

The woman did as she was told. He was surprised at how attractive she was, despite the unwashed hair that fell into her eyes and the rags she wore. Her eyes were a ghostly blue, her features carefully sculpted and delicate.

"You lost a child," Shantow said flatly.

"Yes," she answered quickly, conscious of her station and terrified in the presence of the future Kintaran emperor.

"Tell me about it," he said and Delhia turned away.

"My baby girl was born a hollow. My husband bashed her brains out against the wall, made me watch. It was my punishment, he said. Then he had our marriage—what's the word for when they make it like it never happened at all?"

"Annulled," Shantow said.

"That's it, that's what he did. Now there ain't no man that wants me, 'less I take work as a whore," she said. "That I won't do. I done nothing wrong but love my husband and try to give him children."

"I'm sorry," Shantow said, truly shaken. Her story was one that he had heard many times over the past few months, but that did not diminish its power or its truth, which Shantow still struggled to deny. "I shouldn't have made you go through that again."

"You're very kind," Delhia said. "But it's in the past. It doesn't really matter."

He knew that she was lying. "My wife, my son—" he struggled with the words, then blurted out, "You lay with no man but your husband?"

For the first time, the serving girl briefly came to life. Her gaze bore into Shantow and her pent-up resentment and fury nearly exploded as she somehow kept herself from slapping him. "I don't know how it is in your country, but here it's not right and proper to humiliate—"

She broke off suddenly when she saw the tears that threatened to escape from Shantow. Suddenly he was not a dignitary, he was simply a young man, barely twenty, who had been trapped by his own lies. She had heard the stories of what he had done to his wife and child, and when Akako came to her, her only surprise was that the summons had come so late. Countless nights had passed without sleep as she asked herself a single question that seemed to have no answer: If her own husband were to come to her, repenting his actions, would she find it in herself to forgive him?

Staring into the eyes of the frightened and confused young Kintaran, she suddenly knew the answer. Delhia threw her arms around Shantow, holding him as painful, racking sobs were dredged up from deep within him.

He wept for several minutes, clinging to this complete stranger, and finally whispered that he needed some time to himself. The dark-haired serving girl rose to her feet, his hand still in hers. She squeezed it tightly, smiled with an expression of understanding, then turned to walk to the edge of the roof. Before she moved to climb down over the side, Delhia called his name urgently. Shantow looked up in time to see the serving girl's sky-blue eyes roll up in her skull as she teetered on the brink, then fell from the roof. "No," he said softly.

An instant later he registered the long, bone-white shard that had pierced her chest, identical to the weapons they had found in the guardhouse near the Forest of Bone.

"Shantow, we're under attack!" Akako screamed.

On the roof, the young Kintaran flattened and called upon the power of the Forge to create a pair of crossbows, each loaded and prepared to fire. Akako had taught him how to materialize a new bolt each time he fired, cutting the disadvantage of the minute-long delay between firing shafts from the weapon. Crawling to the edge of the roof, Shantow attempted to see some sign of his enemy.

"Akako, get inside and seal the door with the Forge!"

"I won't leave you," Akako shouted.

"Do it!" Shantow screamed.

Instants later he heard the door slam shut, followed by the whisper of displaced air, the telltale sign of the Forge.

"Akako," he whispered, suddenly aware that he might never again see his teacher and friend.

"I sealed it from the outside," Akako called in their native tongue. "A reasonable compromise. Do you see them?"

"I see nothing," Shantow said. "They maybe do not have their white paint, which would make them easy to spot."

Screams came from the other end of the camp. The hollow were executing the poisoning victims who had been left there in a makeshift hospital. Shantow cried out in frustration. He could see nothing and did not dare leave his position. On the ground before the supply house, Akako was alone and unprotected. He would have forged shields by now, but they would be little help. There had to be a way to get his old friend onto the roof without getting him killed. He looked out at the camp. Before he had asked to see Delhia, all twenty of the fighters left behind had been in position around the camp, all in plain view. Now they were gone. Either the hollow soldiers had already taken them or they were hiding inside the tents, hoping to ambush the hollow after they passed. He asked Akako if he had seen where the warriors had gone and the older man had confessed that he had seen nothing, he had been busy filling and lighting his pipe.

Shantow tried to guess the position of their first attacker from the trajectory of the shard of petrified wood that had killed Delhia. He gazed in that direction. There was nothing but an empty stretch of soil.

More screams drifted toward Shantow from the hospital. "I think there's maybe only one of them out here," Shantow said, wishing that he could somehow signal the guardsmen who were gathered in the valley before the burning fields; he needed them to storm the tent and protect the fallen.

"Let's draw him out," Akako said suddenly, briefly appearing in Shantow's line of vision as he darted to the ladder and scrambled upward. Thick metal shields were tied over his back and he wore the heaviest armors Shantow had ever seen. The young Kintaran blindly fired a volley in the direction where he expected an attack to originate, the area facing the north wall, where Akako climbed. His shafts whistled through the air, skidded across the ground, then rolled and flopped to abrupt stops, harmlessly. Akako's gloved hand was on the parapet of the roof when two white shards of petrified wood sailed through the air from his side. One missed, the other dug deeply into his rib cage, causing him to lose his grip. Shantow anchored himself and reached out for the older man, his hand closing over the man's wrist. The young Kintaran was dragged to the edge of the wall by Akako's armored weight. The older warrior reached out, blinded by pain, and gripped the parapet with his free hand as he screamed, "Shoot him!"

Shantow looked over the side and saw a giant painted in ivory move close to the edge of the wall. The monster was about to throw two more daggerlike shards. Grabbing his crossbow, Shantow fired a bolt in the direction of the hollow warrior as the soulless man threw both of his weapons. The first shard ripped through the fleshy part of Shantow's upper arm, causing him to howl in pain as he dropped his weapon to the ground; the second barely missed his face, sailing into the air with a sharp whistle. Shantow fell back, losing his grip on Akako. The breath was knocked out of him by the impact of striking the roof. Akako vaulted over the parapet, scrambled to his feet, and dragged the ladder with him.

"Shantow," he said, dropping beside his ward. The white shard was embedded in Shantow's upper arm. The major artery had been grazed and the weapon could not be removed without inviting a fountain of blood.

"Did I kill that stinking thing?" Shantow gasped.

"Missed by over a meter," Akako responded, blood leaking from his side. "I saw him running off to his friends."

"By the Unseen," Shantow said as he stared up at the dark

rolling clouds above, the chill making his flesh feel clammy. "Why didn't you maybe just rabbit in the other direction? You could have escaped to warn the Cynarans."

"You were hurt," Akako said proudly. "My place is with you."

"That kind of thinking will get us both killed," Shantow said as he rose to a sitting position and crawled to the parapet. "I see nothing. Perhaps we could still escape!"

Suddenly the hospital tent exploded in flames as one side was torn open and a string of hollow men erupted, screaming with victory as they ran directly for the supply house. The young Kintaran waited for the guards to stream out of their tents, but the enclosures remained silent and dark. The hollow men did not even stop to peer into the tents, they already knew that no one was left behind.

"Shantow, you've got to listen to me. There's only the two of us but we could still have the advantage. Listen to me!" Akako hollered. His young charge turned. Defeat was in the boy's eyes. "You never give up, do you understand me?"

"It's over," Shantow said.

"You wife nearly lost your child *twice*," Akako said harshly. "The second time she was told that to continue the pregnancy might mean her life, but she did it anyway because she knew how much you wanted a son. Chianjur did not lie with anyone but you, Shantow. And if you're to make up for the pain you've caused her, you have to live."

Shantow looked over the side. The hollow men were fifty meters away. "What can we do?"

Akako placed his hand over Shantow's wrist. "Add your vision to mine," the older man said and described an image.

As the pack of soulless warriors approached the supply house they were surprised to see a second wall appear above the parapet. It rose two meters from the slight ledge and was covered with thin slits less than a meter across. The leader of the hollow soldiers was about to give the order for the men to surround the supply house when a metal bolt was fired from the wall into his right eye. The shaft connected with a soft, liquid slap, dropping the soldier to the ground. The momentary surprise of the hollow men allowed the Kintarans to fire three more times, killing a trio of soulless warriors who had been foolish enough to spin and look in the direction from which the bolt had been fired.

"Close to the wall!" the white-skinned sentry hollered as he flattened himself against the black stone of the supply house's east wall, five meters beneath the slot where the Kintarans fired at their enemy. They could only shoot at an angle, not straight down. As long as he was close to the wall he was safe. His fellow soldiers had reacted exactly as the humans had obviously predicted, removing shards of white bone from their quills and throwing them like spears at the wall. The soulless men were enraged and they threw their weapons with blind anger. Nine bounced harmlessly against the wall that had been forged, one miraculously entered the firing slit and did little to stop the barrage that continued to fell the soulless. Eight soldiers were dead in minutes.

That still left thirteen. Laibrook, the white-painted man, could scarcely believe that two wounded humans would have had the strength to forge the walls and rise to the attack. Forging a defensible roof probably would have killed them. He shouted, "Throw your shafts high, let them fall inside their defenses! Then get close to the damned wall!"

Another hollow man was felled as the warriors considered this plan and finally they did as they were told. The white shards flew up, high above the supply house, and seemed to hang in midair for an instant before they sailed downward.

Inside the roofless fort, Akako forced Shantow to the floor of the roof, covering the young Kintaran with his body. Both men were curled into fetal positions to present the smallest targets while Akako held his shields over them and prayed. One by one the white shards fell, sparking against the stone as they struck and shattered. A bone-white projectile pierced Akako's shield and struck the small space on the floor next to their heads.

Silence. The last of the shards had fallen. Akako raised his shield and looked out at the grey sky in time to see a second volley of bone-white daggers turning in the air above them, descending quickly. There had been no order given this time and Akako opened his mouth in surprise. Shantow grabbed the older man's arms, bringing the shields above their heads as they both collapsed to their knees and felt shards fall. One of them ripped through another part of the shield, piercing Akako's hand. He suppressed his cry of pain. Another of the daggers grazed Shantow's leg, tearing open a wide bloody gash. All but one of the other shards rained down around them. The final dagger ripped through the shield and descended toward Akako's chest. Shantow slapped the shard away just as its sharp point touched the chest of his mentor. His movement had been impossibly fast and Akako smiled at his student.

The barrage ended. Silence closed down over them. Then the quiet was rocked by the sound of inhumanly strong fists slamming against the stone walls of the supply house. The hollow men had discovered that there was no longer a door and they would have to bring the walls down to access the supplies. Akako dropped his ruined shield and looked at the young Kintaran. The pride the older man felt radiated from him. Suddenly his expression faltered. Shantow turned and saw what had startled Akako.

A glimpse of a face, then a chest through the slits they had made in the newly forged walls. The hollow men were digging handholds and footholds in the stone and climbing the side of the supply house. They had to have realized that the quickest way inside was through the sealed door, which would be open to them if the caster was dead. Ignoring the horrible, grinding pain from the shaft embedded in his arm, Shantow grabbed his crossbow, which was still loaded, and fired at point-blank range into the gut of the hollow man climbing over the side. Although the soulless warrior moaned with pain, he did not slow.

Akako had seen another soulless man climbing past a slit in the north wall and snatched one of the bone shards from the ground, driving it through the slit, into the face of the soulless man. This one surrendered his grip to place his hands over his ruined face as he plummeted to the ground.

The others weren't foolish enough to climb near the slits. "They're coming over the walls," Akako whispered. "Load your weapon, we'll take a few of them anyway."

"How many could be left?" Shantow said breathlessly.

"Enough," Akako said. "Put your back to mine. Wait for a clear target, go for their eyes."

Shantow's entire body was trembling. Akako's left leg did not appear that it would support him for long. They waited for long seconds. Akako said, "I love you, my son."

"And I you, Father."

Suddenly a hand appeared over the side, followed by another hand with a bone-white shard about to be released. Shantow fired at the hand clutching the weapon, his shaft piercing the wrist. The hollow man outside the wall screamed as the bones in his wrist were shattered, his hand suddenly dangling loosely, held by gristled muscle alone. As he tried to haul himself over the side with his one good hand, a second bolt pierced his left eye, sending him back over the side, dead before he hit the ground.

Another hollow man gripped the outer ridge of the newly forged wall and heaved himself up, his waist level with the ledge, then he leaned in and brought his legs up behind him. For an instant he performed a handstand on the wall, then he pushed off with his hands and spun in midair, landing on his feet directly before the young Kintaran. He opened his mouth and let out a mad scream as his jaws descended toward Shantow's throat. Akako turned and jammed his crossbow against the monster's throat and fired, the bolt tearing open the soulless man's neck. In the confusion, two more soulless warriors had been able to get over the wall. Before Akako could turn, a white bone shard penetrated the upper part of his back, chipping the bone of his shoulder blade.

He teetered as Shantow fired his crossbow, his shaft striking between the eyes of the blue-black-skinned giant who dropped to the ground. The white-painted soulless man leaped forward and three more of his brethren appeared. Shantow forged a scythe and whirled with the weapon, its blade sinking into the painted flesh of Laibrook's face. The man fell twitching and writhing at Shantow's feet. Around his waist was a belt. One of the pouches had come open, spilling the same strange powder Kothra had used to signal his men to set the shores ablaze days ago. The young Kintaran dropped his weapon and reached down, cupping a handful of the spilled powder, and ran to the flaming brazier near the corner of the roof. One of the hollow men reached for him as he threw the powder in the air, then raised the torch. The explosion of blinding white light that followed stunned the hollow men.

"Drop the walls!" Akako screamed.

Shantow released his hold on the walls they had forged. Pinwheels of light flashed across his vision and as they cleared he had a glimpse of the older man rushing forward, shoving him toward the parapet. His legs scraped the meter-high ledge and suddenly he was falling through the air, his back striking the hard ground. He was winded as he looked up to see the last of the hollow men climbing over the ledge, converging on Akako, who had forged the traditional sword of the Yakima family, a two-handed broadsword that he wielded with a vigor that belied his many wounds.

"Akako!" Shantow screamed.

A single word echoed through the grey afternoon as Akako shouted in a voice strangled by pain, "Run!"

The young Kintaran appeared stricken as he came to his feet and ran in the direction of the burning fields. He was crying and screaming in rage as he raced away from the supply house and the camp. Behind him he heard a single human scream of exquisite agony, then silence. He turned and looked back to see three of the hollow men leaping from the roof. The doorway had returned. Torches were tossed down to them, then the last of the survivors leaped from the roof and entered the low building. Shantow was about to run for the supply house when it suddenly exploded from within.

"Akako!" he screamed, although he knew his friend was already dead. The walls collapsed inward as a tower of reddish-black flames rose where the supply house had been. Shantow dropped to his knees in confusion and defeat. The thunder of hooves sounded from behind him and he turned to see mounted warriors racing in his direction. They slowed when they saw the fiery remains of the squat building.

"The supplies!" one of them shouted.

"Are safe," a familiar voice said heavily. Lon Freyr and Wolfram Hilliard rode close. Behind them, Trevelyan was allowed through the line of riders. He dismounted and knelt beside his friend. Black Mask was beside him.

"Akako's dead. Our fallen were slaughtered. The guardsmen disappeared. Dead, I suppose," Shantow said, the pain of his wounds finally becoming real to him. "All dead. And the supplies are gone. We'll starve."

Freyr shook his head. "The supplies were never there. Remember the mountain of waste we buried yesterday?"

Shantow slowly shook his head.

"The liquid fire you brought back was splattered over the walls and floor, the place was drenched with water. We had hoped that a few sparks would be all that was needed."

"Why wasn't I told about this?" Trevelyan demanded.

"There was no need for you to know," Hilliard said.

"I see. Akako died for nothing. He didn't even know—" Shantow broke off, his voice choked with emotion.

Trevelyan glared at Hilliard. "The fallen were mine."

"They knew the risks coming here."

"What happened to the guards?" Shantow asked.

"Their orders were to run if the hollow appeared. We thought there'd be time to evacuate the fallen." Hilliard turned to Trevelyan. "If you wish to discuss it further, we'll do so after the survivors are taken from the field."

"We will talk," Trevelyan said as he turned from the scorched man and placed his hand on his friend's shoulder. Freyr and Hilliard returned to the field. Trevelyan and Shantow stared at the fire. "I'm sorry, Shantow."

They watched the flames. "He died well," Shantow said. "He died for maybe the only thing that's worth giving up your life." The pain was slowly overwhelming him. Before them, the flames were already dying away.

"He died for love."

CHAPTER TWENTY-FIVE

Trevelyan watched as the last of the casualties was removed from the burning field. A healer from Bellerophon was with Shantow. The shard had been removed from the arm of the young Kintaran with a minimum of blood loss and the future emperor had settled into a deep, comforting sleep. The red-haired Maven approached Trevelyan defiantly, prepared for a spirited discussion over her role in the rescue efforts. When she saw the haunted expression on his face, the fight left her and she immediately became concerned. Trevelyan told her the entire story.

"All he talked about was Akako and Chianjur. He understands the mistakes he's made and he wants to make up for them. When we get home, he's going to send for Chianjur and beg her forgiveness. He's sworn to be with her, even if it means giving up his empire."

"Strong words, spoken in grief," Ariodne said. "I hope he still means them later."

"He will," Trevelyan said, recalling the expression on his friend's face. "I know him. He meant what he said."

Together they went to survey the wounded. Rolland Storr had lost none of his men, Kenholm had been killed in the fireball that had consumed the field and his men now looked to Rolland for leadership. Trevelyan met with Rolland and ordered him to protect the wounded at all costs. He would not trust Hilliard again.

The new hospital was erected midway between the field and their main camp. Moving the majority of the wounded was difficult. Soon Trevelyan and Ariodne came upon Chatham, who was crouched beside an unconscious Ruzena. The grey-bearded man gently held the former sentry's limp hand. The strongly built old man remained with his back to the young prince. Trevelyan did not need to see his face to know the bloodlust that flickered in his dark eyes.

"I want to see them dead, Trevelyan. All of them. I want to make them dead!" he snarled.

"Yes," Trevelyan said simply. "There is a way."

Shortly before nightfall, a messenger was dispatched to tell the soulless that the Unseen had indeed provided and the duel would take place in a week. While the confused young man who had been selected for the task of delivering "the word of God" was at the gate, Trevelyan met with Hilliard and Freyr and told them of his plan. After their startling defeat in the burning field, the soldiers from Bellerophon were easy to convince.

"Whoever goes won't be coming back," Trevelyan said flatly. "Getting there will be just as dangerous."

"Then it should be me," Lon Freyr said.

Hilliard studied the face of the red-haired lieutenant. He sensed a fatalism that could not be manufactured. Freyr *was* willing to die for his country. For the first time, Hilliard wondered if he had been wrong about the younger man.

"Your lover," the red-fleshed, bald-headed man said softly, "the Maven. She will take the secret of liquid fire from Kothra once we have captured him."

"Of course," Trevelyan lied. It was unsafe for a Maven to enter the mind of an unwilling subject; she could go mad or die. Freyr glanced conspiratorially at the young prince and maintained his silence.

Afterward, Lon Freyr sought out Trevelyan and met with him alone. "My wife studied to become a Maven. What you told Hilliard was untrue. You don't want to capture Kothra. You want him dead, his secret lost forever."

Trevelyan did not bother denying the charges. "You want something, Freyr. What is it?"

"In the morning, before work begins, you will announce

that *three* tunnels will be made, not one, tripling your chances for success. After all, one of them might collapse.''

''Yours.''

''Or so the story will be told. Your woman was in the mind of the former tunnel worker. She knows the precise layout of the labyrinth beneath the city. The paths of the first tunnels will take the men into the underground, as you had planned. My tunnel will be designed to lead away from Rien, to safety.''

''For this you will maintain your silence?''

''I will,'' Freyr said solemnly.

''And will you release me from the promise I made to you before Hilliard arrived?''

''No,'' the red-haired lieutenant said without hesitation. ''But if I survive, you won't have to honor it.''

''Then it's agreed.'' They sealed the agreement in blood and Trevelyan returned to his friends. Freyr stared at the receding form of the young prince and wondered if either of their plans had a chance of succeeding.

Later that evening, Ariodne led Trevelyan to a deserted hillock where they quietly made love. When they had finished, they lay naked and sweating in each other's arms, their bodies squeezed together as if they were trying to force their flesh to melt away and bond them into a single entity. As Trevelyan relaxed within her, he knew their goal was an impossible one.

''Take him quickly,'' Ariodne whispered. ''Don't let him come anywhere near you. I killed one of them on the wall in a way I didn't know was possible. I'll teach it to you.''

She wanted to tell him that she knew the truth, but she could not bring herself to speak the words that might have saved them both. They made love again, giving themselves without hesitation, without conditions, and without restraint.

Over the next few days, Trevelyan's plan was implemented. Ariodne was kept busy by the designers of the tunnels, helping them to plan the best way to the catacombs. By using the Forge, the warriors were able to blast the earth out of their way in a method similar to that used by sculptors and master builders. They created sturdy concave walls strengthened by support beams. The shafts were camouflaged with newly forged stone buildings without roofs, allowing as much air into the tunnels as possible. The men worked in shifts, a fresh crew in the tunnels at all times.

Occasionally, one or two hollow men would approach the

city. They were outsiders, having heard the call of Rien too late. Rolland and his Black Wolf company hunted down the newly arrived soulless and slaughtered them before they reached the city's fortress walls.

Traders from Knossos were spotted on the trail leading from the Forest of Bone, their goods seized, the merchants questioned and turned away. They had seen no sign of the *Adventure* or Lon Freyr's black ship. Crates of powdered stimulants and marmion roots were taken to the center of the still-smoking field where the humans had been ambushed. The expensive substances were dumped into the smoldering rivulets of liquid fire and destroyed.

Trevelyan had guessed Kothra's plans. The hollow had destroyed the fields because they no longer needed them. They would remain sequestered within their walled city with all the provisions they would need to survive the imminent winter, then march from the city after the weather cleared, fighting their way through the troops gathered outside.

Their target would be the Trader's Reach. The soulless would seize control of the merchant city and disrupt the flow of the world's economy. To this end, they would build war machines that could spray liquid fire at a distance.

Trevelyan sat alone, contemplating a world controlled by the hollow. He heard a familiar padding on the damp earth behind him and did not bother to turn as Black Mask appeared.

The lotus is close, the first wolf said in a voice that only Trevelyan could hear. The young prince stared into the perfect turquoise eyes of the wolf, at the strange black pattern of fur that covered his face, and the sharp teeth that were exposed as the animal panted and moved back and forth in an effort to keep warm. The chill had grown worse.

"Your mate can create gateways," Trevelyan said. "I saw one of them above the wall, when you helped us to escape."

They are not for you, Black Mask whispered.

"Where do they take you?" Trevelyan asked.

A place you could not understand. You would die there. Mortals could not survive where we go.

The dark-haired prince brushed the long shock of hair from his eyes. His beard was growing thick and covered much of his face and his eyes were red-rimmed from lack of sleep.

"If I fall, will the Unseen choose another champion?"

No, Black Mask said. *You are the Arayncourt. Our pledge dies with you.*

Trevelyan laughed. "Yes, you would have to say that. But I expect I'm easily replaced. After all, I wasn't your first choice, was I? You wanted my father. He dreamed of you before his death."

Your actions have honored his memory.

Turning his entire body, Trevelyan pleaded with the wolf. "Tell me if my father's soul has been consumed."

Black Mask stared at him. *Oram's soul has not yet been destroyed. Only* you *have the power to condemn him to what waits for the spirits in the wells throughout Autumn. The next time you call upon the Forge, his soul will be taken.*

Trevelyan became pale. "I can't possibly defeat Kothra in a fair fight. If I don't use the Forge I'll be killed."

Perhaps.

Walks with Fire approached them. She seemed concerned. *Black Mask—*

Leave us. This is not for you. The auburn-furred wolf stared at him defiantly. *Go now!*

The wolf's mate lowered her tail and retreated from him. Trevelyan had nothing further to say. He stared off at the sky and soon Black Mask left him. Twenty minutes later Ariodne found him. "It's time that we practiced," she said.

"Not today," he said softly, remembering his father.

Inside the fortress city, in his private chamber, Kothra sadly looked down at the city. Lady Brynna Celosia was still recovering from her wound and would not be present when he left the city to face the human champion. He had no plans of returning. His age was finally catching up with him.

At first Trevelyan's challenge had seemed absurd. The boy proclaiming that he was the right hand of the Unseen was almost as audacious a lie as the religion that had been founded in Kothra's honor and the myths surrounding his birth. Lady Brynna pointed out how the fight could work to their benefit. If events were left unchanged, the first man of the hollow would pass on from natural causes long before spring, his heart exploding in his chest. The sight of his death in such a quiet, hopeless manner would demoralize his followers, infusing them with a sense of futility. If he were killed while fighting for their ideal, he would die a martyr and would be remembered for all time by the soulless who would soon inherit the world of Autumn.

Abbas Bute appeared. Nothing had been said of his betrayal of Kothra. They had gone on as if nothing had occurred and Abbas waited for punishment. After a time, it came to him that the fearful waiting was in itself a penance.

"Lady Brynna wishes to see you," Abbas said stiffly.

Kothra nodded in response, his back turned to his second in command. Abbas Bute turned and left the chamber.

The first man of the hollow hung his head back, imagining that he was back in the place of his birth, enjoying one of the rare moments when his human parents left him alone. As he was growing they forced him to be their slave, a dog fit for nothing but the sting of the whip and the pain of their boots in his ribs and fists in his face.

He imagined bright, beautiful, warm sunlight. For an instant he felt the heat he so desperately needed. Then a lancing pain shot through him and the chill returned. Opening his eyes, he glanced at the city once again.

He would die for a purpose.

And he would take Trevelyan Arayncourt along with him.

CHAPTER TWENTY-SIX

It was just before dawn in the hollow land. Bright streaks of pastel pink and yellow graced the sky, hanging low on the horizon beneath a deep blue curtain where a few stars were still visible. The temperature had dropped.

Trevelyan stood before the main gates of the fortress city. Kothra was late. If the young prince had not been too busy fighting off the absolute terror that had gripped him from the moment he had awakened that morning, he might have been amused at the hollow man's casual attitude toward their duel. He had arrived late at financial meetings to gain the advantage that came from blinding your opponent with anger, and he was determined not to give Kothra that benefit.

The armors he wore and what weapons he carried had been forged by Ariodne. His refusal to train with the Forge had unnerved her and she insisted that he carry a small arsenal.

Less than an hour before, with Ariodne at his side, he had drawn his *kris* and cut a wide swath in the air with the swordbreaker. Pirouetting, he ducked and stabbed forward with both hands on his sword, as if he were impaling an unseen enemy. The young prince barely noticed the steel plating that covered his body with layers of iron mesh protecting his vulnerable joints and covering the top of his head and his neck. A Bellerophon-style headpiece, similar to the one his father had worn into battle, was handed to him by the red-haired Maven. He locked the headpiece in place, the red-jeweled eyes of a wolf staring out angrily from over his brow. Frighteningly sharp black fangs closed down above his eyes and reached up from below his jaw. Besides the *kris*, he was armed with a matching pair of daggers, two *tallos* stars, pouches containing crushed glass dipped in sticky gel and then covered with salt, and a *nikli* staff. His outfit was completed by the traditional coat of arms of his family, some bright red cloth trim, and the emblem of Cynara, the lone wolf howling in silhouette against a full moon.

He thought of Black Mask's warning not to use the Forge for fear of destroying his father's soul. He wished that he could tell Ariodne the truth, but something held him back.

Despite the matter-of-fact behavior Ariodne displayed once she had finished arming him, treating him as if she were sending him off to a business engagement, Trevelyan sensed that she was hiding something. Finally he convinced himself that all he sensed was her concern and they parted so that he could have a few moments with the others. He gave Chatham a carefully drafted will that named his grandmother as his successor and arranged for the disposition of his personal property, then checked once again on the progress of the tunnels. According to calculations, the two shafts manned with Cynarans were almost through to the catacombs beneath Rien. The "accident" in Lon Freyr's tunnel was due to occur during the fight. At the ridge, riders waited for the chance to alert the tunnelers to proceed through the final walls, to the prize and the glorious death that waited.

Twenty minutes had passed since Trevelyan arrived at the gates and called out for Kothra. A few guards looked down at him with bored expressions. The young prince was beginning to fear that the tunnelers had been discovered.

Suddenly a pair of flame-spitting war machines were brought out to the fortress wall above the gates, their nozzles aimed downward. Trevelyan took a few steps back, although he was reasonably sure he was out of their range. Tongues of flame shot out and struck a slight gully that had been dug before the gate and filled with water. A high curtain of flame rose up, practically obscuring the prince's view of the main gates. He heard the labored mechanism of the steel doors as they were opened behind the flickering wall of fire and looked up to see a select audience of hundreds of hollow men and women on the fortress walls.

The ground began to vibrate.

"Where are you?" Trevelyan spat under his breath. He drew back as a horse and rider suddenly burst from the flames. The warrior raced for the young prince, brandishing a mace in one hand, a newly ignited torch in the other. The horseman was cloaked in the heavy, foul-smelling cloth the Cynarans had developed. The horses the hollow men stole from the field were covered with the material, he thought.

Suddenly the rider was upon him and there was no time to think, only to react. The mace was brought down toward the head of the young prince in a blinding motion. Trevelyan darted back and raised his staff, the heavy chain of the mace wrapping around the thick iron shaft. He was amazed that the weapon did not shatter as he dug his feet into the ground and gave it a sharp tug. The black-garbed rider was yanked from his mount and fell heavily upon the ground. The horse rode on, terrified of the flames at its back.

Trevelyan tried to pull the staff away but the blades at the end caught on the mace and he was forced to abandon the weapon. The hooded figure loosed his hold on the mace as he rose to his feet and pulled back the hood with his free hand, the burning torch still held in the other. The merchant prince drew his *kris* as he saw Kothra's face and noted that the hollow man's cheeks were round and bloated; he looked like a child who was holding his breath to prove a point. Driving forward with his swordbreaker, Trevelyan was caught by surprise as Kothra sidestepped the thrust and spit at him, covering his face with a foul-smelling liquid. The first man of the hollow drove his torch forward as Trevelyan turned and raised his arm in defense. The flaming torch ground against the iron plating of his arm, forcing the young prince to stumble backward as Kothra began to laugh.

"Come on, boy. Surely you can give me a better showing than this!" Kothra shouted and the audience on the fortress wall howled in laughter. The soulless man grinned as he drove Trevelyan back with the torch, then planted a heavy kick that knocked the young prince to the ground. His worshipers exploded in approval as Kothra threw the torch away and stripped off the heavy cloak. He wore all three wolf skulls, one on each shoulder, the other over his eyes. The bones that had been sewn into his flesh glistened with the blood he had bathed in that morning. His razor-sharp teeth were flecked red.

Trevelyan wanted desperately to wipe the stinging liquid fire from his face, but there was no time. He imagined the initial shock of a torch searing his flesh, then the incredible torture as the flames perpetuated themselves until all that was left of his head was charred bone. Keeping a grip on his *kris*, Trevelyan considered how easily he could kill the towering giant if only he could use the Forge. The bearded young prince drew one of the *tallos* stars from his boot and threw it at the soulless man's eye.

Kothra flicked the throwing star away with a barely visible motion. He thought of Skuld's surprised and pleased expression in Telluryde, when Kothra had reached the old man's weapon first. "Come to me, child. Show me something I haven't seen." Kothra allowed Trevelyan to get to his feet. "You're the one who wanted this. Show me something!"

Trevelyan held the *kris* before him and whispered, "No, monster. You're the one who started this. You come to *me*."

Kothra giggled and danced forward, hopping on one foot, then the other, his hands flopping daintily in the air as he recited one of Trevelyan's poems. The creature's head bobbed and wobbled, tilting from one side to the other as he paused to drool and roll his eyes between verses.

The young prince swung repeatedly at the towering, blue-black-skinned giant, who darted out of the way with effortless grace, closing in now and then to tap the flat of Trevelyan's sword with this fingers and pat the young prince on the top of his head.

Kothra ended his rhyme but maintained his taunting demeanor. "Did you know that I've killed men in every country on this planet? Except Modren, that is. Such a peaceful, innocuous lot, they *would* be the type to submit docilely to genocide.

That could provide months of entertainment. But first we're going to take Cynara.''

Kothra abruptly shoved at the young prince, then reached in and snatched one of his daggers from its sheath at his waist, pausing to look at the weapon quizzically as if it were a harmless toy.

Trevelyan had been swinging with increasingly shorter sweeps of his weapon, using it to jab, in an effort to draw Kothra close. The first man of the hollow was attempting to tire the young prince early. Breathing hard, Trevelyan made another strike at the hollow man, stabbing empty air. He stumbled to the ground, faltered awkwardly as he dug his sword into the earth to use the weapon as a crutch and dragged himself to his feet.

Kothra stood over Trevelyan, bending slightly with an open palm to slap the side of the young man's face. The crack from the blow echoed in the still morning and Trevelyan was thrown to one side of the hollow giant, his *kris* wrenched out of the ground. Suddenly the weapon flashed in a tight, controlled arc, aimed at the fragile wrist of the powerful creature. Kothra leaped back, barely avoiding the cutting edge that would have taken his hand in one swift motion.

''Very good,'' Kothra said as Trevelyan shook off the pain of the hollow man's slap, rolling and leaping into a proper fighting stance. ''If I hadn't known you were faking your exhaustion, you might have actually cut me. Now let's see, you have a sword and I do not. That hardly seems fair.''

The two men circled each other warily. From a distance, thunder rolled and lightning flashed. ''Perhaps I should tear one of your arms from its socket and use it as a weapon?''

''You talk too much,'' Trevelyan said, slowly closing the distance between Kothra and himself.

''Someone's got to keep this lively,'' Kothra said. ''But I will say this, Trevelyan. I have a short attention—''

Kothra's features suddenly screwed up in pain. His breath caught and a harsh cry of pain escaped him as he clutched at his chest and doubled over. Trevelyan knew that it could be a feint, but he could see no better opportunity. He swung his *kris* toward the back of Kothra's neck. From the periphery of his vision, the hollow man saw the glint of a blade. His arm shot out, fist striking Trevelyan in the chest, altering the deadly trajectory of the weapon. The sword came down on the side of Kothra's head, cracking open the polished white skull he wore on his head and creating a deep gash that dripped blood into his face.

Trevelyan drove his swordbreaker at the hollow man's chest. Kothra reached up and jammed the fingers of one hand between the arrowhead-shaped grooves as he caught the flat of the weapon between his palms, arresting its motion. He looked up, blood leaking into his red eyes, and screamed as he kicked at Trevelyan's instep, shattering several bones. The young prince was forced to loosen his hold on the *kris* as the blood drained from his face and he cried out in pain. Kothra rammed the hilt of the weapon into Trevelyan's chest, lifting the young prince into the air a few inches before the blade snapped and Trevelyan fell.

Blinding, intense pain consumed the bearded young prince as Kothra tossed the front half of the *kris* toward the wall of flames. Kothra picked up Trevelyan by the back of his neck and dragged the young prince toward the flames.

"Lady Brynna was *wrong*," Kothra hissed. "To die at your hands would be a disgrace. I will find another way—one that does not dishonor my people."

Trevelyan reached up weakly, attempting to claw the hollow man's hand from the back of his neck. His vision cleared and he saw the flames before him. The heat was incredible and his face was still wet from the liquid fire he had been drenched in. The merchant prince had told himself that he had been prepared to die if necessary, but only if his death meant the end of Kothra's threat and the claiming of the lotus. With the harsh yellow and red flames rising and spitting so very close, he knew that he had been lying to himself. He reached down and drew his dagger, raising it so that he could plunge the weapon into Kothra's arm and force him to release his grip. The hollow man looked down contemptuously and flicked the weapon from the prince's hand. He frowned as he gathered up the young man's wrists in one of his massive hands. Trevelyan was helpless, despite the *tallos* and the pouch of ground glass he still carried.

Fear overtook Trevelyan, primal terrors snaked through his mind as Kothra tossed him into the flames. As his body was flung forward, the fires overcame his vision and a distant part of him knew that within seconds his eyes would be scorched from their sockets, his flesh melting from the unbearable heat. That portion of his mind acted from instinct, without engaging Trevelyan's ability to reason, without giving him a conscious choice. From somewhere unbearably close he heard a scream and realized in pure horror that he had called upon the Forge in an effort to save himself from the fire.

He cried, "Father, forgive me—!"

It was too late, he understood dully.

The soul of his father had been destroyed.

Trevelyan allowed the flames to take him.

At the ridge, several minutes earlier, Ariodne waited on horseback with Chatham, Rolland Storr, and Wolfram Hilliard. The Autumn wolves were gathered around them. Together they watched Trevelyan's fight with Kothra. Ariodne had a spyglass, which she used to report some of the details that might have been lost. The hollow man was prancing about, taunting the young prince, who swung his sword at the monster without hope of connecting. Behind them, hundreds of humans served as spectators. Ariodne gazed at the soulless men lined up on the fortress wall. She did not see Lady Brynna Celosia or Abbas Bute and that troubled her.

"Why doesn't he use the Forge?" Ariodne said nervously.

"Because he's waiting for the city to blow," Hilliard growled. "The instant they hear the explosions he's supposed to suffocate the monster until he passes out, then bind him so we can take him with us. The hollow will be too busy saving themselves to come after us."

"There must be another reason," Ariodne said absently. Chatham watched as Black Mask and his mate exchanged glances.

"Yes, why hasn't the city been destroyed?" said Rolland. "We sent riders to the mines the instant Kothra appeared. They should have been through the walls by now."

No one had an answer. Suddenly a single rider appeared, his mount galloping furiously. The red-haired Maven felt her chest tighten at the sight of the horseman who slowed as he rode up beside Rolland. He was a tall, brown-haired man with yellow teeth and a hooked nose who wore the crest of the Black Wolf company. Practically out of breath, the rider panted, "Rolland, the tunnels have been taken by the hollow. There must have been more of them out here, spying on us."

"What of the men we posted?"

"They were ambushed. They didn't have a chance," the soldier said in desperation. "About a half-dozen monsters went into each of the tunnels and more are fighting outside."

Rolland tugged at the reins of his mount, turning the horse in the direction of their base camp, where the shafts and the battle waited. Hilliard stood ready to ride beside him. "Ariodne, Chatham, stay here. If we fail to liberate the shafts, go down and protect Trevelyan."

Without waiting for a reply, Rolland kicked his heels into the side of his mount and signaled for a contingent of his men to go after him as he raced toward base camp. Hilliard followed, two groups of soldiers pulling away from the crowd to join him. The Autumn wolves rallied behind them, prepared to follow, when Black Mask turned on his mate. For the second time, Ariodne was able to hear their exchange.

Stay here, mate. I won't risk your life.

You arrogant, lying fool. The decision is mine.

We are mortal here, Black Mask said impatiently. He knew that he was not winning the argument. *Then stay to protect the keeper of the rose. The pup will not call upon the Forge and may need both of you if he is to survive.*

Black Mask, what have you told him? What have you done? the auburn-furred wolf pleaded. Her mate turned and raced from her, his lieutenant and dog soldiers following.

Ariodne dismounted and looked into the troubled eyes of the first wolf. She reached out and touched the side of the wolf's head. The animal started at first, then remained still, allowing the contact.

You wanted me to hear that, Ariodne said. *Why?*

My husband lied to yours, the wolf replied.

We're not yet married.

In your hearts, you are. That is what matters.

Ariodne felt an even greater fear than the one she felt when she saw Kothra burst from the flames and attack her lover. *How did he lie?*

He told Trevelyan that nothing mortal could survive in the border realms where we go when my gates are open. But we are now mortal, and we survive in that place.

The red-haired Maven swallowed hard. *You could take someone directly into the underground catacombs.*

Yes. But only one. And there is no guarantee that you would not go mad.

Standing, the Maven looked out at the field of battle. Trevelyan and Kothra circled each other warily. The vision of Trevelyan plunging a knife into her chest suddenly returned.

She remembered the haunted, insane glare in his eyes. The vision would not come to pass, she decided.

The tunnelers are going to fail. Take me there.

From above Ariodne heard a thunderclap. She stared at Trevelyan, tears welling up in her eyes. "Good-bye," she whispered. "I love you."

A heavy blue haze descended upon her. Through it she saw Chatham running for her, shouting for her to wait, but then it was too late. The ridge vanished, Trevelyan and Kothra faded, and a blinding streak of lightning fell before her, its brilliance consuming her vision.

Her sight did not return, but she was suddenly aware of other senses that she did not know she possessed, and through them she found herself experiencing an existence that was apart from anything she had ever known before.

She no longer had a body or a conscious will. Around her was a universe of pleasures that reached beyond the realm she had left. A dozen worlds were created and destroyed in a span of a heartbeat. She was a single streak of pure black light racing across the eye of the sun, dipping into its flames, reveling in its comfort and warmth. Suddenly she was drowning— her newly formed *senses* were drowning—and she was in a bright, sparkling stream of knowledge and ideas, a raging tide of experiences carrying her along as she died a thousand deaths, some sudden and painful, others long overdue. She experienced a love that overwhelmed her, then shuddered as all-encompassing fear became her only reality.

The Stream of Life, she thought, fighting against the phantasmagoric flood of images and sensations to retain individuality, and suddenly she felt the presence of another.

Sister, you are needed.

With a disquieting tug her soul was yanked backward from the stream, past nightmarish inverted cliffs upon which a millennium of hatreds given face and form waited to lure her to their realm, past inviting gullies where the jealousies of countless lifetimes writhed and attempted to separate themselves from their bleak, timeworn surroundings, through storm-drenched skies that played host to the forgotten aspirations, the lost dreams, and the frustrations of mankind, which took forms of horrid wraiths eternally clawing at the world but never making contact.

A spinning vortex loomed before her, a beautiful creation with swirling reds and blues, dotted with stars.

He needs you.

Beings created from eternal longing and hopelessness made a final lunge for that which had been the Maven Ariodne Gairloch. Her essence sped past the damning influences, toward the spiraling arms of the gateway, and went through.

Ariodne found herself on the dark, clammy ground of an underground chamber. Walks With Fire was above her, licking her face, the animal's foul breath catching Ariodne unprepared. She sprang to a sitting position where she coughed violently and attempted to acclimate herself to the limitations of her human shell. Already the visions were fading. The creatures she had seen were jealous of the living; they desired nothing so much as the chance to once again walk upon Autumn. She knew instinctively that when the last soul was destroyed, the final well consumed, these horrible beings would take the planet and mankind would never again be given the opportunity to take root.

Ariodne, a voice called insistently.

The red-haired Maven jumped up and surveyed the dank room where the wolf's power had taken them. They were in the mixing chamber, where Kothra labored alone to create the delicate balance that resulted in liquid fire. The wolf had combed Ariodne's stolen memories and placed them in the ideal location. Stores of liquid fire were stacked up along the walls, and the explosive base chemicals the hollow man needed were stocked up in chambers adjacent to this one. Tables with cups and spoons, large basins, glass tubes, and vats of foul-smelling, black liquid were in evidence. If there were guards, they were posted outside the chamber.

Kothra would want no one to know his secrets.

The room was lit by small bowls of liquid fire that burned a deep, flickering reddish-black. From somewhere close she could hear the sounds of fighting. At least one group of tunnelers had come close to this place. Ariodne turned on the wolf. "You could have taken one of us here a week ago. Why did you wait?"

Kothra has to die by Trevelyan's hand. The lotus—

"That's not the reason," Ariodne said.

The wolf lowered her gaze. *My husband forbade me. He was afraid I would be hurt, or killed.*

"Do you always do what your husband tells you?"

The auburn-furred wolf stared at her defiantly. *We're here, aren't we, sister? Your mate is fighting for his life. We must help him.*

Ariodne nodded, and then examined the room. The floor was wet. Jagged holes had been driven through the casks of liquid fire. Even the walls had been splattered. It didn't make sense. None of the tunnelers had made it through.

Sister, I sense—

"Ariodne Gairloch," a familiar voice called out. The Maven turned and saw Abbas Bute standing in a shadowy alcove at the far side of the room. She quickly forged a loaded crossbow and aimed it at the towering man who laughed and said, "There is no need. There was no need for *any* of this."

The fumes from the opened casks rose to Ariodne. The smell had evidently confused the wolf, dulled her senses. "You were going to set fire to this place."

"Of course," Abbas said. "Kothra's mad. And Brynna—"

"You'll die here," said Ariodne. "Help me to set the fire and we'll take you with us."

Sister, it cannot be done. The soulless cannot walk the path between the gates.

The soulless man caught the looks exchanged between the wolf and the Maven. "Talked too soon, did you?" Abbas Bute said. "It doesn't matter. We are, all of us, under a death sentence. We live, at most, five years, our bodies aging a year for every month we exist. We can arrest the process on the outside. But the strain eventually bursts our hearts. If you had laid a conventional siege against us, keeping us locked in this prison, we would eventually have all passed. I will not see my people die so meekly. This way—"

The point of a spear suddenly burst from Abbas's throat. He trembled, clutching at his neck as he sank to his knees making pained, gurgling sounds, then he dropped forward. Ariodne stared at him in shock as his blood spread in an ever-widening pool on the wet floor, mixing with the dark liquid that had already been spilled.

Lady Brynna Celosia wrested the spear from his neck and smiled at Ariodne in greeting. The Maven raised the crossbow, but before she could fire, the auburn-furred wolf bounded across the room and leaped at the throat of the beautiful, silver-haired hollow woman, whose midsection was wrapped tightly in bloodstained cloth. Lady Brynna took a step back and raised the spear in a blinding motion, impaling the wolf in midair, the animal's weight and momentum driving the soulless woman back. Brynna's bare feet slipped on the slick pool of blood from Abbas's wound and she fell back, her staff breaking in two as Walks With Fire landed on her chest, the animal alive and fighting despite its terrible pain. Brynna reached up, ignoring the incredible strong nails that ripped into her flesh, and clutched at the savage jaws of the wolf, forcing them apart, shoving them so wide that with a sudden sickening crack of bone she killed the auburn-furred creature. Walks With Fire shuddered, then fell limply upon the heavily scarred-bluish-black flesh of the soulless woman. Brynna attempted to heave the body of the wolf from her, the wound in her side once again open and sending white-hot messages of pain to her mind.

"You bitch," Ariodne said quietly.

Lady Brynna Celosia looked up to see the red-haired Maven standing directly over her, the crossbow aimed at her left eye. Ariodne held the weapon with one hand and anchored it with the other as she fired, a sudden lance of pain from her recently injured shoulder ruining her aim, sending the bolt to the hard floor beside Lady Brynna's head.

The hollow woman recovered quickly from her surprise at Ariodne's failure to kill her and used her one free leg to sweep the Maven's legs out from under her. Ariodne fell back, against the body of Abbas Bute, surprised that the hollow man gave a slight moan at the impact. Lady Brynna freed herself of the dead Autumn wolf and straddled Ariodne before the Maven could call upon the Forge or make a move to defend herself. The hollow woman delivered a brutal series of blows to Ariodne's face, keeping her unbalanced and unable to concentrate on anything more than the pain she was enduring, forcing her attention away from the Forge.

"You think we didn't expect a betrayal from this idiot? But we needed him alive, at least until today."

Brynna grabbed at Ariodne's hair and pounded the Maven's head against the floor. "Do you know the exquisite irony of this? You've not only given me the opportunity to kill the whore of my husband's enemy, but his bastard child as well."

Ariodne attempted to focus her thoughts. What Brynna had said was impossible. She couldn't be pregnant.

"Go on," Brynna said, giving the Maven a respite from the barrage. "Look deep within, you can sense it, can't you? You couldn't at first, because the child is one of ours. He would have been born without a soul, he would have—''

Lady Brynna gasped as the knife Ariodne had slipped from her waist found a home in her throat. A spray of blood struck Ariodne's eyes as she made a deep, vicious cut with the blade and pulled with all her strength to widen the gash, nearly severing Brynna's head in the process. With her free hand, Ariodne reached up and grabbed the white stalk of hair on the top of Brynna's head and yanked it backward. There was a snap as vertebrae cracked apart, then the hollow woman tumbled backward, her eyes wide and staring in death as she settled against the cold, wet floor made even more slick by the blood that pumped from the ragged wound in her neck.

Ariodne went to the body of the fallen wolf. There had been no mistake, Walks With Fire was dead. Ariodne stared into the eyes of the wolf, searching for the blinding intelligence she had seen there. In death, the creature's shell was that of an animal, nothing more.

The Maven smelled the stink of liquid fire. Beside her, Abbas made another sound. He was still clinging to life, his eyes wide and pleading. She sensed there was something he wanted to tell her, but his throat was ruined and he could not speak. Placing her hand against his face, Ariodne lowered her defenses and entered the mind of the dying man.

Seconds later she withdrew her fingers at the touch of his cold flesh. Her mind reeled. He had just given her the secret of liquid fire, a secret Kothra had shared with him out of necessity in the frozen arena of Telluryde.

The hollow man was dead.

Ariodne rose from the pool of blood at her feet, her boots sliding as she made her way to the other side of the room, where the bowls of burning liquid waited. Above her, Trevelyan fought for his life and his destiny. She had come to this place with the certainty that she would die here. Someone had to remain behind to ensure that the chamber would ignite. Even the Autumn wolf and her gates would not have been fast enough to outrace the waves of destruction that would occur when the volatile chemicals caught fire.

The words of Lady Brynna Celosia came to her. She wondered if she was actually pregnant with Trevelyan's son. As a Maven, she would be able to use her powers to explore her own body and learn the truth, if she so desired.

A hollow child. She knew how Trevelyan would react. He would want the child put to death before it could mature. For all her self-righteous views, at that moment she did not believe her response would be any different.

Don't think about it, she urged herself as she picked up the bowl and prepared to hurl it at the waiting pool of liquid fire, starting a reaction that would consume her in seconds. The bowl trembled in her hands as she considered how much she loved him. "I'm so sorry," she whispered.

She lifted it above her head and closed her eyes.

Outside the main gate of the city, Trevelyan had finally called upon the Forge, creating a thick, black hood that covered his face as he was thrown, head first, into the wall of flames. His body struck the fiery wet mud of the ditch and he felt a staggering heat. Crawling blindly from the burning water, Trevelyan thought the blood would boil in his veins before he reached the other side of the flaming curtain. He could not breathe in the hood he had forged and his flesh was becoming sore and numb.

Finally he made it through the gauntlet of fire and removed the hood. The flames were still close, and he dragged himself away from them. He was on the fortress side of the ditch, separated from Kothra by the flames. He looked up at the wall and saw one of Kothra's war machines pointed in his direction. Behind him, the city gates were open. A flame cart had been wheeled out and was also aimed at him.

"Go back through," the hollow man beside the cart called with a laugh. "Go back or we'll burn you right here!"

There was a flicker of reddish-black flame from the nozzle of the ground machine. Trevelyan knew that Kothra would be waiting for him on the other side of the flaming wall, but there was no other choice.

Despite the agony he felt over what he had done, as much as he felt that he deserved death, and worse than death, the same oblivion to which he had consigned the soul of his beloved father, he knew that he had to live, he had to find a way to atone for his actions.

He was about to put on the hood once again when suddenly a horrible explosion came from deep within the bowels of the fortress city and all those gathered turned in the direction of the low, crackling series of booms. From their vantage at the wall, the spectators saw the ground rip open as the earth shuddered.

Fissures were torn throughout the streets of the city. Fires leaped from one rooftop to another as if carried on the wings of destruction. Burning swaths cut through the masses of blue-black-skinned people screaming and trying to escape. Probing, fiery fingers flexed and stretched to ensnare dozens of people at a time as entire streets filled with mammoth, rolling fireballs. Finally, the flames reached the walls of the fortress city, spitting concentrated bursts of fire that tore away chunks of stone with their power, while deep gashes were driven into the earth below the mighty, five-meter-wide stone walls, causing them to sink and collapse as the flames burrowed deeper, then rose up to engulf the walls and the spectators gathered on the high walls, which crumbled and collapsed, spilling the screaming, burning spectators to the quivering ground and the deep reddish-black pools of liquid fire that waited below in the fissures that were still opening in the ground.

Behind the city, near the stone buildings that held the camouflaged entrances to the trio of tunnels the humans had dug, Rolland Storr, the men of his Black Wolf company, and more than fifty Cynarans fought against two dozen hollow giants. When Rolland had arrived, he had been told that almost as many had already made it into the shafts below. The sight of Black Mask and his fellow wolves had slowed down the soulless men, filling them with a primal, superstitious dread as the animals savagely attacked, ripping the hollow men apart. Hilliard's black-garbed warriors clashed with a second group of soulless that had arrived the moment his battered troops entered the melee. To Rolland's horror, he had spotted Shantow wandering from the hospital, toward the battle, then lost sight of the young Kintaran.

No one was prepared as ripping explosions sounded from the city, bringing their combat to a momentary halt as human and soulless alike stared at the towers of flame that rose from within the fortress walls and tore the streets and buildings of Rien apart. Beneath their feet they felt a strange thundering vibration that grew more violent with every second until it was accompanied by a heavy roar and a trio of shocking explosions that blew apart the stone buildings protecting the tunnels, sending a shower of rock fragments upon the combatants. Fires spouted from the entrance to the shafts and fierce columns of flame were driven into the brisk morning air. A feeling of triumph surged through the condottiere as he watched the flames fall to the earth, creating small burning patches of ground.

He did not yet know the price of victory.

The hollow men wailed in unison, a cry of terror and defeat. They stared at their city, their burning dream carried away so quickly, and screamed again, this time in anger. Many of them surveyed the outlying areas, flight obviously on their minds.

Rolland Storr raised his sword. "Do you yield?" Several of the hollow men turned, the slits of their red eyes narrowing. With a cry of defiance the battle was rejoined.

At the main gates of the fallen city, Trevelyan tried to regain his senses. He remembered the initial series of blasts from within the city and the elation he felt at the sounds of the explosions. Suddenly a tremor had ripped through the earth beneath him and the force of a blast picked him up and hurtled him back through the thin curtain of flames, where he tumbled and ground to a stop. The blinding pain from the broken bones in his foot made him cry out. He felt nauseous and weak, and the blood seemed to drain from his head as he struggled to sit up and found himself staring at the back of Kothra's leg. He scrambled back in fright, favoring his ruined foot, and stopped when he realized that the hollow man was paying him no attention. Kothra's gaze was fixed on the smoking ruins that had been Rien.

"She's dead," Kothra said, his voice just loud enough to be heard over the ripping flames ahead. "I can't feel her in my thoughts anymore." The hollow man allowed his head to sink low. "Young pup, I suppose I should be grateful to you. This is the first time since I came back to these evil shores that I have been myself. I can see now the insanity of what Brynna wished to accomplish. The woman was mad." His hands, hanging loosely at his sides, curled into fists, his fingers digging so deeply into his palms that his skin turned white. "The unfortunate part for you, Lord Trevelyan Arayncourt, is that I *loved* her, and I need someone to vent my anger upon."

"Then take me," a low, guttural voice cried out from behind the young prince, whose heart was thundering so loudly that he hadn't even heard the approach of hooves. Kothra, who had also been distracted, turned in time to see Chatham ride before him, a shaft with three deadly blades aimed at the hollow man's chest. Kothra tried to leap out of the way but he moved an instant too late. All three blades pierced the side of his chest, next to his heart. Chatham's unnatural strength and the momentum he had built from his gallop helped to force the heavy steel shaft deeper into the hollow man. The weapon ripped through his back, the blades dripping with blood and gore as Kothra howled and was dragged along a few meters by the momentum of the old warrior's ride. Then Kothra dug in his heels and grabbed the shaft, using its back end to sweep Chatham from his mount. The powerfully built old man dropped to the ground with an indignant cry. Kothra snapped the shaft from the weapon and stumbled forward, raising it so that he could drive the metal rod into Chatham's chest, when he heard shuffling from behind.

The hollow man looked over his shoulder and saw Trevelyan, his face awash with pain, holding himself up with a sword, a black weapon with a razor-sharp edge on one side, a series of arrowhead spikes on the other. With a speed born of desperation, Trevelyan raised the sword and plunged it into Kothra's side, the blade sinking deep into the creature's stomach. The soulless man spun and reached out for Trevelyan, grabbing him by the back of the throat, holding the teetering young prince up as he pulled back his lips and exposed his razor-sharp teeth. Trevelyan jerked upward with his *kris,* causing the hollow man to squeal with pain. Kothra's teeth came closer to Trevelyan's throat and the young prince yanked his *kris* to the side, causing Kothra to wail in agony. The monster's breath was on Trevelyan's skin when the young prince dug his free, gloved hand into the pouch filled with sticky, salted, crushed glass and ground a handful into the wound he had made in Kothra's belly. The hollow man snapped his head back and screamed in pain as he loosened his hold on Trevelyan's neck and the prince fell to the ground, dragging his *kris* from the monster's body, disemboweling the monster. Barely conscious, his mind attempting to retreat into the pleasant moments of his childhood, Kothra looked down to see his ruined stomach. The sight galvanized him and he fell upon Trevelyan, the swordbreaker once again biting into his flesh. The hollow man's jaws opened and descended toward Trevelyan's throat.

Suddenly Chatham was above the creature, yanking his head back by the hair with one hand while he slid his sword against Kothra's throat.

"No!" Trevelyan screamed as he called upon the Forge. A long, jagged blade with sharp grooves appeared in the hand of the merchant prince and he plunged the knife into Kothra's heart. The first man of the hollow gasped, his eyes rolling back in his head, then he slumped forward, driving the *kris* and the dagger deeper into his lifeless body.

Chatham tore the heavy corpse from Trevelyan. Kothra sank to the ground beside the young prince, his arms limply flopping over his ruined chest. Nearly out of breath, Chatham lay down on the darkened earth on the other side of the young prince. The two men stared at each other and a single thought seemed to occur to them at once, a slight smile stealing across first Chatham's face, then Trevelyan's.

"Lay down and die, boy!"

"I'm the prince. I will die for no man."

Despite the blood that covered them, and the nearness of Kothra's body, they found themselves laughing. Trevelyan shuddered and his laughter turned to tears. Laying a comforting hand on the boy's arm, Chatham said, "The lotus."

Trevelyan spun sharply, half expecting to see the flower blossom from the torn-open chest of the hollow man. There was nothing to be seen but blood and gore. Propping himself on one knee, Trevelyan fought off the bile that rose as he carved the heart from the soulless man.

The lotus was not to be found. "I don't understand," Trevelyan said weakly. Suddenly he looked around, his eyes wide with terror. "Ariodne," he hissed. "Where is she?"

The good cheer drained from Chatham. The old man looked past the curtain of flame, to the fiery remains of the hollow city. "I'm sorry," he said quietly.

"You're lying," Trevelyan shouted as he attempted to stand and collapsed painfully. He started to crawl in the direction of the dying city and Chatham went to him, holding the prince down as he wailed and screamed for release.

"I tried to stop her," Chatham said. "The hollow men infiltrated the tunnels. Walks With Fire took her to the catacombs. There was nothing I could do."

The fight suddenly left Trevelyan. A part of him knew, just as Kothra had known, that the woman he loved was dead. He threw his head back and screamed as if his soul had been torn from him. Chatham held the boy as he cried out in far-reaching agony, sharing in his ward's grief. Behind them, on the ridge, were gathered endless rows of green-and-black garbed warriors, together with those wearing the traditional silver and red of Cynara. The soldiers were Kintarans. The others were survivors from the *Adventure* and the black ship. They streamed toward the city.

"Too late," Chatham said bitterly. Then he heard the screams from the fortress city. Hundreds of hollow men, the survivors of the destruction, poured from the city, many headed their way. Chatham reached down and lifted Trevelyan into his arms, then ran in the direction of the Kintarans.

Before any of the hollow could reach Chatham and the young prince, the Kintarans swarmed past them, attacking the last of the hollow. He saw that Shantow was riding with them, the young heir to the empire refusing to allow his pain and loss to keep him from the fray.

"I loved her," Trevelyan sobbed as the last several thousand troops passed them and the old warrior set him down.

"Yes," Chatham said, surprised that the words he was about to speak were entirely true. "*I understand.*"

He held the young prince, amazed by his own tears.

CHAPTER
TWENTY-SEVEN

The skirmishing continued for another three days. The fires continued to burn for half that long. Rolland guessed that several hundred of the hollow had survived the conflict, driven out of the city's charred, skeletal remains into the hills and the outlying country, although where they would go from here and how they would survive was unknown.

Driven by grief into the lands that skirted madness, Trevelyan refused to leave the city for another week, ordering his men to excavate the ruins where Kothra's palace had been. Black Mask had been at his side, their mutual loss uniting them. Shantow had granted the assistance of his men in the task. The leader of the forces from Bellerophon, Wolfram Hilliard, had rallied his men and left the hollow land as soon as he learned that the secret of liquid fire had been lost. They had not remained behind for the fighting that had broken out and lasted for days after the fall of the city or to search for the body of Lon Freyr in the tunnels.

When it became clear, even to Trevelyan and the first wolf, that nothing could have survived at the heart of the initial explosions that leveled the city and that the bodies of their mates would have been incinerated instantly, the young merchant prince finally gave the order for a full withdrawal from the hollow land. Samples of liquid fire had been taken for closer inspection in Cynara.

He learned that a week and a half earlier, the *Adventure* and the black ship had fled north at the first sign of liquid fire. The closest port they could find that was not guarded by the hollow had been days away. After they docked and disembarked, they had met resistance on their journey back to the fortress city. They were rescued by the Kintaran forces and together the soldiers had come to Rien.

Trevelyan was quiet and unapproachable on the journey home. His leg was heavily bandaged, a cast forged to keep him from slowing the healing process. He was already experienced with crutches. Chatham and Shantow stayed close, keeping those who wished to offer their sympathies as far from their friend as they could. The young Kintaran knew that his proper place was on one of the ships from his homeland, but he refused to abandon his friend. The grey-bearded old man divided his time, also tending to Ruzena, who was in good cheer and refused to give into despair, even after the pronouncement of the healer that she would never again be able to use her legs.

"Now Trevelyan will have no choice but to honor that desk job he offered me as appointment master," she had said brightly. Chatham had smiled and kissed her, but he could not fully mask his pain at her condition.

During the journey, Black Mask was rarely seen out of the company of the young prince. They did not speak of the lotus; they did not speak at all.

Upon their return to Cynara, Trevelyan was plagued with a feeling of unrest that overcame his lethargy. After he said his farewells to Rolland Storr and the many other Cynarans who fought for him, Trevelyan was left with Chatham and Ruzena. A carriage was being prepared to transport the tall, blue-eyed woman from the dock to Arayncourt Hall.

"You've served me well," Trevelyan said gravely.

Ruzena smiled at him, her eyes filled with life. She took Chatham's hand and winked at Trevelyan. "I've served *myself*. You think I was going to let you get this mangy old wolf killed on me?"

Chatham patted her hand. "Thank you for the eloquent description, my dear," he said sourly.

Trevelyan told Ruzena that the position of appointment master would indeed be hers for as long as she wanted it, then asked to see Chatham alone for a moment. The two men walked along the dock, Black Mask staying with Ruzena.

"The quest was a failure," Trevelyan said. "I've lost all that mattered to me. Black Mask lied about the lotus. More are born of the hollow every day. The Well of Souls will not be filled."

Chatham was silent.

"What I'm saying is this: There's no reason for you to feel obligated to me anymore. I doubt the promises Black Mask made to you carry any more weight than the ones he made to me. You have Ruzena and a chance at a life as a mortal." Trevelyan drew a deep breath and sighed.

"If you choose to leave, I'll understand. I can arrange for back pay that will more than cover setting the two of you up with a new life wherever you wish to go."

The grey-bearded old man allowed his heavy hand to clamp down on Trevelyan's shoulder. "As always, boy, you have a lot to learn. First, my mortality was lifted with the fall of Rien. Second, and more importantly, you may have started out as the worst burden I could ever imagine, but you've become a friend. I don't abandon my friends."

They stopped and stared at each other. Trevelyan almost smiled, then his sadness of Ariodne's death returned to him and his eyes once again turned cold. "Very well, then."

"I should say." Chatham smiled and they returned to Ruzena.

Several hours later, after Trevelyan settled in to Arayncourt Hall, having passed dozens of celebrations that appeared to be in his honor, the young prince entered his grandmother's quarters.

"You wished to see me?"

"Sit down, Trevelyan." The young prince complied. "My condolences on your loss. I know that Ariodne meant very much to you. She was your first true love. Just between the two of us, your grandfather was not my first love, and I have yet to get over the passing of either of those two men."

"I understand," Trevelyan said without interest.

The old woman frowned. "Trevelyan, in your absence, I investigated the claims your mother had made of threats from the other families. It may come as a surprise to you—it did to me—that she was correct. Our empire and our lives were in danger. To the best of my ability, the situation has been neutralized. There will be peace between the five families, but it comes at a price that only you can pay.''

''I don't understand,'' Trevelyan said flatly. ''What more do I have to do so that I may live up to my family name?''

''You may come in now, Lyris.''

Trevelyan turned back to the doorway and saw his mother escorting a young woman into the chamber. She was no more than seventeen winters, with soft brunette hair pushed back and held in an ornate headdress. She had a pretty face with dark eyes and full lips that were turned up in a shy smile. The young woman wore a flowing white gown. Gazing into Trevelyan's face she said, ''Oh, they didn't tell me about the beard. My father wears a beard. It's very nice.''

''Trevelyan, I'd like you to meet Rosalind Sancia. A week from tomorrow the two of you will be man and wife.''

Leaping to his feet, Trevelyan slammed his hands on the desk behind which his grandmother sat. ''Is this how you honor my grief, by taunting me? This jest is in poor taste.''

''No jest,'' Mayra said in careful, measured tones. ''Remember, you signed over your empire to me, Trevelyan. If you want it back, this is what you must do.''

The young prince laughed perversely. ''I brought you here because I knew you were capable of something like this. I never expected to be the recipient of your talents.''

''Trevelyan, it must be done,'' she whispered harshly.

''Is something amiss?'' Rosalind said innocently.

Grabbing at his crutches, Trevelyan used one for support as he hobbled close to the innocent young girl. The remaining crutch he pointed in her direction as if it were a sword, driving both women back. ''Amiss? No! How could anything be amiss?'' He laughed again, his tone even darker. ''Understand that there is nothing inside of me. My heart is black. Empty. You and I will be married in name only. Take your pleasures where you will, but be discreet.''

Rosalind's mouth opened and she sputtered but could not form words. Lyris raised her hand to her son. ''You may be used to having your women sullied before they come to you, but Rosalind is pure—''

Trevelyan slapped his mother with the back of his hand. She stared at him in shock for a moment, then grasped Rosalind's hand and led the startled young woman from the chamber. The young prince looked back to his grandmother.

"What would you have done if Ariodne had not been killed?" Trevelyan said bitterly as Mayra leaned forward.

"I would have *urged* you to make a decision."

Trevelyan laughed again. "Draw up the papers, Grandmother. Arrange the ceremony. Let the people rejoice." He turned and his body seemed to shrink as he hung his head and left the chamber. "Their prince is getting married."

Above, in the private set of rooms Shantow had been given, the future Kintaran emperor returned to his quarters and was surprised to find several visitors waiting.

"Father," Shantow said in complete shock.

Koto Yakima was a short man of slight build, but he exuded a power that belied his form. His eyes were a cold sky-blue and his face was lined with tiny scars. Silky black hair framed his hard features. The Kintaran emperor was dressed in bright red, green, and yellow ceremonial robes. Silver fingerless gauntlets, bands of gold around his neck, waist, and thighs, and a jeweled headpiece completed his raiment. Servants stood on either side of him.

Shantow raised his good hand to his face, attempting to cover his disfiguring scars. His father shook his head.

"There is no need. You may wear your scars with pride. I was told that you acquitted yourself well in the war."

Shantow slowly lowered his hand. He saw one of his father's attendants look away, pretending that he was staring at one of the paintings on the wall.

"I was also told that Akako was lost in the battle. His loss is regrettable."

"Yes," Shantow said.

"It would have been better if you had died instead."

The young Kintaran looked stricken. "Father, how could you say that?"

"If you had died in battle you would have retained your honor. This entire matter could have been swept aside. The fact that you live complicates everything. It would have been far better if I had never been forced to say what I have come here to say and if you had not lived to hear my words."

"What are you saying, Father?" Shantow was reeling from his father's words.

"You had a sister, Shantow."

"Mother was with child? Why wasn't I told?"

"We thought it best to keep this a secret, until the child was born, to make sure that it would be—normal."

Understanding slowly came to the young man. "You said I *had* a sister. The child died?"

"The baby was of the hollow. She was put to death."

"Father, you must not punish Mother for what has—"

"The thought never occurred to me. When Chianjur arrived at our palace, your henchmen read off the complaints against her. They did as you said they should, disrupting a meeting of the high council, where Chianjur's father sat beside me. He became enraged when he heard your charges of adultery and when his daughter refused to deny these claims, he disowned her. We had been told your son died in childbirth—not that you had cut his throat."

"But you did the same—"

"The execution of the babe does not enter into the reasons for your punishment."

"My punishment," Shantow repeated dully.

"Chianjur maintained her silence, humiliated and shattered by your betrayal. She was certain no one would believe her word against that of her husband, a man of royal blood. But your mother refused to honor the shame you had placed upon her. She housed Chianjur in a wing of the servant's quarters, and spent considerable time with her. To their mutual surprise, the time of birth came to your mother when she was with Chianjur. Your wife witnessed the birth of the child and knew what would happen to it after it was taken away. The strain was too great upon her mind. She broke down and told us all.

"Once I knew the truth, there could be no turning back. I informed her father, and he insisted, under his rights by law, that you be punished in a like manner. It is with a heavy heart that I gave leave to this punishment."

He gestured and one of his attendants unraveled a large scroll. "Shantow Yakima, you are to be stripped of your family name and all claims to the throne of Kintaro. Furthermore, if you ever again step foot upon the soil of your former homeland, a land that now disavows your claim to liberty, you will be treated as a criminal and incarcerated. During your imprisonment, the one you have wronged will be given full rights over you, including the power to have you put to death should it please her."

Shantow was trembling. "Father, I know that I have erred. I love Chianjur. If you would let me talk to her, plead my case, I know that we—"

"I *have* spoken to her, Shantow. What you want no longer matters. You have killed whatever love she had for you. There is no changing her mind in this."

Shantow's thoughts raced as he tried to find a way to convince his father of his sincere wish to make amends for his past conduct. A terrible sense of finality seeped through him. "Has the rite of succession been performed?"

"It has," Koto said solemnly.

"Who is to take my place?"

The young Kintaran heard a rustling from his private bath chamber. The curtains parted and a beautiful, dark-haired woman appeared. "I will."

"Chianjur!" Shantow said as he took a few steps toward her, then stopped. Once he looked into the dark, endless recesses of her eyes, he knew that she was lost to him. Nothing he could say would ease her pain or quiet the screaming rage he saw within her beautiful eyes. "I am truly sorry," he said. "Forgive me."

"Not likely," Chianjur said.

Shantow stiffened. "By law, I am allowed to undertake a mission of your choosing as penance for my actions."

The beautiful young woman grinned. She had anticipated this moment and was savoring it with particular delight. "The Seers have told me that an object from the ancient myths once again takes root in Autumn. A flower. It is the red-white rose. There will be only one. Find this for me, bring it to my chambers, and I will assure you safe conduct."

"And then?" Shantow said breathlessly. He knew that Chianjur believed that she was sending him on a fool's mission, but he had heard similar rumors.

"Then I will hear your petition," Chianjur said. "If your words and your actions please me, I will *consider* taking you as my consort."

"Our marriage is annulled, then," Shantow said.

"Oh, yes," Chianjur said delightedly. "And even if you fulfill my desires, my former husband, the throne will never be yours. The most you can aspire to is the position I have described, with little more rights and privileges than that of a dog. If that enticement does not appeal to you, then you may stay here in Cynara until you rot."

Chianjur turned to the emperor. "We are done here."

Koto lowered his gaze and gestured for his attendants and Chianjur to leave ahead of him. The young woman brushed past Shantow, smiling maliciously. As Koto walked around his son without addressing him or bothering to say his farewell, Shantow reached out and grasped his arm. *"Father."*

Koto looked up at his son, his expression unreadable. "You must never call me that again, on pain of death. Is that understood?"

Shantow released his father's arm and the older man left the chamber, slamming the door shut behind him. The young Kintaran crossed to the bed where he and Chianjur had conceived their first and only child and sat down hard. On the table across from the bed was a mirror. His own reflection, scarred and twisted, seemed to mock him. Drawing his dagger, Shantow hurled the weapon, handle first, at the glass. The mirror shattered and Shantow was left with nothing but his memories.

That night, Trevelyan unlocked the rooms where his father had dwelt. They had been sealed since the time of his death. The first room had a musty smell. Trevelyan struggled to open the window and soon breathed in the cold night air of his homeland. Soft bluish-white moonlight filtered into the room, illuminating artifacts from campaigns fought by his father and his many ancestors.

He felt guilty for his treatment of Rosalind. After all, the girl had been used just as he had been. She did not deserve his harsh tone, although his words had been heartfelt. There was a scittering on the window ledge and Trevelyan turned to see Black Mask perched on the windowsill.

"How dare you come to me here," Trevelyan said.

The turquoise eyes of the wolf seemed to blaze in the pale light. *There is much to discuss.*

"You lied about the location of the lotus. You lied about your mate's power—you said that she could not take one of us through the gates she created. Did you also lie about my father?"

What reason would I have had?

"Because it's what you do, it's who you are. Chatham tried to warn me about you but I didn't listen."

I spoke the truth about the lotus. I lied about Walks With Fire to protect her. Would you have not done the same for Ariodne?

"Yes," Trevelyan said without hesitation.

Now we are both alone. The wolf hesitated. *The soul of Oram Arayncourt is lost. That is the truth.*

Trevelyan felt his heart sink. "Why are you here?"

To tell you that you must continue on your quest. Soon the lotus will be in your hand, but it will be worthless without the rose.

"You said that I would find the lotus in the heart of my greatest enemy. Kothra is dead by my hand. There was no flower growing in his heart. You *lied*, Black Mask."

The commandments were true. The lotus in the heart of your greatest enemy, the rose in the heart of your greatest love.

"Ariodne," he said softly. "You would have had me kill her."

The decision was not mine. I have also lost a mate. We have been together for millennium. I would not wish this pain on anyone.

Trevelyan did not want to be reminded of his loss. "What of Lady Brynna's words? She claimed that there was another deity, one that guided the hollow to Rien."

Lies.

"Then it was the Unseen that made you and your pack mortal in Rien?"

No. The wolf hesitated. *It is possible that the slumber of one of the sleeping gods has been disturbed. I do not know which it may be.*

"Lying bastard," Trevelyan said as he turned his back on the wolf. "You would say anything to avoid the truth."

Trevelyan.

The prince turned. Black Mask's lips were pulled back, exposing his glinting, white fangs as he growled.

For what I am about to do, I am very sorry.

The wolf suddenly leaped from the windowsill, striking Trevelyan in the chest. The animal's weight knocked him to the floor, where his head struck the hard wood and he blacked out.

In the darkness that followed, he did not dream.

The next morning Trevelyan felt warm fingers of sunlight playing upon his face. His head was throbbing, and pain lanced through him when he tried to rise. Looking down at his body, he saw that his top shirt had been ripped to shreds, and his chest was covered in blood. The gashes he saw upon his breast were already covered over with scars.

In his hand was the black lotus.

From somewhere close he heard Black Mask's voice.

I did not lie, young prince. The lotus was in the heart of your greatest enemy. And your greatest enemy has always been yourself.

Understanding came to the young prince and he began to weep, clutching the lotus in one hand, covering his face with the other. Ariodne, he thought. She died for nothing.

Nothing!

The prince turned on his side and released a scream of agony and grief that echoed throughout the chambers and drifted to the courtyard beyond, where Black Mask lowered his head and raced away in shame.

EPILOGUE

The burnt man hurried through the knee-deep drifts of fine white snow. Night was coming and he did not wish to be caught outside the shelters when the fragile sunlight gave way. Already the deep blue skies had been attacked by twilight, deep red and yellow gashes torn through their comforting veil. The frozen wastelands of upper Bellerophon were merciless after the fall of night and he had no desire to test his mettle against such a challenge.

His legs were supported by strong metal braces, his weak, nearly useless arms dangling at his side as he moved. Soon the village was within sight, and Solvig, an elder in the tribe that had found him, half dead, several kilometers away and adopted him, was approaching, waving his hands high in the air. Their language had evolved from the same primitive roots as the refined dialect he had been taught and before long the burnt man had come to understand most of what the tribesmen had to say. It was only in instances like this when Solvig or one of his companions spoke in a clipped, agitated manner that he could not understand them.

"Slow down," the burnt man called. As he came closer, he was able to make out the words "Red hair!" and "Her time!" Suddenly their excited way made sense. The woman was about to give birth and he had to be there.

They had found her in a deserted outcrop on their recent trek back from the outpost where they had met with traders from Knossos. Several of the items the merchants had for sale were unmistakably of Cynaran design. When asked where they acquired these fineries, they said only, "Witch woman. Red hair! She pay with these!"

The burnt man was intrigued. On the journey back to their village, fires were spotted in a place that had been set aside by all the tribes as accursed. Spirits were said to dwell in the outcrop, and only a being of great power could survive there without tempting their wrath and having the foul skins of the ghosts hung over their shoulders, a fate that would quickly spell their deaths. The men from the village watched the outcrop for several days. When they were certain the intruder was not about to expire from the evil within the cave, the villagers approached and found a beautiful red-haired woman who was heavy with child. Despite this, she had thrived in a place known only for death.

Like him, she had much to offer the people, and so she was quickly accepted into the tribe. Now her time had come, the baby would soon be among them. The burnt man allowed Solvig to pick him up and carry him the rest of the way back to the village, and soon they were within the stone hut where the red-headed woman lay with several women from the tribe in attendance. "You've come," she said between gasps.

"Yes, Ariodne," he said. "I could hear your wailing a kilometer away." She grinned, then cried out in pain. He reached down and held her hand. "I would not leave you."

"Of course," she said, looking down at her swollen belly. "You can't help but find me irresistible, I'm sure."

"Closer to the truth than you know," the burnt man said as he brought her hand to his lips and held it as tightly as he could, although the muscles in his arms barely responded to his desires. He stayed at her side for the entire night. When morning came, the head of the child finally appeared.

It was as he had feared. The child was of the hollow, and it was stillborn. The child was removed from her body, the cord was cut, and the baby was cleaned and brought to her. The attendants were dismissed, leaving Ariodne along with the body of her child and the burnt man.

Ariodne held the unmoving child to her breast and her thoughts abruptly shifted to the final moments in the catacombs beneath Rien. She had been prepared to die, but not to take the life of Trevelyan's son. Her plan was a desperate one. She used the Forge to blast her way through to the tunnel where Lon Freyr and his men fought for their lives. Their tunnel had been designed to come much closer to Kothra's master chamber than she had let on to anyone. When she made it through, she found that Freyr and his men were dead. Two of the hollow men lived. She brought the supports crashing down on the soulless men, killing them. The tunnelers had come close to completing their goal, securing a channel away from the destruction. They had gone back to face the threat of the hollow men who had invaded the tunnel.

The red-haired Maven had returned to Kothra's workroom, laying a winding fuse of liquid fire. Then she set the first flame and hurried into the tunnel, running as far as she could before she collapsed the shaft behind her and used her power to continue the work of Lon Freyr's men. When the explosions began, her tunnel was hit hard and she was knocked unconscious. She woke to find herself buried alive with very little air. There was no choice but to blast her way upward, where she finally found fresh air and the cover of night under which she made her escape.

The decision to leave Trevelyan weighed upon her. She knew, however, that even if her child was born of the hollow, she would not be able to have it put to death; despite his protests, that would have been Trevelyan's choice. Although he would grieve for her, and she would miss him fiercely, as if he were a limb that had been severed from her body, she could not stay and take the risk that he would kill their child. This way, he would believe she was dead, and the wolves would have to find some other hiding place for the red-white rose. Then one day, when the madness was over and the wells were refilled, she would return to him, with their son who would now be human, granted a soul.

In the small, firelit hut, the creature at Ariodne's breast came to life with a horrible scream. Ariodne cried as she stared into its red, catlike eyes.

The burnt man watched her in sympathy. He did not know how much he had in common with Ariodne. She had not told him of her escape from the blazing catacombs beneath Rien, and he had not shared with her his true name, or his escape from the burning arena of Telluryde through a carefully planned underground left by the assassins who once ruled that place.

Erin Branagh reached out with his scarred, disfigured hand and touched the side of the child's blue-black-skinned face.

The crying stopped instantly and the baby fixed its gaze on Branagh's horribly burned face with concern.

"You have a calming influence on him," Ariodne said as she stroked the child's head, her tears beginning to dry.

"Yes," Branagh said softly. His gentle tones masked the anger that welled up within him as he thought of Searle Orrick, the man who had ordered him on his mission against Kothra, sending him to what should have been his death. He had dreamed of having a tool to use against the leader of Bellerophon. One had just been delivered to him. "Your son and I will have much to do together. So much to talk about."

Ariodne smiled weakly.

"His father," Branagh said. "When will you tell him that he has a son? And when will you tell the boy that he has a father?"

As she cradled Trevelyan's child to her breast, Ariodne whispered, "One day. One day I will tell him. . . ."

Her hands caressed the face of her child. She knew it would not be long before the child began to grow.

One year for every month.

"When he's old enough," she whispered. "Soon, when he's old enough. . . ."